Sidney Sheldon's
Reckless

BOOKS BY SIDNEY SHELDON

Chasing Tomorrow

The Tides of Memory

Angel of the Dark

After the Darkness

Mistress of the Game

Are You Afraid of the Dark

The Sky is Falling

Tell Me Your Dreams

The Best Laid Plans

Morning, Noon & Night

Nothing Lasts Forever

The Stars Shine Down

The Doomsday Conspiracy

Memories of Midnight

The Sands of Time

Windmills of the Gods

Sidney Sheldon's
Reckless

Tilly Bagshawe

An Imprint of HarperCollinsPublishers

HarperCollins books may be purchased for educational, business, or sales promotional use. For information please e-mail the Special Markets Department at SPsales@harpercollins.com.

FIRST HARPERLUXE EDITION

HarperLuxe™ is a trademark of HarperCollins Publishers

Library of Congress Cataloging-in-Publication Data is available upon request.

ISBN: 978-0-06-241669-8

15 ID/RRD 10 9 8 7 6 5 4 3 2 1

For Belen.
With love.

Part One

Chapter 1

ROYAL MILITARY ACADEMY, SANDHURST,
ENGLAND SATURDAY, NOVEMBER 22, NINE P.M.

"Sir!"

Officer Cadet Sebastian Williams burst into Major General Frank Dorrien's office. Williams's complexion was white, his hair disheveled, his uniform a disgrace. Frank Dorrien's upper lip curled. If he closed his eyes he could practically *hear* the standards slipping, like turds off a wet rock.

"What is it?"

"It's Prince Achileas, Sir."

"*Prince Achileas?* Do you mean Officer Cadet Constantinos?"

Williams looked at the ground. "Yes, Sir."

"Well? What about him?"

For one appalling moment, General Dorrien thought that Williams might be going to cry.

"He's dead, Sir."

The Major General flicked a piece of lint off his jacket. Tall and thin, with the wiry frame of a marathon runner and a face so chiseled and angular it looked like it had been carved from flint, Frank Dorrien's expression gave nothing away.

"Dead?"

"Yes, Sir. I found him . . . hanging. Just now. It was awful, Sir!" Cadet Williams started to shake. Christ, he was an embarrassment.

"Show me."

Frank Dorrien took his battered attaché case with him and followed the distressed cadet along a windowless corridor back towards the barracks. Half walking, half jogging, the boy's limbs dangled like a puppet with its strings tangled. Frank Dorrien shook his head. Soldiers like Officer Cadet Sebastian Williams represented everything that was wrong with today's army.

No discipline. No order. No fucking courage.

An entire generation of dolts.

Achileas Constantinos, Prince of Greece, had been just as bad. Spoiled, entitled. These boys seemed to think that joining the army was some sort of game.

"In there, Sir." Williams gestured towards the men's bathrooms. "He's still . . . I didn't know if I should cut him down."

"Thank you, Williams."

Frank Dorrien's granite-hewn face showed no emotion. In his early fifties, gray haired and rigid backed, Frank was a born soldier. His body was the product of a lifetime of rigorous physical discipline. It was the perfect complement to his ordered, controlled mind.

"Dismissed."

"Sir?" Cadet Williams hovered, confused. Did the Major General really want him to leave?

Not that he wanted to see Achileas again. The image of his friend's corpse was already seared on his memory. The bloated face with its bulging eyes, swinging grotesquely from the rafters like an overstuffed Guy on bonfire night. Williams had been scared to death when he found him. He might be a soldier on paper, but the truth was he'd never seen a dead body before.

"Are you deaf?" Frank Dorrien snapped. "I said 'dismissed.'"

"Sir. Yes, Sir."

Frank Dorrien waited until Cadet Williams was gone. Then he opened the bathroom door.

The first thing he saw were the young Greek prince's

boots, swinging at eye level in front of an open stall. They were regulation, black and beautifully polished. A thing of beauty, to General Dorrien's eyes.

Every Sandhurst cadet should have boots like that.

Dorrien's eyes moved upwards. The trousers of the prince's uniform had been soiled. That was a shame, although not a surprise. Unfortunately the bowels often gave way at the moment of death, a last indignity. Dorrien wrinkled his nose as the foul stench assaulted him.

His eyes moved up again and he found himself looking into the dead boy's face.

Prince Achileas Constantinos looked back at him, his glassy, brown eyes fixed wide in death, as if eternally astonished that the world could be so cruel.

Stupid boy, Frank Dorrien thought.

Frank himself was quite familiar with cruelty. It didn't astonish him in the least.

He sighed, not for the swinging corpse, but for the shit storm that was about to engulf all of them. A member of the Greek royal family, dead from suicide. At Sandhurst! Hung, no less, like a common thief. Like a coward. Like a nobody.

The Greeks wouldn't like that. Nor would the British government.

Frank Dorrien turned on his heel, walked calmly back to his office and picked up the telephone.

"It's me. I'm afraid we have a problem."

FORMER SOVIET REPUBLIC OF BRATISLAVA
SUNDAY, NOVEMBER 23, TWO A.M.

Captain Bob Daley of the Welsh Fusiliers looked into the camera and delivered the short speech he'd been handed the night before. He was tired, and cold, and he couldn't understand why his captors were going through with this charade. His captors weren't stupid. They must know that the demands they'd made of the British government were nonsensical.

Disband the Bank of England.

Seize the assets of every UK citizen with a net worth above one million pounds.

Shut down the stock exchange.

No one in Group 99, the radical leftist organization that had kidnapped Bob Daley from an Athens street, actually believed that these things were going to happen. Bob's kidnap, and the speech he was giving now, was clearly just a big publicity stunt. In a few weeks his captors would let him go and think of some other way to grab the international headlines. If there was one thing you could say for Group 99, they were masters at self-promotion.

Named after the 99 percent of the global population that controlled less than half of the world's wealth, Group 99 were a self-described band of "Robin Hood Hackers" targeting big business interests on behalf of "the dispossessed." Young, computer savvy and completely non-hierarchical, up until now their activities had been confined to cyberattacks against targets they perceived as corrupt. That included multinational companies like McDonald's, as well as any government agencies seen as being on the side of the wealthy, the hated 1 percent. The CIA had had its systems hacked and seen the publication of hundreds of highly embarrassing personal emails. And the British Ministry of Defence had been exposed with its metaphorical trousers down after accepting bribes to give places at Sandhurst to the sons of Europe's wealthy elite. After each attack, the target's screens would fill up with images of floating red balloons—the group's logo and a tongue-in-cheek reference to the eighties pop song "99 Red Balloons." It was touches like this, their humor and disregard for authority, that had given Group 99 an almost cult following among young people all across the globe.

In the last eighteen months, the group had turned its attention to the global fracking business, launching devastating hacks against Exxon Mobil and BP, as well as two of the top Chinese players. The environmental angle had given them even more cachet among the young, as well as winning them a number of prominent Hollywood supporters.

Captain Bob Daley had rather admired them himself, even if he didn't share their politics. But after three weeks locked up in a mountain cabin in some godforsaken forest in Bratislava, the joke was wearing thin. And now they'd woken him up at two in the bloody morning and dragged him outside to record some ridiculous video in subzero temperatures. The air was so cold it made Bob Daley's teeth ache.

Still, he told himself, at least after this I'll be going home.

His captors had already told him. He would go first. Then, a few weeks later, it would be the American's turn. Hunter Drexel, an American journalist, had been snatched off the streets of Moscow the same week that Bob was ambushed in Athens. Hunter's kidnap had appeared almost random, a spontaneous act to generate publicity back in the U.S. Bob's had been more carefully planned. It was his first trip abroad for MI6, a training exercise, and someone in Group 99 clearly knew exactly where he was going to be and when. Bob was convinced they had someone on the inside at MI6. There could be no other rational explanation. His kidnap had been designed to cause maximum embarrassment to both the army and MI6. It helped Group 99's cause that Bob was also in fact the Honorable Robert Daley, from a wealthy and connected, upper-class British family. No one liked a toff.

"Don't take it personally," one of his captors had told him in perfect English, smiling. "But you are a bit of a poster boy for privilege. Just think of it as an experience. You're doing your bit for equality."

Well, it *had* been an experience. Hunter Drexel had become a good friend. The two men were polar opposites. Bob Daley was traditional, conservative and deeply patriotic, whereas Hunter was a maverick, individualist and lover of risk in all its forms. But there was nothing like three months stuck in a cabin in the middle of nowhere to bring people together. When he finally got home, Bob would be able to sell his memoirs and retire from both the army and his abortive career as a spy. His wife, Claire, would be delighted.

"Look directly at the camera please. And stick to the script."

It was the Greek who spoke, the one they called Apollo. Everyone in Group 99 had a Greek codename, which they also used as their handle online, although members came from all over the world. Apollo was a real Greek, however, and one of Group 99's founding members. The group traced its beginnings to Athens, and the euphoria following the election of the country's most leftwing premier to date, the union firebrand Elias

Calles. Perhaps for this reason, the Greek codenames had stuck.

Bob Daley and Hunter Drexel both disliked Apollo. He was arrogant and had no sense of humor, unlike the rest of them. Today he was dressed in black fatigues with a knitted balaclava covering his face.

Playing soldier, Bob Daley thought. *The big man on campus.*

It was pathetic, really. What were these kids going to do when they grew up? When the whole Group 99 adventure was over? When Apollo was caught, as Bob didn't doubt he would be eventually, he'd be looking at serious prison time. Had he even considered that?

"My name is Captain Robert Daley," Bob began. Looking right at the camera he delivered his lines perfectly. The sooner this was over, the sooner he could get back inside the cabin to his warm bed. Even Hunter Drexel's snoring was preferable to being out here in the snow, jumping through hoops for this muppet.

When he finished, he turned and looked up at Apollo. "OK?"

"Very good," the balaclavaed man replied.

"Am I done now?"

Through the slit in his mask, Bob Daley saw the Greek smile.

"Yes, Captain Daley. You're done."

Then, with the camera still rolling, Apollo pulled out a gun and blew Bob Daley's head off.

MANHATTAN
SATURDAY, NOVEMBER 22, NINE P.M.

Althea watched on her laptop screen as the bullet ripped through Bob Daley's skull. She was sitting with her long legs crossed on the suede couch of her $5-million apartment. Outside, snow was falling softly over Central Park. It was a beautiful winter's night in New York, clear and cold.

Captain Daley's blood and brain tissue splattered across the camera lens.

How wonderful, Althea thought, a surge of satisfaction flooding through her, *to be watching this in real time, from the comfort of my living room. Technology really is quite amazing.*

She reached out and touched her screen with her perfectly manicured fingers, half expecting it to be wet. Daley's blood would still be warm.

Good, she thought. *He's dead.*

The Englishman's body slumped forward, hitting the forest floor like a sack. Then Apollo walked towards the camera. Pulling off his balaclava, he wiped the lens clean and smiled at her.

Althea noticed the bulge in his pants. Killing clearly excited him.

"Happy?" he asked her.

"Very."

She turned off her computer, walked to her refrigerator and pulled out a bottle of Clos d'Ambonnay, 1996. Popping the cork, she poured herself a glass, toasting the empty room.

"To you, my darling."

In a few hours, Captain Daley's execution would be front page news around the world. Kidnap and murder had become commonplace across the Middle East. But this was the West. This was Europe. This was Group 99, the Robin Hood Hackers. The good guys.

How shocked and appalled everyone would be!

Althea ran a hand through her long, dark hair.

She could hardly wait.

Chapter 2

"This is a nightmare."

Julia Cabot, the new British Prime Minister, put her head in her hands. She was sitting at her desk in her private office at 10 Downing Street. Also in the room were Jamie MacIntosh, Head of MI6, and Major General Frank Dorrien. A highly decorated career soldier, Dorrien was also a senior MI6 agent, a fact known only to a select handful of people, which did not include the General's wife.

"Please tell me I'm going to wake up."

"It's Bob Daley who isn't going to wake up, Prime Minister," Frank Dorrien observed drily. "I hate to say I told you so."

"Then don't," Jamie MacIntosh snapped. Frank was a brave man and a brilliant agent, but his tendency to assume the moral high ground could be extremely wearing. "None of us could have predicted this. This is the E bloody U, not Aleppo."

"And a bunch of teenage geeks in red-balloon hoodies, not ISIS," Julia Cabot added despairingly. "Group 99 don't *kill people.* They just don't!"

"Until they do," said Frank. "And now they have. And Captain Daley's blood is on our hands."

It was hard not to take Bob Daley's murder personally. Partly because Frank Dorrien knew Bob Daley personally. They'd both served in Iraq together, under circumstances that neither Julia Cabot nor Jamie MacIntosh could imagine, never mind understand. And partly because Frank *had* warned of the dangers of treating Group 99 as a joke. These groups always began with high ideals and, in Frank's experience, almost always ended with violence. A splinter group would rise up, nastier and more bloodthirsty than the rest, and end up seizing power from the moderates. It had happened with the communists in Russia after the revolution. It had happened with the real IRA. It had happened with ISIS. It didn't matter what the ideology was. All you needed was angry, dispossessed, testosterone-fueled young men with a thirst for power and attention, and in the end bad things, very bad things, would happen.

MI6 had been sitting on intelligence for weeks about where Captain Daley and Hunter Drexel might be being held. But no one had acted on it, because no one had believed the hostages were in serious danger. Indeed, when Frank had proposed sending in the SAS on an armed rescue mission, he'd been shot down in flames by both the government and the intelligence community.

"Have you lost your mind?" Jamie MacIntosh had asked him. "Bratislava's an EU country, Frank."

"So?"

"So we can't send our troops into another sovereign nation. A sodding *ally*. It's out of the question."

So nothing was done, and now hundreds of millions of people around the globe had seen Bob Daley's brains being splattered across a screen. Celebrities who only last week had been lining up to be photographed with red balloon badges on their dinner jackets, in support of the group's lofty aims of economic equality, were now scrambling to distance themselves from the horror. Kidnap and murder, right here in Europe.

"I understand you're angry, Frank," Julia Cabot said grimly. "But I need constructive input. The Americans are screaming blue murder. They're worried their hostage is going to be next."

"They should be," said Frank.

"We all want to get these bastards." Cabot turned to her intelligence chief. "Jamie, what do we know?"

"Group 99. Founded in Athens in 2015 by a group of young Greek computer scientists, then rapidly spread across Europe to South America, Asia, Africa and around the globe. Stated agenda is economic, to address poverty and the global wealth imbalance. Loosely classed as communists although they have no stated political, national or religious allegiances. They use Greek codenames online, and they are very, very smart."

"What about their leaders?" Cabot asked.

"One or two names have cropped up. The guy code-named Hyperion we believe to be a twenty-seven-year-old Venezuelan named Jose Hernandez. He's the fellow who leaked the private emails of the former Exxon boss."

"The chap with the transsexual mistress and the cocaine habit?" Cabot remembered Group 99's sting on the hapless oil executive. Despite the CEO's resignation, hundreds of millions of dollars had been wiped off the share price.

"Precisely. Ironically Hernandez comes from a wealthy establishment family. They may have helped him avoid detection by the authorities. But part of the problem is that there *are* no clear leaders. Group 99 disapproves of traditional hierarchy in all its forms. Because it's web-based and anonymous, it's more of a loose affiliation than a classic terrorist organization. Different individuals and cells act independently under one big umbrella."

Cabot sighed. "So it's a hydra with a thousand heads. Or no heads."

"Precisely."

"What about funding? Do we know where they get their money from?"

"That's a more interesting angle. For a group that purports to be against accumulated wealth, they seem to have a lot of cash washing around. They invest in technology, to fund their cyberattacks. It's an expensive business, staying ahead of the game against sophisticated systems at places like Microsoft or the Pentagon."

"I can imagine," said Cabot.

"We also believe they are behind various multi-million-dollar anonymous donations to both charitable groups and leftwing political parties. Numerous sources have pointed to a female member of the group, an American, as both one of their largest donors and a driving force in Group 99's strategic objectives. You remember the attack on the CIA a year ago, when they published a bunch of compromising private emails from top Langley staffers?"

The prime minister nodded.

"The Americans believe that was her. She operates under the codename Althea, but that's pretty much all anyone knows about her."

Julia Cabot stood up and walked over to the window, aware of Frank Dorrien's eyes boring into her back. She found the old soldier difficult. Only a week ago, she'd met with him to discuss the tragic and diplomatically embarrassing suicide of the young Greek prince at Sandhurst. It struck her then how little compassion General Dorrien had shown for the boy, as well as how dismissive he was of the political ramifications of his death on British soil and in the care of the British army.

"Perhaps he was depressed?" was the closest he'd come to offering any explanation. And when pressed he'd become positively irritated. "With respect, Prime Minister, I was his commanding officer, not his therapist."

Yes, Julia Cabot had thought angrily. *And I'm your commanding officer.*

She wondered whether Dorrien was being so rude because she was a woman, or whether he was always this way.

On this occasion, however, the general was right. Bob Daley's blood *was* on her hands. If the American journalist, Hunter Drexel, died too, she would never forgive herself.

"We must work with the Americans on this," she announced. "Total transparency."

Jamie MacIntosh raised an eyebrow laconically. "Total transparency" was not a phrase that made him feel good. At all.

"They need to get their man, Drexel, out of there. I want you to give the CIA everything you have, Jamie. Possible locations. All of that."

"So we're going to help rescue their man after abandoning our own?" Frank Dorrien looked suitably outraged.

"We're going to make the best of a bad job, General," the prime minister shot back. "And in return we'll expect the CIA to share all of their intelligence on Group 99's global network with us. Up until now their cyberattacks have focused primarily on U.S. targets. American companies and government agencies have been hit a lot harder than we have. I'm sure they already have groaning files on these bastards."

"I'm sure they do, Prime Minister," Frank Dorrien said drily. It was uncanny the way he managed to make every comment sound like a criticism.

"Something made these people change tactics," Cabot said, ignoring him. "Something changed them from hi-tech pranksters into kidnappers and murderers. I need to know what that something is."

"I don't like it. I don't like it *at* all."

President Jim Havers scowled at the three men seated around his desk in the Oval Office. The men were Greg Walton, the diminutive, bald head of the CIA. Milton Buck, the FBI's top counterterrorism agent. And General Teddy MacNamee, head of the Joint Chiefs of Staff.

"None of us like it, Mr. President," Greg Walton said. "But what are the alternatives? If we don't get Drexel out now, right now, we could be looking at his brains being sprayed across a screen. If we don't act on this intelligence . . ."

"I know. I know. But what if he's not there? I mean if the Brits were so damn sure, why didn't they get their own man out?"

President Havers's scowl deepened. He was under enormous pressure, from Congress and from the American public, to save Hunter Drexel. But, if the intelligence they'd just received from the British was correct, saving Drexel meant launching a military offensive in an EU country. The United States had gotten enough flak for sending troops into Pakistan to take out Bin Laden. And this was a whole different ball game.

Bratislava was an ally, a Western democracy. Its president and people would not react kindly to American Chinooks invading their airspace and dropping Navy SEALs into their mountains, mountains that the Bratislavans themselves categorically denied were being used as a safe haven for Group 99, or any other terrorists for that matter.

And what if the Bratislavans were right and British Intel was wrong? What if Havers sent troops in, and Drexel wasn't there after all? If a single Bratislavan citizen so much as spilt their coffee over this, President Havers would be dragged in front of the UN with egg all over his face before you could say "breach of international law."

"They might let him go," the president said, half to himself.

The three men all gave their commander in chief a look that roughly translated as *and pigs might fly.*

"I'm just saying, it's a possibility."

"I imagine that's what the British were thinking, right up until last week," said Greg Walton.

"But maybe what happened to Captain Daley was a one-off," the president countered, clutching at straws. "An aberration. After all, Group 99 have never espoused violence before."

"Well they've sure as hell espoused it now, Sir." General MacNamee said grimly. "Can we really afford to take the risk?"

"What I don't understand is why they even kidnapped Hunter Drexel in the first place." President Havers ran a hand through his hair in frustration. "I mean, to what end? A two-bit journalist and gambling addict, fired from the *Washington Post and* the *New York Times.* Which is quite an accolade in itself, by the way. How is this man representative of the one percent of the people this group claim to despise? From what I understand he can barely pay his bills. How is he representative of anything?"

"He's an American," the FBI man, Milton Buck, observed quietly.

"And that's enough?"

"For some people," Greg Walton said. "These people aren't necessarily rational, Sir."

"No shit." The president shook his head angrily. "One minute they're sending pop-up balloons onto people's computer screens and storming the stage at the Oscars, and the next they're making snuff movies. I mean Jesus *Christ!* What next? Are they gonna start burning people in cages? It's like a bad fucking dream. This is Europe."

"So was Auschwitz," said the general.

A tense silence fell.

If he sent in the SEALs and the operation was a success, President Jim Havers would be a hero, at least at home. Of course, he would owe the British big-time. Julia Cabot was already demanding more information on Group 99's global network and funding sources, particularly "Althea," information the CIA was extremely reluctant to share. If this worked President Havers would have no choice but to give it to her. But it would be worth it. His popularity ratings would be through the roof.

On the other hand, if Drexel wasn't where the British said he would be, it was Havers who'd be hung out to dry, not Julia Cabot. America's reputation abroad would plummet. He could wave goodbye to a second term.

The president closed his eyes and exhaled slowly. In that moment, Jim Havers hated Hunter Drexel almost as much as he hated Group 99.

How in hell had it come to this?

"Fuck it. Let's do it. Let's go in and get the son of a bitch."

Chapter 3

Hunter Drexel pressed the radio against his ear and listened intently. The voice of the BBC World Service newsreader crackled through the darkness.

"As concern grows for the welfare of kidnapped American journalist Hunter Drexel, a minute's silence was held today at Sandhurst Military Academy in Berkshire in memory of Captain Robert Daley, whose brutal murder last week at the hands of terror group 99 shocked the world."

Hunter thought, *So now they're terror group 99.* He laughed bitterly. *Funny how one little murder changes everything.*

Two weeks ago the BBC couldn't get enough of Group 99. Like the rest of the world's media, they'd fawned over the Robin Hood Hackers like groupies at a One Direction concert.

Then again, was Hunter really any better than the rest of them? After all, he'd misjudged Group 99 too.

At the time he was kidnapped he'd been working on a freelance article about corruption in the global fracking business. He'd been particularly interested in the billions of dollars flowing between the United States, Russia and China, and the secretive way in which drilling contracts were awarded, with oil giants in all three countries splitting obscene profits. Handshake deals were being thrashed out in Houston, Moscow and Beijing that blatantly contravened international trade law. Back then Hunter had seen Group 99 as an ally, as opposed to the rampant corruption in the energy business as he was. Ironically, he'd been on his way to meet Cameron Crewe, founder and owner of Crewe Inc. and one of fracking's very few "good guys," at Crewe's Moscow office when he was dragged into an alleyway, chloroformed and bundled into the boot of a Mercedes town car, not by Kremlin thugs but by the very people he'd believed were on his side.

He remembered little of the long journey to the cabin. He changed cars at least once. There was also a short helicopter ride. And then he was here. A few days later Bob Daley showed up and was introduced as Hunter's "roommate." It was all very civilized. Warm beds, a radio, reasonable meals and, to Hunter's delight, a pack of cards. He could survive without freedom if he had to. Even sex was a luxury he could learn to live without. But a life without poker wasn't worth living. He and Bob would play daily, often for hours at a stretch, betting with pebbles like a couple of kids. If it hadn't been for the armed guards outside the cabin, Hunter might have believed himself taking part in some sort of student prank, or even a reality TV show. Even the guards looked halfhearted and a bit embarrassed, as if they knew the joke had gone too far but weren't quite sure how to back out without losing face.

Except for Apollo.

Hunter hated using the stupid Greek codename. It was so pretentious. But as it was the only name he had for the bastard who had shot Bob, it would have to do. Apollo was always different. Angrier, surlier, more self-important than the others. Hunter had identified him early on as a bully and a nasty piece of work. But never in a million years had he thought Apollo intent on murder.

Bob's execution had left the entire camp in a profound state of shock. It wasn't just Hunter. The other guards seemed genuinely horrified by what had happened. People were crying. Vomiting. But no one had the gumption to face down Apollo.

This was it. The new reality.

They were all in it up to their necks.

The radio signal was fading. Hunter twiddled the knob desperately, looking for something, anything, to distract him from his fear. He'd been in dangerous situations before in his journalistic career. He'd been shot at in Aleppo and Baghdad, and narrowly escaped a helicopter crash in Eastern Ukraine. But in a war zone you had adrenaline to keep you going. There was no *time* for fear. It was easy to be brave.

Here, in the silence of the cabin, with nothing but his friend's empty bed and his own fevered thoughts for company, fear squatted over Hunter like a giant, black toad. It crushed the breath from his body and the hope from his soul.

They're going to kill me.

They're going to kill me and bury me in the forest, next to Bob.

In the beginning, in the days and hours after Bob's death, Hunter had dared to hope. *Someone will find me. They'll all be looking now. The Brits. The Americans. Someone will come and rescue me.*

But as the days passed and no one came, hope died.

Hunter's radio crackled loudly, then the signal dropped completely. Reluctantly, he crawled back under his covers and tried to sleep. It was impossible. His limbs ached with exhaustion but his brain was on speed. Images flew at him like bullets.

His mother in her Chicago apartment, beside herself with worry in her tatty chair.

His most recent lover, Fiona from the *New York Times*, screaming at him for two-timing her the day he left for Moscow. "I hope one of Putin's thugs catches you and beats you to death with a crowbar. Asshole!"

Bob Daley, making some stupid wisecrack the night before he made the video.

The night before Apollo blew his brains out.

Would they make him record a video too? Would Bobby's bloodstains still be on the camera lens?

No!

A cold prickle of terror crept over him, like needles in the skin.

I have to get out of here!

Hunter sat bolt upright, gasping for breath, struggling to control his bowels. *Please, God, help me! Show me the way out of this.*

He hadn't realized until this moment quite how desperately he didn't want to die. Perhaps because this was the moment when he knew for certain that he was going to. Any rescue mission would have happened by now.

No one knows where I am.

No one's coming.

And really, why should they come? Hunter Drexel had never felt or shown any particular loyalty to his homeland. What right did he have to expect loyalty in return?

Hunter had never understood the concept of patriotism. Allegiance to a country, or an ideology, was utterly baffling to him. People like Group 99, who devoted their entire lives to a cause, fascinated him. *Why?* Hunter Drexel saw the world only in terms of people. Individuals. People mattered. Ideas did not. Hunter had more in common with Group 99's worldview and political beliefs than he did with Bob Daley's. Yet Bob was a good person. And Apollo, or whatever his real name was, was a bad person. In the end, that was all that mattered, not the labels that either man lived under:

Soldier.

Radical.

Terrorist.

Spy.

They were nothing but empty words.

If Hunter Drexel identified himself as anything, it was as a journalist. Writing meant something. The truth meant something. That was about as ideological as Hunter got.

He looked around the wooden cabin that had been his home for the last few months and tried to slow his breathing. The heavy wooden door was wedged shut with a split tree trunk and armed guards took shifts outside. Since Bob's death two solid iron bars had been nailed across the window. Beyond it lay miles of impenetrable forest, an army of tall, darkly swaying pines above a thick white blanket of snow. In their wilder moments of fantasy, Hunter and Bob had concocted escape plans. All were insanely risky, preposterous really. The kind of thing that would work in a cartoon. And all involved two people. Alone, escape was quite impossible. The only way out of here was the one that Bob Daley had already taken.

Hunter lay back, not calm exactly, but past the hyperventilating stage. Acceptance, that was the key. Letting go. But how did one accept one's own death?

His mind drifted to a story he'd heard on the radio yesterday, about the Greek prince who'd hung himself at Sandhurst. Achileas. It sounded like one of the stupid names Group 99 gave themselves. There was much hand-wringing about the boy's death and an "official inquiry" had been launched.

As ever, it was the human side of the story that gripped Hunter.

Here was a young man with everything to live for, yet who had *chosen* to die.

Perhaps if Hunter could understand *that* impulse, the impulse that drove a young prince to embrace death like a lover, he would feel less afraid?

Slowly, Hunter Drexel drifted into a fitful sleep.

The noise was a low buzz at first. Like insects swarming.

But then it got louder. The unmistakable whir of chopper blades.

"Dimitri." One of Hunter's guards grabbed the shoulder of his companion, shaking him awake. "Listen."

The other guard slowly struggled out of sleep. Like Dimitri he was only nineteen. Both boys were French. This time last year they'd been studying computer science in Paris. They'd joined Group 99 for a lark, because a lot of their friends were doing it, and because they loosely supported the idea of taking the world's super-rich down a peg or two. Neither of them quite knew how they'd ended up in a Bratislavan forest, freezing their tits off and armed with machine guns.

By the time they got to their feet, strobe lights filled

the sky. The whole camp was bathed in blinding light. Then the first shots rang out.

"Shit!" Dimitri started to cry. "What do we do?"

Already the helicopters were so loud, it was hard to hear each other.

"Run!" yelled his friend.

Dimitri ran. He heard shots behind him and saw his friend fall to the forest floor. He kept going. His legs felt like jelly, as if all the strength had been sucked out of them.

The camp was a horseshoe of canvas tents clustered around the cabin. There were also two breeze-block structures, one used as a weapons store, and one as a control center, complete with a generator, satellite phone and specially customized laptop. The second structure was closest. Dimitri staggered towards it. All around him, group members were emerging from their tents, bleary-eyed with panic. Some waved guns around, but others were unarmed. Atlas and Kronos, two German lads, had their hands in the air. Dimitri watched in horror as they were mown down anyway in a hail of bullets, their limbs flailing grotesquely like dancing puppets as they died.

Then something hit him from behind. Not a bullet or a stone. It was a gust of wind, so powerful it blew him off his feet. The choppers had landed. Suddenly all was chaos, light and noise. American voices were shouting. "ON THE GROUND! GET DOWN!"

Dimitri screamed, a child's wail of terror. Then suddenly, arms were around him, under his shoulders, dragging him into the control center.

"You're OK." Apollo's voice was firm and calm. Dimitri clung to him like a life raft.

"They're going to kill us!" the boy screamed.

"No they're not. We're going to kill them."

Dimitri watched as Apollo pulled the pin out of the hand grenade with his teeth and lobbed it toward the men who had just killed his friends. As they were blown into the air, their legs came off.

"Here." Apollo handed him a grenade. "Aim for the choppers."

Inside the cabin, Hunter Drexel cowered under a table.

The noise of the Chinooks was the most beautiful sound he'd ever heard.

They're here! They found me!

Even the gunfire, the all too familiar *pap pap pap pap* of machine guns he remembered from Iraq and Syria sounded soothing to his ears, like a lullaby, or a mother's voice.

Boom! The cabin door didn't so much open as explode, shards of wood flying everywhere. Smoke filled the room in seconds, disorienting him. Hunter's ears were ringing and his eyes stung. He heard voices, shouts, but everything was muffled, as if he were hearing them under water. He waited for someone to come in, a soldier or even one of his captors, but no one did. Crawling on his belly, Hunter began feeling his way towards the space where the cabin door used to be.

Outside, he quickly got his bearings back. Stars up. Snow down. The Americans—presumably?—were mostly in front of him and to the right, directly facing the camp. To his left, what was left of Group 99 had taken up position in the two breeze-block buildings and were firing back. Gunshots flashed in the blackness like fireflies. Occasionally a strobe or flare would illuminate everything. Then you could see men running. Hunter watched as three of the American soldiers were gunned down just feet in front of him. His captors were clearly not giving up without a fight.

A whimpering sound to his left, like a wounded animal, made him turn around.

"Help me!"

Crawling towards the sound, Hunter found the English boy codenamed Perseus sprawled out in the snow. Hunter had a particular soft spot for Perseus with his skinny, chicken legs, cockney accent and thick, dorky glasses. Hunter had nicknamed him "Nerdeus." They often played poker together. The boy was good.

Now he lay helplessly on the cold ground, his eyes wide with shock. A deep crimson stain surrounded him. Glancing down, Hunter saw that both his lower legs had been blown off.

"Am I going to die?" he sobbed.

"No," Hunter lied, lying down next to him.

"I can't feel my legs."

"It's the cold," said Hunter. "And the shock. You'll be fine."

Perseus's eyes opened and closed. It wouldn't be long now.

"I'm sorry," he whispered. "I never meant for . . . all this."

"I know that," said Hunter. "It's not your fault. What's your name? Your real name."

The boy's teeth chattered. "J-James."

"Where are you from, James?"

"Hackney."

"Hackney. OK." Hunter stroked his hair. "What's it like in Hackney?"

The boy's eyes closed.

"Do you have any brothers and sisters, James? James?"

He let out one, long, fractured breath and was still.

Hunter felt his eyes well up with tears and his body fill with anger.

Not anger. Rage.

James was his friend. He was just a fucking kid.

"NO!" He started to scream, all the pent-up fear of the last few days erupting out of him in one wild, animal howl of fury and loss. In that moment he didn't care if he died. Not at all. Stroking James's cold, dead forehead tenderly, he stood up and ran towards the light of the Chinooks.

That's when it happened.

One of the helicopters exploded, sending a fireball hundreds of feet high shooting into the air like a comet. Hunter watched it in shock. It dawned on him then that the Americans might actually lose this battle. This wasn't the clean rescue they'd intended. It was all going wrong. Soldiers were dying. Group 99 were fighting back, fighting for their lives.

Hunter kept running, because really, what else was there to do? He would run until something happened to stop him. Until his legs blew off like James's, or a bullet ripped through his skull like Bob Daley's, or until he was free to write the truth about what had happened tonight. The truth about everything.

The lights grew brighter. Blinding. Hunter thought he was past Group 99's control center now but he wasn't sure. Just then a second Chinook roared back into life, its blades turning full pelt just a few yards from where Hunter was standing. Hunter watched camouflaged men leap into it one by one as it hovered just inches above the ground. Bullets flew over his head. Then, right in front of him, a hand reached out in the carnage.

"Get in!"

The American soldier was leaning out of the Chinook, reaching for Hunter's hand. He was younger than Hunter, but confident, his words a command, not a request.

Hunter hesitated, a rabbit in the headlights.

He thought about the story that had gotten him kidnapped in the first place.

About the truth, the unpalatable truth, that so many people wanted to suppress.

Once he got into that helicopter, would he ever be able to tell it? Would he ever complete his mission?

He looked behind him. Scores of corpses littered the charred remnants of the camp that had been his world for the last few months. It had all happened in minutes. Bad men and good men and naïve young boys lay slaughtered like cattle. Just like poor Bob Daley had been slaughtered.

And now a confident young American was holding out his hand, offering Hunter a way out. It was what he'd been praying for.

Get in!

Hunter Drexel looked his rescuer gratefully in the eye.

Then he turned and ran off into the night.

Chapter 4

"What do you mean, 'he ran'?"

President Jim Havers held the phone away from his ear in disbelief.

"He ran, Sir," General Teddy MacNamee repeated. "Drexel refused to get into the helicopter."

There was a long silence.

"Fuck," said the president.

"What do you mean 'he ran'?"

The British Prime Minister rubbed her eyes blearily.

"I don't know how many other ways to say it, Julia," the President of the United States snapped. "He wouldn't get in the chopper. He ran into the fucking forest. We're *screwed.*"

Julia Cabot thought, *You mean you're screwed, Jim.*

Her mind raced as she tried to figure out the best way to play this.

"I've already had the Bratislavan president on the line, screaming blue murder," President Havers ranted on. "The UN secretary General's asked me for a statement as a matter of urgency."

"What did you tell him?"

"Nothing yet."

"What will you tell him?"

"That Drexel wasn't there. He'd been moved. But that they successfully took out a bunch of terrorists."

"Good," Julia Cabot said.

"I can count on your support?"

"Of course, Jim. Always."

President Havers exhaled. "Thank you, Julia. We need a joint intelligence meeting. To figure out where we go from here."

"Agreed."

"How soon can your guys be in Washington?"

"I think, under the circumstances, Jim, it makes more sense for *your* guys to come to London. Don't you?"

Julia Cabot smiled. It felt good to have the upper hand with the Americans for once. Right now she was the only friend Jim Havers had in the world and he knew it. She must play her cards for all they were worth.

"I'll see what I can do," Jim Havers said gruffly.

"Wonderful." Julia Cabot hung up.

Exactly one week later, four men sat around a table in Whitehall, eyeing one another warily.

"Good of you to come, gentlemen." Jamie MacIntosh rolled up his shirtsleeves and leaned forward, smiling amiably at his American counterparts. "I know you must both have had a difficult week."

"That's an understatement." Greg Walton of the CIA looked desperately tired. He resented being summoned to London, especially at a time when his beloved agency was being ripped to shreds by Congress back home. But he made an effort at politeness. Unlike his FBI colleague, Milton Buck.

"I hope you have something important to add to this operation," Buck snarled at Jamie MacIntosh. "Because frankly we don't have time to waste on handholding you Brits."

Sitting beside Jamie MacIntosh, Frank Dorrien stiffened. "Well, quite," he said sardonically. "After the mess you made of what should have been a perfectly simple rescue mission, based on *our* entirely accurate intelligence, I imagine you want to devote as many man-hours as possible to training your own men. Heaven knows they need it."

Milton Buck looked like he was ready to throw a punch.

"All right, that's enough." Jamie MacIntosh glared at Frank Dorrien. "None of us have time for chest beating. Let's leave that to the politicians. We're here to combine our resources and share information on Group 99 and that's what we're going to do. Why don't I start?"

Greg Walton leaned back in his chair. "Great. What have you got?"

"For starters, we've got a name for Captain Daley's killer."

Walton and Buck looked at each other in shock. "Seriously?"

Frank Dorrien pushed a file across the table.

In the top left-hand corner was a photograph of a handsome, dark-skinned man with a strong jaw, long aquiline nose, and hooded, distrustful eyes. There was a detached air about him and a certain watchful hauteur, like a bird of prey.

"Alexis Argyros," Jamie MacIntosh announced. "Codenamed Apollo. One of Group 99's founder members and a thoroughly unpleasant piece of work. Grew up in foster care in Athens. Possibly abused. A high school dropout but brilliant with computers and obsessed with violent video games from his early teens. Hates women. Sadist. Narcissist. All this is from his social worker's reports."

"Criminal record?" Greg Walton asked.

"Oh yes. Petty theft, vandalism, arson. Two years in youth custody for rape. And he was suspected in a hideous case of animal cruelty where a cat and kittens were burned alive."

"You only get two years for rape?" Greg Walton asked.

"The Greeks can't afford to run their prisons," Jamie MacIntosh said matter-of-factly. "Not since austerity. Anyway, we believe Argyros was the man who pulled the trigger in Daley's execution video. He was running the camp you raided, and his star is on the rise within Group 99. For months now he's been trying to steer the group towards more violent methods, battling against the moderate elements within 99. Argyros appeals to disaffected young males in the same way that the jihadist groups groomed boys in the west after the Syrian war. He offers them a purpose and a sense of belonging, wraps it all up in a pretty parcel of social justice—"

"And then murders people," Greg Walton interrupted.

"Precisely. We are fearful that Captain Daley's death

may mark the beginning of a new era of global terror. It's an enormous pity you didn't kill Argyros when you had the chance."

"How do you know we didn't?" Greg Walton asked.

This time Frank Dorrien answered.

"Because we've picked up internet traffic between Apollo and an unknown contact in the U.S. Alexis Argyros is alive and well and he's out there looking for Drexel, just like we are. Make no mistake. Group 99 want Hunter Drexel dead."

"And you know all this how?" Milton Buck demanded sourly. A stocky, handsome, middle-aged man with dark hair and what ought to have been a pleasing face, Buck successfully concealed whatever charms he may have had beneath a thick veneer of arrogance.

"Our methods are none of your concern," Frank Dorrien snapped back. "We're here to share intelligence, not tell you how we came by it. Now, what do you have for us?"

Milton Buck looked at Greg Walton, who nodded his approval. Buck pulled out an old-fashioned Dictaphone voice recorder and put it on the table.

"While you've been unmasking the monkey," the FBI man sneered, "we've been focused on the organ grinder."

Jamie MacIntosh sighed. He was starting to find Milton Buck's posturing deeply irritating.

"Your man Apollo may have pulled the trigger," Buck went on, "but he was following orders from above."

He pressed PLAY. A woman's voice filled the room. It was American, educated, soft and low and the sound quality was excellent, as if she were sitting right there with them.

"Is everything ready?"

A man's voice answered. *"Yes. Everything has been done as you instructed."*

"And I will see it on live feed, correct?"

"Correct. You'll be right there with us. Don't worry."

"Good." The woman's smile was audible. *"Have him deliver the speech first."*

"Of course. As we agreed."

"And at nine p.m. New York time precisely, you will shoot him in the head."

"Yes, Althea."

Milton Buck hit STOP and smiled smugly.

"That, gentlemen, was the authorization for Captain Daley's execution. The woman on that tape, who goes by the codename Althea, is the real brains behind Group 99. We've been tracking her for the last eighteen months."

"We already knew about Althea," Jamie MacIntosh said dismissively, to the FBI man's visible annoyance.

"But you didn't know she'd directly ordered Daley's assassination. Did you?" Greg Walton countered.

"No," Jamie admitted. "What else have you got on her? An ID?"

"Not yet," Greg Walton admitted, a little uncomfortably.

"You've been tracking this person for eighteen months and you still don't know who she *is*?" Frank Dorrien asked, disbelievingly. "What *do* you know?"

"We know she channels funds to Group 99 through a complicated network of offshore accounts that we've mapped extensively," Milton Buck snapped.

"We have some unconfirmed physical data," Greg Walton added more calmly. "Witnesses at various banks and hotels we believe she's used have suggested she's tall, physically attractive and dark haired."

"Well that narrows it down," Frank Dorrien muttered sarcastically.

Milton Buck looked as if he were about to spontaneously combust.

"We know she orchestrated the attack on the CIA systems and the blackout of the stock exchange servers on Wall Street two years ago," he snarled. "We know she personally arranged the kidnap and murder of one of your men, General Dorrien. All in all I'd say we know a hell of a lot more than you."

"How long have you had this recording?" Jamie MacIntosh asked.

Greg Walton shot Milton Buck a warning look but it was too late.

"Three weeks," Buck said smugly. "I played this to the president the day after Daley was killed."

A muscle on Jamie's jaw twitched. "Three weeks. And nobody thought to share this information with us sooner?"

"We're sharing it with you now," Greg Walton said.

Frank Dorrien slammed his fist down hard on the table. Everybody's water glasses shook.

"It's not bloody good enough!" he roared. "Daley was one of ours. With allies like you, who needs enemies?"

"Frank." Jamie MacIntosh put a hand on the old soldier's arm, but Dorrien shrugged it off angrily.

"No, Jamie. This is a farce! Here we are spoon-feeding the Americans valuable intelligence, detailed intelligence, actually providing them with the *exact* location of their hostage. And all the while they're sitting on vital information about Bob Daley's killer? It's unacceptable."

Buck leaned forward aggressively.

"And just who are you to tell us what's acceptable, General? Has it occurred to you that maybe we didn't trust the British with this intelligence? After all, your men have been dropping like flies lately."

"I beg your pardon?"

"Think about it. First a Greek royal dies on your watch, General," Buck said accusingly, "a young man who just happens to be a personal friend of Captain Daley. Then, only days later, Daley himself is killed, which let's just say is out of character for Group 99, up to this point. Now, you may say there's no connection between those two events—"

"Of course there's no connection!" Frank Dorrien scoffed. "Prince Achileas died by suicide."

Milton Buck raised an eyebrow. "Did he? Because the other possibility is that Group 99 have someone embedded within the British military. Maybe someone at Sandhurst, or in the upper echelons of the MOD—also the subject of a Group 99 attack, if you remember."

"As were the CIA!" Dorrien shouted back. "Prince Achileas was gay. The man hung himself out of shame, you cretin."

"What did you call me?" Buck got to his feet.

"That. Is. ENOUGH." Greg Walton finally lost his temper. "Sit down, Milton. NOW."

Greg was the senior man here. He hadn't flown

thousands of miles to watch his FBI colleague and General Dorrien go at each other like a pair of ill-disciplined dogs.

There was also something about the tone the general used to talk about the Greek prince that put Greg Walton's back up. Greg was also a homosexual. He found the general's lack of compassion for the dead boy both distasteful and disturbing.

"Whatever has happened in the past, in terms of sharing information, has happened," he said, looking from Buck to Dorrien and back again. "From now on we have direct orders from the White House and Downing Street to cooperate fully with one another and that's what we're going to do. This is a joint operation. So if either of you have a problem with that, I suggest you get over it. Now."

Frank Dorrien looked to Jamie MacIntosh for support but there was none forthcoming. He shot a last look of loathing at Milton Buck and sat back in his chair, sullen but compliant. Buck did the same.

"Good. Now, as it happens we do have one other important development to share with you," Greg Walton went on. "Have either of you ever heard of an individual named Tracy Whitney?"

Frank Dorrien noticed the way Milton Buck tensed up at the mere mention of this name.

"Never heard of her," he said.

"Tracy Whitney the con artist?" Jamie MacIntosh frowned.

"Con artist, jewel thief, computer wizard, cat burglar," Greg Walton elaborated. "Miss Whitney's résumé is a long and varied one."

"That's a name I haven't heard in a long time. We thought she was dead," said Jamie. He explained to Frank Dorrien how, along with her partner Jeff Stevens, Tracy Whitney had been suspected of a swath of daring crimes across Europe a decade ago, conning the corrupt rich out of millions of dollars in jewelry and fine art, and even extracting a grandmaster from the Prado in Madrid. But neither Interpol nor the CIA nor MI5 had ever been able to prove a case against her. "I dread to think the man-hours and money we wasted trying to outsmart that woman." He sounded almost nostalgic. "But then overnight it seemed, she vanished and that was that. Jeff Stevens is still knocking around in London I believe, but he seems to be retired." Jamie turned back to Greg Walton. "I'm baffled as to what Tracy Whitney can possibly have to do with all this."

"So are we," Greg admitted. "The day after the failed raid in Bratislava, we received an encrypted message at Langley from Althea in which she referenced Tracy Whitney."

"More than referenced," Milton Buck jumped in. "The two women clearly knew each other."

"What did the message say?" Jamie MacIntosh asked.

"It was a taunt, basically," Walton replied. "'You guys will never catch me. I'm going to outsmart you just like Tracy Whitney did. I'll bet you Tracy could find me. Why don't you have Agent Buck call her in . . .' That kind of stuff. She clearly knew Tracy, but it was more than that. She knew the agency's history with Tracy. She knew that Agent Buck had had dealings with her."

Greg Walton filled his British counterparts in briefly on the operation a few years ago to track down and catch the Bible Killer. How Tracy and Jeff Stevens had both resurfaced at that time, and Tracy had formed an uneasy alliance with both Interpol and the FBI to bring Daniel Cooper to justice. "Agent Buck here ran the operation. It was a success, but it would be fair to say that Milton and Tracy's relationship was"—he searched for the right word—"tempestuous. Althea knew that."

"I see," Frank Dorrien said archly. "So perhaps it's *you* with a Group 99 informant on the inside?"

The comment was aimed at Milton Buck, but Greg Walton replied. "Anything's possible, General. At this point we're keeping all our options open. "

Jamie MacIntosh asked, "Have you contacted Miss Whitney? I'd be curious to know what she has to say about all this."

"Not yet," said Walton. "We want to broach the subject face-to-face. Tracy has a bad habit of disappearing when she gets spooked. If she knows about Althea in advance, she might just run."

"We'd be with her right now if we hadn't been railroaded into flying here to meet with you instead," Milton Buck added ungraciously. "We're wasting valuable time."

"You know, Tracy used to have something of a Robin Hood complex herself," said Jamie, ignoring the jibe. "She and Jeff only ever stole from people they believed deserved it. And she was quite the whiz with computers. I believe international banking was her forte. I wouldn't be entirely surprised to learn that she and Jeff were involved with Group 99."

"I doubt that," Greg Walton said. "I can't speak for Jeff Stevens. But Tracy Whitney's changed. She was an invaluable asset to us last time. I think we can trust her."

Frank Dorrien frowned but said nothing. He did not like the sound of Tracy Whitney, not one little bit. The woman was a professional thief and liar. Hardly the sort of person they needed on the team.

"I don't think Group 99's the link. My guess is that these two women go back way before that," Greg

Walton went on. "Althea might have known Tracy in prison. Or through Jeff Stevens. She might have been one of Jeff's lovers, or a rival con artist, or even someone Tracy and Jeff targeted in their heyday. We know she's wealthy, after all. There are a million possibilities. Hopefully once we speak to Tracy in person, she can shed some light."

"Anything else we need to know at this stage?" Jamie asked, in a tone that suggested the meeting was coming to a close.

"I don't think so." Greg Walton stood up to leave. "Nothing material. Finding Hunter Drexel and bringing him home safely remains the official focus of our operation. But identifying Althea is our most important strategic mission. We're hopeful Miss Whitney can help with that. Of course, it would be nice to get this guy Argyros's head on a plate too. Maybe you fellows can take the lead on that?"

Jamie MacIntosh nodded.

The two Americans walked to the door.

"One last thing, Mr. Walton," Frank Dorrien called after them.

"Yes?"

"Hunter Drexel. Why do you think he refused to go with his rescuers? Why did he run?"

Greg Walton and Milton Buck looked at each other briefly.

Then Walton said with a straight face. "I have no idea, General. But when we find him, believe me, that'll be the first question we ask."

Forty minutes later, Jamie MacIntosh received a call from the prime minister.

"Can you work with them?" Julia Cabot asked, once Jamie had debriefed her on his meeting with the Americans.

"Of course, Prime Minister. Frank's not a fan of their FBI chappie. But they provided some very useful information."

"Do you trust them?"

Jamie MacIntosh laughed. "Trust them? What a quaint idea! Of course I don't trust them."

Julia Cabot grinned. "Jolly good. Just checking."

"They're lying through their teeth about Drexel," said Jamie.

"You think they know why he ran?"

"I think they know, and I think they'll do anything to stop *us* knowing. I would dearly like to find Mr. Drexel before they do and learn what it is they're hiding."

"Well," Julia Cabot said, "we'll just have to make that happen then, won't we?"

"Can you work with them?" President Havers's voice sounded tight with strain.

"Yes, Sir," Greg Walton said. "Agent Buck got off on the wrong foot with one of their guys. But the meeting was constructive. MacIntosh is a reasonable guy."

"Tread very carefully, Greg," the president warned. "There are places we want MI6 sniffing around and places we don't."

"Of course, Sir. Understood. We'll keep them under control."

"What about Tracy Whitney?"

"We'll keep her under control too."

"Good. Just make sure you do. Good night, Greg."

"Good night, Sir."

Major General Frank Dorrien was at home in his living room, watching President Havers on television.

Sitting in the oval office with the American flag behind him, in an expensive dark suit and silk tie with his silver-gray hair slicked back, Havers looked like what he was: the most powerful man in the world.

"A week ago, the United States struck at the heart

of a group of terrorists who wish to destroy our way of life. Group 99 had already brutally murdered a British hostage, Captain Robert Daley. We had reason to believe that their second hostage, the American journalist Hunter Drexel, was about to meet the same fate. We also had intelligence indication that Mr. Drexel was being held in the same camp, in Bratislava, where Captain Daley was killed.

"A carefully planned, covert operation took place, based on that intelligence. And yes, that operation did involve American troops briefly entering Bratislavan territory. The United States makes no apology for this action. Although it appears Mr. Drexel was moved by his captors to another location following Captain Daley's death, we established that both men *had* been held in Bratislavan territory—contrary to that country's denials of harboring terrorists. Moreover, our mission was not in vain. Scores of terrorists were killed, the same individuals responsible for Captain Daley's barbaric murder. Regrettably six American servicemen also lost their lives.

"Make no mistake. The United States remains committed to fighting the terrorists who threaten our citizens, and our security, *wherever* we may find them. And whatever their so-called motivations, or justifications for their actions might be. Now, there may be folks who criticize us for that. But that has always been, and remains, the policy of this administration. Group 99 are not harmless. They are not freedom fighters or champions of the poor. They are terrorists.

"We remain confident that, working with our British partners, we will locate Mr. Drexel imminently. And in the meantime his captors should know this: You can't run. You can't hide. We will find you and we will destroy you."

Major General Frank Dorrien winced and turned off the television. Havers was so dishonest, it made Frank's teeth ache. Of course, most politicians were. But the Americans were such spectacularly *glossy* liars. Virtuosos of insincerity. Masters of misrepresentation.

How he despised them!

Frank's thoughts turned to Hunter Drexel, the man for whom all these lies were being told. The United States had risked near total diplomatic isolation for a man who had not only run away from the soldiers sent to rescue him but who, by all accounts, was a typical, entitled journalist, interested only in his story and loyal to no one but himself. A gambler and inveterate womanizer, Hunter Drexel had left for Moscow with a string of broken hearts, angry editors and unpaid creditors in his wake. Men like that didn't deserve to be rescued.

To have brave, honest, loyal men risk their lives to save them.

Major General Frank Dorrien was big on loyalty. Loyalty to family, to religion (Frank was brought up staunchly Church of England and considered himself a conservative with a very capital C), to his country. But above all, Frank Dorrien believed in loyalty to the British army.

Frank would gladly die for the British army.

He would kill for it too.

In Frank Dorrien's world, one did what one had to do. One did one's *duty,* whatever form that took. Recently, duty had taken Frank in some unexpected directions. He'd been forced to make some difficult decisions. Distasteful decisions. But never once did he question his actions, or second-guess his superiors. That was not the soldier's way.

The army was Frank Dorrien's life. He had his wife, of course, Cynthia, whom he loved. And his opera, and his roses, and the Church choir, and his books on Byzantine history. But these were all fruits of the tree. The army *was* the tree. Without it, Frank's existence would be nothing but a meaningless series of days, without order or discipline or purpose.

What was the purpose of men like Hunter Drexel? Or libertines like Group 99, revolting communists even before they started butchering people? Or women like Tracy Whitney, a thief and con artist who, for some inexplicable reason, Jamie MacIntosh appeared actually to admire?

Not for the first time, Frank Dorrien wondered about the dissolute world in which he now found himself working. *Intelligence.* Never had an industry been more ineptly named.

Still. Duty called.

"Would you like a cup of tea, Frank?"

Cynthia Dorrien's voice drifted in from the kitchen, reassuringly normal and sane.

"I'd love one, darling," Frank called back.

One day, this would all be over.

One day they could all return to normal.

Bundled up against the bitter New York wind in a full-length mink coat and matching hat, her Tiffany diamond drop earrings sparkling like stalactites in the dazzling winter sunshine, Althea ran a black, gloved hand along the top of the gravestone, lovingly tracing a finger over the one-word inscription.

Daniel.

"He's dead, my darling," Althea whispered. "Bob Daley's dead. We got him."

Watching the Englishman's skull explode across her computer screen had been gratifying. But it hadn't brought Althea the closure she'd hoped for. She'd come to Daniel's grave today in hopes that it might bring her some peace.

It hadn't.

Perhaps it's because he isn't really here? The simple marble slab was just a memorial. Nothing lay beneath it. Thanks to them, Althea would never know where her beloved Daniel really lay, or whether he had even been buried. They had stolen that comfort from her, just as they had stolen everything else.

That's why I don't feel closure, she realized suddenly. *Captain Bob Daley was just the beginning.*

I must destroy them all.

Just as they destroyed me.

Althea wondered why the CIA hadn't called in Tracy Whitney yet.

It was vital that Tracy be a part of this. Her message had been crystal clear on that point. Why were they waiting?

If that moron Greg Walton didn't act soon, she'd be forced to take matters into her own hands. As the icy wind bit into her cheeks, Althea hoped it didn't come to that.

Wrapping her mink more tightly around her, she turned and walked to her waiting limousine.

It was nice to be rich.

But it was even nicer to be powerful.

Chapter 5

Tracy Whitney watched the snowflakes fall softly to the ground outside her window as she sewed name-tapes into her son's soccer kit. *Nicholas Schmidt, 9G.* This was the second kit Tracy had had to buy Nick since the summer. At fourteen, her son was growing like a weed. *He must be taller than Jeff now,* Tracy thought.

Nicholas knew Jeff Stevens as Uncle Jeff, an international antique dealer and old friend of his mother's. He believed his real father was a man named Karl Schmidt, a German industrialist, who'd died tragically in a skiing accident while Nick was still in his mother's womb. It was the story Tracy had told him and everybody else in Steamboat Springs, the small Colorado town that had been their home for almost fifteen years now. But it wasn't true. There had never been any Karl Schmidt, or any ski accident. Jeff Stevens was Nick's father. He was also a con artist and a thief, one of the best in the world. Although never *quite* as good as Tracy.

Putting aside the shorts, Tracy got to work on Nick's shirt. The dark blue team colors brought out the color of Nick's eyes—piercing blue, like his father's. He also had Jeff's athletic build and thick dark hair, and that irresistible combination of masculinity and charm that had drawn women to Jeff Stevens like moths to a lightbulb. Tracy hadn't seen Jeff in three years, not since she saved his life, rescuing him from a psychotic former agent named Daniel Cooper. But she thought of him often. Every time Nicholas smiled, in fact.

That last encounter with Jeff Stevens had been a crazy time in Tracy's life, a brief, brutal return to the adrenaline and danger of a world she thought she'd left behind forever. Afterwards, she'd struck a deal with the FBI to grant her immunity from prosecution and returned to the peaceful anonymity of Steamboat Springs. Uncle Jeff had visited once, and kept in touch with postcards from far-flung parts of the world. He'd also set up a trust fund for Nick worth tens of millions of dollars. *What can I say?* he wrote to Tracy. *The antiques business is booming. Who else am I going to leave it to?*

Jeff knew that Blake Carter, the old cowboy who

ran Tracy's ranch and had practically raised Nicholas, was a far better, safer, more solid father than he could ever be. Like Tracy, he wanted their son to have a stable, happy life. So he'd made the ultimate sacrifice and walked away. Tracy loved him for that more than anything.

It bothered her sometimes that everything Nick knew about her and his real father was a lie. *My own son doesn't know me at all.* But she took comfort in Blake Carter's words. "He knows you love him, Tracy. When all's said and done, that's all that matters."

At last the huge pile of kit was named and folded. Tracy stretched, poured herself a bourbon and threw another log on the huge open fire that dominated her open-plan living room. She watched it spit flames high into the air, crackling so loudly it sounded like a gunshot. Warm, comforting smells of pine resin and wood smoke filled the room, mingling with cinnamon from the kitchen. Tracy sighed contentedly.

I love this place.

With her slender figure, shoulder-length chestnut hair and lively, intelligent eyes that could change from moss green to dark jade according to her mood, Tracy had always been a beauty. She was no longer a young woman, but she still exuded an intoxicating appeal to the opposite sex. There was something unattainable about her, a spark of challenge and temptation in those unknowable eyes that transcended age. Even in jeans, Ugg boots and a roll-neck sweater and without makeup, as she was now, Tracy Whitney could light up a room at a glance. Those who knew her best, like Blake Carter, saw something else in Tracy—a sadness, deep as the ocean, and beautiful too in its own way. It was the legacy of loss—lost love, lost hopes, lost freedom. Tracy had survived it all. Survived and thrived. But that sadness was still a part of her.

Tracy sipped the dark liquor, letting its warmth slide down her throat and into her chest. She shouldn't really be drinking—it was only four in the afternoon— but after all that damn sewing she deserved it. Plus it felt like evening. Outside twilight was already making way for darkness, with the indigo sky fading slowly to black. On the ground, snow lay feet thick and pristine, like frosting on a wedding cake, punctured only by the dark green spruce and pine trees, reaching their leafy arms up to the heavens. The house was at its best in winter, when its floor-to-ceiling windows showcased the snowcapped Rockies at their most magnificent. The term "splendid isolation" could have been coined for this place. It was one of the main reasons Tracy chose it all those years ago.

A loud knock on the door interrupted her thoughts.

Tracy smiled.

So much for isolation.

The ranch's position might be remote but Steamboat Springs was still a small town and Tracy was the mother of one of its more troublesome teenagers. Her mind ran over the possibilities as she walked to the door.

School counselor?

Principal?

Irate mother of an eighth grade cheerleader?

Sheriff?

Oh God, please not the Sheriff. Blake would hit the roof if Nick had been running one of his scams again. Last time he'd managed to reprogram the school library computers to show that half of the middle-school students were entitled to rebates. The school had erroneously paid out more than two thousand dollars to Nick's buddies before the head librarian got wise and called the cops.

Sheriff Reeves had gone easy on Nick that time. But one more screw up and he'd have to make an example of him.

Tracy put on her most gracious smile and opened the door.

A waft of freezing air hit her. Tracy shivered.

Two men were standing on her porch. Both wore

long cashmere coats, trilby hats and scarves. One of the men she didn't recognize. The other, very unfortunately, she did.

"Hello, Tracy."

Agent Milton Buck of the FBI attempted a smile, but was so out of practice it came off as a leer.

"This is my colleague, Mr. Gregory Walton of the CIA." Buck gestured to the much shorter man standing next to him, hopping from foot to foot against the cold. "May we come in?"

Five minutes later, Tracy and the two agents stood awkwardly around the kitchen table. Tracy had offered them each a cup of coffee. Coats had been removed, pleasantries dispensed with. It soon became apparent that the shorter man, from the CIA, was in charge of proceedings.

"Thank you for letting us in, Miss Whitney."

Bald, softly spoken and scrupulously polite, Tracy immediately liked Agent Walton a lot more than Agent Buck. Then again there were tapeworms that Tracy Whitney liked more than Agent Buck. The two of them had history together, none of it good.

"It's Mrs. Schmidt here," Tracy said. "And I wouldn't leave a man to freeze to death on my doorstep,

Mr. Walton. However much I didn't want to see him," she added pointedly, looking directly at Milton Buck.

"Please. Call me Greg."

"OK." Tracy smiled. "Greg. Let's skip the pleasantries. Why are you here?"

Walton opened his mouth to say something, but Tracy wasn't finished.

"I had a cast-iron guarantee from the Bureau, after I helped them neutralize Daniel Cooper and arrest Rebecca Mortimer three years ago, that my family and I would be left in peace."

"I understand that," Greg Walton said reassuringly. "And you will be. You have my word on that."

"And yet here you are in my kitchen." Tracy raised an eyebrow archly and crossed one long, slender leg over another.

Greg Walton thought *this lady's quite something.* Not for the first time in the presence of a very beautiful woman, he felt relieved he was gay.

"What we need to talk to you about today, Miss Whitney, has nothing to do with that case or with your past. It's a matter of national security."

Tracy looked puzzled. "I don't understand."

"Perhaps if you listened, you would," Milton Buck snapped. He was still handsome in a brutish, arrogant way, Tracy noticed. And every bit as charmless as she remembered.

"What Mr. Walton is saying is that we're not here to prosecute you for your crimes as a jewel and art thief."

Tracy said, "I should think not as I haven't committed any."

"We're here to demand that you do your duty for your country."

"Is that so?" Tracy's eyes narrowed. As far as she was concerned Milton Buck could stick his *demands* where the sun didn't shine. Three years ago the bastard would have left Jeff to die, strung up on a cross by that maniac Cooper in the hills above Plovdiv, Bulgaria. It was only Tracy, and her friend Jean Rizzo from Interpol, who had saved Jeff and brought Daniel Cooper to justice. Although of course the FBI had basked in the credit, no one more so than Agent Buck.

"Not demand," Greg Walton corrected, shooting Buck a dirty look. "Request. We're here to request—to ask you to help us. The long and the short of it is, Tracy, we need your help."

Tracy studied Walton's face distrustfully. She looked at her watch.

"I'm picking up my son at five thirty. You have my attention for the next hour, but after that you *must* leave."

Milton Buck looked outraged. He opened his mouth to speak but Greg Walton glared at him. "That's a deal, Miss Whitney," Walton said. "Now, let me tell you why we're here."

For the next forty minutes, Greg Walton didn't draw breath. Tracy sat listening to him, leaning forwards over the kitchen table, her coffee growing lukewarm, then cold. Like most people in America, Tracy had seen the story of Captain Daley's gruesome execution at the hands of Group 99 online. She knew about the controversial raid in Bratislava; how for all the government's spin it had clearly been a failed attempt to rescue American journalist Hunter Drexel.

What she didn't know, was that rather than still being in Group 99's hands, as President Havers had explicitly told the nation in a televised statement, Hunter Drexel was actually on the run, for reasons unknown. Or that a woman, codenamed Althea but believed to be a wealthy *U.S. citizen*, was not only masterminding and funding Group 99 but had directly ordered Daley's death.

"Wow," Tracy said, once Walton was finished. "Havers must be out of his mind. To flat-out lie like that? What happens if Drexel suddenly pops up somewhere, Edward Snowden–style, and holds a press conference?"

"That would be extremely unfortunate," Greg Walton admitted. "More unfortunate, however, would be a global escalation of violence and murder such as we witnessed with Captain Daley. Kidnappings, executions, bombings. Anything's possible now that they've crossed this red line. We don't know exactly how large Group 99's network is. But we do know that it's massive, and growing, especially in places where the economic divide is acutely pronounced. Like South America, for example."

"On our doorstep," Tracy mused.

"Precisely."

Tracy processed all this for a moment before turning to Walton.

"This is all very interesting. But I still don't see where I fit in."

Greg Walton leaned forward. "This woman, Althea, sent an encrypted message to us at Langley a little over a week ago. In it, she mentioned you by name, Tracy."

"Me?" Tracy looked suitably dumbfounded.

Walton nodded.

"What did she say?"

"That she'd outsmarted us just like you did. That only you could unmask her. That Agent Buck here should pay you a visit. She almost made it sound like a game. A competition between the two of you."

If Greg Walton's expression hadn't been so serious, Tracy would have burst out laughing. *This had to be a joke, right?*

"Have you any idea who this woman might be, Tracy? Any idea at all?"

Tracy shook her head. "No. I wish I did but, no. This makes no sense to me."

"Listen to this."

Greg Walton played her the same recording of Althea ordering Bob Daley's execution that he'd played for MI6 a few days earlier.

"Have you ever heard that voice before?"

"I'm sorry," Tracy said. "I haven't. Not that I remember."

"Think hard. It may be someone from your distant past. From your childhood, even. Or the Louisiana Penitentiary?"

Tracy allowed herself a small smile. The voice on the tape was educated, sophisticated. Nobody from the penitentiary had sounded remotely like that.

"Could she have been a colleague at the Philadelphia Bank?" Walton pressed. "Or perhaps someone you and Jeff knew in London?"

From my days as a thief, you mean? Tracy finished for him. *No. I don't think so.*

Hearing Greg Walton, a man she'd never met before, reel off places and people in her life as if he knew her intimately was disconcerting to say the least. But she kept her composure.

"No," she said. "I'd remember, I'm sure of it."

"Well, you do know her." Milton Buck lost his patience. "That much is a fact. So if she's not from your past, she must be from your present. What prior contact have you had with Group 99?"

"*What?*" Tracy scowled at him.

There were no words to adequately express her loathing for Milton Buck, a man who was prepared to sacrifice anything, or anyone, for the sake of advancing his career. If Buck had had his way, Jeff would have been left to die at Daniel Cooper's deranged hands. Tracy would never forgive him.

"Think very carefully before you answer, Miss Whitney," Buck warned her. "If you lie to us now, any deal we may have made in the past will be off. Null and void."

"I don't need to think carefully," Tracy shot back. "I've never had any contact with Group 99."

"Hmmm." Milton Buck's upper lip curled. "You admire them, though, don't you?" He seemed to delight in pressing Tracy's buttons. "All that subversive, antiestablishment baloney. It's right up your street."

"I did quite admire them once," Tracy said defiantly. "Before Daley's execution I was impressed by their techniques. But then so were a lot of people. I mean, there's no doubt they're smart. Hacking in to the Langley computers is no mean feat."

"No. It isn't," Greg Walton muttered bitterly.

"They've outsmarted governments and intelligence agencies and Big Oil," Tracy went on. "But, I never shared their views, Agent Buck. Other than their dislike of the fracking industry. And I certainly don't admire terrorists, or murderers."

"So you don't believe in redistributing wealth away from the top one percent?" Milton Buck asked skeptically. "Robbing the rich to help the poor?"

"Certainly not," said Tracy. "Look around you, Agent Buck." She gestured to the expensive oil paintings hanging on the walls and the cabinet full of polished silver in the dining room. "I'm part of the one percent. Then again, from what you describe, so is this woman Althea." She turned back to Greg Walton. "If she's rich enough to funnel millions to Group 99, isn't she part of the problem, in their eyes?"

"There's a lot about Group 99 that doesn't make sense to us right now," Walton replied. "A lot of inconsistencies. Together with the British, we're piecing together a clearer picture of their changing objectives. But what we do know is that their days of peaceful protest are over. We have a hostage out there right now whose life is in imminent danger."

"I know that," Tracy said, chastened. "Hunter Drexel."

"And he won't be the last. We believe Althea may hold the key to the entire network, Tracy. We need your help to find her. Come back to Langley with us."

Tracy's eyes widened. If the situation weren't so serious, she would have laughed.

"You want *me* to come to Langley? Right *now*?"

"We don't want it," Greg Walton's tone was deadly serious. "We need it. You're our best hope."

"No," Tracy said, on autopilot. "I won't. I can't. I have a son . . ."

She stood up and walked over to the window. It was totally dark now. All Tracy could see was her own reflection.

I look like a housewife, standing in her kitchen.

This is ridiculous. I am a housewife, standing in her kitchen.

Turning back to the two agents she said, "Look. I don't know this woman. That's the God's honest truth. We've never met. Clearly she knows who I am. But that doesn't mean the reverse is true."

Greg Walton leaned forward urgently. "Even if that's true, Tracy. Even if it turns out you *don't* know her, you can still help us."

"I don't see how."

"You and Althea have a lot in common."

Tracy frowned. "How do you figure that?"

"You're both wealthy, independent women, with a background in computers, who've successfully evaded detection by the authorities in multiple countries. You both play by your own rules, conceal your identities, and rise to the top in what are traditionally all-male environments. You're both risk takers."

"Not anymore," Tracy said firmly. "My reckless days are over. She's a terrorist, Mr. Walton."

"Greg."

"I'm a housewife."

"She knows you," Walton insisted. "And at a minimum, you can help us understand her strategy, her MO. If we can predict her next move and identify her weaknesses, we stand a chance of stopping her. *How* is she slipping through the net? Who's helping her? What would you do if you were in her shoes?"

"I don't *know* what I'd do." Tracy's frustration was mounting. "Group 99, Althea's world, it's a closed book to me."

"So let us open it." Greg Walton's tone was becoming more insistent. "We'll brief you on Group 99, everything we know and British intelligence knows. Trust me, Tracy, if I weren't certain you can help, I wouldn't be here. The president himself asked us to approach you."

Tracy looked skeptical. "Really?"

"President Havers would be happy to call you himself to confirm it," Walton said, leaping on her hesitation. "Finding Althea and cutting Group 99 off at the knees is the White House's top national security objective right now. Bar none. A call from the White House can be arranged if you'd like that."

Tracy ran her hands through her hair. "I'm sorry, Greg. I'm flattered, I really am. But if the president thinks I can help then I'm afraid he's been seriously misinformed. I give you my word that if I think of any connection between myself and Althea, or any sort of lead you could use, I will pick up the phone. But I'm not coming to Langley. I have a son."

"I know," Greg Walton sighed. "Nicholas."

"That's right. The last time I left him, I almost didn't make it back. I swore then, to him and to myself, that I would never put myself in harm's way again."

"Not even for your country?"

Tracy shook her head.

"I love my country. But I love my son more." She looked at her watch again. "And now, gentlemen, you'll have to excuse me. It's time for me to go pick him up."

Milton Buck got angrily to his feet. "You don't get to

call the shots here, Tracy. Do you think anybody cares about your soccer mom priorities, when Americans are out there being kidnapped and tortured and American companies are having billions of dollars wiped off their balance sheets? Who the hell do you think you are?"

"That's enough." Greg Walton didn't raise his voice, but the look on his face made it plain that he was livid with his colleague. "I apologize, Miss Whitney. We're grateful to you for giving us your time." He handed Tracy a card. "If you change your mind, or have any information or questions, please call me. Day or night. We'll see ourselves out."

He walked to the door, with Milton Buck following like a sullen child.

As they left, Tracy said, "I'm sorry."

Milton Buck waited till Greg Walton was out of earshot before hissing in Tracy's ear. "You will be."

For five minutes the two men drove down the mountain road in stony silence.

Then Greg Walton turned to Milton Buck.

"Fix this," he said. The avuncular tone he'd used with Tracy was gone now. The two short words dripped with menace.

"How?" Buck asked.

"That's your problem. I don't care how you do it,

but you get Tracy Whitney to Langley or your career is over. Is that clear?"

Milton Buck swallowed hard. "Crystal."

Nick and Tracy sat at the dinner table, watching a video on Nick's phone.

"That is *awful*," Tracy said, tears of laughter streaming down her face.

"I know," Nick grinned. "I'm putting it on Vine."

"You are *not*," Blake Carter said thunderously. "Give me that phone."

"What? No!" said Nick. "Come on, Blake. It's funny. I'll bet it goes viral."

"It's disrespectful is what it is," said Blake. Ignoring the boy's protests, he took the phone and deleted the footage of the principal of the middle school glancing around what he clearly believed to be an empty corridor before farting loudly.

"Mom!" Nick protested.

Tracy shrugged, wiping away the tears of mirth. "Sorry, honey. Blake's right. You shouldn't sneak up on people like that."

"Not 'people,' " Blake corrected her. "Adults. Teachers, for crying out loud. In my day you'd have had a whip taken to ya for something like that."

"In your day they didn't have phones," said Nick, still angry. "Your idea of fun was hitting a ball on a string. You know what your problem is? You don't know *how* to have fun."

"Nick!" said Tracy. "Apologize."

"Sorry." The word dripped with sarcasm. "I'm going to my room."

Seconds later Nick's bedroom door slammed.

Blake looked at Tracy. "Why do you encourage him?"

"Oh come *on*. It was funny."

"It was puerile."

"That's because he's a kid," said Tracy. "You don't always have to come on quite so 'Sam Eagle' about everything."

Blake looked hurt.

"I'm not his friend, Tracy. I'm his parent." Realizing what he'd just said, Blake blushed. "Well, I mean . . . you know . . . I'm . . ."

"You're his parent," Tracy said seriously, laying a hand over Blake's. "He's lucky to have you. We both are."

Tracy felt tremendous love for Blake Carter. Pushing seventy now, the old cowboy had been a wonderful father figure to Nicholas and the dearest friend Tracy ever could have wished for. She knew that Blake loved her. He'd even proposed once, years ago. And though she couldn't love him back in the same way, she absolutely considered him family.

"Is something the matter, Tracy?" Blake asked her. "Besides Nick?"

That was the other thing about Blake Carter. He saw right through her. Trying to hide things from Blake was like trying to hide them from God—a wasted effort.

"I had a visit today," Tracy told him. "From the FBI." Blake Carter stiffened, like a deer sensing danger.

"And the CIA," Tracy added. "Together."

"What did they want?"

Tracy told him. Not everything, but the bare bones of what had been said, as well as Greg Walton's proposal that she fly to Langley.

"What did you say?" Blake asked.

"I said no, of course. I've never met this woman, I'm sure of it. And what I know about counterterrorism you could write on the back of a stamp."

"But these guys thought you could help?" Blake said gently.

"Well, yes," Tracy admitted. "They did. But they're wrong. Don't tell me you *want* me to go to Langley?"

"Of course I don't want you to go," Blake's voice grew gruff with emotion. "But maybe it's not about what I want. Or what you want. These 99 people . . . they're out of control. Someone needs to stand up to them. They're against everything this country stands for. Everything America was built on."

"You see, there you go again," Tracy said archly. "Sam Eagle."

"All's I'm saying is, they need to be stopped. Don't you agree?"

"Of course I do," snapped Tracy. "And they will be stopped. Just not by me. I'm not a spy, Blake. I have nothing to offer here. Heaven knows how this woman Althea knows about me, or why she mentioned my name. But now she's got the FBI, the CIA and the White House convinced I have some sort of inside information, some magic power to find her and do their jobs for them. The whole thing's ridiculous! I feel like Alice down the rabbit hole!"

"OK, Tracy. Calm down."

"And even if it weren't ridiculous, even if I could help, which I can't—I'm not leaving Nick. Not ever."

"I understand that."

"Actually I don't think you do." There were tears in Tracy's eyes now. She was angry and visibly upset, although whether it was with Blake Carter or herself she couldn't have said. "I think you'd better go home, Blake."

The old cowboy raised an eyebrow. "OK. If that's what you want."

Before Tracy could gather her thoughts, he'd picked up his hat and left. Tracy heard the sound of Blake's truck pulling away, followed by a loud blaring of angry teenage music coming from Nick's bedroom. Tired and miserable, she cleared away the plates and went to bed.

Two hours later, Tracy was still wide awake, staring at the ceiling.

She thought about Blake Carter. Why did he have to be so good, all the time? So damn selfless and upstanding and righteous? Didn't he realize how annoying it was?

She thought about Nicholas, and how like his father he was. Jeff would have laughed at the fart video. She tried to deny it to herself, but there were times when Tracy missed Jeff so badly it felt like a stone slab pressing on her heart.

Finally, despite her efforts to shut them out, she thought about her two visitors today. The short, charming CIA chief, Greg Walton, with his earnest entreaties; and the bullying, hateful Milton Buck with his not-so-veiled threats.

"I'm sorry."

"You will be."

Tracy hadn't told Blake about that part. She hadn't wanted to worry him. Blake didn't know about the jewel heist Tracy had pulled off only a few years back in L.A., stealing the Brookstein emeralds from under the nose of her rival, Rebecca Mortimer. The FBI had made a deal after the Bible Killer case, promising Tracy immunity on that and a string of other crimes. Tracy had scratched their back, and they'd promised to scratch hers. But if Tracy knew one thing about Agent Milton Buck it was that the man had no scruples. He'd think nothing of reneging on their deal and sending her to jail if he thought it would advance his career.

I'm not going back to jail, Tracy told herself. *Not ever.*

Milton Buck wasn't the only one with dangerous secrets up his sleeve. Blackmail, Tracy had learned long ago, was a two-player game, and Tracy had prepared her own next move long ago. If Buck tried to come after her over this Group 99 business, she'd be ready.

Eventually, sleep began to come to her. As she sank into its embrace, floating in and out of consciousness, Tracy thought about Althea, this mysterious, murderous, wealthy woman that had the President of the United States and all his many minions clutching at straws.

Who is she?

Where is she?

And how does she know my name?

How had she gotten involved with Group 99? And was she the one responsible for turning them from an organization of peaceful, subversive, idealists into brutal terrorists, as bloodthirsty and ruthless as all the rest?

Blake Carter's words came back to her: *It's not about what I want, Tracy. Or what you want. These people need to be stopped.*

Exhausted, Tracy Whitney finally slept.

Chapter 6

Sally Faiers waited patiently for the four keys in front of her to merge into one so that she could unlock her front door. It would help if the door would stop swaying too. But after four large vodka and tonics, one couldn't have everything.

Sally's flat was on Beaufort Street in Chelsea, one of hundreds in a typical, redbrick Victorian mansion block. By journalist standards it was a nice place. Expensive part of London. Decent transport links. Not covered in mold. An award-winning columnist at *The Times*, Sally Faiers was at the top of her game but she would never earn a fortune. No one went into investigative journalism for the money. But Sally owned her own place, paid her own mortgage and even, when the situation demanded, bought her own vodka.

At last, the key went in, so suddenly that Sally lurched forward, bumping her head painfully against the door.

"Arse," she grumbled under her breath.

The four flights of stairs were a killer. She really must go to a gym sometime this century. Staggering, breathless, into her flat, she locked the door behind her and kicked off her heels.

What a night! Sally had filed her latest story, an exposé of one of the top Catholic clerics in England colluding in a pedophile ring, at six o'clock and had gone straight to the nearest pub to celebrate. She was in between boyfriends at the moment, but had made do with snogging John Wheeler from the sports desk in the cab on her way home. She contemplated asking him in for a nightcap—word on the desk was John had the biggest dick in Wapping—but then she remembered what had happened the last time she had a one-night stand with someone at work. Will, the sexy intern on news. Poor Will had mooned over Sally for weeks afterwards, continually "dropping by" her desk for coffee when she was trying to write. In the end she'd had to have a word with the editor and get him transferred to obituaries. She still felt bad about it.

Padding into the bathroom, Sally peeled off her

dress and tights and turned on the shower, glancing at her reflection in the mirror before she stepped inside. At thirty-two Sally Faiers still had a good figure, despite her gym phobia, borderline alcoholism and generally dissolute lifestyle. Her waist was small, her boobs big and remarkably perky, and her long legs just the right amount of toned. She had a small, snub nose that she hated but that men inexplicably found sexy, pale gray eyes like morning mist, and a very wide mouth, that had been known to produce an astonishing number of swear words, curses and profanities, especially when its owner was under a deadline. She wore her blond hair in a blunt bob, and almost always dirty due to a chronic lack of both time and being arsed.

The moment she opened the shower door, her phone rang.

Sally groaned. *Two in the fucking morning!* It wasn't unusual for her to receive calls at odd hours. But once a story was filed, there was usually a lull until her research began again. On this last story, some of the calls had been harrowing. Broken men, sobbing down the line to her as they recalled childhood abuse. Detachment was the one part of the journalist's job that Sally had never been able to master. That, and an ability to ignore a ringing phone.

Wrapping a towel around herself—*Why? Nobody's*

here?—she staggered back into the hallway and picked up.

"Sally Faiers."

"Hello, gorgeous."

Sally's heart dropped to the pit of her stomach. It was a bad line, but she'd know that voice anywhere, the deep, masculine, American voice that was part drawl, part growl.

"Hunter." Just saying his name was painful. "You're alive, then."

"No need to sound so happy about it."

"I'm not happy about it. You're a fucking arsehole."

"Now, that's not kind. You know the only way I got through the last year was by imagining you naked, with those perfect legs of yours wrapped around my waist. Remember Stockholm?"

"No," said Sally. "The only way *I* got through the last year was by imagining you chained to a wall in some godforsaken Group 99 hideout with a pair of electrodes glued to your bollocks."

Hunter laughed. "I missed you."

"They let you go, then?"

"Actually I escaped."

Now it was Sally's turn to laugh. "Bullshit! You have about as many survival skills as a hedgehog trying to shuffle across the M40."

"I've improved." Hunter sounded wounded. "I did have a little help from my fellow countrymen. At the beginning."

Through her drunken haze, Sally read through the lines. "You mean, you were there? In the Bratislava camp?"

"I was there," Hunter confirmed.

"And they left you behind?" she asked, incredulous.

"Not exactly," Hunter admitted. "I made a run for it."

Sally slid down the wall and sat on the floor. "What? Why?"

"It's a long story."

A torrent of emotions rushed through her. The strongest was relief that Hunter was alive. He'd broken her heart into a million tiny pieces when he left her for that slut Fiona at the *New York Times*. But even Sally didn't want to see pieces of his skull flying through the air like poor Bob Daley's.

Hot on the heels of relief was excitement. The whole world was out there looking for Hunter Drexel and speculating about his fate. And she, Sally Faiers, was on the phone with him, listening to him tell her that he'd run from his American rescuers—that President Havers's statement had been an out-and-out lie! Talk about a scoop!

Reaching up, she grabbed a pencil and pad from the hall table.

"Where are you?"

"Sorry," said Hunter, sounding nothing of the sort. "Can't tell you that."

"Give me a clue at least."

"And you can't tell anyone about this phone call either."

Sally laughed. "Fuck off. This is front-page news. The minute you hang up I'm calling the news desk."

"Sally, I mean it, you can't say anything." Hunter's voice was deadly serious all of a sudden. "If they find me they'll kill me."

"If who finds you?" Sally asked.

"Never mind that now," Hunter cut her off. "I need you to do me a favor."

It was astonishing how quickly relief could turn to anger. "In what alternate universe would *I* do *you* a favor?" Sally asked.

"I need you to do some digging for me," Hunter said, ignoring her. "You remember the Greek prince who was found strung up at Sandhurst?"

"Sure. Achileas. The suicide. Hunter, you aren't seriously telling me you're working on a story right now? Because . . ."

"I don't think it was suicide," Hunter interrupted

her. "There's a senior officer at Sandhurst, Major General Frank Dorrien. I need you to find out anything you can about him."

Sally paused. "You think this Dorrien guy murdered Prince Achileas of Greece? Are you on drugs?"

"Just look into it," Hunter said. "Please."

"Tell me where you are and I'll think about it," said Sally.

"Thanks. You're an angel."

"Hey, I didn't say yes! Hunter?"

"You're breaking up." He started making ridiculous, crackling noises down the phone.

"I am *not* breaking up. Hunter! Don't you dare hang up on me. I swear to God, if you hang up now I'm gonna call the CIA right this minute and tell them about this call. Every word. And then I'll run the story in tomorrow's *Times*."

"No you won't," said Hunter.

He hung up.

Sally Faiers sat naked in her hallway for a long time with the phone in her hand.

"Fuck you, Hunter Drexel," she said aloud.

You ripped my heart out. You utterly betrayed me. And now you expect me to sit on the biggest story of my career, and quietly go out and do your dirty work for you on some wild-goose-chase, bullshit story at Sandhurst?

"I'm not doing it," Sally shouted down the empty hall of her flat. "Not this time."

But she already knew that she would.

Hunter hung up the pay phone and stepped out into the howling wind.

How he wished he were in London with Sally! Preferably in bed. He found himself getting hard at the thought of her. Those legs. Those phenomenal tits . . . What had possessed him to leave her in the first place?

She's right, he thought. *I am an asshole.*

He looked around him miserably. Up and down the litterstrewn street, poorly dressed people dived into ugly concrete apartment buildings or offices or cafés, anything to get out of the cold. The few poor souls forced to wait at bus stops huddled together miserably, like sheep en route to the abattoir, stomping their feet and smoking and clapping their gloved hands together repeatedly against the bitter weather.

Romania was a beautiful country. But Oradea, the city where Hunter had spent the last three days, was a dump, full of abandoned, communist architecture and depressed, unemployed people. The hospitals were stuffed full of abandoned children, and filthy Roma families roamed the streets like animals, some of them actually sleeping on top of mounds of rubbish, left to rot or freeze or drink themselves to death.

If Romania's a supermodel, Hunter thought, *Oradea is the pimple on her ass.* There was none of the beauty of Transylvania here, none of the sophistication of Bucharest. No sign anywhere of the much talked about economic revival. Wherever Romania's EU millions had been spent, it wasn't here. Oradea felt like a forgotten city. But that made it perfect for Hunter Drexel. Right now Hunter needed to be forgotten. No one would look for him here.

Not that there was no money to be found in Oradea. In the Old Town, along the banks of the Crişul Repede river, a few magnificent mansions, relics of the pre-communist days, had been reclaimed by wealthy private owners. Stuffed with fine art and priceless antiques, their formal gardens lined with lavender bushes and neatly clipped hedges, these homes glittered like stars in an otherwise pitch-black sky, sparkling incongruously like newly cut diamonds dropped in a pile of manure. Their owners were mostly native Romanians, gangsters, corrupt local government officials, and a smattering of legitimate businessmen, some returning to their hometown now after years of exile abroad.

It was in one of these houses that Hunter was staying. Its owner, a property magnate by the name of Vasile Rinescu, was a keen poker player and a friend of sorts.

"If you're here to play, you're welcome," Vasile told Hunter, when the latter had arrived, shivering and desperate, on his doorstep. "I don't know about blood, but poker is definitely thicker than water."

"Thank God for that," said Hunter.

"I'm hosting a game this Saturday as it happens. Some very interesting players. High stakes."

"Good," Hunter said. "I need the money. I'm . . . in a bit of a tight spot right now."

Vasile laughed. "We may be a backwater, but we do watch the news here, my friend," he told Hunter. "The whole world knows about your 'tight spot.'"

A look of panic crossed Hunter's face.

"Don't worry." Vasile clapped him on the back. "My friends are discreet. No one's going to turn you over to the CIA, or Group 99. Unless of course you lose, and you can't pay. In that case they'll turn you over to the highest bidder."

"Right."

"Once they've finished torturing you."

"Gotcha." Hunter grinned. "I guess I'd better not lose then."

"I would try very hard not to," said Vasile. He wasn't smiling.

Hunter didn't lose. After three days at Vasile's, enjoying the first home-cooked meals and hot baths he'd had since he was kidnapped in Moscow, he'd managed to win enough money to fund at least another month on the run.

Keeping one step ahead of the Americans, Hunter realized now, would be the easy part. It was Group 99 that worried him, in particular Apollo. The sadistic guard was bound to view Hunter's escape as a personal humiliation, one that he would stop at nothing to avenge. If Hunter so much as glanced at a computer, Apollo would find him. That meant no emails, no credit card, no cell phone, no rented car, no flights, no electronically traceable presence of any kind. From now on, until his story was finished and in print all around the world, Hunter must live entirely under the radar.

Luckily, poker provided the perfect opportunity to create this new, cash only, invisible version of himself. Poker players were natural secret keepers, with an inbuilt sense of loyalty towards one another. Through poker, Hunter had "friends" like Vasile Rinescu scattered all across Europe. He could flit from safe house to safe house, earning enough to live, and work on his story between games. Of course, without a computer or a phone, research would be tough. He couldn't do this without Sally Faiers's help. But he knew Sally would help him.

She may not trust me as a man. But she trusts me as a journalist.

She knows this is big.

Once he'd published his story—once the truth, the whole truth about Group 99, was finally out there—he would turn himself in to the Americans. He'd have some explaining to do, of course. But then so would a lot of people.

Wrapping his scarf tightly around the lower half of his face, Hunter headed across the bridge to the mansion.

Vasile Rinescu had been a wonderful host, but his friends were getting tired of losing.

Tomorrow Hunter would move on.

Chapter 7

J eff Stevens eyed the girl sitting at the end of the bar.
He was at Morton's, an exclusive private members
club in Mayfair, and he had just lost heavily at cards. But
something about the way the lissome blonde returned
his smile gave him the feeling that his luck was about
to change.

He ordered one glass of Dom Pérignon 2003 and one
glass of Perrier and crossed the polished parquet floor
to where she was perched, her endless legs dangling
deliciously off the end of a taupe velvet barstool. She
was in her early twenties, with high cheekbones and
the sort of glowing skin that only youth could produce.
If her silver dress got any shorter it would be in clear
contravention of the sales descriptions act.

In short, she was Jeff's kind of girl.

"Waiting for someone?"

He handed her the flute of champagne.

She hesitated for a moment, then accepted, locking her dark blue eyes on Jeff's gray ones.

"Not anymore. I'm Lianna."

"Jeff." Jeff grinned, mentally calculating how many minutes of flirting he would have to put in here before he could take Lianna home with him. Hopefully no more than fifteen. One more drink. He had a big day ahead of him tomorrow.

Jeff Stevens had been a con artist for as long as he could remember. He'd learned the basic skills of his trade as a boy at his Uncle Willie's carnival, and they'd taken him all over the world, to places more dazzlingly glamorous and terrifyingly dangerous than the young Jeff had known existed. With his sharp, inventive mind, easy charm and devastating good looks, Jeff had quickly risen to the very top of his "profession." He had stolen priceless paintings from world-famous art galleries, relieved heiresses of their diamonds and billionaire gangsters of their property portfolios. He'd pulled off jobs on the Orient Express, the *QEII* and Concorde, before that airliner's tragic demise. Working with Tracy Whitney, in the heyday of his career, Jeff had pulled off some of the most audacious and brilliant heists ever accomplished in a string of cities across

Europe, always targeting the greedy and corrupt, and always managing to stay one step ahead of the hapless police as they tried and failed to link him or Tracy to any crime.

Those were happy days. The best days of his life, in many ways.

And yet, Jeff reflected, he was happy now too. After losing Tracy for ten long years—after they married, Tracy suspected Jeff of having an affair, wrongly as it turned out, and disappeared off the face of the earth— they were now back in contact. Tracy had saved Jeff's life a few years back, when a deranged former FBI agent named Daniel Cooper had tried to kill him. It was in the aftermath of that ordeal that Jeff learned he had a son, Nicholas. Unbeknownst to Jeff, Tracy had been pregnant when she took off and had raised the boy alone in Colorado, with the help of her ranch manager, a decent, sweet man named Blake Carter.

Jeff had seen at once that Blake was effectively already a father to Nick, and a damn good one. He'd loved the boy enough not to try to change that. Tracy had introduced Jeff as an old friend, and in the interven- ing years Jeff had become a sort of unofficial godfather to his own son.

Perhaps it was a strange arrangement. But it worked. Jeff adored Nick, but his life was way too crazy to provide a stable environment for a child, or teenager as Nick was now. This way they could be friends, and hang out and send each other stupid videos on Vine that Nick's mother wouldn't approve of. Jeff *did* want to visit the boy more. But he hoped, with time, Tracy would come around on that point.

As for Tracy, the love between the two of them was still there, still as strong as ever. But she too had made a new life for herself, a peaceful, calm, contented life. For Jeff, the adrenaline rush of pulling off the perfect con remained irresistible. It was as much a part of him as his legs or his arms or his brain. Even so, he would have given it up for Tracy, as he did once before when they married. But as Tracy had said, "If you gave it up, Jeff, you wouldn't be you. And it's you I love."

So Jeff had returned to London and his old life. But this time it was different. Better.

Now he knew that Tracy was alive. And not just alive but safe and happy. Even more wonderful, he had a son, a fabulous son. Nick became the purpose of everything now. Every job Jeff took, every penny he made, was for his boy.

He gave up drinking, only gambled occasionally and started turning down any jobs he perceived as too high risk. It wasn't just him anymore. Jeff could no longer afford to be so reckless.

On the other hand, he thought, resting a hand on Lianna's buttermilk thigh and feeling himself growing harder by the second, *a man must have some pleasures in life.*

Jeff would never marry again. He would never love again, not after Tracy. But asking Jeff Stevens to forsake women would be like asking a whale to live without water, or commanding a sunflower to grow in the dark.

Leaning forward, he was about to ask for the bill and bundle the lovely Lianna into a cab when a tall, thin, older man stepped angrily between them.

"Who the hell are you?" the man asked, glaring at Jeff. "And what are you doing pawing my fiancée?"

Jeff raised an eyebrow at Lianna, who flashed him back an apologetic half smile.

"Jeff Stevens." He offered Angry Man his hand but was met by another withering glower. "She never mentioned she was . . . that you were, er . . . congratulations. When's the big day, Mr. . . . ?"

"Klinnsman."

Jeff swallowed hard. Dean Klinnsman was probably the biggest property developer in London after the Candy brothers, and he allegedly ran a sizable organized crime operation. He had a small army of Poles, building contractors by day, whom he used after hours as enforcers paying the kind of visit to Klinnsman's enemies and business rivals that Jeff Stevens definitely did *not* want to receive.

"A pleasure to meet you Mr. Klinnsman. I'll be on my way."

"You do that."

Dropping a wad of fifties on the bar, Jeff practically ran for the door.

"What was his name?" Dean Klinnsman growled at his young fiancée, once Jeff had gone.

"Madely," the girl answered without blinking. "Max Madely. He's here on vacation. Isn't that right, James?"

She looked at the barman, who went white with fear.

"I believe so, Madam."

"He lives in Miami," the girl went on. "I think he makes, like, coffee machines. Or something."

"Hmmm," Dean Klinnsman grunted. "I don't want you talking to him again. Ever."

"Oh, Deano!" Lianna coiled herself around the famous developer like an oversexed snake. "You're so jealous. He was only being friendly. Anyway, you needn't worry. He flies back to the States tomorrow."

Jeff's cab ride home took longer than it should have, thanks to the driver's taking some stupid detour around the park. As they crawled past the grand, stucco-fronted houses of Belgravia, Jeff found himself tuning in to the talk show debate on the driver's radio.

Two men, both politicians, were arguing heatedly about Group 99 and the ongoing but so far fruitless search for both Captain Daley's killer and the American hostage, Hunter Drexel.

"It's the Americans we should be blaming for this," one of the men was insisting. "I mean, if you're going to throw your weight around, trample international law and go guns-blazing into someone else's country, the least you can do is A: make sure your hostage is actually *there* and B: shoot the right bloke when you arrive. Instead, we now have Daley's killer on the loose, Hunter Drexel still being held somewhere, and a bunch of murdered teenagers lying in a Bratislavan morgue."

"They weren't 'murdered,'" his opponent shot back, apoplectic with rage. "They were military combatants, killed in action. Justified action I'd say, after what they did to Bob Daley. They were terrorists."

"They were kids! The fella who shot Bob Daley was a terrorist. But he's not the one with a bullet in his skull, is he?"

"They're all part of the same group," yelled his opponent. "They're all responsible."

"Oh really? So are all Muslims responsible for ISIL?"

"What? Of course not! The two situations are not even remotely similar."

" 'Ere we are, mate."

To Jeff's relief, he saw that the cabbie had finally reached his flat on Cheyne Walk. Tipping the man more than he deserved, Jeff stepped out into the cool night air. The breeze coming off the river, combined with the softly twinkling lights of Albert Bridge, soothed his nerves.

Like many people in England, Jeff was gripped by the twists and turns of the Group 99 affair. On the one hand he found the lazy, anti-Americanism expressed by the first politician on the radio show to be both insulting and wrongheaded. Jeff had lived in England long enough to know that if it had been the SAS going in to rescue a British hostage, they'd have been hailed as heroes and Bratislavan territorial integrity be damned.

Then again, the SAS might not have made such a total balls up of the whole thing.

On the other hand, there was a part of him that agreed with the first politician, when he characterized the men shot dead at the Bratislava camp as "kids." Up until Daley's slaying, Group 99 had never been violent, and were rarely if ever referred to as terrorists. Was everyone who had ever joined the organization now to be tarred with the same brush as the monster who shot Daley?

Jeff Stevens knew he made an unlikely apologist for the Group 99ers. Back when it was trendy to admire them, Jeff had always found their politics crass and their so-called mission wildly insincere. These young men from Europe's broken states might justify their actions under the banner of social justice. But from what Jeff could see, what really drove them was envy. Envy and anger and a growing sense of impotence, fueled by leftwing firebrands like Greece's Elias Calles or Spain's Lucas Colomar. Maybe Jeff was getting old. But in his day, the idea was to earn one's wealth and then enjoy the hell out of it. True, Jeff had broken plenty of laws in his day. Technically, he supposed, he could be described as a thief. But he only ever stole from genuinely unpleasant people. And he did so at great personal risk to himself, boldly and daringly; not by sneaking into the back end of somebody's computer system. To Jeff Stevens's way of thinking, hackers were just a bunch of whining cowards who happened to be good at math. And as for targeting the fracking industry? Really! If there was one thing guaranteed to put Jeff's back up it was a sanctimonious eco-bore. If Nicholas ever turned into one of those entitled, embittered little nerds, Jeff would die of shame. Not that that was likely to happen.

Taking the lift up to his penthouse apartment, Jeff felt glad to be home. The vast lateral flat was his pride and joy. With its elegant sash windows, high ceilings, parquet floor and spectacular views across the river, it felt more like a museum than a private residence. Over the years Jeff had filled the place with priceless antiquities, treasures from his travels, both legally and illegally acquired. The shelves were crammed with everything from ancient Egyptian vases, to first edition Victorian novels, to mummified pygmy heads creepily pickled in jars. There were coins and statues, fossils and burial robes, fragments of arrowheads and an entire Nordic rune stone mounted on a plinth. There was no rhyme or reason to Jeff's collection, other than these were all unique items, things with a history that he loved. An ex-lover once suggested that Jeff surrounded himself with things to compensate for the lack of human closeness in his life, an observation that irritated him deeply. Probably because it was true. Or at least it had been, before he found Tracy again, and Nick came into his life.

Wandering into the kitchen, Jeff slipped a Keurig coffee packet into the machine and walked out onto his terrace while it brewed. Since giving up drinking, coffee had replaced whisky as his nighttime ritual. For some reason it never seemed to keep him awake, and childishly he enjoyed the gadgetiness of the new generation of coffeemakers, all the shiny chrome and buttons to press and the perfectly frothed milk.

It was the week before Christmas, and London was in the grip of a cold snap that covered everything with a sparkling gray frost. There was no snow, yet, but the park still looked like a Victorian Christmas card, timeless and peaceful and lovely. Jeff had always loved Christmas. It made him feel like a kid again, dreaming of candy and presents with his nose pressed against the store windows. Then again, as Tracy used to remind him, Jeff had never really stopped being a kid. The only difference was that as an adult he'd exchanged gazing through store windows for breaking in through the roof. "You've become a permanent fixture on Santa's naughty list," she used to say.

Smiling at the memory, and still half thinking about Nicholas—he missed him at Christmas more than usual—Jeff pulled out his phone and, on a whim, called Tracy's number. Irritatingly it went to voicemail.

"It's me," he said awkwardly. Jeff had never liked leaving messages. "Look, I really want to see Nick. I know we said to give it some time, but I want to come out there. It's been too long and I . . . I miss him. Call me back, OK?"

He hung up feeling annoyed with himself and went back inside to retrieve his coffee. He should have waited for Tracy to answer. Things always went better when they spoke in person.

A loud buzz from the doorbell made him jump.

Who the hell could that be at this time? Jeff's stomach suddenly lurched. Surely not even Dean Klinnsman could have tracked him down that quickly. Or maybe he could. *Someone at the club could have given him my address. It would only take a phone call.*

Jeff darted into his bedroom, unlocked the drawer on his bedside table and pulled out a handgun. Keeping his back to the walls, he edged towards the front door of the flat and peeped nervously through the spy hole.

"Jesus," he exhaled, opening the door. "You scared the crap out of me."

Lianna stood alone in the hallway, wrapped up in a dark gray cashmere coat and winter boots.

"I thought it was your fiancée. Or one of his henchmen. Come to finish me off."

"No," Lianna smiled lasciviously. "Just me."

Undoing the belt of her coat she opened it slowly, her eyes never leaving Jeff's. Other than the boots, she was completely, gloriously naked.

"Where were we?" she asked, advancing towards

Jeff like an Amazon goddess, her pupils dilating with lust.

For the tiniest fraction of a second, Jeff thought about how very, very foolish he would be to sleep with Dean Klinnsman's girlfriend. Then he grabbed Lianna around the waist with both hands and pulled her into the apartment.

As long as Tracy Whitney was alive, Jeff Stevens's heart was spoken for.

The rest of his body, however, was quite another matter.

Chapter 8

Tracy looked around the familiar walls of David Hargreaves's office. Christmas cards from staff and grateful former pupils covered every available surface. School would be out in a few days.

If only Nick could have controlled himself a little longer, Tracy thought desperately.

She'd gotten to know the principal of Nick's middle school almost as well as she'd known his elementary school head, Mrs. Jensen. Poor Mrs. Jensen. It was a wonder the woman wasn't in a sanitarium somewhere, banging her head quietly against a padded wall, after everything Nicholas had put her through.

"The thing is, Mrs. Schmidt, it's not simply a question of money. What Nicholas did was a blatant act of disrespect."

Tracy nodded seriously and tried to rid her mind of the image of Mr. Hargreaves farting loudly into what he believed to be an empty corridor.

Nick, seated beside his mother, adopted a hurt look.

"What about artistic expression? Our teacher told us only last week that art knows no boundaries."

"Be quiet!" Tracy and Principal Hargreaves said in unison.

Nick's decision to break into the faculty recreation room after school hours and paint a series of cartoons on the walls, depicting various teachers in caricature, was likely to mark the end of his career at John Dee Middle School. He and an unnamed accomplice had painted the teachers engaging in different "humorous" situations (the mean, overweight math teacher, Mrs. Finch, was re-imagined by Nick as a hot dog, lying in a bun and being squirted with ketchup by the football coach). As a piece of art it actually wasn't bad. But as Principal Hargreaves said, that wasn't the point.

"I'll talk to the board over the weekend," the principal told Tracy. "But to be frank, I don't see that we have much wiggle room here. Nicholas has had a lot of chances."

Principal Hargreaves didn't want to lose the beautiful Mrs. Schmidt as a parent. Tracy's son might be a tear away, but she was a lovely woman. More importantly she'd donated very generously to the school over the years, and was offering to "more than compensate" for the damage Nick had caused to school property this time. But his hands were tied.

Tracy said, "I know. And I appreciate your even discussing it. Please let the board know that I'm grateful."

After the meeting, Tracy waited till they were in the car and safely off campus before turning furiously on Nick.

"I don't understand you. You have to go to school, Nicholas. It's the *law*. If they kick you out of here, you'll just have to go somewhere else. Somewhere farther away, and stricter, where you don't have any friends."

"You could homeschool me," Nick suggested guilelessly. "That would be cool."

"Oh no." Tracy shook her head. "There is zero chance of that happening, mister. I'd rather stick pins in my eyes."

Homeschooling Nicholas would be like trying to teach deportment to a newly captured chimpanzee.

"I could send you to boarding school," Tracy countered. "How about that?"

Nick looked aghast. "You wouldn't!"

No, Tracy thought. *I wouldn't. I couldn't live without you for one day.*

"I might."

"If you did I'd run away. Why do I need school anyway? Uncle Jeff left school at twelve. He learned all he needed to know on his Uncle Willie's carnival."

"Uncle Jeff is not a good role model."

"Why not? He's rich. He's happy. He has a great business, traveling the world."

"That's . . . not the point," said Tracy, increasingly desperately. She didn't want to talk about Jeff and his "great business."

"Well what about Blake?" said Nick. "*He's* a good role model, isn't he?"

"Of course."

"Well he went to work on his daddy's ranch when he was my age. Full-time."

They'd reached home now. It was still only lunch-time. Tracy debated sending Nick to his bedroom—minus his computer, phone and any other means of escape—but the thought of him stuck indoors all day, brooding, didn't seem right. Instead, she sent him out with two of the hands to go and clear the snow drifts that had built up on the high pastures.

"You want to work on a ranch full-time?" she told a stricken-looking Nick as she pushed him into the back of the truck. "You may as well get started now."

With any luck a few days of backache and chilblains would cure of him of that romantic notion at least. Still, Tracy wasn't looking forward to explaining Nicholas's latest shenanigans to Blake Carter. She could already hear the old cowboy's "I told you so" ringing in her ears.

"**I told** you so," said Blake. "I'm sorry to say it, Tracy, but I did."

"You don't look sorry to say it," Tracy complained, handing him a bowl of steaming beef and vegetable soup. On stressful days, Tracy liked to destroy things in blenders. "I didn't tell him to go in there and do those paintings, you know. He's not a toy that I control."

"No," agreed Blake. "He's a boy that you influence. And you keep encouraging him to act out."

"I do *not!*" Tracy said furiously. "How did I encourage this?"

"You told him the artwork was good."

"It was good."

"Tracy." Blake frowned. "When Principal Hargreaves showed you the math lady in the hot dog bun, you laughed! Right in front of Nick! You told me that yourself."

Tracy shrugged helplessly. "I know. I shouldn't have,

but it was funny. Nick *is* funny, that's the problem, Blake. And I love that about him."

The truth was that Tracy loved everything about her son. Every hair on his head, every smile, every frown. Becoming a mother had been the great miracle of her life. Creating Nicholas was the one, pure, wholly good thing she had ever done, untinged by regret, untouched by loss or pain. Whatever the boy's faults, Tracy adored him unconditionally.

"It was tough to keep a straight face in that office," she admitted to Blake. "Every time I looked at Hargreaves I couldn't stop thinking about the farting thing." She started to giggle. Once she started, she couldn't stop.

Blake sat in stony silence as tears of mirth rolled down Tracy's cheeks.

"I'm sorry," she said eventually.

"Are you?" Blake said sternly. "'Cause I don't see it, Tracy. Do you want that boy to wind up like his father?"

Tracy recoiled as if she'd been stung. Blake never brought up Nick's parentage. Never, ever. He knew Jeff Stevens was Nick's real father. Seeing the two of them together that time Jeff came to stay at the ranch had hardened Blake's suspicions on that score into incontrovertible fact. But he'd never discussed it with Tracy. Never asked for any details or cast any judgments. Till now.

To her surprise, Tracy found herself suddenly defensive of Jeff Stevens.

"Do I want Nick to be funny, you mean? And charming and brave and a free spirit?"

"No," said Blake angrily. "That's not what I mean. I mean do you want him to be a criminal, a liar and a thief? Because if you do, you're going the right way about it."

Tracy pushed away her bowl and stood up, her eyes brimming with tears.

"You know what, Blake? It doesn't matter what I want, or what you want. Nick *is* like Jeff. He just is! You think you can lecture it out of him, or punish it out of him, but you can't."

Blake stood up too. "Well, I can try. I'm gonna take him out for a meal tonight in town. Talk to him man to man. One of his parents needs to tell that boy the difference between right and wrong."

"What's that supposed to mean?" Tracy shouted. Blake was already heading for the door. "You are so goddamned holier than thou, Blake Carter. Did you ever wonder why I'm your only friend? You're not perfect, you know."

Blake kept walking.

Tracy yelled after him. "If Nick's a hoodlum, he's a hoodlum *you* raised! Not Jeff Stevens. You! Take a look in the mirror you . . . hypocrite!"

Blake shot her a look of real pain.

Then he walked out, slamming the door behind him.

For the rest of the afternoon Tracy caught up on paperwork. Then she cleaned the kitchen until every surface sparkled and reorganized the books in her library. Twice.

Why did Blake have to be so judgmental?

Worse than that, why did he always have to be right?

Afternoon turned to evening, then to night. When the hands came back in from the fields, Nick wasn't with them.

"Mr. Carter came and picked him up," one of the men told Tracy. "They were headed into town, I think. Did you want us to bring him back here, Ma'am?"

"No, no. That's OK," Tracy said. "You go on home."

It was a bitterly cold night, not snowing, but with a wind blowing that could flay the skin from your bones like a razor blade. Usually Tracy loved nothing more than to curl up in front of the fire on a winter's night like this, luxuriating in the warmth and savoring the precious hours alone with her book. But tonight she found she would read a page and take nothing in. She wandered into the kitchen to make herself some food, then found she wasn't hungry. If Nick were here they'd have watched a show together—something mindless and funny like *The Simpsons*—but Tracy hated watching television alone. Eventually she gave in to her jitters and began pacing the room, going over and over the argument with Blake in her mind like a child stubbornly picking at a scab.

I shouldn't have called him a hypocrite.

High-minded maybe. And rigid. But not a hypocrite.

He'd looked so hurt when he walked out. That was the killer. Then again, Tracy had been hurt too. Did she really deserve to be punished for loving the free spirit in Nick? For finding him funny and charming, even when he was being exasperating? For being on his side?

Tracy's parents, both long dead, had always been on her side. Especially her father. Then again, as a child Tracy had never given them cause to worry. She'd never stepped out of line or been in trouble at school.

I was the archetypal good girl. And look how my life turned out.

For all Blake Carter or anyone else knew, Nick might grow up to be a missionary or an aid worker. Rebellious boy didn't necessarily translate into rebellious man. Did it?

Still, she shouldn't have said what she said to Blake. She'd apologize as soon as he dropped Nick home. And thank him for tonight.

Tracy looked at her watch. 10:15 P.M. They were very late. Most restaurants in Steamboat stopped serving at nine. Tracy pictured Blake ensconced in a booth somewhere, haranguing Nick about moral responsibility until the poor boy's ears melted.

I hope he's OK.

A banging on the front door broke her reverie.

They're back!

Blake must have forgotten his key. Tracy flew to the door. Pulling it open, the first thing she noticed were the lights of the squad car, blinking blue and white in the darkness. Then she focused on the two cops standing in front of her.

"Mrs. Schmidt?"

"Yes," Tracy said cautiously.

One of the cops took off his hat. He gave Tracy a look that made her knees start to shake.

"I'm afraid there's been an accident."

No, there hasn't.

"It seems Mr. Carter ran his truck off the road up at Cross Creek."

No, he didn't. He didn't. Blake's a very careful driver.

"I'm so sorry, Mrs. Schmidt, but I'm afraid he was killed instantly."

Tracy clutched the doorframe for support.

"What about Nick? My son?"

"Your son's OK. He's been taken to the hospital. Yampa Valley Medical Center."

Tracy's legs gave way beneath her. Blake was dead—her Blake, her rock—but all she felt in that moment was relief. Nick was alive! It shamed her to admit it, but that was all that mattered.

"He had to be cut out of the truck. But he was conscious going into the ambulance. We'll take you to him now if you'd like?"

Tracy nodded mutely. She started walking towards the squad car, stumbling through the snow like a zombie.

"Do you have a coat, Ma'am?" the cop asked. "It's pretty cold out tonight."

But Tracy didn't hear him, any more than she felt the cold.

I'm coming Nick. I'm coming my darling.

Everyone at Yampa Valley Medical Center knew Tracy Schmidt. She was one of the hospital's most generous local donors.

A nurse led her to Nick's room. To Tracy's immense relief, he was awake.

"Hi, Mom."

His face was bruised and his lower lip was trembling. Tracy wrapped her arms around him like she would never let go. He started to cry.

"Blake's dead."

"I know." Tracy held him. "I know, my darling. Do you remember what happened?"

"Not really," he whimpered. "Blake thought someone was following us. A woman."

"What woman?" Tracy frowned. "Why would he think that? "

"I don't know. I didn't really see her. But Blake was kind of distracted I guess. One minute we were driving and the next . . ." He started to cry.

"Shhhh. It will be all right, Nicky. I promise."

Tracy stroked the back of his head. Beneath her palm she could feel a lump the size of a hen's egg.

Forcing herself not to panic, she asked, "Do you feel OK?"

"Sort of. I feel dizzy. And super tired. The doctors ran some tests."

"OK," Tracy said brightly. "You get some rest. I'll track down that doctor and see what's what."

She didn't have to go far. Dr. Neil Sherridan was already walking down the hall towards her as she closed Nick's door behind her. Tracy knew Dr. Sherridan from the hospital fund-raiser she'd been to with Blake last summer. She remembered she'd worn a red ball gown and the diamond earrings Jeff had given her on their wedding day. Blake had beamed with pride to be escorting her, even though everybody knew they were mother and son. It all seemed like another life now.

"Mrs. Schmidt?"

"I felt a lump," Tracy blurted. "On his head. Is he OK?"

"I'm afraid not," Dr. Sherridan said gravely.

Tracy felt her stomach lurch, as if she were in an elevator and someone had just cut the cable. "What? What do you mean you're afraid not?"

"We need to operate immediately."

Tracy blinked, uncomprehending. At the gala, she remembered thinking that Dr. Sherridan was handsome. Now he looked hideous, like a devil. Why was he saying these dreadful things?

"I have the consent forms here."

Tracy looked at the doctor, then at the forms he'd thrust in front of her.

"B . . . but," she stammered. "He was talking to me. Just now."

"I understand that. It's not uncommon after car accidents. These sorts of head trauma often take hours to present."

"But, he was fine," Tracy insisted. "He *is* fine."

Dr. Sherridan placed a hand on Tracy's arm.

"No, Mrs. Schmidt. We ran the tests. He's not fine. I'm sorry. The lump you felt is the result of a massive trauma to his brain. He was lucky not to have been killed instantly."

Tracy wobbled. *I'm going to faint.*

"He still stands a solid chance of recovery," the doctor informed her. "However, without an operation, your son *will* die."

The word "No" formed on Tracy's lips. But no sound came out.

"I'm sorry to be so blunt about it but time isn't on our side here. I need you to sign these forms, Mrs. Schmidt. Right now."

Tracy stared at the pen in her hand. Her throat was dry. She tried to swallow but nothing happened. Looking back over her shoulder she watched an unusually tall nurse slip into Nicholas's room. She had mud on her sneakers that left a trail on the clean hospital floor. Tracy fixed her eyes on the mud stains, trying to hold on to anything real. Because what Dr. Sherridan was telling her wasn't real. It couldn't be.

This is a practical joke. A really, really awful one.

When I sign my name with this pen, water will squirt in my face and we'll all start laughing.

"Right here."

Dr. Sherridan pointed to the bottom of the paper.

Tracy scrawled her name.

"Thank you. We'll prepare him for surgery right away."

"He will . . . be OK?" Tracy croaked. She hated the fear in her own voice. "Once you operate? You can fix this, can't you, Dr. Sherridan?"

Dr. Sherridan looked her in the eye.

"We'll know more once the operation's under way. I'm hopeful. But scans only tell us so much."

"But . . ."

"I promise to let you know as soon as we're done, Mrs. Schmidt."

He walked away.

Tracy sat outside the operating theater, praying.

She didn't believe in God. But she tried to make a deal with him anyway.

Let him live and I'll do anything you ask.

Let him live and take me instead.

If only she hadn't had that stupid argument with Blake! He was always such a careful driver. Had he been distracted because he was still upset with her?

I shouldn't have let him take Nick out. Not until he'd calmed down.

The *what ifs* rolled endlessly through Tracy's mind until she couldn't think anymore. *What if I'd sent Nick to his room instead of out on the ranch? What if I'd taken him out instead of Blake? What if they'd taken another route home?* Exhausted, she put her head in her hands. She wished Blake were here to hold her hand. But Blake Carter would never be here again. Blake was dead, gone forever, and Tracy hadn't even found a second to mourn him. Nick filled every atom of her being.

Just let him live, God. Please, please, let him live.

Dr. Sherridan was the best brain surgeon in Colorado, and one of the very best in the whole country. Never mind God. Dr. Sherridan would save Nick.

A shadow fell over Tracy and she jolted awake.

How could I have fallen asleep at a time like this? she thought guiltily.

Then she looked up into Dr. Sherridan's face and the guilt was replaced with something else. Something far, far worse.

The last thing Tracy heard before she lost consciousness was the sound of her own screams.

Chapter 9

"Oh Jeff! Jeff! Oh God!"

Jeff Stevens felt Lianna climax beneath him and grinned. Jeff never tired of the thrill of giving a beautiful woman pleasure. Many women had told him over the years what a wonderful lover he was. But each new girl was a new challenge.

"What about you, darling?" Lianna rolled over on top of him, her wonderful, heavy breasts resting on Jeff's chest like twin jellies turned out of their molds. Dean Klinnsman was a lucky man. With her blond hair and endless legs this girl was phenomenally sexy, although in the absolute opposite way to Tracy.

Jeff never slept with girls who looked like Tracy. They broke his heart.

"Don't you want to come too?" Lianna cooed. "What can I do for you?"

She gave Jeff a knowing look and began to work her way down his body, snaking towards his groin.

"Actually, Angel," Jeff said, pulling her gently back up, "all I really want right now is some food. I'm starved. D'you fancy a Byron Burger?"

"But . . . you're not satisfied?" The girl pouted.

"On the contrary, I'm very satisfied," Jeff assured her.

It was partly true. The simple truth was he was too tired to come. At least not without putting in some effort. Now that Lianna was satisfied, his mind was already drifting to other things. Specifically a bacon cheeseburger with all the trimmings.

Not that Jeff didn't still enjoy sex. Jeff adored women. All women, give or take the odd humorless feminist, although even they provided an interesting challenge. But these days he kept his sexual liaisons strictly compartmentalized. He had been in love twice in his life, and had married both women. Louise Hollander, his first wife, was a twenty-five-year-old, golden-haired heiress who'd hired Jeff to work on her yacht and promptly seduced him. Jeff had loved Louise, right up until the day he learned she'd been cheating on him with a string of wealthier lovers. After their divorce, Jeff swore he'd never become vulnerable to a woman again.

Of course, that was before he met Tracy Whitney.

Tracy was not so much a woman as a force of nature, the adored love of Jeff's life. After their last job together in Holland, brilliantly stealing the Magellan diamond from under the nose of both local and international police, Jeff and Tracy had married. Perhaps, with hindsight, that had been their mistake? The beginning of the end? Domestic bliss had certainly proved a lot more elusive once the adrenaline of their old life was gone.

But if we'd never married, we'd never have had Nick, Jeff reminded himself.

"You should go home, darling," Jeff told Lianna, kissing her on the cheek as he pulled on his jeans. On reflection, stunning, twenty-three-year-old Russian models were rarely big cheeseburger fans. "We don't want your future husband getting suspicious."

"No," she agreed. "But I will see you again? You'll call me, won't you?"

There was already a hint of doubt in her voice.

"Of course," Jeff said.

"Soon?"

"Just as soon as it's safe," he assured her. Which of course would be never if she really did marry Dean Klinnsman. Bedding Lianna once had been dangerous. Making a habit of it would be positively suicidal.

As soon as he heard the front door to his flat close,

Jeff let out a sigh of relief. These days he didn't know what he enjoyed more—really great sex, or a really great burger afterwards, safe in the knowledge that he would never have to see the girl in question again.

He was about to head out the door when his phone rang.

Jeff sighed. Damn it. Lianna could only just have left the building. She hadn't seemed like the clingy type earlier at the bar, nor just now in bed. He sincerely hoped he hadn't misjudged her. Playing dodge-the-bunny-boiler while Dean Klinnsman attempted to have him beaten to death was not Jeff's idea of a merry Christmas.

He let the call go to message.

"Jeff."

Tracy's voice tore through him like an arrow. Lunging for the phone, he tripped over a pile of books, almost concussing himself in his desperation to reach it in time.

"Tracy? Thanks for calling back so quickly. Does this mean it's OK for me to come out there? You have no idea how much I'm dying to see him and I . . . ."

Tracy cut him off.

For years afterwards, Jeff Stevens would dream about that phone call. He would recall everything. Exactly how the handset had felt in his palm. What his flat smelled like in that moment. The distant, empty echo of Tracy's voice, how it was her but *not* her. How she hadn't cried, or shown any emotion, merely laid out for him the cold, terrible, incomprehensible fact of Nicholas's death.

My Nick.

My son.

Dead.

"I'm coming, Tracy," Jeff told her numbly. "I'll get the next flight out."

"Don't. Please."

"Tracy, I have to. I can't let you go through this alone."

"No."

"*I* can't go through this alone."

"Don't come, Jeff."

It was like talking to a zombie.

Jeff's voice broke. "For Christ's sake, Tracy. He was my son too."

"I know. That's why I called you," Tracy said logically. "You had a right to know."

"I love you, Tracy."

Tracy hung up.

For about a minute, Jeff stood frozen, allowing the shock to pass through his body like an electrical current. Then he picked up the phone and booked himself a flight.

There would be time for other emotions later. An eternity of time in which to mourn the son he never really knew, not properly. Time for all the questions, all the whys and hows that he'd been unable to articulate on the telephone.

Right now he had to get to Tracy before she did something stupid.

It took almost exactly thirty-six hours from the moment Jeff received Tracy's phone call in London until he pulled into the driveway of her isolated Colorado ranch.

The last time he came here—the only other time he'd been to the house, in fact—Jeff had been so weak he could barely walk. His ordeal at the hands of Daniel Cooper, the former insurance agent turned rogue vigilante, compelled by a murderous obsession with Tracy, had left Jeff physically broken. But in the end, ironically, Daniel Cooper had done Jeff Stevens a favor. Perhaps the biggest favor of Jeff's life. OK, so Cooper had tried to crucify him and bury him alive in the walls of an ancient Bulgarian ruin. But he'd also achieved what Jeff had failed to achieve in a decade of searching. He'd brought Tracy back to him, and with her, Nicholas. For that, Jeff Stevens would always be grateful. Tracy had found Jeff and rescued him and saved his life. In return, Jeff had agreed to let Tracy live *her* life, as an unassuming mom in a small town in the mountains. He would leave her to raise their son with the help of her ranch manager, Blake Carter, because he knew Carter was a better man than he was. And because Blake loved Nick and vice versa.

It was the right decision, Jeff told himself now, failing to fight back tears. *Nick was happy. He was!*

Jeff had told himself he would have time to make things up to his son once the boy was older. When Nick was a grown man, when the time was right, Jeff and Tracy would sit down with him, together, and tell him the truth. As an adult, Nick could make his own choices. Jeff didn't know why, but he'd always felt confident his son would forgive him. That Nick would understand, and that the two of them would have a full and warm relationship, making up for lost time.

But now both Blake and Nick were dead.

There was no more time.

Everything was lost.

The pain was indescribable. Jeff spent the entire flight sobbing. Passengers around him asked to be moved. The regret was like a physical weight, a Mack truck parked on Jeff's chest, snapping each rib one by one before crushing his heart to pulp.

Why did I do it?

Why did I let him go?

I made a terrible, terrible mistake. And now I can never put it right.

It's too late.

By the time the plane landed in Denver, Jeff had no more tears to cry. He wasn't relieved so much as spent, emotionally and physically emptied. On the long drive up into the mountains, he thought about Tracy. If the pain was this bad for him, what must it be like for her? Jeff had lost the idea of a son, the hope for a relationship. Tracy had lost the reality. Nick was the child she'd longed for all her life. The child she believed she would never have. She had carried him and given birth to him and loved him every day of his life with the fierce passion of a lioness protecting her cub. Even her own body must remind her of Nick. For Tracy there could be no escaping the grief, no end to the tears.

With a loss that great, Jeff thought, *suicide must seem like a pretty rational option. Perhaps the only rational option.*

Panic swept through him as he recalled Tracy's strange, empty voice on the line.

"There was an accident. Blake died at the scene. Nick died the next morning from his injuries. I'm sorry."

She spoke like she wasn't there. Like she'd already checked out.

Jeff drove faster. When he finally reached the ranch

he was hugely relieved to see lights on at the house and two cars parked outside. People were moving around inside, walking past the windows.

Good. Tracy has friends, people who knew she mustn't be left alone.

Jeff wondered briefly how he was going to explain himself to those friends—who should he say he was?—but he soon dismissed the thought. It didn't matter now. He would see Tracy, he would hold her, they would cry together. After that . . .

Jeff couldn't think about after that.

He ran up the steps to the front porch and was about to knock on the door when he realized it was already open.

"Hello?" He stepped inside. Half-packed crates littered the entryway. The table where Jeff had played cards with Nick was upside down, its legs swaddled in bubble wrap. An officious-looking woman with an iPad hanging around her neck on a string was taking paintings down from the walls.

"What's going on?" Jeff demanded. "Who are you?"

"Karen Cody. Prudential Real Estate." She was about to scowl, until she noticed how attractive the dark-haired man was. His eyes looked tired, and he was graying at the temples, but the firm jaw, sensuous mouth and toned athlete's physique all more than made up for any shortcomings. Karen fluttered her false eyelashes. "May I help you?"

"Where's Tracy?"

"Mrs. Schmidt is on the East Coast right now." The Realtor chose to ignore Jeff's rude tone.

"Where?"

"I understand she's staying with relatives."

Jeff thought, *Tracy doesn't have any relatives. Not living anyway.*

"Such a tragedy." Karen shook her head sadly. "Are you a . . . close friend?"

Jeff didn't answer. Instead he ran upstairs, desperately opening and closing doors, as if Tracy might suddenly materialize. At last, despondent, he returned to where the Realtor was standing.

"Did she say when she'd be back?"

Karen Cody gave the handsome man a pitying look.

"I'm afraid she won't be. She's put the house up for sale. That's why we're here." Karen Cody gestured to the crates around her.

"But . . . wh—what about the funeral?" stammered Jeff.

"There's a memorial for Mr. Carter on Wednesday. I believe Nicholas's remains were already cremated."

"Already?" Jeff looked stricken.

"His mother wanted things expedited. I understand

she scattered the ashes privately. If you wanted to pay your respects, the middle school is holding a vigil on—"

"Did Tracy leave an address?" Jeff interrupted her. He wasn't interested in vigils or memorials. He didn't want to "pay his respects." He wanted answers. How had Nick died? Tracy said an accident, but *what* accident? What the hell had happened?

"A contact number? Anything?"

"She did not. To be honest with you, I think the poor woman just needed to get away. The sale of the ranch is being handled through Mrs. Schmidt's trustees. Perhaps you could talk to them?"

Jeff's heart sank.

Tracy knew I was coming. She knew I couldn't stay away.

She knew, and she ran.

I scared her off.

The Realtor said, "I can give you a contact for the trustees' office if you'd like one, Mr. . . . what did you say your name was again?"

"I didn't," Jeff said. "Where's Nick's room?"

Karen Cody bristled. Handsome or not, this man was beginning to irritate her. "At the top of the stairs, first on the right. But you can't just . . ."

Jeff started up there.

"We're in the middle of packing," Karen called after him. "This really isn't a good time."

Jeff called back over his shoulder. "Don't touch his things."

"My instructions come from Mrs. Schmidt," Karen shouted back. "She made it perfectly clear that . . ."

"I SAID DON'T TOUCH HIS THINGS!" Jeff roared.

The Realtor's eyes widened. Who *was* this guy?

Upstairs Jeff sat down on Nick's bed, too exhausted to cry.

Why did Tracy run?

Why wouldn't she see me?

He didn't even know what had happened, not really. A car accident. A head injury. Tiny fragments of fact, with no context, no explanation. An empty room and a cupboard full of clothes. That was all that Tracy had left him.

Jeff was angry.

A dirty t-shirt lay crumpled on the floor. Nick must have dropped it there before the accident.

Two days ago. Two days ago he was alive. How was that even possible?

Jeff picked it up, pressed it to his face and closed his eyes, inhaling the scent of his son. In a day or two,

the smell would fade. In a week it would be gone altogether. Then there would be nothing left.

Clutching the shirt, Jeff ran downstairs, passed the
Realtor, and out of the front door. He didn't stop till he
got to his rental car.

If Tracy had run, it was because she didn't want to
be found. Jeff Stevens had spent half of his adult life
trying to hunt Tracy Whitney down. He couldn't go
through that pain again. Not after this. He wouldn't
survive. But he couldn't let his son down either.

He would find out the truth. The whole truth.

He would lay Nick to rest.

Turning the key in the ignition, Jeff drove back to
the airport and caught the first flight back to London.

He fell asleep over the Atlantic, with Nick's t-shirt
in his arms.

Sitting bolt upright and wide awake on another plane,
Tracy read the message on her phone for the hun-
dredth time.

"May have information related to your son. Please
contact us. G.W."

Greg Walton had provided a secure number at
Langley for Tracy to call.

Tracy hadn't. What could Greg Walton possibly
have to tell her about Nick?

How dare the CIA try to toy with her at a time like this? To play on her grief for their own cynical ends?

Boom! The plane suddenly slammed into turbulence so violently it felt as if they'd hit a wall. Tracy's phone flew out of her hands. All around her drinks were spilling and bags were tumbling out of overhead bins. A number of people screamed as the aircraft dropped suddenly, losing hundreds of feet of altitude in a few seconds.

"Please return to your seats and fasten your seat belts." Even the Captain sounded agitated. "Cabin crew, take your seats now please."

Tracy watched the flight attendants exchange frightened glances. The woman beside her, eyes closed and fists clenched, was muttering furiously.

Praying, Tracy thought, pityingly. *There's no God, you know. Nobody's there.*

A profound sense of calm washed over her as the plane jerked and shuddered through the storm. She felt detached and warm. Deeply at peace.

Nothing mattered now.

Greg Walton woke up late on Christmas morning.

His partner, Daniel, was away for the holidays this year, taking his elderly mother on a Caribbean cruise.

Daniel was Jewish, so he didn't do Christmas anyway. Greg was Presbyterian, and on prior years had made an effort, trimming the tree, attending the carol service at Western Pres on Virginia Avenue, a stone's throw from the White House, and cooking a turkey for the two of them. But truth be told it was mostly out of guilt, or some misplaced sense of tradition. Christmas was for children. There was something weird, something forced and discordant, about two nonbelieving gay men pulling crackers, eating overpriced pecan pie and singing "Hark the Herald Angels Sing," just because everyone else was doing it.

This year, Greg had their beautiful, historic house in Georgetown to himself. He intended to spend the day on the couch watching trash TV and eating chocolate and trying to put Group 99, Bratislava and Hunter Drexel out of his mind.

Greg was under no illusions. President Havers had put his balls on the line by ordering the raid in Bratislava. If they didn't find Drexel, or Althea or the butcher Alexis Argyros, soon, Havers was going down. And if Havers went down, he would take Greg Walton with him. Nobody cried when the CIA took a hit. *We're the guys everyone loves to hate*, Greg thought bitterly. Then again, he knew what he was getting into. Greg Walton had been a spy all his adult life. And this was what intelligence agencies did—saved all the lives and got none of the glory. Took the fall for politicians and the army, even for stupid-ass, attention-seeking journalists like Hunter Drexel. As for the British, their so-called "staunch allies," Greg Walton knew he wouldn't see them for dust if Havers failed to turn this around, to pluck some kind of victory from the jaws of defeat.

But as of today, they'd got nothing.

Tracy Whitney had been the Great White Hope. Althea's fascination with Tracy was the one solid lead they had. Tracy had a link to Group 99, an important one, whether she knew it or not. But, despite Greg's threats, Milton Buck had utterly failed to get her to cooperate. *Once again, the FBI does not deliver.* Now, with her son in the morgue, Whitney had gone off grid completely. Greg Walton had been with the agency long enough to know that if Tracy Whitney didn't want to be found, she wouldn't be. He'd texted her directly in desperation. But, as he expected, the radio silence had been deafening.

Merry Christmas to you too.

Greg showered, made himself some eggs, and rearranged the cushions in the formal sitting room. Then he lit a fire and the imported Italian scented candles, the ones he and Daniel had discovered in Venice, that smelled of oranges and cloves and incense and cinnamon, all intermingled in a delicious spice bomb. Finally he put on music, carols from King's

College, Cambridge, letting the pure boys' voices soar through the house, as if hosts of angels were singing.

Perfect.

With the scene set, he settled down to his guilty pleasures—a Kurt Wallander DVD and a packet of Reese's Pieces (cheap chocolates were always the best)—when to his intense annoyance, his doorbell rang.

Really? On Christmas Day?

Clicking on his iPad, Greg scanned the images from the twelve CCTV cameras surrounding the property. He and Daniel had discussed it when Greg took the top job at the agency, and they'd decided to decline the offer of a 24/7 physical security presence. Yes, there were always crazies out there. Always risks. But technology could go a long way towards providing protection, without the intrusion of a permanent human presence. The cameras were only one part of a comprehensive system that included a panic room, bulletproof windows and bomb detection software. It wasn't perfect, but it left Greg and Daniel with some semblance of privacy, and the feeling that they lived in a home, not a fortress.

The figure on Greg's iPad screen was no terrorist, however.

A lone, white-haired woman stood forlornly on the stoop. She looked frail, hunched at the shoulders, and was possibly confused. This Greg inferred from the fact that she carried no bag, kept looking around her as if she weren't quite sure what she was doing on his doorstep, and wasn't wearing a coat, let alone gloves or a scarf, which was borderline suicidal in a DC winter.

I'll have to ask her in, he thought resentfully. *Try to reach her family. Or social services.* Really, people ought to keep a closer eye on their own elderly relatives, especially on Christmas damn Day.

He opened the door. "Hello there. Can I help you?"

"Yes," the woman said, a tiny handgun emerging miraculously from the inside of her cardigan sleeve. "You can tell me the truth, Mr. Walton. The whole truth. Or I will kill you."

Greg's eyes widened. He stifled a gasp. "Tracy?"

The white hair wasn't a wig. It was real, just like the weight loss. Tracy Whitney must have aged twenty years in the two weeks since he saw her last.

"Inside," she commanded. "Slowly."

"You can put that down, you know," Greg Walton said, closing the door behind them and walking calmly back into his living room. "We both know you're not a killer, Miss Whitney. I'm so sorry about your son."

"You wrote me that note," Tracy said, still pointing her pistol firmly at Walton's head.

Greg sat down on the couch. "Yes."

"Why? You can't possibly know anything about Nick's death."

"Can't I?"

"No. Nick's death was an accident."

Greg Walton thought, *Is she trying to convince me, or herself?*

"It may have been. It may not have been. Either way, Miss Whitney, I'm not sure what you think is to be gained by shooting the messenger."

Tracy hesitated. Her head throbbed and her body ached. She hadn't slept properly in two weeks and she'd barely eaten either. She'd come to Walton's house in a fit of anger, convinced he was the enemy. In her grief-addled state, that had made sense. Walton and Buck had come to the ranch. Blake and Nick had been killed. Now Walton was trying to lure Tracy to Langley. In Tracy's mind, those three events had merged into a sinister chain. But now that she was standing here, looking at Greg, doubts overwhelmed her. To her embarrassment, and intense surprise, she found herself starting to shake uncontrollably.

"It's OK." Greg walked over and gently relieved her of the gun. Wrapping an arm around her shoulder to help her to the couch, he was horrified by how thin she was. He could feel every bone. "You've had a huge shock." Tracy sat beside him, still shaking. "I'll make you some tea."

A few minutes later, wrapped in a heavy blanket like a shipwreck survivor and sipping hot, very sweet tea, Tracy apologized.

"I needed someone to lash out at. I needed to *do* something," she told Greg.

"I understand, really. No need to apologize. To be frank with you, Tracy, I'm just glad you're here."

"What do you know about my son?" Tracy asked.

"We don't *know* anything," Greg admitted. "But there are suspicious circumstances surrounding the accident."

"What circumstances?"

"The FBI took a look at Blake Carter's truck. It appeared that the steering may have been tampered with."

Tracy's hand flew to her mouth. "No! That's not possible. Who would want to hurt Blake? He didn't have an enemy in the world."

"I agree," Greg Walton said. "*He* didn't."

He paused a few moments for the import of his words to sink in.

"We've had reports of a woman at the diner Blake and Nick went to that night. Tall, dark-haired, attractive. None of the locals knew her. She left the restaurant right after Mr. Carter did. She was driving a black Impala."

Tracy's mind flashed back to her last conversation with Nick.

"*Blake thought someone was following us. A woman. He was kind of distracted.*"

"Nick said something," she murmured, as much to herself as to Walton. "In the hospital. Before he . . . He said a woman was following them."

Greg Walton leaned forward earnestly. "Her physical description tallies with what we believe Althea looks like."

Tracy shook her head, disbelieving.

"It's only a theory," Walton went on. "But we know this woman knows you, Tracy. That she wants to draw you into this whole mess with Group 99 and the hostages. Someone messed with Blake's truck—Blake who, as you said yourself, has no enemies."

Tracy shook her head more vehemently.

No. This can't be because of me. Nick and Blake can't be dead because of me.

"An unknown woman, fitting Althea's description, then followed Blake and your son, possibly driving them off the road."

With a huge effort of will, Tracy forced herself to be logical.

"It doesn't add up. For one thing, how would harming Blake or Nick help her?"

"I don't know," Greg admitted. "Maybe she simply wanted to hurt you. Or maybe she thought, with your family out of the picture, you'd agree to come help us. To get involved."

There was a horrible, twisted plausibility to this that made Tracy's heart race. Even so . . .

"It's so messy, though. A car accident," she said. "What if they'd survived? I mean Nicholas almost did. When I saw him afterwards, at the hospital, he . . ."

She stopped dead. All of a sudden she looked as if she'd seen a ghost.

"What?" Greg Walton asked. "Tracy, what is it?"

"At the hospital," she whispered. "I saw someone go into his room."

"Who?"

"A nurse. I thought it was a nurse. She was in uniform. But . . ."

Greg took her hands in his. "Tell me, Tracy. What did she look like?"

"I only saw her from behind. But I noticed her because she had mud all over her sneakers. Like she'd been out hiking or something."

"What else?"

Tracy looked right at him. "She had long, dark hair. And she was really, really tall."

After Tracy checked into a hotel, Greg Walton picked up the phone.

"How is she mentally?" Milton Buck asked.

"Shaky. She's still in shock."

"And physically?"

"Terrible. She looked like she'd aged twenty years. Her hair's completely white."

"Jesus." Buck whistled through his teeth. "But she'll do it? She's in?"

"Are you kidding me?" Despite everything, Greg Walton couldn't entirely keep the smile out of his voice. "Tracy Whitney won't rest until she finds Althea now. She's in all right. To the death."

Milton Buck hung up, turned to his wife and hugged her tightly.

"What was that for?" Lacey Buck giggled. Milton had been like a bear with a sore head these past few weeks. He was always this way when work was going badly.

"Oh nothing." Buck grinned. "Sorry I've been such a Grinch. Turns out it might just be a merry Christmas after all."

Part Two

Chapter 10

LAKE GENEVA, SWITZERLAND, ONE MONTH
LATER . . .

"When will you be home, Henry? Remember we have dinner with the Alencons tonight."

Henry Cranston looked at his wife, Clotilde, and wished she were younger. And prettier. And less demanding. Had he ever been attracted to her? He couldn't remember. Maybe, before the twins were born and her stomach got all saggy and wrinkly, like the skin on an overblown apple.

"I'll be home when I'm home," he said rudely. "I have a lot on at work today."

Clotilde Cranston tried to pout but last week's Botox injections had rendered her lower face almost immovable. She really must change dermatologists. Dr. Trouveau was supposedly the "top man" in Geneva, but that wasn't saying much. Clotilde missed New York. At least there she had girlfriends to distract her from her loveless marriage. Girlfriends and a decent dermatologist. And Bergdorf's.

"I love you!" she called after Henry, desperately and untruthfully.

"You too," Henry Cranston lied back.

Closing the door of his Bentley with a satisfyingly heavy *thud*, he immediately felt better. He *did* have a lot on at work today. He would spend the morning banging his new secretary, a perky little brunette barely out of her teens and wonderfully eager to please.

Then he would sign off on the bribes to the Poles and nail down his latest deal, winning Cranston Energy Inc. the fracking rights to a vast swath of Polish countryside bursting at the seams with shale gas. It wasn't quite as good a deal as the one he'd struck for exclusive fracking rights in Western Greece, on land still owned by the exiled royal family. Unfortunately, thanks to their stupid, faggot son hanging himself, that had all unraveled faster than a politician's promises after the election. But the Polish deal was a decent consolation prize.

After sewing that up, Henry would have a late lunch with his mistress, Claire. Claire was also becoming too demanding. He'd have to get rid of her soon, but not until he'd completed his home video collection and browbeaten her into having anal sex with him. I mean, really, what did the silly bitch think she was for? If he wanted boring, vanilla sex he could have it with his wife, without paying an extra half million euros a year on a rented penthouse apartment!

Henry Cranston slipped his key into the ignition and started the engine.

At the Reuters office in Manhattan at that exact same moment, journalist Damon Peters watched his computer screen go blank, then fill with a familiar computer-generated image of red balloons.

The same thing happened at the London *Times*, the *New York Times*, the *China Post* and the *Sidney Morning Herald*, along with hundreds of other newspapers and media organizations around the world.

Except this time, the first balloon to reach the top of the screen popped. Tumbling out of it, in heavy, dark block letters, came the chilling message:

VIVA GENEVA. HENRY CRANSTON R.I.P.

In Manhattan, Damon Peters spun around in his

chair. Looking at his colleague, Marian Janney, he asked, "Who's Henry Cranston?"

"No idea."

"And what the hell just happened in Geneva?"

Locals reported the explosion could be heard up to two miles away.

Clotilde Cranston was blown backwards through the front door of her house, shattering her pelvis and breaking four ribs.

Miraculously, she lived.

So did their dog, Wilbur.

Henry Cranston was blasted into a million, lying, cheating, mean-spirited pieces.

Tracy Whitney studied the pictures of the Geneva bomb scene again.

There wasn't much to see. Twisted lumps of metal. Fragments of rubble from what had once been a garden wall. A single, severed finger.

Greg Walton asked, "How soon can you be out there?"

Tracy was in Gregory Walton's office at Langley, being briefed on the latest development in the fight against Group 99. It was February, three days since Henry Cranston's murder. Tracy had spent the last month in Washington, regaining her strength physically and mentally. At Greg Walton's insistence, she'd been placed on a strict, high-calorie diet and although she remained extremely slim, she was no longer the skeletal waif who had shown up on Greg's doorstep. Her white hair had been dyed back to its original chestnut brown, and she'd been prescribed strong sleeping pills, which seemed to be working.

The only part of the CIA's treatment program that wasn't working was the therapy. Tracy had answered all of the therapist's questions politely and cooperatively. But she refused to even begin the work of processing Nick's death.

"If I open that door," she explained simply, "I won't survive."

Her certainty on that point was unshakable, so much so that even the CIA therapist had begun to think Tracy might be right. Instead of talking, Tracy had made work her therapy, immersing herself psychologically in the classified files on Althea.

After multiple briefings and hours spent poring over every thread of evidence, both electronic and physical, Tracy now knew as much about Althea as anybody in the world.

Except who she is.

Or how she knows me.

Or why she's involved with Group 99.

Or whether she really did murder my son.

Tracy was itching to get out there and look for her. But until the Geneva bombing there had been no new leads.

Now, however, suspicious e-traffic intercepts strongly suggested that Althea was physically *in* Switzerland when the Cranston bombing took place. She may even have attended a meeting at a Private Bank in Zurich two days prior to the attack. The CIA were still trying to get their hands on CCTV footage from that meeting, as well as permission to interview the banker in question, although so far with no success.

"Trying to get information out of the Swiss is like trying to get a straight answer from a lawyer," Greg Walton had complained yesterday. "Seriously, you'd think we were the enemy."

Tracy raised an eyebrow. "Imagine that."

Greg Walton grinned. "What happened to the trust, eh, Tracy?"

The two of them had developed a good working relationship, friendly and respectful. This was partly because Milton Buck had been too immersed in the hunt for Hunter Drexel—who at this point appeared to have disappeared off the face of the earth entirely—to show up to meetings. And partly because the only thing on earth that mattered to Tracy Whitney was finding out the truth about what happened to her son.

For that she needed Greg Walton, just as much as he needed her.

"I can fly tonight if you need me to," she told Greg now.

"I think it would be a good idea. If you're up to it."

"I am." Tracy smiled.

"Good." Greg smiled back.

In a classic white silk blouse and black cigarette pants, with her newly dark hair tied back and her skin glowing from a combination of drug-induced sleep and enforced healthy eating, Tracy looked terrific today. Poised. Beautiful. Well.

"You can pick up your ticket at the airport," Walton told her. "Remember, you don't officially work for us. That may give you more wriggle room with the Swiss."

"Got it."

"See if you can charm them. Failing that, see what . . . alternative channels . . . you can come up with to find Althea."

Tracy nodded. This she could do. "Alternative channels" was her specialty. At least, it had been once.

"I know you'll be resourceful." Greg Walton handed her a written file with the word "Classified" printed on the cover. "Some light reading for the plane. Good luck, Tracy."

"**You set** me up!"

Alexis Argyros, aka Apollo, held the phone away from his ear. Althea was screaming at him, hissing and spitting with impotent fury like a snake beneath his foot. How the tables had turned!

It felt wonderful.

"Don't be ridiculous," he answered, when she finally fell silent. "Our Swiss brothers organized this. I had nothing to do with it. I'm too busy hunting our friend, Hunter. Or had you forgotten about him?"

"You had everything to do with it! Are you saying it's just coincidence that this happened here, while I'm in the country?"

"Not everything revolves around you, Althea."

A few months ago he would never have dared to speak so boldly. But now? Now he had the power.

Sensing his enjoyment, Althea fired back. "You're sick, Apollo. Everybody knows it. You had Henry Cranston murdered because it aroused you to see him die."

"And watching Bob Daley's brains explode didn't arouse you?" Apollo scoffed.

To his delight, Althea sounded shaken when she answered. "Of course not. Bob Daley was different. You *know* why he had to die."

"Do I?" Apollo teased, like a cat toying with a mouse.

"There were never meant to be others!"

"Oh, but there will be others, my dear. Many, many others. One percent of the world's population is a big number, you know. The righteous oppressed have tasted vengeance at last. And they want more!" His voice quivered with excitement. "Greedy, grasping, earth-raping bastards like Cranston deserve to die."

Earth-raping. It was an expression that Group 99's eco-warriors had long used to describe fracking. Althea had always found it laughable in the past, immature and melodramatic, something only a self-righteous student could have coined. There were sides to Group 99 that had always bothered her, but she'd stuck with them, for Daniel's sake. But hearing the term from Apollo's lips now, hijacked as a cause in which he could wrap his sadism and blood lust, chilled her to the bone.

Apollo started to laugh. "Just remember, Althea," he sneered. "*You* opened the gates of hell. Not me."

Is that what I did? she thought, once the phone went dead, gazing out across the lake to the mighty Alps in the distance. *Did I open the gates of hell?*

She pulled out her suitcase and hurriedly started to pack.

"Something to drink, Ma'am?"

The flight attendant's voice jolted Tracy back to the present.

"Coffee, please. Black."

She was going to need it. The file Greg Walton had given her—his idea of "light reading"—had turned out to be a practically impenetrable analysis, not only of Henry Cranston's business, but of the fracking industry in general. Group 99 had long been opposed to hydraulic fracturing, or fracking, believing the new techniques for extracting shale gas by pumping vast amounts of pressurized water deep underground to be deeply harmful to the environment. *Was this why Cranston had been murdered?*

If so, it marked a departure from Group 99's prior MO. Prior attacks aimed at the fracking industry had all been both cyber and financial in nature. And indeed, only hours before Cranston's death, four million dollars were mysteriously siphoned out of two of his corporate accounts; accounts held at the same private bank in Zurich where Althea was believed to have had meetings. It was all suspiciously incestuous, especially as Tracy now knew that Hunter Drexel had been working on a story about the fracking business at the time of his kidnap. Drexel's past stories had all been very much of the exposé variety, as explosively controversial as they were riveting. In his checkered journalistic career, he'd tackled such taboo topics as child abuse in the Catholic Church, police brutality and rampant corruption in the world of international humanitarian aid.

So why would Group 99 kidnap a man who was about to write the equivalent of an op-ed piece on their behalf, taking down the fracking industry?

And why would they murder Henry Cranston when they'd already gone to the trouble of carrying out a brilliant and successful economic attack?

Captain Daley's brutal execution certainly seemed to have been a watershed moment in terms of Group 99's willingness to embrace violence. Overnight, it seemed, they'd made the leap from activists to terrorists.

Why? Tracy wondered, as she worked her way through the material. *How does killing people advance their cause?*

The last third of Greg Walton's file was devoted to a man he wanted her to meet on her return from Switzerland, an American billionaire oil and gas magnate by the name of Cameron Crewe.

Tracy had seen profiles of Crewe from time to time. There'd been something in the *New York Times* a few years back, and a piece in *Newsweek* more recently, about his extensive charity work. If fracking had an "acceptable face," Cameron Crewe was it. Crewe Oil was well known for its ecologically sensitive drilling practices, at least versus others in the industry, and for plowing back millions of dollars in aid and grants to the communities in which they worked. Crewe Oil had built schools in China, medical centers in Africa, and affordable housing projects in Greece, Poland and a number of impoverished former soviet republics, including Bratislava. They had created jobs, planted trees and endowed hospitals around the globe. Perhaps for this reason, uniquely among the big five fracking companies, they had never been targeted by Group 99.

Cameron Crewe himself had been touched by tragedy. His only son, Marcus, had died from leukemia at fourteen—the same age as Nicholas. Crewe's marriage had collapsed soon afterwards. Somehow these bald, sad facts served to humanize the billionaire in the public consciousness. People liked Cameron Crewe.

Ironically, Hunter Drexel had been en route to an interview with Crewe in Moscow when he was snatched off the streets by Group 99 heavies. And the links didn't end there. Henry Cranston was also a direct competitor of Cameron Crewe's. In fact, Tracy read now, Crewe Oil had been the under bidder on Cranston Eneregy Inc.'s latest landmark deal to begin fracking for shale gas in Poland. In the wake of Henry Cranston's death, they now looked likely to take over that contract. There were rumors that they'd already moved in behind the scenes on the original Greek deal that Henry had been working on, before Prince Achileas's unfortunate suicide at Sandhurst.

The lights in the cabin dimmed. Tracy's fellow passengers began to settle down to sleep. Switching on her reading light, Tracy sipped her coffee instead. Pressing her face against the window for a moment, she looked out into the blackness.

Thoughts of Nicholas came to her then. She could only ever hold them off for so long. Sleep was the worst. As soon as she let herself slip under, the dreams would begin. Strangely, they were never nightmares about the accident. They were always beautiful dreams, snapshots from the past. Blake was in some of them. Jeff was in others. But always there was Nicholas, smiling, laughing, his hand holding Tracy's, their fingers entwined in love. In Tracy's dreams she could hear her son, feel him, smell him. He was so real. So alive.

And then she would wake up and the loss would crush her again afresh, like an anvil being dropped onto her heart. She couldn't remember the last time she'd woken without screaming, or crying out, her hands grasping at the air in front of her as if she could somehow hold on to Nick, reach into her beautiful dreams and pull him back to her . . .

She thought about Jeff.

Did Jeff have dreams like that too?

Was he out there tonight somewhere, soul-dead and

hopeless like she was, clawing at the void that Nicholas's death had left?

Tracy had felt guilty, running out on Jeff. She knew he must be hurting too, desperately. But the truth was she simply didn't have the strength to see him. Nick had looked so like him, had been so like him. It would be too hard. Besides, in Tracy's experience, a grief shared was never a grief halved. Human loss was not a team game. Each person dealt with tragedy differently.

Tracy Whitney dealt with it alone.

Turning back to the CIA files, Tracy forced Jeff's image out of her mind, along with dear Blake Carter's, and her darling Nick.

There would be time for tears later. A lifetime of tears.

Right now Tracy was going to find the woman who killed her son.

Chapter 11

Tracy stormed out onto the Rue de la Croix Rouge in a white-hot fury.

A light dusting of new snow covered the sidewalk, and a bitter wind blew as Tracy stalked across the street towards the Cathédrale Saint-Pierre. But her blood was boiling so furiously, she barely felt the cold.

Arrogant asshole! How dare he?

Monsieur Gerald Le Doux, the managing partner of Ronde Suisse Private Bank, had been as sexist, condescending, superior and generally obnoxious as he possibly could be during Tracy's brief meeting in his office. He reminded her of a Swiss version of Clarence Desmond, the senior vice president at the Fiduciary Bank & Trust in Philadelphia where Tracy had once worked as a computer specialist, a hundred lifetimes ago. Desmond had been seen as a dinosaur even back then, with his constant innuendos and knee patting and "harmless" in-jokes that were very pointedly only for the boys. Yet here was Monsieur Le Doux, at the pinnacle of banking's new age of modernity and transparency, still flying the flag for entitled chauvinists everywhere.

"How may I help such a beautiful lady?"

"You ladies have your secrets, Miss Whitney, and so must we."

"I daresay you're not familiar with our banking laws here in Switzerland, young lady. But I'm under no obligation whatsoever to provide you information about our private clients, still less with video footage."

"I assume you'll be shopping while you're in our beautiful city?"

Hateful little man.

Tracy might have felt better about this fruitless meeting had the rest of her encounters in Geneva been more productive. Her visits to Henry Cranston's widow, mistress and secretary had all contributed to a picture of a man so thoroughly unpleasant, it was a wonder no one had blown him to smithereens years ago. Between the women he'd betrayed, business partners he'd double crossed and employees he'd bullied, Henry Cranston had a list of enemies as long as both Tracy's arms. And yet there was nothing, beyond the general nature of his business, to tie him to Althea or Group 99.

However, the latter had now formally claimed responsibility online for his murder, although Althea herself had remained pointedly silent. No cryptic messages had been sent to the CIA, or to Swiss Intelligence. Tracy had done her usual trawl of hotels and guesthouses and a comprehensive computer search of airline, train and car rental records. But Althea, like Henry Cranston's missing $4 million, had vanished into thin air.

With Greg Walton's words about "being resourceful" ringing in her ears, Tracy had reached out to two old contacts from her con artist days. Pierre Bonsin was an ex-banker turned occasional thief, although Pierre himself would never have used that word. A wizard with financial models of all kinds and a demon cracker of algorithms, Pierre saw himself as a sort of rogue chess player, outsmarting the machine that was the international banking system. Tracy had asked him to see if he could find any evidence of Althea having been in Ronde's systems.

She'd asked her other old friend, Jim Cage, a yacht broker and safe-blower by night, whether any of his contacts knew anything about a woman sourcing explosives in the weeks leading up to Cranston's death.

"She'd be American, educated, attractive and wealthy. Tall, with brown hair, although she may well have disguised her appearance."

To Tracy's intense disappointment, both had drawn a blank. Ronde's systems had indeed been attacked, and potentially compromised.

"Unfortunately it happened four times in the last six weeks," Pierre Bonsin explained. "Any one of them could have been your girl, but we've no way of knowing. This is the age of the hacker, Tracy. You know that. These kinds of cyberattacks are a part of daily life now, for all the big banks."

Jim Cage was equally downbeat.

"No female of the description you gave me has been sourcing bomb-making equipment here," Jim told Tracy, in his luxurious, modernist office overlooking the lake. "No female of any description come to that."

Jim Cage was handsome in a classic, aging matinee idol sort of way, tall and dark with a little too much tan and extremely white teeth. He'd always fancied Tracy, and was pleased to see how well she'd held up over the years. She was a bit too thin these days. The bottle-green cashmere dress she was wearing today showed her ribs, a look that some men liked but that was a bit too much for Jim. But Tracy was still a knockout. It was those emerald eyes that really did it. Or were they jade? Either way they were looking at him reproach-fully now. She'd hoped for better news.

"The thing is, Tracy, you and I are old school. We still like to do things in person. Talk to the experts, the artists. Group 99's not like that, are they? They're kids. Anything they need to build a bomb they can get online. There's no romance anymore."

Althea's not a kid, Tracy thought. *And there was precious little romance in Henry Cranston's death.* But she took the point. Althea was too smart to risk being seen or leaving evidence when she didn't need to.

Now, drawing her fur coat more tightly around her as she approached the bridge towards Saint-Gervais Les Bergues, Tracy did something she hated doing: she admitted defeat. If either Althea or Henry Cranston's missing $4 million were still in Geneva, or even in Europe, she'd be very surprised. Monsieur Le Doux's patronizing stonewalling back at the bank had been the bitter cherry on the top of an already thoroughly disap-pointing cake. Tracy's entire trip had been a total waste of time.

"Whoa there!"

Tracy had been so lost in her own thoughts, she didn't look where she was going and collided suddenly and forcefully with a man on the sidewalk. Losing her footing from the impact, she managed to drop her briefcase, which promptly burst open, scattering papers all over the place.

"Let me help you," the man said, as Tracy scrambled to retrieve them. His response in English was the first thing that threw her. The second was his smile. Broad and genuine, it lit up his entire face.

"Thank you," Tracy muttered, embarrassed. Between them they managed to pick up all the stray documents. "I'm so sorry," she said afterwards. "I'm afraid I was miles away."

"I can see that." The man was still smiling. Handing her a sheaf of letters, he noticed the name on the top of one of them. Looking at Tracy astonished, he asked, "You're not . . . Tracy Whitney, are you?"

Tracy frowned. "Do we know each other?"

"Not yet." The man's smile broadened still further. "But I believe we were supposed to meet next week in New York. I'm Cameron Crewe."

Chapter 12

Over dinner that night at Rasoi by Vineet, the Michelin-starred Indian restaurant at Tracy's hotel, Tracy learned a lot about Cameron Crewe.

The first thing she discovered was that the beaming smiles he'd bestowed on her earlier were rare. Not that he wasn't friendly, or kind or warmly disposed towards her. He was all of those things. But his default manner was definitely serious.

Tracy opened with the obvious question. "What are you doing in Geneva?"

Crewe had already explained how he knew about *her*. Greg Walton had called him a couple of days ago and suggested that they meet. But he hadn't told her what he was doing here, in Switzerland.

"I'm here for the same reason you are, I imagine," said Cameron. "Or a related reason anyway. Henry

Cranston's death has serious ramifications in our business. There are certain deals that Cranston Energy have pulled out of, where my company may step in. I flew here to meet with Henry's partners and discuss terms."

"No offense," said Tracy, "but isn't that a bit vulture-like? I mean, the man has just been murdered. What's left of him is barely cold."

Cameron Crewe shrugged, not callously, but in a matter-of-fact way. "It's business. Henry and I weren't personal friends. Although to be honest, even if we had been, I would want to move quickly on the Polish deal. Fracking is a very fast-moving sector. If we don't get in there, believe me Exxon or the Chinese will."

"It's what got Henry Cranston killed," Tracy observed.

Cameron sipped his wine. "Perhaps."

"Doesn't that make you nervous?"

"No. Not really. To be honest, Tracy, not many things make me nervous."

They ordered and ate and talked. The food was exquisite—Tracy's chicken dopiaza was the best she'd ever tasted, better even than in Delhi—but afterwards it was the conversation that she remembered.

Cameron Crewe was a fascinating man, and not at all what Tracy had expected. In Tracy's experience, most billionaires were conceited and arrogant men, even the philanthropic ones. But Cameron was neither of those things. Instead he was controlled, a little serious and extremely polite. He could be warm—his smiles, when they came, were like sunlight bursting through clouds. But the main thing that struck Tracy about Cameron Crewe was the haunting sadness in his eyes.

It wasn't as if he looked upset. Quite the opposite, in fact. He was clearly as engaged and interested in the conversation as Tracy was, especially when they began discussing Group 99, their involvement in Henry Cranston's death and their apparently changing tactics. The sadness was simply *there*, a permanent fixture, like a black curtain at the back of a stage set. The actors might be singing or dancing or laughing. But behind them, always, the darkness remained.

Tracy had that same curtain. It had come down first when she lost her mother to suicide. Then again, years later, when she thought Jeff Stevens had betrayed her. With each loss it had turned just a shade darker. Nick's death had turned it midnight black.

Was it his son's death that lowered the curtain for Cameron?

Instinctively, Tracy felt a connection with him, a common bond.

The waiter started to pour more of the chilled Chablis, but Cameron politely put a hand on his arm.

"I can do it," he said. "We need to talk privately."

"Of course, Mr. Crewe."

They know him here. Tracy was surprised. But perhaps he came to town often on business? It was the business of expensive restaurants to remember patrons as rich and powerful as Cameron Crewe.

"You asked my thoughts about Group 99," Cameron said, refilling Tracy's glass.

"Yes."

Tracy had changed for dinner into a simple black shirtdress and pumps. On another woman the outfit might have looked boring and staid, but on Tracy it was wonderfully elegant, emphasizing her slender arms and smooth, alabaster skin. Her chestnut hair was loose, and she wore a small emerald pendant at the neck that seemed to glow the same green as her eyes. Cameron realized with a start that he was powerfully attracted to her. It had been a long time since he'd felt that for any woman. Too long.

He must be careful.

"To tell you the truth, I'm fascinated by Group 99," he told her. "In some ways they're different from any terrorist threat we've seen before. Yet in other ways they're as old as the hills."

Tracy waited for him to elaborate.

"I mean, on the one hand, their 'model,' if you can call it that, is unique. There's almost no bureaucracy. No official hierarchy or leadership. No barriers to entry. They took a simple idea, and they spread it around the globe. Very quickly and very effectively."

"And the idea is?"

"That the world is unfair," Cameron said. "That a system that allows one percent of the population to control well over fifty percent of the world's wealth and resources is inherently a broken system. It's tough to argue with that."

Yes, Tracy thought. *It is.*

"Group 99 told people that *they*, the ninety-nine percent, didn't have to sit back and take it. That people could *do* something about the injustice. All they needed was a computer screen and a little ingenuity and to stick together. That's a compelling message. And it worked."

"And that's what's new about them?" Tracy clarified.

Cameron nodded. "That and the technologies. I mean think about it. With a computer these days, the possibilities are just about limitless. Anything with a computerized element can be hacked. *Anything.* Intelligence agencies. Nuclear weapons systems. Banks. Governments. Armies. Disease control facilities. There are satellites out there, not just predicting weather but affecting it, that are vulnerable to attack. Imagine *that*." His eyes lit up. "Being able to control the weather, to harness natural disasters, say, or control the flow of water. What if terrorists could unleash floods or tsunamis? Or spread bubonic plague?"

Tracy frowned. "Come on. That's a bit sci-fi, isn't it?"

"Is it?" Cameron raised an eyebrow. "Ask Greg Walton about the CIA's program on weather terrorism. I'm serious, Tracy. And we aren't the only ones looking into this. Everyone's thinking about terrorism 2.0. It was Group 99 that brought that agenda forward, pretty much single-handedly."

"OK," Tracy said, nibbling thoughtfully on her poppadum. "So let's say you're right. Let's say all of that is possible, at least theoretically, and Group 99 were on the front lines of that change. Why go back to the old-school stuff? Kidnap. Execution. Car bombings. I mean, if they have all this potential power at their fingertips, isn't that a retrograde step? Not to mention a major PR blunder. They've gone from heroes to villains overnight."

"Exactly!" Cameron slammed his fist down on the table. The smile was back. "And that's the paradox. Group 99 are new and different, but they're also *not* new at all. Forget tactics for a moment—although that's important—but let's look at their motivations. Strip away the Robin Hood, social good, eco-warrior façade and what have you really got? I'll tell you what. You've got envy. And you've got anger. And you've got testosterone. Young, impotent, dispossessed males, spoiling for a fight."

"There are plenty of women in Group 99," Tracy countered. "Just look at Althea."

Cameron waved a hand dismissively. "She's one. The only senior woman, as far as we know, in that group. And senior in the loosest sense as they have no central leadership."

"Even so . . ."

"Even so nothing." Cameron was firm. "That's like pointing at Benazir Bhutto and saying 'Wow, a woman president. Pakistan must be a great place for women's rights!' Make no mistake, Tracy. Group 99 is all about men. It's the same phenomenon you'll see in just about all terrorism of the last hundred years. Maybe thousand years. Think about it. The Islamists, the IRA, the Basque Separatists, even the Black Panthers. They all hide behind some ideology or other—religious, nationalist, racial, it doesn't matter. With Group 99 it's economic. Not important. What they really are, in all these cases, is a bunch of young men at the bottom of the economic ladder. Men who feel powerless and angry. Men who feel they have no future. Maybe they can't get a job. Maybe they can't get laid. Doesn't matter. They aren't fighting for a cause. Fighting *is* their cause. They turn to violence because it makes them feel good. Simple as that. I call them the Lost Boys."

Tracy listened intently, taking all this in.

"If Group 99 were smart they'd play their advantage and stick to cyberattacks. But they aren't smart. Or at least, the smart elements are having their voices drowned out by the Lost Boys. You know they started in Greece, right?"

"I know," said Tracy. She was a little surprised by how much Cameron knew. Then again, he was a CIA asset/advisor, just like her. Maybe they'd read the same files?

Does he know about Hunter Drexel, running from his American rescuers? Tracy wondered. Greg Walton had stressed to her that this was top-secret information. She mustn't assume anything. Still, she wished she knew more about just how close Cameron Crewe and the CIA really were.

"I know Greece," Cameron continued. "We do a lot of business there and I'm involved in numerous charities. It was a tragedy what happened to that country. A classic case of what happens when you push a people beyond their limits."

"Their prime minister called it a humanitarian crisis," said Tracy.

"He's right. Like Germany with the reparations after World War I, the suffering of the man on the street simply became too much to bear. Politically you start to see the rise of men like Calles. And beneath the surface, men like Argyros starting Group 99. Alexis Argyros might be smarter than your average ISIS militant. But his agenda was always violence, in the end."

The waiter cleared their empty plates. Tracy wasn't hungry but she found herself ordering dessert anyway, some sort of milk pudding made with rice that Cameron recommended. It sounded disgusting, but was in fact quite ambrosially delicious. They kept talking.

"What about the tactics issue," Tracy said. "Drexel and Daley's kidnaps, Daley's murder, the Cranston bombing. Surely you don't put that down solely to testosterone-fueled boys lusting for blood and guts?"

"Not solely, no," Cameron agreed. "Even if the Lost Boys are taking over Group 99, and the likes of your Althea are being pushed out, they'd have had to try to sell the idea of a shift towards old school violence internally."

"And how would they do that?"

"There are plenty of arguments you could use," Cameron said breezily. "Kidnap and murder have proved highly effective tools for other terror groups, especially if the aim is to engage the enemy, to escalate conflict. Plus it's a shock to the enemy's system. People are used to seeing medieval barbarism in the Middle East and Africa, but not in Europe. The irony is, it's precisely *because* hacking has gotten so sophisticated and so virtually unstoppable that we're seeing a return to old school methods. U.S. nuclear codes are stored on paper files these days. Once you know the Pentagon can be hacked to the core, it's only a short step to the major powers moving back to cannons and bows and arrows."

Tracy laughed.

"OK, maybe not bows and arrows. But technological weaponry like drones might easily fall out of favor. And once armies start heading back to the dark ages, why not companies, or banks? It would certainly suit Group 99's ends to see a return to bartering, for example. The abolition of financial markets, maybe even of paper money itself. I know it sounds crazy to us, sitting here, about to pay for a five star meal with our platinum visa cards."

"*Your* platinum visa card," Tracy corrected him.

Cameron laughed. "You really are old school, aren't you?"

"I try." Tracy raised her glass.

"But it could happen. Financial anarchy. Or utopia,

depending on how you look at it. Group 99 embracing more traditional terror tactics could certainly be presented as a step in that direction. That would make it consistent with their views."

Tracy changed the subject. "Tell me about Hunter Drexel." She found Cameron fascinating and could listen to him theorize all night. But she was here to find Althea, and to do that she needed facts, not theories. She felt sure that there must be a connection between Althea and the abducted American journalist. Something none of them had thought of yet.

"I'm sure you know far more about Mr. Drexel than I do," Cameron answered cautiously.

"I know he was on his way to meet you in Moscow when Group 99 abducted him."

"That's right."

"Why had you agreed to meet him that day?"

Cameron looked surprised by the question.

"Drexel was working on a piece about the fracking industry. As I assume you already know. Specifically about corruption in the business."

"I hear there's a lot of it about."

"I hear that too." Cameron smiled briefly. "I imagine that's what he wanted to talk to me about but I'm not certain. He was rather cryptic on the telephone. And of course, we never actually met, in the end."

"You don't usually give interviews," Tracy said. "In fact you never give them. According to the CIA files you're notorious for avoiding the media."

"Notorious? Am I really?" Cameron gave Tracy a wry look, taking a sip of his jasmine tea. "What else do Greg Walton's files say about me?"

Tracy blushed, thinking about Marcus, Cameron's only son, lost to leukemia, and his divorce. It was embarrassing to know these private things about a person. She'd already said too much.

"It's all right," Cameron said. "It's true I'm a very private man. After my son died I withdrew pretty much completely from public life. It's also true I don't like journalists. They all bang on about how we need to break our dependence on Saudi oil, yet they have no qualms in slagging off the fracking business, or in tarring all oil and gas companies with the same brush."

"So why meet Drexel?"

"I was curious. Hunter Drexel was just different from all the others."

"In what way?"

Cameron considered for a moment. "Better, I suppose. A better man and a *much* better writer. Did you read his article in *Time* about the Nazi hunters?"

Tracy admitted that she hadn't.

"You must," said Cameron. "It's a beautiful piece of

writing, moving without being schmaltzy, meticulously researched. Hunter Drexel is really, really good at his job. He's also fearless. But of course, there's a downside to that, as he learned in Moscow. I imagine the man has a lot of enemies."

"Such as?"

"Ex-lovers. Disgruntled poker players. Drexel's reneged on a lot of debts in his time. He's a serious gambling addict. The subjects of his op-eds. Pretty much any editor he's ever worked with." Cameron calmly listed the potential Drexel-haters out there. "He's a great writer but he's also a maverick. Erratic. Famously impulsive. He's one of those guys who puts a lot of store by his instinct, without necessarily always having the facts to back it up. When someone sues for libel, it's the editor who ends up picking up the pieces."

"But you said his *Time* piece was well researched?" Tracy reminded him.

"It was. But they haven't all been. He's written some outrageous takedowns of public figures—like Senator Braverman, remember him?"

Tracy cast her mind back. "The orgy guy?"

"Yes, except he wasn't. Drexel's source was flat-out wrong on that story, had him confused with some other sleazy republican. The magazine that ran that story's gone now. Filed for Chapter Eleven just to pay

Braverman's damages. But the Senator's career never recovered. Drexel walked away without a scratch, or a shred of remorse. He's been sued more times than a tobacco company and fired more times than a cheap shooting range pistol."

"And Group 99? Why would they want to harm him, do you think?"

"I don't know," Cameron admitted. "Perhaps something he'd uncovered in his research had rattled them? On the face of it, they don't make natural enemies."

Tracy decided to cast a fly over the water. "What about the U.S. Government? Were they his enemy?"

Cameron frowned. "What do you mean?"

Greg Walton had given Tracy strict instructions not to tell anybody about Hunter running from the task force sent to rescue him. Unfortunately for Walton, Tracy had never been a big follower of instructions. Like Hunter Drexel, she trusted her instincts, and her instincts told her that she could trust Cameron Crewe.

With a deep breath, she told Cameron the whole story. How Hunter had run. How the CIA and MI6 were working jointly to find him, before Group 99 did, so far with no success. How President Havers had lied outright to the world's media about what happened that fateful night in Bratislava.

"Holy shit," Cameron said, once she'd finished.

"But, why? Why would he run from his rescuers? Especially after what happened to poor Captain Daley."

"I don't know," said Tracy. "But I expect the answer lies with Althea. There's a connection between her and Drexel. I feel it in my bones."

It was getting late, but neither Cameron nor Tracy was ready to end the conversation. Cameron paid the bill and they moved to one of the Mandarin Oriental's smaller, more intimate bars. Settling themselves into a corner, candlelit table, Tracy ordered a Cognac and Cameron a single malt.

"Tell me about you, Tracy," Cameron said. "Walton told me you were helping them try to track down Althea. But he didn't say why. Where do you fit into all this?"

Tracy gave him the summarized version. How Althea had sent a coded message to the CIA, after she'd directly ordered Bob Daley's brutal murder, mentioning Tracy by name. "She thinks she knows me. She certainly knows *of* me."

"But you don't know her?"

"I've been wracking my brain, obviously. Trying to think of a connection. There are a number of different chapters in my life where our paths may have crossed. I've had what you might call a checkered past," Tracy admitted.

Cameron's eyebrow shot up playfully. "Really? Greg told me you were a retired art specialist."

Tracy laughed loudly. "That's one way of putting it I suppose."

"What's another way? Come on. I'm curious. I won't breathe a word, I promise you."

"It's complicated," said Tracy. "I spent some time in prison in my twenties. But I'm sure I never knew Althea there."

"What for?" Cameron found it hard to imagine this poised, beautiful, intelligent woman behind bars.

"Something I didn't do." Tracy smiled sweetly. "I've also worked in banking, as a computer specialist."

"That sounds more Althea-like."

"It does," Tracy agreed. "But I was the only woman I knew at that time in my bank, other than the secretaries. Later I, er, developed an interest in fine art," Tracy said tactfully. "And very expensive jewelry."

"Other people's very expensive jewelry?" Cameron guessed.

"Not for long." Tracy grinned. "I was living in London then but traveling a lot. I met a lot of interesting people in that chapter of my life, but still no one like Althea comes to mind at all. Then, after my marriage ended, I moved back to the States with my son."

She hadn't intended to mention Nick. It had just slipped out naturally. As if he were still alive. The instant Tracy said it a cloud passed across her face. The change in her was so sudden and so total, Cameron couldn't fail to notice it.

"Tracy?" Without thinking he reached across the table and put his hand over hers. "Are you all right?"

"I'm fine," Tracy lied. She was trying not to meet Cameron's eyes. There was something incredibly intense about his eyes that made her feel panicked. It was only in that moment that she realized what it was.

He reminds me of Jeff.

Cameron said kindly. "You're not fine. Please tell me what's wrong."

To her own surprise, Tracy looked up and heard herself say, "My son died."

She wasn't sure if she'd ever said those words before out loud. She realized now she'd been holding them in, as if by not saying them she could make them less real. Of course, it hadn't worked. Blurting them out to Cameron Crewe, an almost total stranger, was a profound relief.

"I'm so sorry." Cameron squeezed her hand more tightly. "What was his name?"

"Nicholas. He was killed in a car accident."

"When?"

"Six weeks ago."

Cameron couldn't hide his shock. "Six *weeks* ago? My God, Tracy, that's horrible. This just happened?"

Tracy looked at him blankly. *Had it just happened?* It felt like a lifetime ago to her. Eons of loss had come and gone since the day of the accident.

I must stop calling it an accident. It was murder.

Althea, whoever she is, murdered my son.

Her face hardened.

"You shouldn't be here, you know. Working," Cameron said. "You must give yourself some time. Six weeks is nothing. It's the blink of an eye. You can't possibly have processed what happened yet, never mind come to terms with your grief."

Tracy said simply, "If I didn't work, I'd die."

Cameron nodded. He understood this better than anybody. It was a mistake. But he understood it. The need to be distracted. The need to find a purpose, any purpose, beyond the pain.

"I lost a son too, you know," he told Tracy. "Marcus. He was fourteen."

"I know," Tracy said numbly. "The same age as Nick. He had leukemia. Your foundation has made large donations towards cancer research and developing stem cell treatments."

She's reciting from my file, Cameron realized. Poor thing. It was as if she were in a trance. He'd been there himself, in those early, dark months after Marcus's death.

"That's right," he said calmly. "Marcus was sick for a long time. That was hard, but it also meant we had time, his mother and I. To prepare. I'm so grateful for that now. I'm not sure I could have coped with losing him suddenly. Like you did with your boy."

"How did you cope?" Tracy found herself asking. Cameron seemed so calm, so together. Not like her. Was there a trick to this, a path of some sort that she'd missed?

Cameron quickly disabused her of that notion.

"Very badly," he replied. "Charlotte and I tried to hold it together afterwards. But we grieved so differently. She needed to talk. I needed to work."

Like me.

"And I know it sounds stupid, but just looking at her face was a constant reminder of Marcus." Cameron added. "I couldn't handle it."

Tracy thought about Jeff. How Nick had been his clone, alike in every way. How the thought of seeing Jeff again and talking to him about Nick had filled her with such indescribable panic, such dread, that she'd run out on both him and her old life in Colorado, slamming the door so hard behind her that its echo was no doubt reverberating through the mountains to this day.

"Greg Walton thinks Althea may have been involved in Nick's death," she told Cameron. It was bizarre the way the words kept tumbling out of her mouth, as if her body were vomiting out a sickness. "That's why I'm here. Why I agreed to get involved. He thinks she may have sabotaged the car that my son was riding in that night. She may even have meddled with his drugs at the hospital later, when the doctors were trying to save his life."

"Jesus Christ," Cameron gasped. "Why?"

"To force my hand? So I would try to find her? Or just to hurt me. I don't know, because I don't know who she is. But I will know," Tracy said darkly. "I'll know everything in the end."

Knowledge won't make you happier, Cameron thought. *It won't bring him back. And it won't bring you closure, because there's no such thing.*

"Being Nick's mother made me a different person. A better person. But now that he's gone, that side of me is gone too," Tracy announced. "All the softness. All the caution, the holding back, the setting a good example. There's no one to protect anymore."

"Except yourself," Cameron reminded her.

"But that's just it," Tracy said. "I'm not sure I *have* a self now, at least not one I care about. It sounds terrible but it's actually amazingly freeing. I have no boundaries, no limits. I feel reckless." Incongruously, she started to laugh. "I daresay I sound like a lunatic!"

"Not to me."

As suddenly as it had started, Tracy's laughter stopped. When she spoke again she was deadly serious.

"She was here, in Geneva. Althea. I know she was. I lost her this time but I'm getting closer."

"Well, if I can help in any way, any way at all, I'd like to," said Cameron. Reluctantly releasing Tracy's hand, he pulled a business card out of his pocket. Scrawling a separate, private cellphone number on the back he handed it to her. "Call me any time, Tracy. About anything."

Tracy took the card. "I will," she said gratefully. "And thank you for dinner."

"The pleasure was mine." Cameron stood up. "I'd better go. I have early meetings tomorrow."

Tracy watched him leave. She still couldn't quite believe she'd spent the entire evening talking so intimately with a man she barely knew. But perhaps it was because they barely knew each other that she felt able to talk to Cameron Crewe. To reveal her true feelings, her true pain. *We're like two Vietnam vets. Strangers, but also family in a way, bonded by the loss of our children.*

The curtain of loss that had fallen over both their lives had given them a sort of emotional shorthand. Like a fast forward button in their relationship. *But fast forward to what?*

Tracy could still feel the warmth of Cameron's palm over hers. Guiltily, she recognized the long-forgotten stirrings of arousal in her body. Faint traces of a part of her that had once been there, once known intimacy of a different kind.

Life goes on. Isn't that what people say? Tracy didn't agree. It seemed to her that life had no business going on, not without her darling Nicholas. What she was doing now wasn't living. It was existing. A mere mechanical matter. Inhale, exhale. Eat, sleep. Day, night. Anything more would be a betrayal.

Tonight had felt like something more. Talking to Cameron Crewe, looking into his sad, intense eyes. It had felt good.

That mustn't happen again.

Back at his Geneva apartment—Cameron Crewe kept apartments in every city where he did business— Cameron lay awake, staring at the ceiling.

That mustn't happen again.

He'd been too open with Tracy Whitney. Too unguarded. Cameron knew from experience how dangerous it was to open one's heart. What devastating consequences could follow.

And yet he'd felt a powerful connection to Tracy. He'd felt compassion. And kinship. And something else too. Something much more dangerous.

Desire.

Cameron wanted Tracy.

The realization filled him with excitement, and with fear.

He closed his eyes, switched on his iron discipline, and forced himself to sleep.

Chapter 13

"Full house."

The fat man grinned, revealing a set of the ugliest teeth Hunter had ever seen, and reached forwards across the table to scoop up his winnings. Hunter's arm shot out to stop him.

"Sorry, Antoine." Hunter slowly laid four beautiful jacks slowly out on the table. "I believe that's my game."

The Frenchman made a noise that was part anger and part disbelief. Jack Hanley, or whatever his real name was, had shown up in Riga a week ago and proceeded to clean up at every major poker table in the city. The stakes weren't particularly high tonight. The Frenchman could afford to lose, as could the Latvian businessmen at tonight's game. Still, there was something about Jack Hanley, a certain American arrogance dressed up as humility, that was starting to get on everybody's nerves. That and the fact that he always quit when he was ahead.

"Is that really the time?" Hunter glanced at the antique grandfather clock in the corner of the room. "I think I'd better call it a night."

Ignoring the grumbling of his fellow players—it was after midnight after all—Hunter grabbed his coat and headed into the night.

He preferred Latvia to Romania, and especially liked Riga, a city steeped in both history and romance. His hotel looked directly over the dome cathedral in Vecrīga, the old city, a building that dated back to the thirteenth century and still whispered of knights in shining armor and damsels in distress. Only two weeks ago, Group 99 had orchestrated a flyover of the cathedral, dropping hundreds of red balloons filled with cash for the beggars who still flocked there, hoping for alms. In the last month alone, the group had redistributed well over a million euros to Europe's poor, through balloon drops or less dramatically, by simply depositing cash into the bank accounts of impoverished citizens as well as filling the coffers of various charities and NGOs, particularly in Greece.

Hunter spent his days in Riga working on his story and his nights playing cards. He would have liked to stay longer, but it was too risky. After Romania he'd started using aliases and taking small steps to change his appearance. The CIA would find him eventually, he knew that. He just hoped to stay under the radar long enough to finish his story, to get the truth out there. If . . .

Wheesh! The bullet whistled past Hunter's left ear. He'd been in enough war zones to recognize that sound, even though the shot itself was silent. *Professional.* Instinctively Hunter dropped to the ground, scrambling on his hands and knees to the walled side of the alley, away from the glare of the streetlamps. *Wheesh!* Another shot. This time it clattered against something metal. A trash can, perhaps, up ahead? Or a fencepost.

Hunter looked around him. The narrow streets around Antoine's apartment were utterly deserted at this time of night. He couldn't see his attacker, or anyone, in the darkness. His only hope was to run, to try to make it to one of the main streets or squares where he might find safety in numbers.

Sprinting towards Remtes Street, Hunter's mind spun faster than his legs. He had about $5,000 in his pockets, but he was pretty sure whoever was shooting at him wasn't interested in money. He'd assumed the Americans wanted him alive—clearly they had back in Bratislava. But something had obviously changed. *Unless it wasn't the CIA. Unless it was . . .*

Wheesh! Another shot, and this time he could hear running behind him, boots pounding the cobblestones just like his own. The lights of a tram up ahead shone straight at him, momentarily blinding him. Panicked, Hunter turned around. The last thing he saw was Apollo's face staring back at him, his sadist's eyes alight with excitement as he raised the gun. Pointing it between Hunter's eyes, he calmly pulled the trigger.

Sally Faiers was deep asleep when her mobile rang.

"Can you talk?"

It was the first time she'd heard from Hunter in almost a month. He sounded out of breath and antsy. *Probably just climbed out of some married lady's bedroom window with the husband in hot pursuit.* In typical Drexel style he'd asked Sally to do something for him, something complex and time-consuming and of no benefit to her whatsoever, and then gone completely AWOL. Admittedly he was being hounded by the most powerful government on earth, not to mention a group of potentially murderous terrorists. But it was still deeply annoying.

"No."

"Did you find anything out? About Major General Frank Dorrien?"

"What part of 'no' do you not understand, Hunter? It's one in the fucking morning."

"Don't hang up!" It was a yell, panicked and desperate. For the first time Sally detected real fear in Hunter's voice. "Please."

"Where are you?" Her tone softened. "What's happened?"

Hunter hesitated.

"Either you trust me or you don't," Sally said angrily, rubbing the sleep out of her eyes. "Because if you don't, I'm done busting my balls for this stupid story of yours. And I'm done keeping your secrets."

"I'm in Riga," Hunter said. "Group 99 just tried to kill me."

He told her about Apollo, his captor in Bratislava and the man who'd shot Bob Daley.

"He was firing right at me. This truck came out of nowhere and blocked the shot. By the time it passed he'd gone."

"Does he know where you're staying?"

"I assume so," Hunter panted. "He must have followed me to the poker night. Unless one of the players tipped him off. In any case I can't go back to the hotel. I left a bunch of notes there. Research. FUCK!"

Sally sat up in bed. "It's OK. You're alive. And it's all in your head anyway, right?"

"I guess." Hunter's breathing began to normalize. "So did you find anything?"

"That depends on your definition of anything," Sally said, fully awake now. "General Frank didn't kill Prince Achileas. That much I'm pretty sure of."

Hunter let out a long, disappointed breath.

"But he does work for MI6. And he's part of the team that's looking for you."

"MI6 is looking for me?"

"Yes," Sally said. "After Bob Daley's murder the U.S. and UK governments formed a joint intelligence task force to counter Group 99. As part of the information sharing I guess the Yanks told our boys the truth about what happened in Bratislava, that you're on the run. They seem to believe you might be in league with Group 99. That your abduction might have been staged."

Hunter said nothing.

"Was it?" Sally asked.

"I just told you, they tried to kill me," Hunter said. "What else did you find out?"

"This is all hearsay. But it looks like the Brits are anxious to find you before the Americans do. Your man Frank Dorrien, in particular, doesn't trust the CIA."

"We have something in common after all," Hunter quipped.

"I'm not so sure about that," Sally said. "The picture I get of Dorrien is of a highly disciplined, deeply conservative man. He disapproved of Prince Achileas. Evidently the boy was gay. General Dorrien may not have killed the boy but he certainly bullied him. You could argue that he drove the poor kid to suicide."

Hunter wasn't sure he'd call the privileged Prince of Greece a "poor kid" but he took Sally's point.

"Achileas did know Bob Daley. They weren't friends exactly, but they seemed to get along. General Dorrien knew both men, and liked Daley."

"Bob was easy to like," said Hunter. This wasn't the news he'd been hoping to hear about Frank Dorrien. It meant he was going to have to rethink some things. But it was interesting nonetheless, especially the part about the British being on the hunt for him too.

"Hunter?" Sally's voice sounded very far away suddenly.

"Yeah?"

"Tell me what you're working on. Send me your notes, anything, as backup."

"I can't do that."

"You almost got killed tonight," Sally reminded him. "If you die, do you want this story to die with you?"

"No. But I'd rather it died with me than with you."

"I don't understand."

Hunter said, "It's not me they're all trying to bury, Sal. It's the truth. I can't put you at risk."

"*I'm* putting me at risk," said Sally.

"Thanks for the help."

Sally thought about asking him not to hang up, but she knew it would be pointless.

After he rang off she slumped back on her pillow and stared at the ceiling.

What the hell are you up to, Hunter Drexel? What's this really all about?

She wondered how differently things might have turned out between them if she'd ever been able to trust him.

Frank Dorrien waited until his wife was sleeping soundly before creeping out of bed.

Downstairs in his study, he turned the desk lamp on low and switched on Prince Achileas's laptop. There'd been very little time after the boy died to go through his room. But the Greek's MacBook Air was vital. Frank had slipped it into his briefcase while the Prince was still swinging. He felt not the slightest twinge of guilt.

MI6 had retrieved scores of deleted emails, many of them encrypted.

Frank Dorrien had read them all.

His upper lip curled with distaste now at the pornographic images in front of him. All were of deviant young men in various stages of sexual abasement. *What was wrong with the world? Disgusting.*

A female journalist had been sniffing around the barracks in the last few weeks, asking questions. No doubt another bleeding-heart liberal who expected the British army to conform to civilian rules, while somehow magically keeping the country safe from harm. Didn't people realize there was a war on? Not a war between nations, but a war of ideologies, a war of right and wrong?

Frank Dorrien was aware of Miss Faiers. For now he had bigger fish to fry. But he would not tolerate anyone who tried to come between him and his duty. Miss Faiers had better watch her back.

Turning his attention back to the emails, Frank stared transfixed at the top left-hand corner of Achileas's last deleted message.

There, hovering cheerfully, was a solitary red balloon.

Agent Milton Buck was having a bad day.

It was about to get worse.

The British were lying to him. He was sure of it.

They claimed to have made no progress tracking down either Apollo or Althea, and to have heard nothing about Hunter Drexel's fate. But from the tone of General Dorrien's voice alone, Agent Buck knew the man was lying through his teeth. *They're closing the net. They're going to make fools of us all!*

Of course, two could play at the concealing-information game. The problem was that U.S. intelligence had made no progress of their own to withhold from MI6. Tracy Whitney's trip to Geneva had been a bust, a total dead end. Group 99 were dancing on Henry Cranston's grave and there was nothing the FBI or the CIA could do about it. Tracy's failures reflected directly on Milton Buck. He loathed having to work with her, but Althea's bizarre connection had left him no choice. He was sure Tracy was lying to him too— she must know who Althea was, or at least have her suspicions—but of course he had no way to prove it.

On top of which, Milton Buck had Greg Walton breathing down his neck day and night. Presumably because the president was breathing down Walton's neck, but Agent Buck didn't care about that. He cared about the fact that, once again, a chance for major career advancement was slipping through his fingers thanks to Tracy Whitney's ineptitude. And to top it all off, his wife was on her period and bit his head off every time he walked through the door. Which explained why Milton Buck was still at his desk in his office, staring mindlessly at his computer screen, at eight o'clock at night.

Clicking open his documents folder, Milton's screen suddenly went blank.

What the hell?

He tried a few other applications. One by one, they all shut down like dominoes.

He picked up the phone. "Jared. Get up here," he barked at the systems manager. "My laptop just died."

"Everybody's has, Sir," the technician replied. "It looks . . . it seems we've had a breach. Something . . . Oh shit."

Milton Buck looked back at his own screen.

One by one, the blackness was being filled with red balloons.

Greg Walton picked up on the first ring.

"I know," he told Buck. "The same thing's happening at Langley as we speak. Our guys are on it. We're tracing the attack."

He hung up.

Ten minutes later he called back.

"The hacker's in London."

"Are you sure?" Milton Buck asked.

"Positive. Tracy managed to trace her there."

"Her?"

"Uh-huh. It's Althea. Less than a minute after Tracy got a location, she messaged us directly, claiming responsibility."

"But that's impossible," Buck ranted. "How the hell did she get in again? We rewrote the entire system after the last breach. Every firewall, every password, every line of code."

"I know what we did, Milton," Greg Walton snapped. "Evidently it wasn't enough. This virus is a lot more powerful than the last one. Three-quarters of my files have been corrupted. And it gets worse."

"Worse? How?" Milton Buck's head was starting to throb.

"According to Tracy, the virus originated from 85 Albert Embankment, SW1."

"Albert Embankment?" The throbbing got worse. "Isn't that . . ."

"Uh-huh." Greg Walton sighed heavily. "MI6 headquarters."

Chapter 14

"There's no way it originated here. No way. To be frank, Miss Whitney, I can't believe we're even discussing this."

Jamie MacIntosh seemed like a decent man. But Tracy could see that his nerves were frayed to breaking point over this latest Group 99 cyberattack. He constantly worried at his fingernails and his left foot tapped an anxious rhythm as he listened to Tracy talk.

Tracy thought, *No wonder he's worried.* Not only had Althea devastated and deeply embarrassed U.S. intelligence, but she had successfully managed to implicate British intelligence in what happened, thereby setting the two allies at each other's throats at precisely the moment that cooperation was vital.

"I agree with you," Tracy said placatingly. "No one's suggesting that Althea is one of yours."

According to Tracy's research, less than 12 percent of MI6 employees were women, and the vast majority of those were in lowly administrative or secretarial positions. Of the women educated or senior enough to have the wherewithal to plan a sophisticated cyberattack, none came close to fitting Althea's profile.

"But she did compromise your systems, just as she compromised ours. She deliberately set this up to make it look as though this hack came from within. That tells us things about her."

Major General Frank Dorrien looked at Tracy suspiciously. "Such as?"

From the little he knew of Tracy Whitney, Frank Dorrien wasn't a fan. Thieves and con artists were not people to be trusted, no matter how reformed they claimed to be.

"Such as the fact that she knows how Western intelligence services operate. My guess is she's either a former spy, or she knows someone on the inside."

"She knows you, Miss Whitney," Frank Dorrien reminded Tracy. "I suppose it's too much to hope that your memory has been jogged? That some connection has suddenly come back to you?"

Tracy's eyes narrowed. She resented the general's implication that she was lying about not knowing Althea. That she was hiding something. She also resented the way the general had looked down his superior, patrician nose at her from the moment she walked in.

"She knows *of* me," Tracy corrected him. "But so would anyone else who worked here fifteen years ago."

"OK." Jamie MacIntosh rubbed his eyes. "We'll look into the former spy angle. Greg Walton should do the same, although I'll admit I think you're barking up the wrong tree."

"Any alternate suggestions?" Tracy asked him.

"I have a suggestion," the general piped up. "There's a journalist at the *Times*, a young woman by the name of Faiers. Sally Faiers. She's been up to Sandhurst, asking questions about me and about Prince Achileas's death. She seems to be pursuing some preposterous conspiracy theory that I did the young man harm in order to silence him."

"Silence him over what?" Tracy asked.

"I have no idea." Frank sounded bored. "But I do know she's been asking about Captain Daley as well, and whether he and the prince knew each other."

"Did they?"

Frank looked Tracy right in the eye. "No. They may have passed in the corridor or on the parade ground but it was no more than that. Captain Daley was an exemplary soldier. Prince Achileas . . . was not. The idea that they were friends is frankly insulting."

Dorrien's dislike of the young Greek was palpable. It struck Tracy as odd that he made no attempt to hide it. The boy was dead, after all.

"It turns out Miss Faiers is also an ex-girlfriend of the elusive Mr. Hunter Drexel," Dorrien continued.

Tracy's eyebrows shot up.

"And she's written a number of influential op-eds in the past, arguing against hydraulic fracturing, including a withering article about Henry Cranston's company. That's rather too many connections to Group 99 for my liking."

And mine, thought Tracy. She remembered what Cameron Crewe had told her, about Henry Cranston having a deal with the Greeks to extract shale gas that got shelved after Achileas's suicide. Crewe Oil had that deal now. Not for the first time, Tracy felt as if there were dots swirling before her eyes, dots that revealed a clear picture if only she could look at them in the right way.

Tracy didn't warm to Frank Dorrien. The man was arrogant, rude and wildly judgmental. But she had to agree with him on this one. Miss Faiers sounded interesting.

"Have you spoken to her?"

"Frank's not the right person," Jamie MacIntosh jumped in. "Clearly this Faiers woman already distrusts him. As she may be our only link to Hunter Drexel, we can't afford to alienate her. We thought perhaps you might try?"

After Tracy left, Frank turned to Jamie.

"I don't trust her."

"You don't trust anyone, Frank."

"I'm serious. Someone needs to follow her. We can't let her out of our sight for a second."

If it irritated Jamie MacIntosh to be told his job by a subordinate, he hid it well.

"Don't worry, General," he replied smoothly. "It's taken care of."

Jeff Stevens stepped out of his club onto Piccadilly and into the pouring rain. Water cascaded off his umbrella as he scanned the streets in vain for a cab with its light on. All around him people were diving for cover, scurrying into shops or cowering under bus shelters.

"Mr. Stevens?"

A sandy-haired man in a crumpled Macintosh appeared at his side, apparently out of nowhere.

"Might I have a word?" The man gestured towards a gleaming black Daimler with diplomatic plates that had pulled up to the curb. "In private."

Jeff frowned suspiciously. "Do I know you?"

"Not yet." Jamie MacIntosh smiled affably, adding, "It's about Tracy Whitney."

Without hesitation, Jeff closed his umbrella and climbed into the car.

Leaving the iconic MI6 building on Albert Embankment, Tracy decided to walk for a while to clear her head. Crossing Vauxhall Bridge she turned left towards Belgravia and Chelsea, her old stomping grounds. The rain began as a light drizzle, but was soon falling hard. Ducking into a newsstand, Tracy bought a cheap umbrella and kept going.

For an hour she walked aimlessly, thinking about Sally Faiers and how best to make her approach tomorrow. Sometimes Tracy panicked that she was no nearer finding Althea than she had been when she arrived. Was the interview with Sally a diversion? Had General Dorrien set it up deliberately as a red herring, to throw Tracy off the scent? She didn't trust Frank Dorrien, that much she knew. On the other hand, as she'd told

Cameron Crewe, she felt in her gut that Hunter Drexel was a crucial link in all of this. Hunter and the fracking industry, together, held the key to Althea's identity and her connection to Group 99. If Sally Faiers could tell Tracy anything, anything at all, that shed light on Hunter Drexel and the mysterious story he was working on, then it was worth making the trip to see her. Whatever General Dorrien's motives.

Tracy found herself wishing she had someone to talk to about all this. With a pang it struck her that all her life's confidantes were gone, either dead or lost to her forever. Her beloved parents. Jeff. Blake Carter.

Then it came to her. *I know where I need to go.*

The cemetery was just off the Fulham Road, on the border of Chelsea. By the time Tracy got there twilight had already fallen. Rain soaked graves glistened eerily beneath a silver moon. The rain was still beating down, as it had been all afternoon, pounding the gravel paths like a million angry bullets flung down by a spiteful heaven. Deep puddles forced mourners and dog walkers alike to veer off the paths onto the sodden grass, more mud than turf in places.

Gunther Hartog, Tracy and Jeff's former mentor and a father figure to Tracy in her wild, con artist days, had always loved this place. Personally Tracy never understood it. To her the solid, Victorian graves cut from dour gray stone were deeply depressing. But not to Gunther. Tracy could hear his voice now as if he stood beside her.

"It's the thrill of the Gothic, my darling! The kitschness of it all. One half expects Ebenezer Scrooge to jump out from behind a plinth and grab you. Muuuah ha ha ha haaa!"

His deep, melodramatic cackle used to make Tracy laugh.

She wondered if she would ever laugh like that again.

The night she'd had dinner with Cameron Crewe in Geneva, she'd felt some faint stirrings of happiness. But the guilt that followed was so profound and debilitating, she was in no hurry to repeat the experience.

I'm afraid to be happy, she realized. *Afraid to live.*

And yet she knew she must live. She must live to avenge Nick's death.

Unexpectedly, a feeling of defeat swept over her. *I'm never going to find Althea. I'm never going to know what really happened to my darling Nick.*

Tracking somebody electronically was one thing. But it didn't count for much in the real world. Trying to anticipate an invisible woman's next move was like trying to play chess with a ghost.

Was that how the police felt, trying to catch me and Jeff all those years?

Was that frustration what turned Daniel Cooper mad?

No, Tracy reminded herself. *Cooper was a homicidal lunatic long before he even met me.*

It's not you, Tracy. It's not your fault.

At last she arrived at Gunther's grave. For all his love of Gothic pastiche, in the end his good taste had won out and he'd gone for a simple, understated headstone, devoid of gargoyles or roses or crosses ringed with thorns.

The inscription read simply *Gunther Hartog—Art Collector* and the dates.

Tracy stood next to the stone, so that her umbrella covered both of them. She hadn't brought flowers or anything. Now that she was here she wasn't even really sure why she'd come. Only that she'd needed the comfort of an old friend. Of someone who had loved her.

As the rain beat down on her umbrella, Tracy closed her eyes and allowed herself to feel the pain. The loss. Like a roll call, the faces of her loved ones floated before her.

Her father.

Her mother.

Gunther.

Blake.

Nicholas.

Jeff Stevens was still alive, of course. But with Nick gone, it would be too painful for Tracy ever to see Jeff again. He might as well be dead.

"I'm alone, Gunther," Tracy murmured in the darkness. "I'm completely alone."

Standing in the muddy London graveyard, Tracy fell to her knees and wept.

Jeff sat in the back of the car in stunned silence.

Jamie MacIntosh had been talking for almost forty minutes. For all of that time, Jeff had listened, processed, considered. Now, for the first time, he spoke.

"You believe this Althea woman really killed Nick?"

"I don't know," Jamie said honestly. "I know Tracy believes it. But it's possible that the CIA put that idea into her head just to get her involved."

Jeff considered this, nodding. "OK."

Jamie said, "I know Althea ordered the murder of Captain Daley, and probably Henry Cranston. I know she's a grave threat to Western security."

"I don't care about any of that." Jeff waved a hand dismissively.

"But you care about Tracy?"

"Of course."

"So you'll help us? I know your history, Jeff." Jamie MacIntosh softened his tone. "We have a file on you and Tracy as big as the Koran, going back almost twenty years now."

"I'm sure you do," said Jeff, not without a touch of pride.

"If anybody understands how she thinks, how she operates, it's you. Please. For her sake, if not for ours."

Jeff closed his eyes. What this man wanted—what the British Government wanted—was for him to follow Tracy. Not just to track her physical movements. But to anticipate her strategy, spy on her, outsmart her. *Play* her. MI6 wanted to find Althea, and Hunter Drexel, before the CIA did. They wanted to win. Tracy was the Americans' star player. Jamie was asking Jeff to become theirs.

Following Tracy. Outsmarting Tracy. Protecting Tracy, or trying to. It was how Jeff Stevens had spent most of his adult life. The best parts of it, anyway.

Of course, she'd probably hate him for it.

He opened his eyes and looked at Jamie MacIntosh. "When do I start?"

When Tracy woke up, sunshine streamed brightly through the window. For a moment she thought she was back home in Colorado. The light in Steamboat Springs was always dazzling, even in winter. But reality soon reasserted itself.

She was in London, in the modest Pimlico hotel that the agency had paid for. The red damask curtains were pulled back. Traffic was honking outside. The clock by the side of Tracy's bed said 11:15 A.M.

11:15? Tracy rubbed her eyes. How was that even possible? She must have slept for fourteen hours, the first unbroken, dreamless night she'd had since Nick's death. She couldn't remember how she'd got back to her hotel from the graveyard, or how long she'd sat, slumped over Gunther Hartog's grave, sobbing until her body had no more to give. But she remembered getting back to her room and feeling incredibly cold. Peeling off her wet clothes, she'd intended to take a hot shower, but exhaustion must have overtaken her before she could make it to the bathroom. Crawling under the covers, she'd sunk into a sleep so deep it was closer to a coma.

She'd needed to cry and she'd needed to sleep. Thanks to Gunther Hartog, she'd managed both. *Thank you, Gunther darling.* Her body felt wonderful, her mind alert. But there was no time to enjoy these novel sensations, not if she were going to catch Sally Faiers before she left the *Times* offices for her lunch.

Leaping out of bed, Tracy pulled on jeans and a sweater.

Ten minutes later she was in a black cab, heading for Wapping.

Chapter 15

S ally Faiers was rushing for the tube when a waiflike woman approached her.

"Sally!"

"Yes," Sally said uncertainly. The woman said her name as if she knew her but Sally was sure she'd never seen her before. The huge, sad green eyes, high cheekbones and tiny, birdlike body that was closer to a child's than a grown adult's were all striking enough that she would have remembered them. "Have we met?"

"No. My name is Tracy Whitney."

Was that supposed to mean something?

"I need to talk to you."

"What about?" Sally looked at her watch. She didn't have time for guessing games with tiny women. Her boiler was on the blink and the annoying people from Eon were due at the flat in half an hour to fix it. "If it's about a story you can call the news desk." She fumbled in her pocket for a card.

Tracy said, "It's about Hunter Drexel."

Sally froze.

"Not here," she whispered. Scrawling an address on a piece of paper, she handed it to Tracy. "It's a café, off East Street market. I'll meet you there in twenty minutes."

The café was grimy, with steamed-up windows. It smelled of frying bacon and strong PG Tips tea and its clientele seemed to be made up entirely of Polish builders. Tracy loved it immediately.

"Your local?" she asked Sally.

"Not anymore. I was a student in this area. Briefly." Sally wasn't in the mood for small talk. "Who are you?"

They ordered tea and Tracy told her, the edited version. That she was working with the CIA counterterrorism division dealing with the threat from Group 99. "Specifically I'm trying to track down an American woman believed to be one of their leaders. We think she played a part in Captain Daley's murder and in Hunter's abduction."

Sally looked skeptical. "So you're a CIA agent?"

"Not exactly." Tracy heaped sugar into her tea. "I work with them, not for them. I guess you could say I'm a consultant. Of sorts."

"How did you find me?" Sally asked. Reaching into her pocket she pulled out a Dictaphone and placed it on the table, pressing the record button as Tracy looked on. "Just a precaution. Do you mind?"

"Not at all," said Tracy. "General Frank Dorrien gave me your name."

"Ah." Sally rolled her eyes. "The general."

"You're not a fan?" Tracy asked.

Sally smiled. "Is anyone?"

Tracy smiled back. "Mrs. Dorrien, perhaps?"

I like this woman, Tracy and Sally thought simultaneously.

"So what did General Frank tell you?" Sally asked.

"Just that you've been asking questions about him and about Prince Achileas's suicide. And that you and Hunter Drexel were close."

"Hunter's close to a lot of women," Sally said archly.

"Not that he would trust to chase down a story for him. While he's on the run from Group 99 and the U.S. government, and probably in fear for his life," said Tracy.

Sally looked at her admiringly.

"He's alive, then? He's contacted you?"

Sally focused on her tea. She liked Tracy Whitney instinctively, but her instincts had been wrong before. And she'd sworn to Hunter that she wouldn't breathe a word about their contact to anyone.

Sensing her hesitation, Tracy said bluntly, "If Group 99 finds him before we do, they'll kill him. Whether Hunter believes it or not, we're trying to save his life. But we need your help, Sally."

A heavy silence descended over the table. Finally, Sally broke it. "OK. Yes, he's alive. Yes, we've spoken. But I don't know where he is. And even if I did I wouldn't tell you."

"What's he working on? His story."

"I don't know."

"You must know something," Tracy pressed her. "He asked you to look into Frank Dorrien, didn't he? Why?"

"I swear to you, I don't know." Sally ran a hand through her dirty-blond hair in frustration. "Hunter would rather die, literally, than let anyone else in on his scoop. Even me. I know he suspected the general of having a hand in the Greek prince's death. That's why he asked me to check him out."

"And did he?" Tracy tried to make the question sound casual.

Sally shook her head. "No. It was suicide. Like I told Hunter, there *is* no dirt on this guy. And I mean none.

He may not be warm and cuddly, but Frank Dorrien's as clean as a whistle. The man's never gambled, barely drinks, never been disciplined, never cheated on his wife. I wouldn't mind betting his shirts are all perfectly color-coded in his closet. He's rude and a bit weird, maybe, but being OCD and a stickler for good form doesn't make you a killer."

"No, it doesn't," Tracy agreed. "But Hunter still suspects him?"

"He suspects him of something," Sally said. "I don't think even he knows what exactly. One of Hunter's problems is his stubbornness. When he gets an idea in his head, it can take a lot more than facts—or in this case a complete and utter lack of facts—to change his mind. It's the same way with his gambling. Once he's playing his hand at poker, or he's put his money on a horse, it's as if, for him, the outcome is already decided. He must win, so he will win. It's as if he thinks he can make something true by believing it hard enough."

Tracy remembered that Cameron Crewe had told her something very similar about him.

"Not a good trait for a journalist," she observed.

"No," Sally agreed. "Hunter has his strengths. But he can be willfully blind when he wants to be."

"Do you know why he ran from his rescuers?" Tracy changed tack abruptly.

Sally shook her head. "I mean clearly he didn't trust them. But if you're asking why, I have no idea."

"And he never mentioned Althea to you? Or anyone else in Group 99?"

"No." Sally drained her mug of tea. "The weird thing is, they are trying to kill him." She told Tracy about Hunter's near miss with Apollo, being careful not to let slip any locations. "But I get the strong sense that this story he's writing goes way beyond Group 99. It's something big. Big enough for your friends at the CIA to want to bury."

Tracy considered this, chewing on her bacon sandwich in silence. Suddenly Sally said, "Do you know why Hunter and I broke up?"

"Another woman?" Tracy hazarded a wild guess.

Sally smiled. "That didn't help. But the straw that broke the camel's back was actually his gambling. We owned a place together, a lovely garden flat in Hampstead. Most of the money came from my parents. Hunter remortgaged it behind my back to pay off a poker debt." She laughed but there was no happiness in the sound. "I love him. But he is *so* dishonest, it takes your breath away. I lost that flat, and honestly, he wasn't even sorry about it. He just kept saying it was 'only' money, 'only' bricks and mortar. You're wondering why I'm telling you this, aren't you?"

"A bit," Tracy admitted.

"The thing is, Hunter and I *are* close. But I've never understood him. I'm probably the last person you should ask about his motivations. I never know what he's going to do next."

Tracy paid the bill and they walked out onto the street. They swapped numbers, and promised to stay in touch.

"Does anyone else know you've heard from Hunter? Or about him running from the SEALs?"

Sally shook her head. "No one. I'm only telling you because, honestly, I'm scared. All Hunter cares about is his stupid story. But like you said, if Group 99 find him, they'll kill him. Whatever it is that he doesn't want your lot to find out, I don't believe it's worth dying for."

"You really do love him, don't you?"

Sally pulled her coat around her shoulders forlornly. "Unfortunately, yes. I do. He's an asshole and a player. Totally toxic. But there literally is no one else like him. Once you've loved someone like Hunter, it ruins you for normal, stable men." She laughed, embarrassed. "You probably have no idea what I'm talking about."

An image of Jeff Stevens's face popped, unbidden, into Tracy's mind.

"Oh, I do," she told Sally. "Believe me. I absolutely do."

Tracy was woken at six the next morning by a phone call from Greg Walton.

"We've had complaints."

Tracy rubbed her eyes. *Good morning to you too.* "What sort of complaints?"

"Serious complaints. From the British Home Office. According to them you were uncooperative and obstructive in yesterday's meeting."

"That's absurd." Tracy cast her mind back to her conversation with Jamie MacIntosh and Frank Dorrien at MI6 yesterday, trying to think of anything she said or did that might be construed as obstructive. "They asked me to interview a journalist, a contact of Hunter Drexel's, and I did that. Who complained, Greg?"

"That doesn't matter."

"It does to me," Tracy said hotly. "It was Frank Dorrien, wasn't it?"

"Like I said, that's not the issue."

"He made it clear yesterday he didn't trust me." Tracy could feel her anger growing. "But you know what? The feeling's mutual. He's more involved in all this than he lets on. Hunter Drexel doesn't trust him."

"How do you know that?"

Tracy filled Greg in on yesterday's meeting with Sally Faiers. He was excited.

"That's huge, Tracy. Great work. We'll have the Brits subpoena her phone records."

"No, don't," Tracy said hurriedly. "Let's keep them out of this for now. Sally trusts me. If she feels she's being used or spied on, she'll shut down. She dislikes General Dorrien almost as much as I do."

"Hmm." Walton didn't sound happy. "I don't know about that . . ."

"You won't find anything anyway. Hunter Drexel's a pro. He's bound to be on disposable phones."

"All right. We'll leave it for now. But stay close to her. And remember, General Dorrien's on our side. You're there to find Althea, not to investigate the general."

"But what if the two are connected?"

"They aren't, Tracy." A note of firmness had crept into Walton's voice. He quickly replaced it with a warmer, more flattering tone. "I'll be sure to tell the president about your great work over there. Believe me, he'll be delighted to learn that Drexel's still alive at least. That's a lot more than we knew yesterday."

"Hopefully it's only the beginning. There's a lot more I need to do here. Althea's not part of MI6, I'm sure of that. But . . ."

Greg Walton cut her off. "Actually, Tracy, I'd like you back in the States by tomorrow, Thursday at the latest."

"What? Why?" Tracy was bewildered.

"Agent Buck has some potential new leads."

"What new leads? The best leads we have are right here in London."

"Buck will fill you in when you get back here," Greg Walton said, in a way that made it clear Tracy's return was a command, not a suggestion. "Like I said, we're grateful for what you've achieved. But diplomatically it's important you come home."

"OK," Tracy said, deadpan.

Walton seemed relieved.

"There'll be a ticket waiting for you at the BA desk at Heathrow."

"Right."

"Good job again."

Walton rang off.

Tracy sat in bed for a long time, staring at the phone in her hand.

Something's wrong.

Someone wants me gone.

Is it General Frank Dorrien? Good old, upright, squeaky clean Frank?

She started to get dressed.

Greg Walton hung up the phone. He was seated in the Oval Office, across the desk from the president; Agent Buck of the FBI sat beside him.

President Havers looked at Walton. "So he's alive?"

"Yes, Sir."

"But we don't know where?"

"No, Sir. Not yet."

President Havers stared bitterly past his intelligence chiefs to the framed picture of himself on the wall above their heads. It had been taken on his inauguration day, less than a year ago. He must have aged a decade since then, thanks to Hunter Drexel.

Havers's reelection campaign would begin in earnest in a few months' time. Some of his big donors had already written checks. But others, including Cameron Crewe, were hesitating, waiting to see how the Group 99 crisis resolved itself. The situation in Europe was as tense as it had been in decades. The president needed a win and he knew it.

"What about Whitney? How much does she know?"

"She knows nothing," Agent Buck sneered. "She's a tool. Nothing more."

President Havers hoped Buck was right. Tracy Whitney had proved useful in tracking Althea to London and in getting a lead on Hunter Drexel. But her skills of deduction could be extremely dangerous if she wasn't kept in check. She was already showing an unhealthy interest in the unfortunate events at Sandhurst Academy. Not to mention antagonizing British intelligence into the bargain.

A secretary stuck her head around the door.

"So sorry, Mr. President. But I have the British Prime Minister on the line. I don't think she's too happy."

President Havers sighed deeply. Since the disastrous Bratislavan raid, Julia Cabot was the only friend he had left in Europe. He needed her.

Turning to the two intelligence officers, he hissed, "Get Tracy Whitney back here. She's causing too many waves."

"Yes, Sir." Greg Walton stood up. "It's already done."

"And keep her on a tight leash from now on."

As Walton and Buck left the room, they heard the president putting on his warmest, most conciliatory voice.

"Julia!" Havers was practically purring. "To what do I owe the pleasure?"

Camilla and Rory Daley lived in a handsome Georgian rectory on the outskirts of one of Hampshire's most sought after villages. The immaculate gardens and grounds sloped gently down to the River Test, where generations of Daleys had enjoyed exclusive rights to some of the best trout fishing in the country. Inside, polished parquet floors liberally scattered with antique Persian rugs led into spacious, elegant rooms, with original sash windows, generous fire-places and traditional English furniture. Two Turner watercolors hung on the drawing room walls, above a Knowles sofa on which two rather scruffy wire-haired dachshunds slept soundly at opposite ends.

All in all, Tracy thought, it was quite the most charming, upper-class, English country house she'd been in since Gunther was alive. Clearly Captain Bob Daley's parents were paid up members of the top 1 percent, if not the top 0.1 percent.

"Are you sure I can't get you a cup of tea, Miss Arkell?" Lady Daley asked, for at least the third time. Tracy had adopted a perfect, cut-glass English accent and introduced herself as Harriet Arkell, an author, researching a biography on their son. She felt bad lying to the sweet, elderly couple. But she knew that the moment she mentioned the CIA, or the Daleys heard an American accent, they would be on their guard. Years living in England had taught Tracy that the English upper classes were far more forthcoming among those they perceived to be one of their own.

"It's very kind of you but I'm fine, thank you," Tracy said. "I won't intrude too long. I really only wanted to clear up a few minor points about Bob's time at Sandhurst."

"Of course." Camilla Daley beamed, her eyes twinkling the same cornflower blue as her country casuals twin-set. She clearly relished any opportunity to talk about her son. "Bob adored Sandhurst. Absolutely loved the place, didn't he, Rory?"

"Both times," the old man confirmed. "As a cadet with the Welsh Fusiliers, and then later as an instructor. I don't think he missed active service at all."

Lord Daley had jowls that quivered when he talked, like a bulldog's, and pale, rheumy eyes. He seemed older and more tired than his wife. Tracy wondered whether their son's gruesome murder had hit him harder and felt her guilt at her deception redouble.

"Did he have many friends at the academy?"

"Oh, Bob had masses of friends. From school, from the regiment and of course from Sandhurst too."

"Anyone who stands out?"

"Well, yes." Lady Daley's face fell suddenly. "Although he probably stands out for the wrong reasons. Poor Achileas."

"Prince Achileas? Of Greece?"

"I daresay you read about him." Camilla nodded sadly. "He and Bob were great friends. He came here more than once you know. But I'm afraid the poor chap killed himself. We hadn't the slightest idea he was depressed. It was the same week that Bob . . . that we lost Bob."

Tracy's mind raced. General Dorrien's words rang through her skull like a clanging church bell: *They may have passed on the parade ground. But it was no more than that. They weren't friends.*

Tracy thought, *You little liar, Frank!*

"Achileas was an officer cadet," Tracy observed. "So he was a good deal less senior than your son. A lot younger too. Do you know how they became close?"

"Greece," Lord Daley said wheezily from his chair. "Bob was a classicist, you see. Obsessed with Greece since he was a small boy. He was in Athens, you know, when these cowards took him."

"Of course Harriet knows that, darling," said his wife, rolling her eyes. "She's written a book about what happened."

"I thought she was writing a book about Robert?" The old man sounded confused suddenly. He reminded Tracy so strongly of her father in his later years, it was all she could do not to run over and hug him.

"I am, Lord Daley," she assured him. "I am." Turning back to Camilla she asked, "I don't suppose you have any photographs of Bob with Achileas?"

"I'll have a look." Camilla frowned. "I don't think so though. We're not huge picture takers. And of course, Achileas being a royal and all that. I'm not sure he would have liked us snapping away at him like a pair of goggle-eyed tourists."

Any two people less like "goggle-eyed tourists," Tracy couldn't imagine.

"We were so upset though, when we heard what happened," Lady Daley went on. "According to some of Bob's friends, somebody broke into Achileas's rooms after he died and pinched things. Can you believe it? Royal souvenir hunters gone mad. I mean really, who would stoop so low?"

"I can't imagine," said Tracy, suitably horrified.

Although in fact she could imagine very well.

Cameron Crewe was just stepping out of his home gym in New York after a grueling session with his trainer when Tracy called.

"Cameron?"

It took him a moment to place who it was. He hadn't heard from Tracy Whitney since their dinner in Geneva, much to his disappointment, and didn't know if he ever would again.

"Tracy!" he panted, leaning against a wall for support. "What a nice surprise."

"Are you OK?" she asked. "You sound like you're having an asthma attack."

Cameron laughed. It was wonderful to hear her voice. More wonderful than it should have been.

"I'm fine. Just old. And unfit. Where are you?"

"I'm in London. Walking up Wandsworth Bridge Road, to be precise."

"OK."

"Listen, I need some advice."

Cameron Crewe allowed himself a small smile.

She wants my advice. She trusts me.

"Shoot."

For the next ten minutes, Tracy gave him an edited version of developments in the Group 99/Althea/Drexel case since they last met. Without divulging anything classified, she gave him a summary of her meeting with Sally Faiers and managed to convey her suspicions about British Intelligence, and in particular Major General Frank Dorrien.

To Tracy's surprise, Cameron already knew about the Group 99 hack on the CIA and FBI systems. She kept forgetting that Cameron had also worked with Greg Walton for many years. She wasn't the only outsider the agency had ever called on for help. But he didn't know Tracy had traced the hack back to MI6, nor that Hunter Drexel was definitively still alive. He listened intently while she filled him in.

Finally, Tracy told Cameron about her trip to see Bob Daley's family.

"I'd call that serious progress in five days," Cameron said, when she finally drew breath. "I'm guessing Greg Walton's loving your ass right now."

Tracy said, "You'd think so, wouldn't you?"

She explained that the CIA had recalled her to Washington. That she was supposed to be on a plane tomorrow, in fact.

"I'm telling you, General Dorrien's gotten to them somehow. He's behind this. He made some trumped-up complaint against me and now he's got everyone running scared. But the fact is he lied to me outright about Daley and the Prince not being friends. I know that for a fact now." She was speaking very quickly, excitedly. Cameron found it hard to keep up.

Tracy said, "I think he was the one who stole the Prince's stuff."

"Who?"

"General Dorrien."

"I'm confused," said Cameron. "Dorrien is MI6?"

"As was Captain Daley."

"And you think he stole things from the dead Prince's room at Sandhurst?"

"Yes. Including his computer."

"And the Prince's death is connected to Group 99 . . . how?"

"I don't know," Tracy admitted. "But I think Dorrien knows. That's what I need your advice about."

"OK." Cameron waited.

Tracy took a deep breath. "I'm thinking of breaking into his house."

Cameron started to laugh, but stopped in the face of Tracy's silence.

"You're not serious?"

"Completely. I break in, find the computer and whatever else it was he took and doesn't want me to find. And I bring it back to Walton as a fait accompli."

"Right. May I suggest an alternate plan?" said Cameron.

"You may."

"Get on the plane tomorrow, come to New York and have dinner with me."

"Come on. I really need your advice."

"My advice on breaking and entering?" Cameron laughed. "I just gave it to you! Don't do it, Tracy. What you're suggesting is utter madness. Walton would hit the roof and he'd have every right to."

"But if I found proof Dorrien's not who he says he is? Prove that there's a link between Group 99 and Hunter Drexel's story about fracking, and the Prince's death, and that Major Dorrien's involved up to his neck . . ."

"You won't find proof!"

"Why do you say that?"

"Because you'll be arrested, Tracy! Or worse, you'll break your neck. Either way you'll cause a major international incident. Look, I hate to be the one to rain on your parade. But really, what the hell do you know about housebreaking?"

Tracy allowed herself a small smile.

"Hold that thought on dinner," she said, and hung up.

Jeff Stevens watched from the corner of Studdridge Street as Tracy ended her phone call, glanced quickly around her, and hopped onto a number 19 bus towards Chelsea.

She was wearing skinny black jeans and a dark green sweater, and her chestnut hair blew in the breeze behind her and she stepped up into the bus, flashing her Oyster card at the driver. She looked beautiful.

Jeff felt a sharp, stabbing pain in his chest.

He recognized it as longing.

"I'm right behind you, Tracy," he whispered out loud, sticking his arm out and hailing a black cab.

Waving a fifty-pound note at the driver he said, "Follow that bus."

Chapter 16

Tracy's old friend, the fine-art dealer, Jacob Bodie, had prepped the job for her.

Thank God for Jacob.

Now a sprightly sixty, Jacob Bodie no longer stole art himself. It was a very, very long time since he'd broken into a gallery or a private home. But he'd been the best in his day, and he still worked with the best, thoroughly researching and vetting every job he was involved in. Like Tracy and Jeff, Jacob only ever stole from the underserving: philistines, cheats and hoarders.

Tracy trusted him.

"Mrs. Dorrien—Cynthia—always goes out to bridge on a Tuesday night. She leaves the house at six on the dot and is usually back by nine," Jacob explained to Tracy in his deep, gravelly voice.

"Usually?"

"Usually. Come along, Tracy. There are no guarantees, you know that. But that's a three-hour window for a three-minute job. You go in, get what you need, get out. Simple."

Tracy felt sick.

How many times had she heard that word, "simple"?

It was what Conrad Morgan had told her before her first job, stealing Lois Bellamy's jewels from her house in Long Island. She could hear Conrad's voice now, low and soothing, like a snake charmer's song.

It's ridiculously simple, Tracy.

But of course it wasn't. Tracy had come within a hair's breadth of being caught that night, of being sent back to the Louisiana Penitentiary for good.

I wasn't caught though, Tracy reminded herself. *I outsmarted the police, and Jeff Stevens too. I'm good at this. This is what I do.*

Jacob Bodie had provided her with a plan of the Dorriens' modest house, as well as the code to the couple's safe and burglar alarm, and a copied front door key.

"How on earth did you pull all this together so quickly?" Tracy asked him.

Jacob gave a satisfied smile. "I have my ways, dear girl. Although I must say I'm thrilled to have impressed you. It's not easy to impress the great Tracy Whitney."

Tracy wanted to say that the "great" Tracy Whitney had died a long time ago. If she ever really existed. But she didn't.

"What about the general?" she asked.

"He'll be at the barracks, don't you worry," said Jacob. "He's a workaholic. Almost never gets home before ten."

Tracy didn't like that *almost*. Not one bit.

"And this Tuesday he definitely won't be back early," Jacob reassured her. "There's a review meeting for all the senior officers up at the military academy. Dorrien's leading two of the sessions."

Tracy left Jacob Bodie's Bond Street gallery feeling confident and well prepared.

The next night, sitting in the pitch dark outside Frank Dorrien's house in a rented car with the engine switched off, all her confidence had deserted her. Tracy was as frozen with fear as she had been on the Bellamy job, and every job since.

What the hell am I doing here?

There's a plane ticket waiting for me at Heathrow. If I leave now, I'll still have time for dinner before takeoff. Maybe a nice, relaxing glass of red wine.

But it was too late for that now. Tracy was here. The decision was made.

She opened the car door.

In black overalls, gloves and boots and with a cap pulled low over her head, she was close to invisible as she approached the house. Not that it mattered. The entire street was deserted. The Dorriens' neighbors were all at home watching the *Strictly Come Dancing* final on TV, their curtains firmly drawn.

Tracy's heart was beating so loudly, she could hear nothing else. She'd forgotten quite how nauseous adrenaline made her.

She was at the front door now, Bodie's copied key in her hand. Once she opened it she was committed.

Cameron Crewe's voice rang in her ears.

You won't find proof!

You'll be arrested, Tracy.

Tracy slipped the key in the door and turned the handle.

The alarm exploded into life. No bells were ringing yet, but the system was beeping loudly, very loudly, like an angry bee calling back to its hive for reinforcements. Any minute now there would be sirens and lights and . . .

Shit! Where the fuck is the keypad?

Flustered, Tracy felt desperately up and down the wall. Finally she found it, hidden behind a hanging coat. *Thank God!* Heart hammering, she keyed in the code.

Nothing happened.

Damn it! Her hands were shaking. In her panic, she must have got the numbers in the wrong order. Tracy knew she only had twenty seconds to disarm the system. Jacob had been very clear about that. Ten of those seconds must have passed already, at least.

Sweat poured down Tracy's back like a river. She didn't care about being caught for herself. Her own life, her own safety, meant nothing to her anymore. But she had to know what Frank Dorrien was hiding. She had to put the pieces of this puzzle together, for Nicholas's sake.

Forcing herself to stay calm, she typed the code in again, slowly this time, whispering each number as she pressed.

Five. Three. Five. Six.

The beeping stopped.

Tracy laughed. For the first time since she opened her eyes this morning, she began to relax.

Frank Dorrien's house was small and neat and orderly and a little bit soulless, at least to Tracy's way of thinking. There were no family photographs on display, no flowers, no novels or newspapers left casually on a side table. It was more like an office than a home. There was also far too much brown, heavy furniture, nothing colorful or feminine or light. Although perhaps things looked worse in the gloom? Frank and Cynthia had left a few lights on downstairs—no energy saving going on in the Dorrien household. No doubt Frank thought that was for hippies and lefties, but the illumination was patchy at best. Upstairs, everything was pitch-dark.

As black as the general's heart, Tracy thought. *As black as my world without Nick.*

She headed to the master bedroom. This, too, was a dull space, as uninspiring as any corporate apartment. There was a simply upholstered Habitat bed with plain white linen, a chest of drawers with a carved, Chinese box on top and some built-in closets with mirrored doors. A lone cushion in the shape of a sausage dog, propped up against the pillows, was the only sign of humor or personal taste of any kind. Clearly, General Frank was as controlled and uptight at home as he was at work.

The safe was exactly where Jacob said it would be, at the back of the large master closet. Tracy didn't know what she was looking for, exactly, but the safe seemed a good place to start. She entered the code and this time there were no mishaps, no alarms or lights or warning signals. The thing popped open as obligingly as a hooker's legs, as Jeff used to say.

Why must she always think of Jeff at times like this? Irritated, Tracy focused on the job at hand.

Gingerly removing the safe's contents, item by item, she examined each one with her flashlight.

The general's will.

Deeds to the house.

A string of pearls that Tracy's expert eye could see immediately were of more sentimental than material value.

Twenty thousand pounds in cash.

That was unexpected. Twenty grand was a lot of money for a family of modest means to keep at home, stuffed into a dirty envelope. But Tracy put her curiosity aside for now. She didn't have time to waste wondering where Dorrien might have come by such a sum, or what he intended to do with it. Instead she looked through everything again, carefully separating each banknote and each sheet of the legal documents, forcing herself to slow down so she didn't miss anything. But it was no good. She was right the first time.

There's nothing of Achileas's here.

Tracy relocked the safe and looked at her watch. It was still only 6:45 P.M. Plenty of time before Cynthia Dorrien got back from her bridge game.

Tracy retraced her steps back downstairs to Frank's study.

The general's desk was as orderly as everything else in the house, clean as a whistle and perfectly devoid of clutter. Infuriatingly, his computer was gone. He must have taken it with him to tonight's meeting at the barracks. Tracy couldn't get a break tonight.

She started opening drawers, looking for papers, photographs, a thumb drive, anything.

Nothing.

Nothing, nothing, nothing.

There has to be something here, she told herself. *There must be something in this house.*

Tracy searched each room in turn. At first she was methodical, closing kitchen cupboards behind her, replacing carpets that she'd peeled back, covering her tracks. But as the minutes ticked by, then the hours, she grew more and more frantic, pulling paintings down off walls, sweeping piles of books onto the floor.

She was on the point of giving up when she found it. Of all places it was in the loo. A tissue box beside the washbasin felt heavier than it ought to. Tracy ripped it apart like a wild woman, pulling out the precious hard drive like a diver plucking a pearl from its oyster.

She stared at the little black square for a moment, overwhelmed that after so much disappointment she'd actually found it. *This is it. This has to be it.*

I did it!

There was no time to stop and celebrate. Stuffing the drive deep into her rucksack, Tracy stepped back into the hallway. She was almost at the front door when the beams from a car's headlights suddenly blinded her.

Shit!

Tracy froze. She heard the unmistakable noise of an engine drawing closer, then idling and finally switching off. The headlights went off.

Cynthia Dorrien was home.

Worse, she wasn't alone.

Parked a few yards down the street, in an unremarkable Ford Transit, Jeff sat in the darkness, watching the police arrive.

Things had gotten complicated the moment Jeff realized that Tracy was hitting General Dorrien's house. Then again, things always got complicated with Tracy.

Should he tell Jamie MacIntosh what she was planning? Or keep it to himself?

It hadn't taken Jeff long to decide on the latter. If Tracy didn't trust the MI6 officer then Jeff didn't either. On the other hand, he was concerned for Tracy's safety. Even more so now that the boys in blue were on the scene.

He longed to intervene, to do something to save Tracy, but he was powerless.

Come on, sweetheart, he willed her. *Think of something.*

Tracy recognized the familiar blue and white lights of the British police. She heard male voices, hushed but urgent.

Instinctively, she dropped to the floor. She must have been visible, at least partially, from the window. But something told her the police hadn't seen her yet. The car engines switched off one by one, and with them the lights. Everything was dark again and eerily hushed. The calm before the storm. Tracy listened. Every sense was on high alert. She felt like a violin whose strings had been tightened till they were about to snap.

How had the police found her? Had someone seen something? A neighbor, perhaps?

She knew Jacob wouldn't have turned her in, and he was the only one who knew she was here tonight. Her mind raced.

She heard footsteps, walking towards the front door. Other feet were scurrying around the back. Desperately, Tracy looked around for a means of escape. But even if she found one, there was no time! In a matter of seconds the door would burst open. She'd be caught red-handed, arrested. Cameron was right. At best she'd be sent back to the U.S. in disgrace. Or perhaps the CIA would disown her and leave her to rot in a British jail. Save themselves the embarrassment.

Then she would never find Althea. Never learn what happened to Nick.

There was a hammering on the front door.

"Police! Open up!"

Tracy made her decision.

Major General Frank Dorrien was tired. He loathed meetings. *If I'd wanted to witter on about mission statements and best practices or waste my evenings on PowerPoint presentations, I'd have gone into business,* he thought resentfully as he drove home. It was bad enough having to waste half his day indulging in cryptic "chats" with MI6. But one expected spies to beat around the bush. Officers in the British Army ought to know better. Tonight's SFCR (Sandhurst Funding Committee Review) had been torture by any other name. It ought to have been banned by the Geneva bloody Convention. All Frank wanted now was a whisky, a bath and his bed.

Two police cars passed him as he turned into his street. He was just thinking how unusual that was, when he saw a third car with its engine running still parked in his driveway. A uniformed officer was standing on his doorstep, talking seriously to a worried-looking Cynthia, who'd obviously just returned home from bridge.

"I'm so sorry, General." The policeman accosted Frank as he stepped out of the car. "Are the others on their way?"

Frank frowned. "Others? What others?"

"The cadets." The policeman adopted a conspiratorial tone. "It's all right, General. The explosives specialist already filled us in."

Frank was starting to get irritated. It had been a very long day. "Explosives specialist? What the devil are you talking about, man?"

"Captain Phillips. The explosives specialist who let us in to the property earlier. The Captain explained about the training exercise, and how important it was to leave the house untouched, once it had been set up."

Frank's eyes widened.

"We do understand that these 'surprise' exercises are important, General," the policeman went on. "Your cadets need to know how to respond to bomb threats in the community, and real terrorists don't give advance warning. We get it. But this *is* a residential area. In future we'd appreciate a heads-up if you're planning this sort of drill. At a minimum we'd like to warn your neighbors."

"How about warning *me*?" Cynthia piped up indignantly.

"Old Mr. Dingle across the street thought you were being burgled," the policeman chuckled. "So did we, when we first arrived."

Frank Dorrien pushed past the policeman into the house. He ran straight to the downstairs lavatory. The remnants of the tissue box lay in pieces on the floor.

Frank felt the bile rise up in his throat.

Racing back outside he asked the policeman, "When did the explosives specialist leave?"

"About ten minutes ago. Just before your wife got home. She said she was heading back to the barracks but that the others would be on their way shortly. We tried to contact you on your mobile, General, but . . ."

Frank interrupted him. "She?"

"That's right, General."

"Captain Phillips . . . was a woman?"

Now it was the policeman's turn to look confused.

"Yes, Sir. But surely you knew that? If you ordered the exercise?"

Slowly, painfully slowly, the penny began to drop.

Jeff Stevens drove away, his shoulders shaking with laughter.

Darling Tracy! He smiled to himself. *You've still got it.*

Hunter Drexel gave two hard, animal thrusts and climaxed.

The girl underneath him, Claudette, rolled over onto her back, smiling up at him languidly.

"Encore une fois?"

Hunter shook his head. He was far too exhausted to screw her again, or do anything other than sleep. It was a long time since he'd been with a woman, even longer since he'd been with a professional. He'd picked up Claudette at the Crazy Horse, where she was a dancer. At 500 euros a night her rates were steep, but well worth it. She was also clearly prepared to work hard for the money. If only Hunter weren't too shattered to take advantage of it.

He'd taken a big risk coming to Paris. There was much more chance of his being recognized in a cosmopolitan city like this one. But if he was going to publish this story before Group 99 put a bullet between his eyes or the CIA spirited him off to some torture camp somewhere, he needed help. Sally was doing her best but that only went so far, and it was far too dangerous for Hunter to go to London. He had friends in Paris, journalists and subversives, who could help him. And the poker was outstanding.

Drifting into sleep, a parade of images danced before his eyes.

Sally Faiers, naked in his bed.

The Navy SEAL holding his hand out in the Chinook in Bratislava. *"Get in!"*

Bob Daley smiling at him, right before his head was blown off.

Apollo standing in the dark alleyway in Riga, smiling down the barrel of his gun.

Waking with a start, Hunter leaped out of bed and pulled Claudette's right arm painfully behind her back. The little bitch was rifling through the pockets of his pants, trying to rob him!

"Qu'est-ce que tu fais?" Hunter hissed at her, turning her to face him. *"Putain."*

"Asshole!" the girl shot back in English. "I know who you are."

Hunter's face darkened menacingly. All of a sudden, Claudette's stomach liquefied with fear. She'd gone too far. This man was dangerous. Very dangerous. He'd seemed so handsome in the club, so charming. But the look in his eyes now was cold as ice.

Hunter muttered darkly. *"Tu connais rien. Je pouvais te casser. Comme un poulet. Tu comprends?"*

She nodded mutely.

"Get dressed and get out."

He released her, watching in satisfaction as she grabbed her clothes, terrified, and ran.

Cameron Crewe was about to go to bed when the doorman buzzed his apartment.

"What is it?" he asked curtly. He was in no mood for visitors.

"I'm sorry, Sir. But there's a lady here to see you."

"A lady?"

"Yes, Sir. A Miss Whitney. She says it's urgent."

Cameron's bad mood evaporated like a puddle of rain in the sun. He hadn't heard from Tracy since their phone call of a few days ago, and had fully expected her next call to be from a police cell. In fact she was here, in New York, on his doorstep.

"That's quite all right, Billy. Show her up."

Cameron barely had time to change his shirt and splash on some cologne before Tracy burst through the door, a ball of nervous energy.

"Hi." Peeling off her wet trench coat she tossed it on Cameron's expensive B&B Italia couch where it dripped excessively onto the suede. "I'm sorry I didn't call in advance. I needed to see you."

Cameron was thrown by how happy this statement

made him. "No need to apologize. You can come by any time. Can I get you a—"

"I need you to see this," Tracy interrupted him, pulling the black hard drive out of her pocket and waving it in front of Cameron. "Where's your computer?"

"In my study. But slow down, Tracy. This is General Dorrien's?"

"No. It's Prince Achileas's."

"But you broke into the home of an MI6 agent and stole it?"

"I didn't *steal* it. I *retrieved* it," Tracy corrected him. "Frank Dorrien stole it."

"I'm not sure that's the way British intelligence will look at it. Or the CIA for that matter." Cameron ran a worried hand through his hair. "Greg Walton *recalled* you, Tracy. He specifically instructed you to stay away from Dorrien."

"Yes. And did you ever wonder why?"

"No. Not really. But I'm sure he had his reasons. I can't believe you actually did it. You went and burgled the guy's house!"

"Computer," said Tracy.

Still frowning, Cameron led her through into the study.

He watched as Tracy sat down, uploaded the drive and began tapping away, writing code into his computer at a ridiculously rapid rate, her long fingers flying across his keyboard like a swooping flock of birds.

"What are you doing?"

"Retrieving files," Tracy said, not looking up. She was wearing a dark blue cashmere dress that softened her slender frame and her hair was swept up messily at the back. She smelled faintly of irises. Cameron felt a rush of desire shoot through him. "Frank Dorrien's smart," Tracy said. "He erased these pretty good."

"But I take it you're smarter?"

"Naturally." She grinned. "Let's start with the pictures, shall we?"

A large cache of fairly soft core gay porn was interspersed with pictures of Achileas himself, engaged in various sex acts with another, unknown man.

"So he *was* gay."

"Or bi–very curious indeed," quipped Tracy.

"Yeah. That's six hard inches of curiosity right there," said Cameron.

Tracy said, "He may have been being blackmailed. I found twenty thousand pounds cash in the general's safe."

"Which would support suicide," Cameron reminded her.

"Right. But that's not all. Look at this."

Tracy clicked open images of Achileas relaxing at a picnic with Bob Daley. He was playing with Daley's children. Bob's wife must have taken the pictures. The two were obviously close. In one of the shots, at the far right of the picture, another woman could be seen. Standing off to the side with her back to the group, apparently looking down at a river, she was tall and slender with long dark hair cascading around her shoulders.

"Achileas knew Bob Daley well," Tracy said. "And so did *she*."

"Who is that?" Cameron asked.

"I don't know. But I went to visit Bob's wife, Claire, and asked about her. She said her first name was Kate. She was an American, a friend of Achileas's. She thought maybe a girlfriend."

"That seems unlikely," said Cameron.

"Very," agreed Tracy. "But 'Kate' was close enough to be asked on that picnic. So what was their connection?"

Cameron assumed this to be a rhetorical question.

"Take a look at these."

Tracy brought up a string of emails, around thirty in all. Cameron instantly noticed the famous red balloon logo at the top of each one.

"No." He looked genuinely shocked. Pulling up a chair, he sat beside Tracy and started reading the notes. "Why on earth would a wealthy, connected, *royal* Greek kid get involved with Group 99? He was the walking embodiment of everything they hate."

"I can think of lots of reasons," said Tracy. "Rebellion. A desire to piss off his parents. Or maybe he actually believed in what they stood for? He didn't ask to be born rich or royal after all."

Cameron looked skeptical. "Maybe he was funding them? He could certainly afford it."

"Maybe," Tracy agreed excitedly. "And maybe the woman in that picture is Althea. Maybe she got him involved. Maybe she helped to channel the funds. And maybe Frank Dorrien knew about it, and . . ."

"Whoa. Hold on there." Cameron put a hand on Tracy's shoulder. "That's a whole lot of conjecture. Are you sure you aren't putting two and two together and making seventeen?"

Turning off the computer, Tracy turned to face him.

"Perhaps. But the point is, I'm putting two and two together. There is a link here, Cameron, a whole bunch of links in fact. Frank Dorrien doesn't want anyone to find them. And the CIA are right behind him on that, trying to scare me off. Why?"

Without thinking, Tracy found she had put her hand over Cameron's. It was a long time since she'd been this physically close to anyone, never mind an attractive man. Once again desire and guilt competed for her attention.

Guilt won. Tracy pulled back.

"If this is Althea," Cameron said, "it's the only picture anyone has of her."

"I know," said Tracy.

"Have you shown it to Greg Walton yet?"

"No. Only to you."

Cameron flushed with pleasure. He liked that Tracy came to him first. *Only to you.* She looked incredibly sexy tonight, her green eyes alight with intelligence and purpose.

"Are you going to show Walton?"

Tracy thought about it.

"No," she said at last. "Not for the moment anyway. The truth is, I don't trust the CIA. Not fully. And I know for a fact that they don't trust me."

"Don't take it personally," Cameron said. "They're spies. It's their job not to trust people."

"I'm not taking it personally. I'm just not prepared to work for them blind. I think they already know why Hunter Drexel didn't get into that helicopter."

"You do?"

Tracy nodded. "It was something to do with this story he was working on. Something to do with fracking. That's the only thing that makes sense. Achileas's family wanted to sell land to Henry Cranston, land rich with shale gas. Now Achileas and Cranston are both dead. The U.S. government has a huge vested interest in fracking. We're talking about a multibillion-dollar business, vital to American interests."

"You don't need to tell me," Cameron reminded her.

"You're lucky you haven't been hit so far," Tracy told him. "Group 99 aren't the only ones who want a share in those billions, a piece of that pie. People will kill for that sort of money."

"Nobody's going to kill me."

Leaning forward Cameron kissed Tracy once, gently, on the lips.

She didn't kiss him back. But she didn't stop him either.

This is not supposed to happen. This cannot happen.

When she opened her eyes, Cameron was smiling at her.

"How about that dinner you promised me?"

They stayed in.

Cameron's private chef had gone home for the night, but to Tracy's surprise he whipped up a passable spaghetti supper for the two of them.

"I'd never have pegged you as the domestic type," Tracy said.

Cameron noticed she was wolfing down her pasta as if she hadn't eaten in days. For such a tiny person, she ate like a horse.

"When you're divorced, you learn." He poured them both more wine. "I'm not the next Jamie Oliver, but I can get by."

They ate at the kitchen counter. Tracy had assumed they'd talk more about Group 99 and what she'd found in General Dorrien's house, but in fact the conversation quickly turned to more personal matters. It was strange how easily things flowed between them. This was only the second evening Tracy had spent in Cameron's company, but even before the kiss, an intimacy had been established between them that belied their short acquaintance.

Maybe it's the shared grief, Tracy thought. *Or maybe it's the fact that I trust him. That we trust each other.*

Trust was a commodity in increasingly short supply in Tracy's world. She suspected the same was true for Cameron. He was so laid-back, it was easy to forget that he was worth billions of dollars. That fact alone would have earned him scores of enemies, and even more false friends.

Or maybe I'm kidding myself. Maybe this is nothing more than straightforward sexual attraction.

Certainly there could be no denying the chemistry between them. Tracy had felt it the moment she walked in to the apartment. She'd felt it again when they sat at the computer desk together. When they kissed. And just now, watching Cameron at the stove. Sex could make old friends of total strangers. It could also seriously cloud judgment.

"What?" Cameron was looking at her oddly. "What's wrong?"

"Nothing." Tracy stared down at her spaghetti.

"It's not nothing. Your face just changed. You're feeling guilty, aren't you?"

"Why would I be feeling guilty?" Tracy tried not to show how unnerved she felt. Cameron shouldn't be able to read her like this.

"Because you're happy. Even though Nick is dead."

It wasn't said unkindly. Quite the opposite in fact. But it was too much for Tracy. Tears swam in her eyes.

Cameron reached over and took her hand in his, just as he had back in Geneva at the restaurant. But this time Tracy didn't snatch it away.

"Being happy is not betraying your son," Cameron told her. "At least, if it is, then we're both guilty."

He squeezed her hand. Tracy squeezed back.

They didn't need words.

After dinner they sat together in Cameron's living room, sipping Cognac in front of a vast baronial fireplace.

Out of nowhere, Cameron said, "I think you should show Walton the pictures."

Tracy's eyes widened. "What? Why?"

"Two reasons. One, because as long as you're in possession of that hard drive, your life is probably in danger."

Tracy didn't argue.

"And two because this woman Althea needs to be stopped. You may be able to find her on your own. But finding her and capturing her are very different things. You can't stop her alone. The CIA have resources."

Tracy studied his face. The broken nose, the intense gray eyes. Cameron had beautiful eyes. There was something honest about them, the perfect complement to the matter-of-fact, direct way he expressed himself.

He'd be terribly easy to fall in love with, Tracy thought. *If I were capable of falling in love again.*

That was one roller coaster ride that was most definitely behind her. Thank heavens.

"What if I weren't alone?" she said. "What if you helped me? What if we found her together?"

Cameron laughed. "Me?"

"Why not? You have resources too, after all."

"I have money. That's not quite the same thing."

"Sure it is. And anyway, it's not only money. You have a vast network of contacts all over the world.

Not just in the fracking industry but in politics, journalism, the charity sector. You know people."

"Yes, but Tracy, I'm a businessman. I'm not a spy or a paramilitary. I don't have the wherewithal to stop terrorists."

"Six months ago I was a soccer mom," Tracy reminded him.

"Hardly." Cameron gave her a knowing look.

Tracy's eyes narrowed. "You've been researching me?"

"Maybe a little." Cameron smiled sheepishly. "I liked what I found, though."

"OK, so maybe I wasn't your average soccer mom," Tracy admitted. "But the point is I was a civilian. And now I'm not."

"No," Cameron agreed. "Now you're not."

"Please think about it. I know we could do it. We could find Althea *and* Hunter Drexel."

"The world is out there looking for Hunter," Cameron said. "What makes you think we could find him?"

"We have Sally Faiers. She trusts me and I think she'll help me. Especially if Hunter wants to be found."

"If he wanted to be found he'd have gotten into that helicopter," Cameron said reasonably.

"Not if he thought the CIA might harm him. Or silence him. You and I are different. All we want is the truth. My bet is that's exactly what Hunter Drexel's been trying to do. Tell the truth. Remember, he was on his way to see you when he was kidnapped."

"So?"

"So he had something he wanted to tell you. Or ask you. I'm guessing he still does."

"It's a theory," Cameron said skeptically.

"Do you have a better one?" asked Tracy.

"I guess not."

Cameron moved closer. Suddenly Tracy felt powerfully aware of their touching hands. The heat of Cameron's body, its strength, its nearness. The sexual tension between them was electric and stifling at the same time, like a New Orleans thunderstorm about to break.

Sliding a hand around the back of Tracy's neck, Cameron pulled her to him and kissed her. Not gently, like he had earlier, but forcefully and passionately. Tracy responded instinctively, losing herself in the moment. The kiss was an explosion, wild and urgent, as if they were both racing against an invisible clock. Reaching down, Cameron grabbed the hem of Tracy's dress and yanked it up over her head in one fluid movement.

Tracy gasped, closing her eyes. His hands on her back felt heavenly, warm and rough. Doubt and fear and guilt all came flying at her like bullets whizzing through a jungle. But they all fell short of their target, melting into nothing against the raging heat of her desire. It was as if she'd descended, body and soul, into a thick, hot soup of longing. And she wanted nothing more than to drown.

"Make love to me. Please. Now."

The back of Tracy's hand brushed against Cameron's leg. Beneath his jeans, his thighs were tight and muscular and rock hard, like concrete.

"Are you sure, Tracy?" Cameron's voice was hoarse with his own need. "This is what you want?"

"I'm sure."

And suddenly she found that she was. Totally, blissfully sure.

Cameron carried her to his bedroom. The room was both grand and oddly impersonal, all taupe carpets and black silk table lamps, like a very expensive hotel suite. Not that either of them was focused on the décor.

Peeling off Tracy's underwear, Cameron laid her down naked on top of his extra-wide king bed. Then, taking off his own clothes, he knelt over her, gazing down at her body in wonder. Every ounce of blood in his body raced to his groin. He was so aroused it was painful.

"You're beyond beautiful."

Tracy reached up and wrapped her arms around his neck. Pulling him lower, she coiled both legs around his waist, encircling him, her willing prisoner.

"No more talking."

Cameron didn't need to be told twice.

The next few hours were like magic. Tracy had the body of a girl half her age but the sensuality and sexual confidence that only older women possessed. For her part, she found Cameron to be an incredible lover, skilled and responsive and loving and greedy, all at the same time. They made love for hours, again and again, till it was almost light and neither one of them had the energy to move another inch. Then they lay in each other's arms and, as the sun rose, spoke to each other about their dead sons, their grief and their guilt, their memories and their pain, each knowing that the other would understand in a way that nobody else ever could.

As they drifted off to sleep, Tracy rested her head on Cameron's chest.

"You will help me, won't you?" she whispered.

Cameron stroked her hair. A part of Tracy Whitney would always be on the job. That was her nature. Pleasure and business went hand in hand.

Something else we have in common, he thought.

If I'm not very careful indeed, I'm going to fall in love with this woman.

But Cameron Crewe was careful. He had to be.

"You know I will," he told Tracy. "Good night, my darling."

Chapter 17

It was a glorious morning in Neuilly-sur-Seine. The sun shone warmer than it had for weeks and the blue sky dazzled, a first promise of the coming summer and the longer, carefree days ahead.

Lexi Peters had had misgivings about spending the year in France. Turned down by Teach for America— *You have a lot of promise. It's just that the bar was set really high this year. We'd love you to reapply.*—she still wanted to make a difference. She'd been about to take a post at a tiny school in rural Kenya when her dad told her about the Camp Paris job.

"The pay's great. You could actually save something. And Teach for America specifically said a second language would boost your application next year."

Lexi still wasn't sure. Yes, the pay was great, but that was because the camp for wayward teens in the

exclusive Parisian suburb of Neuilly was so outrageously expensive, only the super-rich could afford to
send their kids there.

"I'm not interested in pandering to a bunch of
spoiled, entitled rich kids," she told her father. "I want
to do something meaningful."

"Don't be such a reverse snob," Don Peters countered robustly. "You think rich kids don't suffer? You
think addiction and mental illness give a shit how much
your mom and dad are worth? Camp Paris kids all have
problems, Lex. Helping them would be meaningful. I
think you'd learn a lot."

Well, he was right about that, Lexi thought, leaning
her bicycle up against the stable wall. *I've learned so
much here. I'll be sad to go home.*

The château that housed Camp Paris was a
ridiculously grand, pre-revolutionary pile, complete
with stable blocks for equine therapy, three different swimming pools and six of the most perfectly
manicured lawn tennis courts Lexi had ever seen. Most
of the staff left their bikes or cars at the stables, a short
walk up a beautiful tree-lined drive to the school.

Pulling a pile of psychology books out of her bike
basket, Lexi started towards the stable yard gate when
a dark gray Nissan pulled in.

The driver stepped out and looked around him. He
was very handsome, and oddly familiar, although he

didn't work at Camp Paris. There were only fifteen full-time staff and Lexi knew them all.

"*Bonjour*," she said cheerily. "*Vous êtes nouveau ici?*"

"You could say that." He smiled back.

"Oh, you're American. Me too. I'm Lexi Peters."

"Hi, Lexi."

"I'd be happy to . . ."

The first bullet blew a hole in Lexi's chest the size of a plum. She staggered backwards. The second and third shots hit her shoulder and neck, and the fourth cleanly bored through her skull.

It had started.

Cameron Crewe was on a business trip in Poland when the news broke. Tracy was his first call.

"Have you seen the reports?"

Tracy's voice was hoarse with emotion. "I'm watching the news right now. Twenty-six dead, they're saying. Four teachers, twenty-two kids. I can't bear it."

"It's definitely Group 99?"

"Looks like it. Four gunmen. One shot at the scene, but three still unaccounted for. How is that possible? How did the French police let them get away?"

Cameron said grimly, "I don't know."

For a moment both he and Tracy were silent. The senseless slaughter of teenagers with their whole lives ahead of them had revolted the entire world. But Cameron and Tracy felt it more keenly than most.

"I wish you were here," Tracy heard herself saying.

"Me too. I miss you. Has Walton said anything? About what happened in England?"

"No. Everyone's focused on Neuilly now."

"Of course."

"I'm actually on my way into Langley," Tracy said. "Most of the kids were American. President Havers is expected to make a statement in the next few minutes."

"Any leads?"

"Just one."

Cameron's ears pricked up.

"According to our sources, guess who popped up in Paris last week?" Tracy said.

"Who?"

"Our old friend Hunter Drexel. Have you noticed how, wherever Drexel is, people start to die?"

Cameron Crewe had noticed.

He put the phone down with a deep sense of foreboding.

Althea was at home in her New York apartment when she saw the news flash up on her computer screen ticker.

Tragedy in Paris suburb. Group 99 massacre 26 in school shooting.

She turned on the television. Children, screaming, bloodied and terrified were running into the arms of police. Teenage corpses, some not even covered, lay where they fell, brutally murdered as they tried to flee.

No! No no no!

She felt the bile rise up in her throat.

This wasn't supposed to happen. This wasn't what Daniel would have wanted. No sane person would want this.

She ran into the bathroom and vomited. For a full minute she knelt on the tiled floor, pressing her forehead against the cool porcelain, trying to calm herself down, to think clearly.

Perhaps it wasn't us.

Perhaps it was someone else? Another group, trying to blacken our name?

One of the attackers had been shot dead. Within hours, details would come out about who it was. In her heart, she already knew the dead man would be one of them.

A sadist like Apollo? Or just another angry, misguided boy, poisoned by the Greek's rhetoric, firing off his gun as if it weren't real, as if he were in some violent computer game?

How had it come to this? How had it all unraveled?

And *her* money, *her* support had helped make it happen.

She clutched her head. A violent throbbing had replaced the nausea. Dark spots swam before her eyes.

Was Tracy Whitney watching this too?

Tracy would blame her. The whole world would blame her. And yet she was the one who'd been wronged! All she'd ever tried to do was win justice, justice for Daniel.

Staggering to her bedroom she pulled the curtains tight and curled up in the darkness.

Somehow she slept. When she woke, hours had passed. Almost a whole night. Yet she still felt utterly exhausted.

No rest for the wicked.

Drawing back the curtains, she watched the first faint rays of sun bleed dark red into the city skyline.

She was in the shower when the phone rang, trying to wash herself clean. It wasn't working. The images from Neuilly would never leave her.

Turning off the water, she grabbed a towel then she picked up.

"Kate?"

The towel slipped to the floor. She gripped the back of the couch for support. No one called her Kate. Not anymore.

She was Althea now. Kate was dead.

"Who is this?"

"Oh, I think you know who it is. We need to talk, Kate. Don't you think?"

She stifled a sob. "Yes."

It had been more than ten years since she'd heard it.

But Hunter Drexel's voice hadn't changed.

Part Three

Chapter 18

Tracy opened one eye and saw a hummingbird hover just in front of her, plunging its long beak into a bright orange kou flower before flitting away. It was no bigger than a moth, and so delicate with its iridescent feathers and frantic, dance-like flight. Magical, like everything in Hawaii.

"Ah, you're awake."

Cameron Crewe wandered out onto the balcony. Tracy lay on a sun lounger, her athletic figure already turning brown. Cameron had taken Tracy to the Ritz Carlton in Maui for a romantic getaway, booking them into a palatial suite with ocean views and a private balcony so full of flowers it was more like a miniature jungle.

Group 99's Neuilly massacre had gotten to both of them, but especially Tracy. Her own teenage son might have been murdered at the group's hands, after all. When Cameron called her from Poland, he could hear the strain in her voice. *She feels guilty, responsible somehow, because she hasn't found Althea yet.*

He needed Tracy to know that none of this was her fault.

More important, he needed to be with her. Flying straight home from Warsaw, he'd expected Tracy to put up a fight about coming away with him, with the CIA's fight against Group 99 at such a crucial stage.

I'm needed here, he could hear her saying. *We can focus on us later.*

But she hadn't. To his surprise and delight, Tracy craved intimacy now as much as he did.

"I wasn't asleep," she murmured groggily. All this sun was making her drunk. "Just relaxing."

"Well, don't let me stop you."

Perching on the end of her sun lounger, Cameron began rubbing sun cream into her back. Tracy closed her eyes again. Everything smelled of coconuts. She could hear the waves crashing below her. How wonderful it would be to stay here forever and forget everything, to melt away.

Well, almost everything.

She would never forget Nick, of course. And she would never rest until she'd learned the truth about what had happened to him. But slowly, with every hour

Tracy spent in Cameron's company, the raw anguish of his absence was fading. It wasn't her love for him that she was losing, but the pain of that love. Just a little. And it was a relief.

Other things were harder to let go. While Tracy was here, sipping Kahlúa cocktails with Cameron, Group 99 were still out there killing people. Killing kids.

I shouldn't have come, Tracy thought now for the thousandth time. *I should never have let Cameron talk me into it.* But the truth was she was so exhausted she knew she was close to the breaking point. Physically, Tracy's body greedily accepted the rest. Mentally, it was a different story.

The French security services had yet to catch the other gunmen from the Neuilly attack, and with each passing day it looked less and less likely that they were going to. Meanwhile, despite the fact that good intelligence pointed to Hunter Drexel having conveniently been in Paris at the time of the school shootings, Greg Walton and Milton Buck were doing everything they could to keep Tracy off Drexel's scent.

"You're here to find Althea," Greg Walton reminded her, whenever Tracy raised Hunter's name. "You're the one with a connection to her, Tracy. Let us focus on finding Hunter. You mustn't get distracted."

And yet they hadn't found Hunter Drexel. Once again he'd slipped through the net. Even Sally Faiers was claiming he'd gone to ground.

"I haven't heard anything in weeks," Sally told Tracy. "I'm worried about him."

So am I, Tracy thought. The little voice inside her, telling her that Hunter was the key to everything that had happened, had become a deafening roar. She also couldn't shake the disturbing feeling that if Walton and Buck *did* find Drexel, she might never learn the whole truth.

"The CIA think he was involved in the Camp Paris shootings, don't they?" Sally asked Tracy bluntly. "They think he's a terrorist."

"I honestly don't know," Tracy replied. "If he was in Paris at the time, it certainly raises suspicions."

"He wouldn't do that," Sally said fervently. "I know he ran from the Americans in Bratislava. And maybe he does have some sympathy with Group 99's beliefs. He denies it, but I could see him going native to some degree. Being turned by them or whatever. But he would never, never be a part of something like what happened at Neuilly. I know him."

Do you? wondered Tracy. *Do any of us really know anyone else, deep down?*

How many murderers and rapists are there in prisons around the world right now, whose girlfriends didn't have a clue?

Still, she shared Sally Faiers's concerns. The fact that Walton and Buck were being so secretive about their search for Hunter didn't bode well. Did they really want to rescue him? Or to silence him, permanently? Tracy didn't know the answer. But the question haunted her. Because whether he was a terrorist or not, Tracy needed to find Hunter Drexel alive. She couldn't get answers from a dead man.

Tracy sat up suddenly. "I feel guilty," she told Cameron.

"Why?" He kissed her neck lovingly.

"Because I shouldn't be here. I should be in France right now. And we both know it."

Cameron sighed. "Come on, Tracy. We've been over this."

He traced a finger lazily along the top of Tracy's thigh. In a tropical-print bikini, her long legs glistening with oil, and with her wet hair slicked back, she looked even sexier than usual.

No one was more surprised than Cameron by his feelings for Tracy—both how quickly they'd happened and how intense they were.

Then again, Cameron Crewe's life had been one long string of surprises. Some wonderful. Some terrible. He'd become a master at expecting the unexpected, or at least of adapting to new realities.

"You've nothing to feel guilty about," he told Tracy. "Paris isn't going anywhere. You'll be there in a few days. And in the meantime, it's not as if you haven't been working. This is the first time I've seen you without a laptop in your hands since we arrived."

This was true. Though Tracy wasn't sure what good it had done her. So far there was nothing at all to link Althea to the Neuilly attack. With the exception of Bob Daley's execution—and perhaps Nick's "accident"—Althea's actions for Group 99 had all been sophisticated, slick and nonviolent. After each one she'd left a clue of some sort, a virtual calling card, not because she was careless, but because she was proud to take responsibility for her work.

Neuilly was different. Sending gunmen into a school to massacre teenagers, simply because their parents were rich? That wasn't Althea's style. Her deafening silence online and everywhere confirmed it.

It seemed to Tracy that Group 99 was becoming ever more like the mythical hydra: strike at one head, and two more grew before your eyes, each more lethal than the first.

And meanwhile, Hunter Drexel was still out there, holding on to his secrets until he could find somebody brave, or reckless, enough to publish them, to snatch away all the masks and mirrors and show all the players in this dreadful, violent drama as they truly were . . .

"Come here."

Cameron pulled Tracy onto his lap and slipped his arms around her waist. "Please stay a little longer. I need you."

From a villa across the bay Jeff Stevens watched the scene on Tracy's balcony through a high-power telescope.

A range of emotions flowed through him, none of them good.

Jeff tried not to hate anyone. But he was finding it extremely hard to warm to Mr. Cameron Crewe.

What's a billionaire fracking magnate doing sniffing around Tracy? Who just happens to be working for the CIA in their fight against Group 99? Who just happens to view billionaire fracking magnates about as positively as the rest of the population views pedophiles?

And how convenient that he's whisked her away to Maui just as the shit's hitting the fan in France.

Jamie MacIntosh had informed Jeff yesterday that Hunter Drexel was definitely in Paris and that MI6 were "very close" to apprehending him. The Americans, according to Jamie, were still stabbing around in the dark.

Jeff knew he should be cheered by this news. And by the fact that Tracy was safe on the other side of the world, at least for now, and out of imminent danger.

But he was finding it increasingly hard to focus.

According to Google, Hawaii suffered an average of three shark attacks per year.

Was it too much to ask that Crewe be one of the three?

Tracy sat at her computer, cross-referencing French intelligence files on Henri Mignon, the dead Neuilly shooter, with CIA data on known Group 99 operatives working within the United States. A number of survivors from Camp Paris had confirmed that one of the masked gunman had an American accent. So far Tracy had failed to find a single link.

Rubbing her eyes tiredly, she decided to take a break and try something else.

Hunter Drexel. If the sightings were accurate and he really was in Paris, he was doing a good job of living under the radar electronically. He wasn't using a credit card or a mobile phone or any of his known email addresses. He'd also managed to cross a number of European borders without a passport, or any ID. That meant one of two things was happening. Friends were helping him. And/or he was living on cash.

"Poker." Tracy said aloud.

"Hmmm?" Cameron wandered in from the bathroom with a towel wrapped around his waist. He'd spent most of the afternoon in the hotel gym while Tracy worked, and had just taken a long shower prior to dragging her away from her computer and out to dinner.

"Hunter Drexel plays poker. I'll bet that's where he's getting his cash."

"Maybe," Cameron said. "Does that help us?"

"It might." Tracy looked up at him excitedly. "I could go to Paris, posing as a dumb Texan divorcee with a gambling habit and money to burn. Get myself invited to all the high-stakes games in town."

"And what, run into him?" Cameron asked skeptically.

"Stranger things have happened," said Tracy. "Even if I don't find him, I'll hear rumors. Pick up clues. Maybe learn what alias he's using, what his plans are . . . something. It's worth a shot."

"Greg Walton will have you shot if he finds you're still hunting for Drexel when you're supposed to be looking for Althea," Cameron reminded her, pulling on a pair of white linen pants.

Tracy said, "I don't care about Greg Walton. Besides, I am looking for Althea. That's exactly why I need to find Hunter before they do."

A knock on the door interrupted them.

Cameron scowled. "Who the hell can that be?"

"Did you order room service?" Tracy asked.

"No."

The knocking was getting louder and faster. Hammering.

"What on earth . . . ?" Tracy got up to answer it when Cameron suddenly grabbed her.

"Wait. Don't open the door."

"Why on earth not?"

"We can't afford to take chances, Tracy."

Pushing her to one side, Cameron pressed his face to the glass peephole. Tracy saw his shoulders relax and his jaw tighten. Tension was replaced with irritation. He sighed deeply.

"You have *got* to be kidding me."

"Who is it?" Tracy asked.

Cameron pulled open the door. "My ex-wife. Tracy, meet Charlotte. Charlotte, this is Tracy."

Charlotte Crewe burst into the suite like a Greek Fury, slamming the door behind her. She wore simple white shorts and tennis shoes, with her hair tied back in a girlish ponytail.

She's terribly pretty, Tracy thought. *And so young.*

But the most striking thing about Cameron's ex-wife was the expression of boiling, tight-lipped rage on her face. With her clenched fists and almost comically aggressive body language, Charlotte Crewe looked like a human bomb that might go off at any moment.

"What are you doing here?"

Cameron's greeting was less than affectionate. Perhaps understandably given the way Charlotte was glaring at him. It was all rather odd. Cameron had told her the marriage ended amicably, and the CIA files said the same thing.

"Take a wild guess," Charlotte hissed.

"I really have no idea." Cameron sounded bored. "Although, whatever it is, I can't imagine that we couldn't have discussed it over the phone."

"Oh, you can't imagine? Is that right? You, who haven't taken a single one of my phone calls, or my lawyer's phone calls, in the past eighteen months, *can't imagine* why I didn't just ring?"

Tracy stepped forward for the first time. "Tracy Whitney. Nice to meet you."

She offered Charlotte her hand. To her surprise, Charlotte took it and shook it warmly. "You too."

Was it Tracy's imagination, or was there suddenly something compassionate, even pitying, in Charlotte's tone?

Whatever it was, it evaporated the moment she turned back to her ex-husband.

"You haven't made a payment in eight months," she snarled at Cameron.

"That's not true," Cameron said smoothly.

"It is true! You know it's true. You're one of the richest men in America, sitting here like Croesus on your dirty empire of shale gas. And I'm being evicted from my apartment while you live it up here in the Presidential Suite with your latest, trusting little girl-friend. No offense to you, Miss Whitney," she added to Tracy. "It's not your fault he's a lying, conniving snake."

Tracy frowned. *Dirty empire.* What did Charlotte Crewe mean by that? Was it just a bitter ex-wife talk-ing? It could be, of course. And yet something seemed off. Charlotte and Cameron had had a son together after all. Lost a son together. Didn't that mean any-thing? For all her ranting and raving, Charlotte didn't come across as the spiteful type to Tracy.

She found herself watching Cameron closely for his reaction.

"Charlotte, this is ridiculous," he said curtly. "Please stop. You're embarrassing me and you're embarrass-ing yourself. No one's evicting you. This is a complete fantasy." He glanced apologetically at Tracy. Then turning back to his ex, he asked, "When did you last see Dr. Williams?"

That seemed to push Charlotte over the edge.

"Fuck Dr. Williams!" she yelled. "And fuck you, Cameron. You're a disgrace. Playing these pathetic little power games, with all the money you have? Marcus would be ashamed of you."

Something very close to hatred flashed in Cameron's eyes. "Don't you dare bring Marcus into this."

"I'll bring Marcus into it whenever I want," Charlotte said defiantly. "He was my son. You don't own his memory, Cameron. You can't buy that, like you buy everything else. And you can't fucking silence me!"

She turned back to Tracy. "Do you think I'd be here if I weren't completely desperate? I could barely afford the flight. Please. Talk some sense into him. Tell him to pay what he owes."

"Charlotte." Cameron's tone was measured but firm. "You are not well. You need help, and I will get you that help. No one is evicting you. But I need you to leave now. I don't want to call security, but I will if I have to. Please, darling. Go home."

He reached for her arm but she shrugged him off furiously.

"Like I have a home to go to. Don't worry, I'm leaving. But you haven't heard the end of this, Cameron. I want my money and I'm going to get it. You do *not* scare me."

She emphasized the word "not" by jabbing him in the chest with a finger. Tracy saw a small muscle in his jaw leap twice, then go quiet. He looked positively murderous.

A prickle of unease swept over her. She felt the hairs on her forearms stand on end.

"Goodbye," Charlotte said to Tracy. "And good luck."

She left, slamming the door behind her.

For a moment, neither Tracy nor Cameron said anything. Then Cameron pulled Tracy into his arms.

"I'm sorry about that. You OK?"

"I'm fine," Tracy lied. "Just surprised. I thought you said that you and Marcus's mother had a good relationship."

Cameron let go of her and sat down on the edge of the bed.

"We do," he said.

Tracy's eyebrows shot up.

"When she's well," Cameron explained. "You mustn't judge Charlotte too harshly. It's no wonder she's mentally unstable. She's been through hell, as you know."

"Yes," said Tracy. She did know. And the truth was, she wasn't judging Charlotte harshly. The woman had seemed perfectly sane to her. Angry, certainly, and emotional. But not crazy.

"It's been a long time since I've seen her like that." Cameron shook his head sadly.

"Like what?"

"Well, you saw her. Delusional. Lashing out with these insane conspiracy theories."

"So she's not being evicted?" Tracy asked calmly.

Cameron looked wounded. "Evicted? What? No! Of course not. I would never let that happen. Financially Charlotte has more than she could ever need, and she always will."

He stood up, walked over to the wardrobe and pulled out a jacket. Savile Row tailored, classically cut, it fit him perfectly. Walking back to Tracy, he kissed her on the top of the head.

"Don't let it worry you, angel. You have enough on your plate. I'll call Dr. Williams first thing tomorrow, see if I can get him to reach out to her. I'll also talk to the trustees, just to check she hasn't been wiring all her alimony checks to Scientology or something. She'll be OK. I promise. Let's have dinner and try to forget the whole thing."

"Ok. I'll put some makeup on."

She slipped into the bathroom and locked the door behind her, gazing intently at her reflection in the mirror.

Everything Cameron had said made sense.

Grief could make people delusional. And the CIA files had described Charlotte Crewe's divorce settlement as financially generous, including the deeds to their Park Avenue apartment and a large monthly allowance.

If he's honoring those terms, Tracy thought.

But then, why wouldn't he be? Wasn't it more likely that a grieving mother was still struggling with paranoia, than that a man as rich as Cameron would nickel-and-dime an ex-wife he clearly still cared for?

Of course it was.

I'm being silly, Tracy told herself.

By the time she'd finished fixing her makeup, she almost believed it.

Lucy Grey smiled warmly at the young woman perched nervously on her couch.

"It's been a long time, Kate. How are you?"

"Fine." The young woman didn't smile back. Instead she carefully smoothed out a crease in her skirt and stared out of the window.

Dr. Lucy Grey had been a therapist for more than twenty years, and she had counseled hundreds of patients. But few of them made as much of an impression on her as Kate.

It was always the failures that Lucy remembered.

The young widow had first started coming to therapy five years ago, right after her husband died. She'd attended sessions regularly for more than a year before gradually drifting away, although she'd come back intermittently since. And yet Lucy was ashamed to say she'd made no real headway with her in all that time. She still knew next to nothing about Kate's daily life. About her job, her social world, her friendships. Lucy did know about Kate's grief. About the longing for her dead husband that consumed her, like a fireball burning gas. But that was all she knew, all that existed between the two of them. It was almost as if Kate Evans *was* her grief. And that shouldn't be the case. Not after five years.

Having smoothed out her skirt to her satisfaction, Kate now flicked a barely visible piece of lint off her cashmere sweater. As usual she was immaculately groomed, her long legs perfectly waxed and her mane of dark hair gleaming like an oil slick as it spilled over her shoulders.

That was another thing that bothered Dr. Lucy Grey about Kate Evans. How *careful* the young widow was. How cautious, how controlled, her every movement and utterance measured to the last degree. Somehow it made things less real between them. Less honest. More insulated.

It made Lucy feel as if she were in a play, playing the role of therapist. Which was extremely disconcerting.

"Why are you here?" she asked gently.

Kate looked up at her with tortured eyes. "Have you ever done something, started something, for the right reasons, that ended up having consequences beyond your control? Terrible consequences?"

Lucy looked at her steadily. "I've done things that didn't turn out as I'd expected. As I'd hoped."

"But nobody died. Did they? Because of your mistakes?"

"No, Kate. Nobody died. Do you want to tell me what this is about?"

She shook her head. She *did* want to tell Dr. Grey. Desperately. To tell someone, anyway. To unburden herself. But how could she? If only Daniel were here!

Then again, if Daniel were here, none of this would have happened.

Since Hunter Drexel's call she'd barely slept. He wanted to see her, to meet. She couldn't do it! Just the thought brought her out in hives.

As Althea she'd been powerful, protected, invincible. But Hunter Drexel knew the truth. He'd called her Kate. Just the sound of his voice had undone everything, shattered the illusion like Dorothy pulling back the Wizard of Oz's curtain.

But it wasn't just Hunter who haunted her. Images of the teenagers from Neuilly, their young bodies riddled with bullets, flooded her head day and night. Henry Cranston's death was different. Unnecessary, yes, and excessive. But it was hard to shed too many tears for such a loathsome man. But those children!

Had she started all this violence, this horror, by orchestrating Captain Daley's death?

Had she opened Pandora's Box?

She'd been so sure of that at the time, so certain. After what Bob Daley did it had felt right. Just. Necessary. But now she'd started to doubt even that decision. It was as if she'd lost the ability to tell right from wrong. What had seemed so clear, so black-and-white, now looked murky and gray.

Was that what it was like for you, Tracy? On the run from the law for all those years? On the run from us? Did you always feel like one of the good guys—like Robin Hood—or did you ever doubt? Wake up in the night and think to yourself, "What have I become? I'm just a liar and a thief."

Tracy Whitney had changed, of course. Gone straight. Settled down.

But could you ever really escape your past? The dark side of your nature?

"Kate?"

Dr. Lucy Grey's voice broke her reverie. She wondered how long she'd been sitting there, lost in thought.

"Please let me help you. Tell me what's happened. You obviously came here today for a reason."

Kate Evans stood up.

"I can't. I'm sorry. I shouldn't have come."

She was about to leave when a sudden, searing pain shot through her head, as if she'd been struck by lightning. With a terrible moan she sank back onto the couch, pressing both hands against her skull.

"What just happened?" Lucy rushed over to her patient. "Are you OK?"

Kate moaned again, a terrible, animal sound, full of anguish.

"I'll call an ambulance."

"No! Please." Panic flashed in the young widow's eyes. "It will pass. It's those children. In France. Their bodies, shot to pieces . . . I can't stop seeing them!"

Lucy's ears pricked up. This was a clue. This was something.

She was talking about the Camp Paris shootings, at Neuilly. They'd been all over the news.

Kate's husband, Daniel, had been killed in Iraq, on some mission for the CIA. Probably shot. Had the latest Group 99 atrocity brought back painful memories?

Perhaps the haunting images on television reminded Kate of Daniel's death? Or the children that the two of them would never have.

"You've been dreaming about the Neuilly School shootings?"

Leaning forward suddenly, Kate grasped the therapist's hands. "Dreaming, yes. But it *happened*. I made it happen."

Lucy said, "It may seem that way to you, Kate. But you didn't cause this. You don't have that power. No one does."

"But that's just it. I do!" Kate wailed. "Daniel's gone. Those kids are gone. Gone, gone, gone. Dead and gone. Never coming back."

"That's right," Lucy said calmly. "They are never coming back. But you're not responsible. For their deaths, or your husband's."

Kate slumped back again, clutching her head and moaning, as if she were in labor. It was distressing to watch. But Dr. Grey felt on firmer ground now. She'd seen these episodes countless times in her career. Psychotic breaks, brought on by stress, or grief, or a single, traumatic event.

She would call her psychiatrist friend, Bill Winter.

Bill would get Kate on the right meds. After that it was just a question of rest.

"You lay here for a while." She covered her client in a blanket as you would a sleeping child. "I'm going to make a call."

An hour later, Dr. Lucy Grey watched as a heavily sedated Kate Evans was driven away in an ambulance.

"You did the right thing to call me," Bill Winter assured her. "Two weeks of sleep and she'll be a new person."

"I hope so," Lucy said. "I really do. She's been through so much. And I don't feel I've helped her. Not really."

"I'm sure you have." Bill got into his car. "By the way, does she work? Will her insurance cover an in-patient stay?"

"Oh yes." Dr. Lucy Grey smiled. "That's one thing she doesn't have to worry about. Kate's husband, Daniel, was a CIA lifer. He died in Iraq on some special op, but the agency still pays all her bills. She's covered for life, I believe."

Chapter 19

Hunter Drexel admired his reflection in the mirror.

He'd been nervous about the blond hair. That it would look like an obvious dye job. But actually it worked. Cropped short, and paired with newly dyed blond eyebrows, it transformed his appearance. He looked younger, tougher, cleaner cut. He looked like a soldier.

Which, in a way, he was. *A warrior for truth.*

Laughing at his own pretensions, he pulled on a fake Rolex watch and began fastening his cuff links.

His current rooms were a step down from what he'd been used to. After Neuilly, the entire city was swarming with police, searching for the three escaped gunmen. Hunter had immediately left the expensive hotel where he'd been staying on Avenue Montaigne and moved here, to a much more low key pension close to the Bois de Boulogne.

It was from here that he'd called Kate. A triumphant moment and a turning point in the story he was writing. Of course he still had to speak to her face-to-face. But he'd made huge strides in Paris, and would soon be ready to go to print. Then, at last, he could come out of the shadows and face the world, friends and enemies alike.

Soon.

Right now his priority was to get out of France. He really should have left the day after Neuilly, but he'd been tempted into staying by one last poker game.

Pascal Cauchin would be there tonight. Pascal had bought and single-handedly destroyed thousands of acres of ancient Chilean forest, pumping water deep into the ground to extract hundreds of millions of dollars' worth of shale gas. Not only had he effectively robbed the Chileans, swindling them out of their land at a knockdown price, but he'd devastated the local ecosystem for hundreds of miles around. Cauchin was right up there with Henry Cranston as one of fracking's least responsible, most obnoxious kingpins.

Not like the positively saintly Cameron Crewe.

The thought of getting to look Cauchin in the eye across a card table, whilst concealing his own identity *and* successfully relieving Pascal of thousands of dollars in winnings was more temptation than Hunter Drexel could resist. He would play tonight as Lex Brightman, New York theater impresario and amateur poker enthusiast.

One last game. Then I'm out of here.

Jeff Stevens sat at a corner table at Café Charles, near Notre Dame Cathedral, opposite Frank Dorrien.

"Do you have any idea how English you look?" Jeff asked the general, glancing at Frank's off-duty uniform of brogues, dark green corduroy trousers, Turnbull & Asser striped shirt and MCC tie. "Not exactly the gray man in the crowd, are you?"

"What would you prefer?" Frank quipped. "A Breton shirt, beret and a string of onions around my neck?"

Despite their profound, even seismic differences as people, Jeff and Frank had developed a productive working relationship. As Jamie MacIntosh had succinctly put it, "Frank can be a bit abrasive. But if you want to help Tracy Whitney, suck it up."

Jeff had taken this to heart. Even though "a bit abrasive" turned out to be something akin to wearing a pair of sandpaper underpants. He could handle Frank.

"How was Hawaii?"

Jeff scowled. "Awful."

"Any useful intelligence?"

"Not really. Tracy's tight with Cameron Crewe of Crewe Oil. But we knew that already. It looks as if the two of them are working together, cutting Walton and Buck out of the loop."

"Hmm." Frank considered this. "That may be to our advantage. The less the CIA knows, the better."

"Spoken like a true ally," said Jeff.

Tracy working closely with Cameron definitely wasn't to Jeff's advantage. He didn't trust Crewe as far as he could spit.

Frank said, "And now Tracy's here in Paris?"

Jeff nodded, sipping his coffee. It was ridiculously strong, like tar, but it helped with the jet lag. "At the Georges V."

"Alone?"

Jeff winced. "So far."

"Have she and Crewe been in contact?"

Jeff shook his head. "No."

Shadowing Tracy had been no fun. In fact it had been the dictionary definition of no fun. Nor was Jeff convinced that his presence was protecting Tracy from anything, or anyone. Not so far anyway. He was starting to feel like the worst kind of Peeping Tom. Bugging her hotel room and tapping her phone had both been relatively easy. But he dreaded having to hear her be intimate with Cameron Crewe over the phone, and he'd stopped short of installing cameras in her suite.

"Stay close to her," Frank Dorrien instructed. "Hunter Drexel's still in the city. We think he's going to make a move soon. We're close, Jeff. But we can't let Tracy get to him first, maybe scare him off again. Or worse."

Jeff frowned. "What do you mean 'worse'?"

Frank pushed a classified file across the table.

Jeff read it in silence. Then he read it again.

Finally he looked up at Frank, an expression of pure horror on his face.

"Are you *sure*?"

"Of course we're not sure," Frank snapped. "That's why we need to bring him in. But I think it's safe to say that Hunter Drexel is not who the world believes him to be. If Tracy were to try to corner him alone . . ."

He didn't have to finish the sentence.

Jeff drained his coffee. "Don't worry. I won't let her out of my sight."

Tracy looked at her watch, an exquisite, delicate 1920s antique with a white gold strap and diamond-studded face.

6:15 P.M. Exactly two hours to go.

Putting on a pair of diamond drop earrings to match the watch, Tracy winked at her reflection, ashamed of how much she was enjoying herself. She liked being Mary Jo. Tracy had always enjoyed creating new and different characters. Together she and Jeff had been the masters of it for more than a decade. But now, since Nick's death, stepping out of her own tortured existence and into someone else's was more than just a game. It was an escape. Tracy hadn't realized till now quite how much she needed one.

Her old contacts in Paris had been a gold mine of information when it came to the city's high-stakes poker scene. Which was a good thing, as so far Cameron's had come up with precisely nothing. It was almost as if Cameron didn't *want* Tracy to find Hunter Drexel. *He probably thinks he's protecting me,* Tracy thought. But perhaps it was better this way anyway? She'd grown used to working on her own. Working with Cameron might put a strain on . . . whatever it was that was happening between them. Tracy still couldn't quite bring herself to call it a relationship. That sounded far too permanent. But it was something, and she wasn't ready to break it, not yet.

If I find Hunter—when I find him—I'll bring Cameron in then.

As soon as Tracy heard the name Pascal Cauchin—her dear old friend, the master forger and long-term Paris resident Harry Blackstone, had mentioned Cauchin's monthly poker parties—her hopes soared. Cauchin was huge in the fracking world, right up there with men like Cameron and Henry Cranston. It was inconceivable that Hunter Drexel hadn't heard of him. The fact that he also hosted private poker nights at his penthouse apartment in Montmartre with a secret and closely guarded guest list was almost too good to be true. It would be reckless in the extreme for Hunter Drexel to show up at one of Cauchin's games. But as Sally Faiers had told Tracy, Hunter *was* reckless. Taking big risks was his oxygen, his adrenaline, his raison d'être.

It had once been Tracy's too.

I know you, Hunter, she thought, adjusting her earrings. *I know how you operate.*

I'm going to find you. And when I do, you're going

to lead me to Althea. You're going to help me lay my son to rest.

Alexis Argyros was aroused.

The violently pornographic rape fantasy playing out on his computer screen helped a little. But Alexis had become so used to images of sexual depravity, they were no longer enough on their own.

What really turned him on was power. The power to inflict pain, to create fear. The power to end life.

Hunter Drexel believed that knowledge was power. Knowledge and truth.

Alexis knew differently. Who cared what you knew when pieces of your brain were flying out of your skull and being splattered across the walls?

Violence was power. Violence and terror and death.

Neuilly had excited Alexis. He watched the news reports endlessly, picturing the fat American rich kids screaming and running for their lives, like squealing pigs.

Tonight, at long last, it would be Hunter Drexel's turn to squeal.

The Americans, the British, Interpol, they were all here in Paris, swarming the city like flies on shit, searching for Hunter and the three Group 99 gunmen who had wreaked such delicious havoc. But they knew nothing. He, Alexis Argyros, had outwitted them all.

The pleasure of killing Hunter Drexel would be his and his alone.

Tonight.

In his dingy caravan at the campsite, he slipped on his overalls and the thin black balaclava he would use, right up to the moment of the kill. He wanted Drexel to see him then. Not just the look in his eyes but the smile on his face as he took the American's life, the ultimate act of domination.

The days of his humiliation were over.

I am Apollo the Great.

The God of plague and destruction.

Scourge of the boastful.

Slayer of Giants.

It would be done tonight.

Jeff Stevens called Major General Frank Dorrien.

"It's tonight. Tracy's going to a poker game at Pascal Cauchin's apartment."

Frank took a sharp intake of breath. "Drexel's going to be there?"

"Possibly. All I know for sure is that Tracy's going to the game posing as a rich Texan widow with a hundred thousand euros in cash."

"Shit." Jeff could hear the general's mind racing. Presumably Tracy Whitney must believe Hunter Drexel would show up tonight, or she wouldn't be going. And it made sense. Cauchin was probably the biggest name in the fracking industry in the whole of France. "Does the CIA know about this?"

"I don't think so. Walton thinks she's tracking Althea."

"And Cameron Crewe?"

"She hasn't called him today," Jeff said. "I think she's working alone on this. We have to get down there, Frank. We have to protect her."

"Of course," Frank Dorrien said smoothly. "We're on it. Just sit tight."

"Sit tight?" Jeff said. "I'm not sitting anywhere. I'm going to that game."

"Don't be ridiculous! You'll blow your cover. The moment Tracy sees you she'll . . . Jeff? Jeff!"

The line was dead.

Pascal Cauchin was in an excellent mood.

He'd just finalized a lucrative deal to joint rights in a new gas pipeline, running from Bratislava to Poland and the East. His mistress had returned from a trip to Florida last night with even bigger breast implants that Pascal couldn't wait to get his hands on. And tonight's poker game looked set to be extremely interesting.

Lex Brightman, the flamboyantly gay New Yorker, was attending. Pascal Cauchin had only met Brightman once before, at a house party last weekend, but in that short time the theater producer had impressed him as displaying a uniquely American combination of arrogance and stupidity that boded well for tonight's game. "I'm a pretty great poker player, if I do say so myself," Brightman had informed Pascal, proceeding to talk him play by play through some of what he considered to be his top techniques for outwitting his opponents.

Pascal was looking forward to relieving Lex Brightman of a considerable sum of money.

Another new player was expected too, a last-minute addition by the name of Jeremy Sands. Pascal's good friend, the art dealer Antione de la Court, had called just an hour ago to have Sands added to the guest list.

"You'll like him. He's a good player. Funny. Very well connected."

Pascal wavered.

"He invested four hundred million in alternative energy companies last year."

Sands was in.

And finally there was the lovely Mrs. Morgan Drake. *Mary Jo.* The Texas widow wasn't Pascal's usual type. He normally went for curvy blond girls, and rarely looked at anyone older than twenty-five. Mary Jo was a grown woman, and slender to the point of boyishness. When he'd bumped into her at the Ritz bar last week, her small, apple breasts had been discreetly concealed beneath an expensive gray silk blouse and her dark hair swept up in a demure chignon. And yet there was something intensely sexually compelling about her. Perhaps it was the intoxicating green eyes? In any event, in the week since they met Pascal had found himself fantasizing more and more about taking Mrs. Morgan Drake to bed, ripping off those demure clothes and unleashing what he very much hoped would be the tigress within. When she admitted an interest in cards, he immediately extended an invitation to tonight's game and arranged for his wife, Alissa, to pay a visit to her sister in Lyons.

He would make sure that Mary Jo won a few hands at least, and that her cocktails were double strength. After that, it should be plain sailing.

"Excuse me, Sir." A liveried butler appeared in the doorway of Cauchin's palatial salon. "Mrs. Morgan Drake has arrived early. Should I have her wait in the library?"

Pascal smiled broadly.

Perfect! She's the first to arrive. She's obviously keen.

"No, no, Pierre. That's all right. You can show her straight up."

Jeff sat in the back of the taxi, his fists clenched. All around him drivers were leaning on their horns, a cacophony of stress that was having precisely zero effect on the crawling rush hour traffic.

"Can't you do anything?" Jeff asked the driver, in faltering French. "Try another route?"

The man gave a nonchalant, Gallic shrug. "Friday night. *Les embouteillages sont partout.*"

"It's very important I get there quickly."

Antoine de la Court, an old friend from Jeff's days as an art thief, had pulled some serious strings to get Jeff invited to tonight's game. But if Hunter Drexel got there before him . . . and if Tracy tried to confront him alone . . . Jeff felt his blood pressure soaring.

"Please!" He thrust a fat wad of euro notes at the driver. *"C'est très important."*

Reaching back to take the money, the driver smiled, leaned uselessly on his horn, and inched forward into the gridlock.

"What's happening?"

Jamie MacIntosh paced tensely around his London

office. The Thames crawled sluggishly beneath his window, which was smeared by a steady stream of gray drizzle. It was the most inauspicious of days. Rainy. Dull. Lifeless. And yet in Paris, Jamie's team might be just minutes away from apprehending Hunter Drexel.

"Have you got eyes on Drexel?"

"Not yet." Major General Frank Dorrien sounded equally tense. Jeff Stevens was planning to go rogue and show up at the poker game as a player, revealing himself to Tracy and potentially blowing the whole operation out of the water. Frank was in a café directly opposite Cauchin's apartment building. He had a man on the roof, one more in the lobby, and two on the street entrances at front and back of the building.

"What about the others?" Jamie asked.

"Tracy Whitney's inside. So are the other three players. Stevens is a no-show so far."

"Maybe he couldn't get on Cauchin's list so late in the day?" Jamie suggested hopefully.

"He'll get in there somehow," Frank said grimly. "He's terrified for Tracy. I showed him Drexel's file yesterday."

Jamie erupted. "You *what*?!"

"It was a calculated risk."

"Miscalculated! Are you out of your mind?"

Frank's voice dropped to a whisper.

"He's here."

"Who? Who's there? Drexel or Stevens?"

"Gotta go."

"FRANK!" Jamie MacIntosh roared. But it was too late.

Slamming the phone down in frustration, he started pacing again.

"Mary Jo. Let me get you another drink."

Pascal Cauchin was leaning over Tracy on the chaise longue, so close that she could smell the toothpaste on his breath and the desire seeping through his pores. Cauchin was tall and thin, with dry skin and thin lips that he kept darting his tongue over to keep them moist. He had long fingers and large, wide-set eyes that bulged and swiveled constantly around the room, as if searching for danger. Or perhaps opportunity. He reminded Tracy of a lizard. Cold-blooded, quick, and slippery, with a nasty bite.

"Oh, ahm fine thanks, darlin'," Tracy protested. Her last gin and tonic had been ridiculously strong. She still hadn't formulated a definite plan for what she would do once Hunter Drexel arrived, but she knew she would need her wits about her.

"I insist," Cauchin purred. "Pierre? Another gin for the lady."

"Isn't it time we got started, Pascal?"

Albert Dumas, a newspaper mogul and regular at the Montmartre poker evenings, was getting irritated. It wasn't like Pascal to wait for latecomers. If the two Americans, Jeremy Sands and the other chap, Brightman, couldn't be bothered to show up on time, they didn't deserve to play at a top French table.

"We'll give them five more minutes," Cauchin said, not taking his eyes off Mary Jo, who had pulled out all the stops tonight in a backless green dress that was making it very hard for him to concentrate. The drunker he could get her before they started, the better.

Hunter saw Frank Dorrien first. He recognized the man in the café from Sally Faiers's description, although even without it the general's hiding behind *Le Figaro* was crashingly obvious.

So. The British are here.

From the direction of Dorrien's glances, he ascertained that they had a man on the roof and possibly another at the back of Cauchin's building. There was no sign of the CIA.

It's risky, Hunter thought. *Very risky. But not impossible.*

From his alleyway vantage point he saw the other players arrive. He recognized Albert Dumas, but not the quirky little fellow in the bow tie, nor the over-dressed but beautiful woman in the green evening dress.

Hunter wanted to play tonight, badly. He wanted to beat Pascal Cauchin, to see the look on his face when he lost his shirt. But not at any cost.

Sliding farther back into the shadows he watched and waited.

"I expect Jeremy's stuck in traffic," Antoine de la Court said nervously. "He's usually very punctual."

Albert Dumas gave the art dealer a disdainful look. He'd never been fond of the mincing de la Court, with his bow ties and gossipy anecdotes about the art world and affected way of tossing his bald head back when he laughed. It didn't help that Antoine was an excellent poker player, as cunningly skillful as he was charming. Albert had lost a lot of money to the ghastly little fag over the years.

Apparently one of the newcomers Cauchin had invited tonight was another queer, a theater type from New York. *Pascal probably wants to limit his compe-tition for the Texas woman,* Albert thought bitterly. *Pathetic the way he's all over her.*

The doorbell rang.

"That's probably Jeremy now," Antione de la Court said, sounding relieved.

"Good." Pascal beamed at Mary Jo. "That only leaves Lex Brightman. As soon as he gets here, we'll get started."

Jeremy Sands. Lex Brightman, Tracy thought. *One of them is Hunter Drexel. I'm sure of it.*

Was Hunter about to be shown into the room?

Tracy's heart began to beat faster. Maybe she did need that second drink after all?

Alexis Argyros pulled down the visor on his motor-cycle helmet.

Where the hell is he?

Where's Drexel?

A laundry van passed him, pulling round to the back of the building and disappearing into the underground garage. Alexis felt his stomach churn.

Had he missed Hunter somehow? Was the bastard already inside?

He turned on his engine.

"That's Stevens!" Frank Dorrien hissed at the man stationed in front of Cauchin's building. "He's crossing the road now. For God's sake stop him."

The man started walking towards Jeff, when another voice in his ear made him hesitate.

"Target sighted!" It was the man on the roof. "Repeat, Drexel sighted."

"Where?" Frank scanned the street frantically.

"Coming towards you, General. You should be looking right at him in about twenty seconds. Blond hair, black jacket."

"Shit!" Frank jumped to his feet, spilling hot tea all down his crotch. "Keep him in sights but don't shoot," he told the man on the roof. "Jim," he told the first man, "get over here, now!"

Jeff Stevens stood on the doorstep of Pascal Cauchin's apartment building, panting and mopping the sweat from his brow.

He was late, but only by a few minutes.

Had Drexel arrived already? Was he inside? Was Tracy?

More than anything it was the prospect of coming face-to-face with Tracy again that made his heart race and his palms sweat uncontrollably.

Get a grip, Jeff told himself sternly. *You are Jeremy Sands. You are a wealthy energy investor from Manhattan.*

Tracy wouldn't give him away. She couldn't risk blowing her own cover. But once she saw him the game would be up. Tracy would want to know how he'd found her, not to mention why he was following her. Jeff would have to tell her the truth, or some version of it. *I'm here to protect you,* wouldn't go down well. Tracy didn't appreciate being protected. She could take care of herself. She would also doubtless be furious with Jeff for ruining her chance of confronting Hunter Drexel.

Too bad. She should never have run out on me after Nick died. She's the one who owes me an explanation, not the other way around.

The door swung open.

"May I help you?"

Jeff drew back his shoulders and smiled. "Jeremy Sands. I'm here for the game."

Hunter had been about to blag his way into the service entrance when he heard the motorbike engine revving just a few yards behind him.

Even before he looked over his shoulder he knew.

Apollo!

Risky had just turned into fatal. He had to get out of here. Darting out of his shadowy hiding place like a cockroach out of its nest, Hunter forced himself to keep to a walking pace as he turned the corner into the street.

Left was a dead end. Right took him straight towards the café where MI6 were waiting.

No. I can't let it end here. Caught like a rat in a trap.
I won't.

The front entrance to Cauchin's building was directly opposite him now. A smartly dressed man was standing on the stoop. A doorman opened the door and was talking to the man.

Changing course suddenly, Hunter ran towards the open door.

Tracy was still fending off Pascal Cauchin's advances when she heard the first shot.

"What the hell was that?" Antoine de la Court asked.

"Probably somebody's car backfiring," said Albert Dumas.

Then came the second and third shots, in quick succession, followed by loud screaming from the street below.

"That's gunfire!" Pascal dropped Tracy's hand like a hot stone and dived for the panic button on the far wall. "Everybody get down!" His voice had shot up an octave with fear. Despite this, everyone in the room flattened themselves to the ground as commanded.

Everyone except Tracy. Moving calmly to the window, she pulled back the curtain and surveyed the street below. A man dressed in black and driving a Ducati motorbike roared past and out of sight. The shooter, presumably. But had he found his target?

At first it was hard to tell what was happening. People were running everywhere, scattering in panic, screaming. But Tracy's trained eyes swiftly settled on three individuals amid the melee.

The first was Major General Frank Dorrien, standing in the street yelling into his telephone, gesticulating wildly.

So MI6 knew Drexel would be here! Interesting that they never said a word to the CIA.

The second was a blond man who appeared to be trying to hide a limp. Tracy couldn't make out the man's face from this angle but she saw his muscles tense in pain as he attempted to run in the direction of the river.

The third individual who drew Tracy's attention she could only see from behind. This man was tall, well dressed with dark curly hair, and he was the only person walking, rather than running, toward the metro station.

Tracy's heart sank into the pit of her stomach.

I recognize that walk.

Just then, a hand grabbed her roughly by the waist and manhandled her down onto the floor.

"*Mon Dieu*, Mary Jo, have you lost your mind?" Pascal Cauchin hissed in Tracy's ear. "Stay away from the window. It could be a terrorist attack! The police are on their way but you must stay down."

"Sorry, Pascaaaal," Tracy drawled. Decades of practice had taught her never to slip when in character. "Ah guess ah was just curious."

Lying on Pascal Cauchin's parquet floor, Tracy's heart and mind raced.

I must have made a mistake. It can't be him.

It just can't be.

Hélène Faubourg almost jumped out of her skin. A handsome, blond man with wild eyes and a terrifying expression on his face stepped right in front of her Renault Clio, practically hurling himself across her windscreen.

"Help me," he panted, wrenching open the passenger door and climbing inside once Hélène screeched to a halt.

"Get out!" she screamed. "Get out of my car!"

She had pepper spray in the glove box, but would have to reach across him to get it.

"Please. I won't hurt you. I've been shot. See?" The man pulled up the leg of his pants to reveal rivers of blood.

"I'll take you to the hospital," Hélène said. " The one on Rue Ambroise Paré is the closest. You'll be OK."

"No," said the man. "No hospitals. Please. I need to get out of Paris. Just drive."

Reaching into his jacket pocket, he pulled out what must have been tens of thousands of euros, maybe more, in cash.

"Take it," he wheezed, wincing in pain. "Please. Just get me out of here."

Hélène looked at the money. Then she looked at the man's face. And made a decision.

What the hell. You only live once.

Chapter 20

Tracy might not be a real poker player. But she could certainly do a good poker face.

Two days after the mysterious shooting incident in Montmartre—despite multiple witnesses, both the would-be assassin and the victim he apparently wounded disappeared without a trace—Tracy paid an official visit to the Neuilly crime scene.

"Miss Whitney's a special advisor to the CIA on Group 99," Greg Walton explained over the phone to Benjamin Liset, his French intelligence counterpart in Paris. "I trust you'll give her every assistance."

Benjamin found he had no trouble assisting Miss Whitney, who turned out to be not only polite, intelligent and attractive, but thin and well dressed, a positive barrage of surprises from an American female.

The same could not be said of Tracy's colleague from the FBI, Agent Milton Buck, an arrogant, overbearing boor if ever Benjamin Liset had seen one.

"Forensics went over the entire campus, I presume?" Buck asked, in a tone that made it quite clear he presumed nothing of the sort.

"Naturally." Benjamin's tone was frosty.

"Why haven't we seen a report?"

"Because this isn't your investigation, Agent Buck. I hope I don't need to remind you but you are here as our guests, solely as a courtesy."

"Courtesy?" Buck laughed rudely. "I wouldn't say that's what you French are known for. I hope I don't need to remind *you* that your government has promised the president full disclosure and total cooperation. I mean, let's face it, Ben, you could use the help, right? What's it been now, two weeks? And still no leads?"

Tracy watched in an agony of embarrassment as the Frenchman turned and walked away.

"It's jerks like you that give Americans a bad name, Buck."

Milton Buck shrugged. "The truth hurts. Just calling it like I see it. Speaking of 'no leads,' your latest report on Althea made depressing reading, Tracy. You're no closer to finding her than when you started, are you?"

Tracy glared at him. "You asked me to look for links between Althea and what happened on this campus."

"Exactly," said Buck.

"Well, there are none. I realize you're not the sharpest knife in the drawer, Agent Buck. But I'm not sure I can simplify that any further, even for you," Tracy shot back. "How's the hunt for Hunter going? From what I hear the tumbleweed's still rolling."

It was hard not to blurt out to the odious Milton Buck that she'd already tracked down Hunter Drexel; that she'd come *this* close to confronting him face-to-face; and that the British had too, leaving him and his tragically arrogant agency in ignominious third place. The only person she'd told about what really happened in Montmartre was Cameron Crewe. And even with him she'd left out the part about seeing Jeff.

Because you didn't see him. You couldn't have. You made a mistake in the heat of the moment.

"As usual, you don't know what you're talking about," Milton Buck said caustically. Leaning in closer, he hissed in Tracy's ear. "Walton won't protect you forever, you know. If you don't come up with something on Althea soon, people are going to start asking questions. Like whether you know more than you're telling."

"Like you with Hunter Drexel, you mean?" Tracy hissed back.

Buck looked for a moment as if he might hit her. "Do yourself a favor and forget about Drexel. I'm a senior FBI agent, Miss Whitney. You're an ex–con artist who's in danger of outliving her usefulness."

To Tracy's relief, a charming Frenchwoman from ballistics interrupted them and led Tracy away for a detailed briefing on exactly what had happened at Neuilly. Getting away from Buck was a joy, but as always after her encounters with him, Tracy felt a dull residue of fear lingering in the pit of her stomach.

He's loathsome, but he might end up running the bureau one day.

If he does he won't rest till I'm back in jail and they've thrown away the key.

Tracy took copious notes with the ballistics expert, then made her way up to the château that had been the main school building for lunch. She soon lost her appetite, however, when she spotted Major General Frank Dorrien making his way towards her in the buffet line.

"Miss Whitney." Frank gave Tracy the same blank, robotic smile she remembered from their last meeting in London. The man was about as sincere as a fortune cookie compliment. "I trust you've had an informative morning?"

"Thank you. Yes. You?"

"It's been very interesting."

The last time Tracy had seen Frank he'd been standing in the street in Montmartre, flapping his arms like a distressed chicken as his quarry, Hunter Drexel, got away, along with his would-be killer. Tracy had decided that the blond with the limp must have been Hunter.

As she told Cameron later that night, "It was him, I know it. I think he'd been shot in the leg."

As usual, Cameron ended up playing Devil's advocate. "It could have been a bystander, hurt in the crossfire."

Tracy wasn't buying it. "A bystander would lie there and wait for help, especially once the gunman had made a run for it. But this man was as desperate to get away as the shooter. He couldn't risk being identified."

And Hunter Drexel *had* gotten away, again, leaving Major General Frank Dorrien red-faced and empty-handed. For the second time that day, Tracy found herself resisting the temptation to shame a man she loathed. Not least because, if she had seen *him* that day, there was at least a chance that Frank had seen *her* entering Pascal Cauchin's apartment, but was choosing to keep quiet about it.

Maybe we're both keeping secrets?

From each other and from the CIA?

"Do you know the most interesting thing I learned today?" Frank asked casually, helping himself to a large slice of Brie and proceeding to slather it over his baguette. "One of the teenagers murdered here was Jack Charlston."

Frank gave Tracy a questioning look, but the name meant nothing to her.

"Jack was Richard Charlston's son. Only son, as it happened."

Richard Charlston. It rang a bell. Tracy dredged her memory, trying to place it.

"Richard was the MEP who opposed Crewe Oil's attempts to secure fracking rights across the EU, including right here in France," Frank Dorrien reminded her. "Vociferously opposed. And successfully."

That's right. Cameron had mentioned the name Richard Charlston to Tracy the very first night they met, in Geneva. He'd been in Switzerland trying to drum up support in the European parliament for an expansion of his European business, and the British MEP was speaking against him.

"I remember," Tracy said.

"Richard Charlston was due to give a speech here, at Camp Paris, on the day of the shooting but pulled out at the last moment. I daresay nobody informed Group 99 of the change of plans. Still"—Frank smiled—"at least they got his son. I daresay that's better than nothing from your boyfriend's point of view."

Tracy put down her plate. "What do you mean by that?"

"Merely that Cameron Crewe was an enemy of Richard Charlston. Just as he was an enemy of Henry Cranston. Doesn't it strike you as curious the way that Group 99 seem to target your boyfriend's enemies?" Frank helped himself to a large handful of dates and some pâté. "Almost as if they're doing Crewe Oil's dirty work."

A surge of absolute loathing ran through Tracy's body.

"Cameron lost a son," she told Frank. Her voice was quiet but she was shaking with anger. "Marcus. He was a teenager, just like the children murdered here."

"Yes, I . . ."

"I'm not finished." Tracy cut the general off furiously. "I lost my son, too. At the same age. So you see, General, we *know* what it feels like. Cameron and I. We know what the Neuilly massacre parents are going through. In a way that you never will. If you think for one second that Cameron is capable . . . that he would ever be involved in the murder of children, or support that in any way . . . then you're even more bigoted than you look. You're deranged."

Frank looked at Tracy calmly. "I believe that all human beings are capable of terrible things, Miss Whitney. Just as we are all capable of greatness. Don't you?"

Tracy glared at him in silence.

What a hateful, hateful man, she thought, as the general walked away.

But the names Jack and Richard Charlston haunted her for the rest of the day.

Group 99. Fracking. Cameron.

There was a link there. Not the link that Frank Dorrien was insinuating. But *a* link. Something connecting Cameron, or at least his industry, with these vile and cowardly acts of terror.

Did Hunter Drexel know what that link was? Was that why he had run?

Had Hunter seen whatever it was that Tracy was missing?

And where did Althea, whoever she was, fit into the puzzle?

Not for the first time, Tracy was left with the unsettling feeling that nothing and nobody were what they seemed.

Upstate New York was beautiful at this time of year. From her bedroom window at the rehab facility,

Kate Evans enjoyed glorious views across rolling countryside. Bright green fields and wildflower meadows stretched as far as the eye could see, dotted with cows, picket fences, oak trees and the occasional white clapboard farmhouse. There was nothing ugly out here. Nothing noisy or unpleasant, no poverty or disease or filth or pain. Not a blade of grass out of place, in fact. Just the sort of sanitized, unthreatening, almost manicured beauty that occurred when human beings took nature in hand and bent it to their will. All was order and peace. It was the perfect place to rest, and Kate had rested. But now it was time to go.

"I wish you'd reconsider."

Bill Winter, Kate's psychiatrist, tried again to change her mind. Tall and thin, with a craggy face like a dried-up riverbed and intense, thoughtful brown eyes, Dr. Winter reminded Kate of her father. Owen Evans had died during Kate's first year of high school—a massive heart attack had felled him instantly, like a lightning-struck tree. That was the first time Kate's heart had broken. It hadn't healed, not fully anyway, till she met Daniel.

"I know you do." She smiled at Dr. Winter. "But I really can't stay any longer. There's someone I need to see. And I really do feel so much better."

That last part was truthful. But most of what Kate had revealed to her doctors and therapists here at Westchester Meadows had been a web of half-truths, interwoven with outright lies. That was one of the benefits of a life spent working in intelligence. Once you knew what it meant to go into deep cover—to become somebody else, for your own safety and the safety of others—you learned how to hold on to that other self with an iron grip. Even under hypnosis, Kate could be whoever she needed to be. And yet when the time came to break cover, she could walk away without a backward glance.

Daniel used to say it was like a snake shedding its skin.

Althea had been a necessary cover, a role she had needed to play. But it was time to let her go.

Hunter Drexel's phone call had started the process. Here, at Westchester Meadows, Kate had finished it. The drugs had helped. So had the therapy. And the sleep. But the biggest factor had been Daniel, coming to her in her dreams.

You must forgive yourself, Kate.

Everything you did you did for me. For us.

But you can let go now. Move on.

Darling Daniel! She still missed him so much sometimes, it was hard to breathe.

She could let go of Althea and what Althea had done. But she couldn't move on. Not yet. Not until she'd seen Hunter Drexel face-to-face. Not until she'd closed the circle.

"Where will you go?" Bill Winter asked. "As long as you're in New York I'd still like you to see me at least once a week. And you should start going back to Lucy Grey regularly as well. Don't let things unravel again. It's easier than you think."

"I won't." Kate hugged him, zipping up her bag. "And I promise to come and see both of you as soon as I get back."

"Back?" Dr. Winter frowned. "Where are you going?"

Kate smiled. "To Europe. Like I said. There's someone I need to see there. He's been waiting a long time."

Sally Faiers huddled under her umbrella and lit another cigarette.

It was raining, and she wasn't even in bloody England. The bad weather, clearly, was following her. Just like bad luck seemed to follow her. Or perhaps it was bad choices?

Bad pennies.

Bad men.

She knew she shouldn't have come here. Standing outside Chimay Castle, a lone tourist in this historic but obscure Belgian town, just a few miles from the French border, she felt the full, humiliating stupidity of her decision.

What if Hunter didn't show up?

Or what if he did show up, dragged her into a world of trouble—and not just editor trouble, but the deep, real-world, kidnap and torture and murder trouble he seemed to have got himself into lately—and then left her? For another woman? Another story?

Of course, Sally had her own story now. Tired of waiting for Hunter to let her in on his scoop, she'd spent the last couple of months doing her own digging into the murky world of global fracking. It would be the first thing she published on her own, assuming the *Times* sacked her for this latest extended period AWOL. Ironically, it was the best piece of work she'd produced in years. But Sally knew herself well enough to know that that wasn't why she was here.

As usual it was not her head that had pulled her back to Hunter Drexel, but her heart.

Her stupid, weak, womanly heart.

I hate myself.

The worst part of it was, Hunter hadn't even called Sally himself to ask for help. He'd had some girl do it—Hélène—no doubt the latest naive, trusting young floozy he was screwing.

"A friend of yours is very sick," the girl had told Sally, in broken English.

"A friend?"

"Yes. You know who. He won't go to hospital. He wants you to meet him in Belgium."

Sally had established that this girl, Hélène, had picked up Hunter on the street in Paris—evidently he'd been shot in Montmartre—and he'd convinced her to get him out of France. Money may have changed hands. In any event, since then the girl had clearly thought better of the whole thing. Something had gone wrong between them. Now Hunter's wound was infected, and she was panicking.

"He scares me. He says . . . crazy things. I have to go back to Paris but if I leave him alone he will die."

Stupidly, moronically, Sally had found herself agreeing to a meeting in the grounds of Chimay Castle early on Monday morning. And now, of course, she was here. And Hunter, god damn him, was not.

To pass the time, she started playing the "if" game.

If he doesn't show up in the next ten minutes, I'm leaving.

If he wants my help, he'll have to credit me on his story. But I'll make sure mine runs first.

*If he wants to get back together, I'll shut him down
immediately. There is no way we can ever . . .*

She heard the little blue car before she saw it,
straining up the hill like an asthmatic mule, its engine
wheezing and spluttering in the rain. Sally was standing outside the castle walls, a few meters from the
empty carpark where her own rental car kept a lonely
vigil. The carpark was at the top of a long winding
driveway. But instead of continuing its labored journey
to the top, the blue car pulled into a lay-by halfway up.
Sally watched as a skinny blonde in jeans and a trilby
hat hopped out of the driver's seat, pulled a small duffel
bag from the boot, and threw it unceremoniously on
the side of the road. Every movement, every gesture,
was rushed. Frantic.

That must be Hélène.

Next she yanked open the passenger door. Sally
watched in confusion as a man stepped out, slowly and
gingerly, onto the road. The girl waited anxiously for
him to step away from the vehicle. Then, slamming the
door closed behind him, she ran back around to the
driver's side, got in and turned the car around, speeding
off into the distance in a thick smog of exhaust fumes
and desperation, back towards France.

Skinny and frail, with ragged clothes and white-
blond hair, her poor abandoned passenger looked

utterly bereft and bewildered, standing next to his suitcase as the rain poured down.

Sally's first thought was. *There's been a mistake.*

The man looked nothing like Hunter.

Before she had time for a second thought, she watched in horror as he sank to his knees and then collapsed completely, facedown and apparently lifeless on the ground.

Shit! Sally looked around her.

There was nobody else there. Just the two of them.

Shit, shit, shit!

Closing her umbrella, she started to run.

Tracy's premier suite at the Georges V in Paris was like something out of a storybook. More like a Marais apartment than a hotel room, it boasted a luxurious king-size bed draped with the finest silk and linen bedclothes, a deep marble bath, an antique walnut writing desk and salon area hung with refined artwork and spectacular views across the city. At almost six thousand euros a night, it was outrageously expensive. But it wasn't as if Tracy had anything else to spend her money on. Besides, after the day she'd had today, not only walking through the horrors of Neuilly but having to contend with two of her least favorite people, Milton Buck and Frank Dorrien, she deserved a little luxury. Sleeping at the Georges V was like laying one's head on a bed of clouds. For once Tracy could hardly wait to drift away.

Throwing her Dior purse, phone and laptop down on the bed, she lit a Diptyque candle, filling the room with the scent of fig flowers, and smiled at the picture of Nicholas she had propped up on the nightstand. He was nine years old in the photograph, standing on the banks of the Colorado River with Blake Carter, holding an enormous salmon and grinning from ear to ear. Tracy adored the picture, because it showed Nick's cheeky character as well as his love for Blake. And because, when he smiled, he looked exactly like Jeff. That was the Jeff Tracy wanted to remember. The Jeff she had loved so passionately. Before life got complicated and pulled them apart with a current too strong for either of them to resist.

But she mustn't dwell on the past. Cameron Crewe had helped her with that.

"Don't shut it out. That only gives it more power. But don't let it consume you." That was Cameron's mantra. It was how he'd survived after his own son died. And it was working for Tracy too. Cameron was the one who'd encouraged her to travel with Nick's photograph.

"His face is in your head, so why not in a picture frame? He'll always be with you, Tracy. Let him be."

Thank God for Cameron, Tracy thought for the millionth time, peeling off her clothes and stepping into the shower. *I would officially be a basket case without him.*

Remembering Frank Dorrien's vile insinuations about him at lunch today, she felt the anger surge back up inside her. It also angered her that Frank had referred to Cameron as her "boyfriend," twice. Firstly because Tracy had no idea how the British General knew anything about her personal life. And secondly because she didn't consider herself to be in a relationship. Whatever Cameron Crewe was to her—friend, lover, therapist—it was temporary. Once this was all over, once Tracy had found Althea and knew the real truth about Nick's death, they would part ways. Neither of them had said so in so many words. But it was understood.

At least, Tracy hoped it was. Frank Dorrien, damn him, had begun to make her doubt. Did Cameron think of himself as her boyfriend? Did he imagine them having a future together?

Slathering lavender shower gel over her body, Tracy struggled to untangle her emotions. Thinking about Cameron Crewe made her feel happy and sad at the same time. Happy because, in so many ways, he had brought her back to life. He was interesting and funny and passionate and Tracy loved being in his company.

But she felt sad too, because she knew she was no longer capable of the sort of love that would make *him* happy. Cameron had shown her that there was life after Nick's death. But he'd also confirmed what Tracy already knew: that a part of her *had* died with her son. Yes, she could still feel pleasure. She could still taste food and savor music and experience affection, perhaps even love. But these things were only an inch deep now, where once they'd been bottomless. Tracy felt them on her skin, but not in her soul. Her soul was deep beneath the Colorado earth, with Nick.

Before Tracy met Cameron Crewe, that hadn't mattered to her.

Now it did, if only for his sake.

Drying herself, Tracy slipped into a toweling robe and wrapped her hair up turban style in one of the hotel's butter-soft towels. Walking to the bathroom window, she gazed out at the Paris skyline. The rooftops of the city were a world of their own, a mishmash of tiles and stone and copper, of piercing spires and majestically curved domes. In the distance, above it all, the Eiffel Tower loomed, iconic, watching over everything like an amused wrought-iron god, surveying his kingdom.

Tracy loved Paris. France, generally, was a country of happy memories. The Château de Matigny at Cap d'Antibes, where she and Jeff had made off with two million dollars' worth of jewels and a Leonardo; Biarritz, where she'd outsmarted the repellent Armand Grangier. But Paris had always held a special place in Tracy's heart, perhaps because she'd never pulled off a job here. To her and Jeff, Paris had meant pleasure, a respite from the stress and adrenaline of their lives as con artists. Paris meant food and art and love. Paris meant beauty.

Tracy had always meant to bring Nicholas here one day, when he was older.

But of course, Nicholas would never be older.

There were no more "one days."

She was still gazing out at the city when she heard it. A very soft *click* so quiet it was almost inaudible. But Tracy's trained ear recognized it as a door being opened.

She froze. The door to her suite was locked. She hadn't ordered room service, and the maids never cleaned at this time. Besides, if it were housekeeping they would make more noise.

Someone's breaking in.

The bathroom door was open a crack. In the mirrored wall, Tracy glimpsed movement, a man's shadow crossing the room. Her mind raced. Any second now he could come into the bathroom and attack her.

Her suite was eight floors up and it was a sheer drop from the bathroom window. No ledges or fire escapes. She could make a run for the bathroom door, try to lock it from the inside. But he would likely get there before her. And even if he didn't, assuming he had a gun he could blow off the bolt in seconds.

Deciding attack was not just her best but her only form of defense, Tracy picked up a heavy marble soap dish from beside the bath, wielding it over her head and ran screaming like a banshee into the bedroom. The man was standing over the bed with his back to her. He'd pulled one of her dresses out of the closet and was holding it up to the light admiringly. He only had time to half turn in surprise as Tracy leaped on him, bringing her right arm down with as much force as she could towards his skull.

But his reflexes were quicker than she'd bargained for. In an adrenaline-fueled haze, Tracy felt his fingers grip her arm like a vice, forcing it backwards painfully and shaking it like a terrier shaking a rat until the soap dish fell from her hand and clattered noisily onto the floor.

"Tracy!"

She was struggling so hard, she didn't hear her name.

"Tracy, for God's sake, relax. It's me."

For the second time in as many minutes, Tracy froze.

He let her go and for a long moment the two of them sat on the bed in shock, staring at each other.

Then Jeff Stevens smiled broadly.

"Put this on." He handed Tracy the dress he'd been holding, a red silk Chanel shift. "I'm taking you to dinner."

Chapter 21

"Well, this is nice, isn't it, darling? Just like old times."

Tracy and Jeff were sitting in a corner table, tucked away at the back of a nondescript bistro about a hundred yards from Tracy's hotel. Jeff looked as dapper as ever in a perfectly tailored dark suit. Tracy was wearing a lightweight black sweater and knee-length skirt, with no jewelry and minimal makeup. She'd purposefully refused to wear the red dress that Jeff had picked out for her in the hotel room. Partly because Jeff had picked it out. Tracy didn't like having decisions made for her. And partly because the dress was far too sexy. Whatever tonight's dinner turned out to be, it wasn't a date.

"What are you *doing* here, Jeff?" It wasn't a question so much as an accusation.

Jeff sipped his wine. "Having dinner with a stunning woman."

"I mean what are you doing in Paris," Tracy said firmly.

"It's a beautiful city." Jeff snapped a breadstick playfully. "And I hear the poker's wonderful here."

"I wouldn't know," said Tracy.

"Of course you wouldn't, darling." Jeff chuckled to himself. He'd always loved playing these games with Tracy. They both knew that the other had been there at Montmartre that night, but neither of them would be first to admit it.

"I mean it, Jeff. Why are you here?" Tracy said, suddenly serious. "The truth, please."

Jeff looked hurt. "When have I ever lied to you?"

Tracy's eyebrows shot up so far they almost disappeared altogether.

"OK, OK," said Jeff. "The truth. I'm working for British intelligence."

Tracy burst out laughing. "*You?*"

"And why is that so funny?"

"Well now, let me think . . . Perhaps because the last I heard you were on their Most Wanted list?"

Jeff shrugged. "Times change. You're working for the CIA, after all. Or is it the FBI?"

"That's different."

"How? In a world where you and Agent Buck are colleagues, I'd say we're all pretty far down the rabbit hole. Wouldn't you?"

Tracy couldn't deny this. Even so, she found it very hard indeed to picture Jeff as an MI6 stooge.

"OK. So you're working for the Brits. On what? Group 99?"

Jeff nodded, dropping his voice to a whisper. "I'm here for the same reason you are. The British want to find Hunter Drexel. Badly. Julia Cabot doesn't trust President Havers as far as she can spit. She wants MI6 to find Drexel first so that they can discover whatever it is the Americans are hiding."

"And what does she think that is?" Tracy asked.

"No idea," said Jeff. "Let's order."

They both ordered green salads. Tracy followed hers with a light bouillabaisse. Jeff, predictably, opted for steak frites.

"This whole thing clearly has something to do with fracking," Jeff said, once the salads arrived. "Europe's being carved up according to an underground map of shale gas reserves. It's the new Wild West, with billions of dollars at stake. Right now the U.S. is the world leader in that industry with China close behind. But that could change. Poland, Greece, Bratislava, they all have gas. Ordinary people there are suffering, yet they have a fortune in natural resources quite literally sitting beneath their feet."

"You can see why that angers Group 99," Tracy agreed. "It's the same old story. Like Africa's diamonds or Saudi Arabia's oil. A tiny minority are becoming unimaginably wealthy while the rest of the people starve."

"But the governments let it happen because the tax revenues are huge."

"And the GDP soars up."

"Right." Jeff smiled. It was wonderful talking with Tracy again. Seeing through the bullshit together. Seeing eye to eye. He'd missed this.

"So that's the backdrop," Tracy said. "I understand MI6's interest. But where do you fit in? What's your connection?"

"My connection?" Jeff laughed. "My connection is you, Tracy."

She looked confused.

"I was brought in to keep tabs on *you*. To find out what you were doing for the Americans. And what you

might be doing behind their backs," Jeff added knowingly. "They had other applicants, but I was the only
one with twenty years of experience following you
around the globe."

He grinned, but Tracy didn't find it funny.

"Let me get this straight. So the plan was for *me* to
do all the legwork. Find Althea, and Hunter Drexel.
Figure out the connections. And then *you* would swoop
in and take all the glory?"

"Something like that," Jeff beamed. "After all, it
worked in Madrid. When you helpfully stole the *Puerto*
for me. Remember?"

"How could I forget?"

It still stung. Jeff had roundly outsmarted Tracy
on that occasion, presenting Gunther Hartog with the
famous Goya masterpiece that Tracy had painstakingly
procured in a brilliant con that had been months in the
making. Back then the rivalry between them had been
fun and exciting, a foreplay of sorts, although neither
of them recognized it at the time. Now, everything was
very different. This wasn't a game. This was real. And
Group 99 wasn't a gallery or a rich collector. It was a
terrorist organization. Innocent people were being
kidnapped and tortured and murdered. Government
systems were being hacked. Children were being shot

to death, all in the name of a group that had once stood for justice and equality, for righting the world's wrongs.

The violence had started with Bob Daley's brains being splattered across a screen. And it was still going on. Althea was still out there, Hunter Drexel was still missing. There was no end in sight.

The waiter cleared their salads and returned promptly with the entrees. Jeff took a bite of mouthwateringly tender steak before turning back to Tracy.

"You do realize I'm not doing this just because MI6 asked me to," he said, refilling Tracy's glass. "I had my own agenda."

"Which was?" Tracy looked up at him questioningly. "Let me guess. There's a Renoir in a château somewhere you need to liberate? Or a Fabergé egg collection desperate for a new home?"

"No," said Jeff. "I came here to protect you."

Tracy frowned. "I don't need protection. I can take care of myself."

"I disagree." Jeff sipped his wine. "From what I've seen you've made some dangerous friends recently."

Tracy's eyes narrowed. "Meaning?"

"Oh, I think you know. Do you realize how many of Group 99's actions in the last six months have ended up benefiting Crewe Oil? Directly or indirectly?"

"Not you as well . . ." Tracy muttered darkly.

"I mean it," said Jeff. "Think about it. How well do you know this guy? I mean *really* know him."

"Well enough to know that he's a good man," Tracy shot back angrily. "This is Frank Dorrien talking, Jeff, not you."

"That's not true."

"No? Well let me ask *you* a question. Has it ever occurred to you to ask *why* the General's so keen to prove a link between Group 99 and Cameron Crewe? Could it be to take the heat off himself?"

Now it was Jeff's turn to frown. "The heat? What heat?"

"Frank Dorrien's using you, Jeff! He's in this up to his neck. Starting with Prince Achileas's suicide. That was a cover-up if ever I saw one."

"Maybe it was," admitted Jeff. "But you're wrong about Frank. He's a decent man."

"Decent?" Tracy's eyes widened. "He ransacked the kid's room after he died. Stole his computer. That much I know for a fact. He's a liar, a sexist and a homophobe, not to mention anti-American. And *I* think he's a killer."

"That's ridiculous, Tracy."

"Is it?"

"Yes! I know Frank Dorrien. You don't."

"Oh yeah? Well, *I* know Cameron Crewe. And *you* don't. Cameron's a decent man, Jeff. More than decent. He's one of the best."

"I know you want to believe that, Tracy," Jeff said, trying and failing to block the images of Tracy and Cameron together in Hawaii out of his mind.

"I don't want to believe it. I *do* believe it. And if you don't it's either because Frank Dorrien's poisoned you against him, or because you're jealous!"

As soon as the words were out of her mouth, Tracy regretted them. The last thing she wanted to do was to make things personal between her and Jeff. To open up a door to the past, their shared past. But that was exactly what she'd just done.

Reaching across the table, Jeff took her hand.

"I came to look for you, you know. After Nick died. When you called me in London. I got the next plane out."

"I know," Tracy croaked.

"Then why did you run?"

She shook her head silently. Tears welled in her eyes.

"You owe me an answer, Tracy."

She looked up at him. "I told you not to come."

"He was my son too, you know."

To Jeff's surprise, she reacted angrily to this.

"No! It's not the same," she insisted. "It's nowhere close to the same. I raised him, Jeff. I raised him alone."

"Only because I never knew he existed!" Jeff protested.

But Tracy wasn't listening. "Nick was my world. My whole world. You don't know what it's like, to lose that, to have it taken from you."

"You're right," Jeff said quietly. "I don't. But I did love him. And I wanted to be there. Not just for him but for you."

They sat silently for a moment, suspended in a fragile bubble of grief.

Then Jeff burst it. "I love you, Tracy."

Tracy fell painfully back to earth.

"Please. Don't."

"Don't what? Don't love you? Or don't say it out loud?"

"Both!"

Tracy tried to pull her hand away but Jeff tightened his grip.

"Why not? It's the truth. I love you and you love me. You can't run from that forever, Tracy."

"Oh yes I can! Don't you see?" She looked at him in utter exasperation. "You are the one person, the *one* person, who I absolutely cannot be with. Ever."

"Why not?" Jeff's voice wavered. He felt close to tears himself.

"Because everything about you, your face, your voice, your walk, everything brings him back to me. When I look at you, I see Nick."

"But you love me, Tracy. We love each other," Jeff pleaded.

"It isn't enough," Tracy said sadly. " Seeing you drags me back to the darkness."

"And I suppose Cameron Crewe pulls you into the light, does he?" Jeff said bitterly. He knew he was being unfair but he couldn't help himself.

Tracy didn't answer. A gloomy silence fell as the waiter cleared their plates and returned with a dessert menu.

Jeff broke it first. "I have a proposal."

As he leaned forward across the table, his eyes were sparkling again. It was the old Jeff. Irrepressible. Tracy thought, *He's still alive inside. And I'm not. That's the real difference between us. The chasm that can never be bridged.*

"Let's find Hunter together. As a team," said Jeff. "Cabot and Havers may not trust each other. And the CIA and MI6 certainly don't. But we do. You and I can achieve far more than the lot of them put together."

It was an interesting proposal, the same proposal

that Tracy had made to Cameron not so long ago. Although even she had to admit that Cameron hadn't been much practical help so far, other than as a sounding board. At least she and Jeff knew how to get things done.

"What would we do when we found him?" Tracy asked. "Hand him over to the British? Or the Americans?"

"That depends," said Jeff.

"On what?"

"On what he has to say for himself. On what he's hiding. By the way, I do love the way that you said 'when.'"

Tracy thought for a moment. It would be helpful to pick Jeff's brains, not just on finding Hunter but on getting him to tell them the truth. Having a partner to work with would make things a lot easier. But if Jeff was prepared to risk everything to help her, to play a double game with his British paymasters, she owed it to him to be honest about her own involvement.

Taking a deep breath, she said, "There's something I need to tell you."

Slowly, and without once making eye contact, she told him the story he'd already heard from Jamie MacIntosh. About Althea requesting that Tracy be brought onto the CIA team, mentioning her by name. About a woman fitting Althea's description tampering with Blake's truck before it ran off the road, and later showing up at the hospital where the doctors had battled to save Nick.

"If it's true," Tracy finished, twisting her napkin round and round in her hands, "if she really did murder Nicholas, then it happened because of me. It's my fault he died."

Jeff gripped Tracy by the shoulders. "No it is not. It is not your fault, Tracy. Look at me. You can't think like that."

"But she knew me! She knows me! She wanted me to be a part of this, and when I refused to do it, Nick died."

"That doesn't mean anything. Not on its own. You're putting two and two together and making twenty."

"Do you have any idea who she could be, Jeff?" Tracy asked him desperately. "Any idea how she knows me? What she wants with me?"

"No," Jeff said. "I don't. But I'd lay good money that Hunter Drexel does. And when we find him that'll be the first question we ask. OK?"

Tracy nodded, grateful. "OK."

"He's already left Paris," Jeff said.

"How do you know?"

Tracy suspected as much, but she was surprised to hear Jeff confirm it.

For the last five days Tracy had been unable to get any answer from Sally Faiers. Sally's phone was off and she'd stopped opening her emails, which was very unusual. Sally had mentioned to Tracy a month ago that she was working on something—a story—but she'd been very cagey about what it was. Could her silence be connected with that?

Tracy suspected not. That Hunter Drexel had made a move, and that Sally Faiers might be swept up in it, keeping his secrets once again. But she had no hard evidence.

Did Jeff?

"Here."

Scrolling through pictures on his iPhone, Jeff showed Tracy a string of grainy images. They showed a slim, blond man at a gas station, getting into a beat-up Renault Clio with a pretty young girl. A young girl who was definitely not Sally Faiers.

"That's him?" Tracy squinted at the man in the picture. The resolution was terrible.

"We think so."

"And the girl?"

"The car's registered to an Hélène Faubourg. Twenty-three years old, art student from Paris. No known links to Group 99. None of her friends have seen her since the Montmartre shooting. Car was dumped a few miles from the Belgian border. No leads since."

"OK," said Tracy, waving to the waiter for the bill and smiling at Jeff for the first time. "So I guess we're going to Belgium."

"Not we. You."

"But I thought you said . . ."

"We can't make it too obvious we're collaborating," Jeff said. "Not unless we want the spooks getting suspicious. Say what you like about Frank Dorrien, but he's not stupid."

No, Tracy thought, *he's not.*

"I'll join you in a week. Or as soon as either of us finds something."

They said their goodbyes and agreed to meet the next day at noon. In the intervening hours, Tracy would come up with a suitable cover story to tell her bosses at the CIA, and Jeff would do the same with his British paymasters.

Jeff waited until Tracy was completely out of sight before jumping into a cab and heading to a different, equally nondescript bistro in another quarter of the city.

Frank Dorrien greeted him warmly.

"Well done. You did it."

"Yeah," Jeff said without enthusiasm. Reaching

under his shirt he ripped off the tiny recording device stuck to his chest and handed it back to the general. "I did it."

"You strayed from the script once or twice," Frank said, still smiling. "I'm not sure there was any need for all that 'Julia Cabot doesn't trust the president' business."

"It's the truth," said Jeff.

"I daresay. But Tracy Whitney didn't need to know it. However, I'm not complaining. You got the job done. She trusts you."

Yes, Jeff thought. *She trusts me. And I just betrayed her.*

Reading his thoughts, Frank said firmly, "You're doing this for her, Jeff. Don't forget that. You're saving her from a very dangerous situation. She thinks she can handle this but she can't. We'll protect her. "

"Will you?"

"Of course." Frank sounded almost impatient. "You have my word."

Your word.

The two men looked at each other. Tracy's words echoed in Jeff's head: *Dorrien's using you, Jeff. He's in this up to his neck.*

"I have to go." Jeff pushed back his chair. He was feeling more like Judas Iscariot by the minute.

"Why did you tell Tracy to go to Belgium alone?"

Frank asked suddenly. "You said you'd follow her later."

"That's right. I need a break."

"A break?" Frank's face darkened.

"Yes. I need some time off. Alone. A week should do it."

Frank looked at him incredulous. "A week? Have you gone mad? This is no time to take a holiday, Stevens. We are *this* close to getting Drexel. We need to stay on Whitney now more than ever."

"Stay on her, then." Now it was Jeff's turn to get angry. "That's your job, isn't it?"

"I'm serious. You can't leave."

"So am I," said Jeff. He didn't like that "can't." "I'm taking a week, Frank."

"And just what, exactly, do you need this week *for?*"

"It's personal."

"That's not good enough! This is a matter of national security. A matter of duty."

Jeff shrugged, as if to say *not my problem.*

"There's something I need to do, that's all. I'll be in touch."

Frank Dorrien watched Jeff Stevens leave the café. Beneath the table, his fists were clenched so tightly that the muscles in his fingers began to spasm.

That's not how it works, Stevens, he thought furiously. *You and Whitney don't get to call the shots.*

Frank had warned Jamie MacIntosh that this would happen. That bringing in amateurs was the thin end of the wedge. But of course, no one had listened to him.

Frank paid the bill and slipped out into the night.

Regrettably, it was time to take matters into his own hands.

Tracy's mind was racing too fast after dinner with Jeff for her to go back to her hotel and sleep. She decided to take a walk along the river.

Before she got a hundred yards from the bistro, her cellphone buzzed with a text.

It was from Cameron.

I miss you.

Tracy texted back. *I miss you too.* Then she felt guilty because it wasn't true. Not in that exact moment anyway. Or perhaps the guilt was because she'd just seen Jeff—not only seen but agreed to work with him again—information she already knew she wasn't going to share with Cameron.

Why not? she asked herself now. *Is there something about Jeff Stevens that brings out the liar in me? The con artist?*

When Jeff was around life always got more exciting. But it also got more complicated. More gray.

Or perhaps Tracy was blaming Jeff for her own uncertainty? Right now she had no idea how she felt about Cameron, or Jeff, or anything. *I barely know who I am anymore.* She still hoped that when she solved the mystery of Althea there would be some sort of closure on Nick's death, and that she could move on. But move on to what?

Without Nick, who was she?

Who did she want to be?

Cameron Crewe loved her. He hadn't said it in so many words yet. But since their trip to Hawaii, Tracy knew.

The question was, did she love him back?

Unfortunately, Tracy didn't have an answer. She was happy when she was with him and sad when she left him behind. Was that love?

She felt calm around him. Was *that* love?

Her darling dad always used to tell her that if you had to ask whether you loved someone, you didn't. Tracy had never had to ask with Jeff. Then again, loving Jeff had brought her more pain than anything else in her life—apart from losing Nicholas, obviously. Perhaps loving Cameron Crewe would be different? Calm and easy and painless.

Could love be like that?

Perhaps having dinner with Jeff tonight had been a mistake? It had stirred everything up again, filled Tracy with doubts and fears and emotions that, up till now, she'd convinced herself she had under control.

The fact that Jeff was so obviously jealous of Cameron only made things worse.

On the other hand, the idea of working with Jeff again *was* exciting. If anyone could outsmart Hunter Drexel and help Tracy find Althea, it was Jeff. Together, Tracy and Jeff could do anything.

Except stay together, Tracy chuckled to herself. *For some reason that's always been the hard part.*

Gazing across the still waters of the Seine, shimmering like molten silver beneath a full moon, Tracy realized she'd walked farther than she'd intended. Across the water she could make out the gardens of the Sorbonne. It was a good hour walk back to the Georges V from here, and the evening breeze had turned from cool to distinctly chilly.

Pulling her scarf more tightly around her shoulders, she turned to retrace her steps when she felt the first blow. Something hard and heavy, like a metal bar, slammed painfully into her back, sending her flying forwards in the darkness. Before Tracy could see where it had come from she heard a scream. Someone behind her must have seen Tracy's attacker.

Then the second blow slammed into the side of her head. The last thing Tracy remembered was the sickening crunching sound of her own skull cracking.

Then nothing.

Chapter 22

J eff Stevens parked his car outside the Mountain Mall in downtown Steamboat Springs and walked into Jumping Beans coffee shop.

The place was busy. Young moms with toddlers in strollers competed for space with high school kids, glued to their phones, and a healthy smattering of cowboys, their hats cluttering up the tables as they waited in line for their morning brew. Jumping Beans was a classic small town joint. Everybody seemed to know everybody. Jeff found himself wondering whether Nick used to come here, and if any of the kids had been friends of his, when he saw her.

Karen Young, a nurse at the Yampa Valley Medical Center, was sitting at a table in the corner, hiding nervously behind her copy of the *Steamboat Herald*. She smiled at Jeff and he came over to join her.

"I didn't know if you'd come," Karen said, lowering her voice almost to a whisper.

"Why wouldn't I?" Jeff smiled broadly. "I have a story to write after all. I said I'd be here, and here I am."

Posing as an award-winning investigative journalist from New York City, Jeff had spent the last four days in Steamboat, researching a book on cowboy culture. He'd been asking a lot of questions around town about the late Blake Carter.

"The Carters were one of the oldest cowboy families in this part of the state, as I'm sure y'all are aware. Blake was the last of the line. The more y'all can tell me about him, the better."

At first, Blake's fellow hands up at the ranch had been happy to talk, as had his fishing buddies and the local Baptist minister. But as soon as Jeff's questions began to focus on the accident—how thorough or otherwise the police report had been; whether a strange woman had been seen around town or up at Tracy Schmidt's ranch in the days leading to the crash; which doctors had attended the scene—suspicions were raised. Doors began closing and locals stopped talking.

Which was why Nurse Young was so important. In a tight-knit community like this one, run on gossip but big on loyalty, Jeff knew it would be tough to find someone willing to help him. By now just about everybody at the Yampa Valley Medical Center knew better than to talk to the *New York Times* writer. So when Jeff caught Karen Young's eye at Ruby's, a local dive bar, last night, and learned she was a nurse, he'd turned up the charm to full throttle.

"I appreciate your trust in me, Karen." Reaching under the table, Jeff squeezed her hand. "You know the very last thing on my mind is disrespecting Blake Carter's memory. Or hurtin' this community."

"I know that." Karen squeezed back.

For an older man, he really is terribly handsome, she thought.

Karen had been off older men ever since Neil—Dr. Sherridan—had broken off their affair and gone crawling back to his wife, like the snake that he was. But Jeff Stevens seemed different.

Honorable.

Interested only in the truth.

The fact that Neil might wind up in a whole heap of trouble, if it turned out Blake Carter or the boy *could* have been saved after all, and Jeff wrote an article about his negligence in the *New York Times*, shredding his reputation and destroying his career, would merely be an unavoidable by-product of the truth telling.

Karen Young was all about telling the truth.

"I'll help you in any way I can, Jeff." She fluttered her sky-blue eyes at Jeff. "We just have to be discreet is all."

"Discretion is my middle name," said Jeff, pressing his leg against Karen's, and wondering why on earth she'd chosen to meet in a crowded coffee shop if she didn't want people to see them together. The young lady clearly had the IQ of a bird dropping. "Of course, what would really help me . . ." He looked away suddenly, drawing back his leg and releasing her hand. "No. It's too dangerous."

"What?" Karen looked crestfallen. "What's too dangerous?"

"No, no. Forget it. I couldn't possibly ask you."

Jeff took a big swig of his coffee and pushed his chair back, as if preparing to leave.

"Please. Just tell me!"

Jeff shook his head. "You could lose your job."

"There are more important things than jobs," Karen said earnestly, leaning forward to give Jeff an enhanced view of her ample cleavage. "If something bad happened to Mr. Carter or that poor boy and I stood by and did nothing, I'd never forgive myself."

Jeff took her hands again and looked deep into her eyes.

"Karen?"

"Yes, Jeff?"

"I don't suppose you happen to know anyone who has access to the hospital's CCTV archives?"

The girl's face fell. "Gosh, I . . . I don't. I'm real sorry but I don't know anything about security. Is there anything else you need?"

The rest of the day crawled by.

Frank Dorrien and Jamie MacIntosh had left him so many messages since he got to the States that in the end Jeff had disabled his phone and bought a disposable, pay-as-you-go handset. That, by contrast, never rang. Suddenly, it seemed, nobody at the ranch or the local garage remembered seeing a woman, unusual or otherwise. No one at the cop shop had access to the police report. All the staff at Yampa had been exemplary and none of Nicholas's school friends or teachers could remember anything unusual in the days leading up to the crash. Or, indeed, any other days. If Jeff Stevens the New York journalist was looking for scandal, he could look elsewhere. Steamboat Springs had closed ranks like a threatened clam snapping shut its shell.

After his dinner with Tracy in Paris, Jeff knew he had to come here. He had to find out for himself what had really happened to his son. After all, it was

Nicholas's death that had dragged Tracy into all this in the first place. Group 99, Althea, Hunter Drexel, Cameron Crewe. None of those names would have touched Tracy if Blake Carter's truck hadn't plunged off the road that night, right here in Steamboat Springs.

And now Jeff, too, had been drawn in. This wasn't their world, his or Tracy's. They weren't spies or counterterrorism experts, for God's sake. And yet here they were, running around Europe fighting other people's battles, solving other people's riddles, like pawns in some giant game of chess. A game in which, increasingly, Jeff doubted there would ever be a real winner.

Meanwhile Tracy, his Tracy, was blaming herself. Tracy thought Althea had killed Nick. That Nick, and Blake, were dead because of her. And she was turning to another man to assuage her of that guilt, to comfort her in her grief.

But what was the truth, really? What had happened here?

Perhaps, Jeff thought, *if I could answer that one question, I could stop the madness. I could save Tracy, spare her the torment.*

I could save myself.

The problem was, he couldn't answer it. Rumors swirled around him, taunting him like blowing leaves he could never quite catch. But he had no actual evidence of anything. As far as Jeff could tell, there was a woman at the diner that night, who may or may not have taken the same road Blake Carter did. But that was it. Maybe the police could have dug a little harder, or the ambulance crew driven a little faster, or the surgeons operated on Nick's brain an hour earlier. But every accident had its "maybes," every tragedy its "what ifs." Jeff had seen nothing in Colorado to make him believe that Tracy's crazy conspiracy theory about Althea was true. The whole thing was smoke and mirrors.

I'll fly back to Europe tomorrow, Jeff thought. Nurse Karen Young had been his last hope, but even she had always been a long shot. Chances were there was nothing worth seeing on the CCTV footage anyway.

Jeff's hotel was in town, a simple but cozy Victorian with a wraparound porch and a fire permanently lit in the parlor. Ski season was over and the tourists had poured out of Steamboat like water through a sieve, so there were plenty of parking spaces out front. Dusk was starting to fall when Jeff got back, tired and defeated. He'd spent most of the day roaming uselessly around Blake Carter's old haunts, getting the cold shoulder from wary locals. But despite his bad mood, he took a moment to look up and appreciate the beauty of his surroundings. Mountains rose like giants from behind the hotel, their snowy tips blushing pink in the sunset. A rainbow of colors oozed into the blue sky like spilled paint, every shade of orange, red, purple and peach, shot through with flashes of turquoise.

No wonder Tracy was drawn to this place.

What a magical corner of the world for Nick to grow up in.

Walking up the porch steps, Jeff felt a stab of loss and longing, a visceral wrench of pain for all the years he'd missed. With Tracy. With their son. It struck him forcibly then that the whole idea of closure was ridiculous. Knowing what happened wouldn't change anything. He couldn't save Tracy from the agony of Nick's death, any more than he could save himself.

"Ah, Mr. Stevens, there you are." Jane, the hugely overweight receptionist, smiled at Jeff warmly. "I'm so sorry, but the young lady just left. She waited more than an hour but I think she had to get to work in the end. I would have called you but I didn't have a number and—"

"What young lady?" Jeff interrupted her.

Jane blushed. "Oh Lord. How stupid of me. All this time she was here and I never got her name. She was young. Blond. Very attractive."

Karen.

"She left you this."

The receptionist picked up a sealed brown paper envelope in her pudgy hands and passed it to Jeff.

His heart rate shot up. He could feel immediately that there was a USB chip inside.

Bounding up the hotel stairs two at a time, Jeff hurried into his room, locking the door behind him. Drawing the curtains, he sat down at his computer and loaded in the chip.

The footage was time-stamped. There was a little under two hours' worth in all. *Thank you, Karen!* Images were streamed from the Yampa Valley Medical Center's car park, front entrance, reception desk and waiting room, and from three corridors inside the building. One clearly led to a surgery suite of some kind. The others looked like regular corridors on a ward, with patients' rooms to the right and left.

Jeff settled back to watch, not sure what he was looking for exactly, but hoping it would jump out at him when he saw it.

Minutes rolled by. Ten. Twenty. Thirty. An hour.

When he finally saw the figure, sauntering confidently up to the reception desk, he had to pause the footage and rewind.

It can't be. Jeff leaned forward, staring at the screen as if he'd seen a ghost. *It can't possibly be.*

Jumping up, he pulled open the bedside drawer and started reassembling his phone, sliding in the sim card and battery.

I have to call Tracy. Right now.

Waiting impatiently for the home screen to load, Jeff tried to think of what he was going to say exactly. What words would he use to break this news? To tell Tracy she was wrong. To tell her . . .

The phone rang loudly, startling him.

"Hello?" He answered without thinking.

Frank Dorrien's voice boomed in his ear, angry and doom-laden. "Stevens! Where in Christ's name have you been?"

"I can't talk now," Jeff said dismissively. "I need to speak to Tracy."

"Jeff . . ."

"I'm sorry, Frank. This can't wait."

"Well, it'll have to," Dorrien shot back hurriedly, before Jeff could hang up. "Tracy's in a coma, Jeff."

Jeff froze. The room had started to spin.

"What?"

"She was attacked the night you left Paris. Bludgeoned from behind."

Jeff held on to the desk for support. He felt terribly light-headed suddenly. Dark spots swam before his eyes. When he spoke his voice sounded strangled. "I don't understand. Who attacked her?"

"We're not sure. Various witnesses—"

"Why didn't you tell me sooner?"

"We tried," said Frank. "Repeatedly. None of us could reach you."

"Well, what have the doctors said? I mean, she's in a coma. But she's going to recover, right? She's going to be OK?"

"She hasn't woken up since it happened," Frank said bluntly, although not without compassion. "I'm sorry, Jeff, truly I am. But it doesn't look good."

Chapter 23

Tracy heard Blake Carter's voice first, out in the corridor.

"Where is she? I need to see her. I need to explain."

And the doctor. "She's not up to visitors yet, Mr. Carter."

I am up to visitors!

Blake's alive? He's been alive all this time? And now he's here to see me?

Blake! She sat up in bed, tried to call out his name, but no sound came out. Then the pain came back, the agony, like a herd of elephants stampeding across her skull, pulverizing her bones into dust one after the other. *Blake, I'm here! Don't leave!*

She passed out.

Frank Dorrien was in the room.

Tracy couldn't see him. She couldn't see anything. She couldn't move, or speak, or do anything except breathe. And listen.

"Who's her next of kin?" the doctor was asking.

General Dorrien's voice. "She doesn't have one."

"Is there no one we can notify? A friend?"

"No. We'll take care of it."

"But there must be . . ."

Frank's voice again, more hard-edged this time. "There isn't. Come on, Doctor. Let's be honest. We both know she isn't going to wake up. So it's all a moot point anyway."

Tracy thought, *I'm not going to wake up.*

Profound peace overwhelmed her.

She would be with Nick at last.

"Wake up!"

Someone was shaking her. Shining a light in her eyes.

She'd been having the most wonderful dream. She and Nick were playing chess, back in the kitchen at Steamboat. Blake wasn't there—he'd gone out riding— but Jeff was, whispering in Nick's ear, teaching him how to cheat, or at least how to outsmart his mother.

They were both laughing. Tracy didn't approve but she was laughing too.

Until Althea walked in, her long dark hair billowing behind her, her face a mask of death. Sitting down at the table, she swept away the chess pieces. Tracy watched, frozen, as they clattered to the floor. Something was wrong. Terribly wrong.

"I hate chess. Let's play poker."

And then the kitchen was gone, Nick too, and they were at a table in a casino—the Bellagio?—and Hunter Drexel was dealing. But the cards weren't playing cards, they were Tarot cards, and Tracy turned over the Lovers and Althea looked at Jeff and started laughing and laughing and then Hunter Drexel grabbed Tracy by the shoulders and shouted:

"WAKE UP! Look at the light! The truth's right in front of you, Tracy! Wake up!"

Tracy opened her eyes.

Loving, familiar eyes stared back at her.

"It's you!" she smiled.

And sank back into the darkness.

It was the longest night of Cameron Crewe's life. Longer, even, than the night he lost Marcus. He'd been numb then, too shocked to process fully what was happening. He remembered Charlotte sitting beside him at Marcus's bedside, the two of them holding hands. If someone had taken a photograph then and given it a title, they would probably have called it *United in Grief.* Except, of course, that grief didn't unite anything. All it did was destroy. Dismantle. Unravel.

Cameron Crewe hadn't known that then but he knew it now, watching Tracy fight for her life. Seeing her struggle up into the light, only to lose her footing and tumble back down, helpless, into the darkness.

It was Greg Walton who called him, a full twenty-four hours after Tracy was attacked. Cameron was furious.

"Why the hell didn't anyone contact me sooner?"

"We didn't know ourselves," Greg Walton insisted. "Agent Buck's in Paris but the FBI have been running their own investigation, separate from what Tracy's been doing for us. It was the Brits who alerted us. MI6."

"General Dorrien?" Cameron practically spat out the name.

"Yes." Walton sounded surprised. "Do you two know each other?"

"No. But Tracy knows him. And she doesn't trust him an inch."

"The British think it may have been Hunter Drexel

who attacked her. Despite my express instructions it appears Tracy's been trying to track Drexel alone, off-book. You wouldn't know anything about *that*, I suppose?"

But Cameron wasn't interested in CIA guessing games. Instead he flew his G650 directly into Le Bourget airport, making it from his New York apartment to Tracy's bedside in under ten hours. Once there, he pulled every string in the book to make sure that Frank Dorrien and any other intelligence officers were refused all further access. Luckily Don Peters, the new U.S. ambassador to France, was a close personal friend. So was Guillaume Henri, the hospital's largest donor.

"Tracy Whitney's a friend of mine. I'm the closest thing she has to family," Cameron insisted to Guillaume. "Nobody sees her but me."

"Your wish is my command, old friend. She must be quite a woman."

"She is," Cameron said.

Within hours of his arrival, Tracy had opened her eyes and spoken for the first time.

"It's you!" she said when she saw him. And then she smiled, that bewitching, sad, intelligent smile that danced on her lips but always started with her moss-green eyes. The smile that had conquered Cameron Crewe from the very beginning.

But seconds later the smile had faded and Tracy's eyes had closed once again.

That was two days ago.

Now, according to Greg Walton, Jeff Stevens was on his way. The British government was up in arms, demanding to be allowed to see Tracy and assess her condition.

"They're pissed. MI6 are saying she's compromised their operation against Drexel, that it's our fault for failing to control her. And they want *your* head on a plate."

"Too bad."

"They're claiming Stevens is her next of kin," Greg Walton said. "If that's true you won't be able to stop him seeing her. And he'll bring Frank Dorrien and anyone else Dorrien wants in with him."

Cameron Crewe was distraught.

He couldn't let that happen. He had to get Tracy to wake up.

He'd been on the point of giving up when suddenly, in the early hours of this morning, he'd woken suddenly in the chair by Tracy's bed to hear her moaning loudly, asking for water and complaining about her head. She'd been confused at first. Delirious. But within a few short hours she was sitting up, sipping sweetened tea and holding his hand, talking to him quite normally.

"Do you know what happened to you?" Cameron asked her. "Do you remember anything?"

Tracy looked away guiltily.

"I know you had dinner with Jeff Stevens," Cameron said. "It's OK."

He was trying to reassure her, but Tracy's eyes instantly narrowed with suspicion.

"How do you know?"

"Greg Walton mentioned it," Cameron said, a little too breezily. The last thing he wanted was to alienate Tracy now. He'd let her out of his sight once, against his better judgment, and he was in no hurry to repeat the experience. "Do you have any idea who did this to you?" he asked, changing tack.

Tracy shook her head. "Do you?"

"I have a couple of theories."

"Shoot."

"You won't like them."

"Try me."

"OK. Jeff Stevens."

"Jeff?" Tracy started to laugh, but it made her head hurt. "That's ridiculous."

"Is it?" Cameron looked at her intently. "I don't see why. He knew where you were. It would have been the easiest thing in the world for him to follow you that night. He'd already pumped you for information over dinner. Found out what his paymasters wanted to know. He didn't need you anymore."

"Jeff would never hurt me." Tracy was unequivocal.

"Are you sure? What if he felt he'd told you too much that night at dinner? What if he regretted it? Maybe he was scared?"

Tracy shook her head. "You're way off base."

But Cameron wasn't giving up. "Maybe he was jealous. Angry. Lashing out in a blind fit of rage."

"About what?"

"You and me," Cameron said. "Being together. That can't be easy for him."

Tracy blushed scarlet. She wanted to say, *We're not together! Who said we were together?* But this didn't feel like the right time. Besides which, she really didn't know what her romantic feelings were at this moment, for Cameron, or Jeff, or anyone.

"You told me yourself he has a temper," Cameron went on. "It makes sense, Tracy."

"It doesn't. Move on. What's your other theory?"

"General Frank Dorrien."

Tracy's ears pricked up. "Go on."

Cameron outlined his theory. Like Jeff, Dorrien knew where Tracy had been that night and could easily have followed her after dinner. Perhaps he knew about the harddrive Tracy had stolen from his house in

England, the evidence tying him to Prince Achileas's death? That alone would be motive enough for him to try to kill her. He'd made no secret of his dislike of Tracy from the beginning. Now, according to Greg Walton, Dorrien's MI6 bosses were equally displeased with her efforts to corner Hunter Drexel privately, not to mention her failure to make progress on Althea.

"No one in Whitehall would be crying into their Earl Grey tea if you met an untimely end, Tracy," Cameron said bluntly. "They want to catch Drexel first. They want the glory. That's why they brought Jeff Stevens in in the first place, to cut you off at the knees."

Tracy thought, *It's possible. Jeff basically admitted as much over dinner.*

"What if Dorrien saw his chance and he took it?" Cameron warmed to his theme. "But he screwed up. You didn't die right away. There was a witness. So he swoops in as a 'bystander,' has you brought here, controls all access to you. He didn't even tell the CIA you'd been attacked until a day and a half after the fact. That doesn't strike you as suspicious?"

The problem was, everything struck Tracy as suspicious. She was more than prepared to believe that Frank Dorrien had attacked her. She knew for a fact he was capable of it, especially if he felt impelled by some warped sense of duty. Or even just to save his own skin. And yet something was niggling at her. Something that didn't quite ring true.

"What about Hunter Drexel?" she asked Cameron.

"What about him?"

"He could have attacked me. If he thought I was close to finding him. Close to finding out the truth."

"It's possible, I suppose." Cameron sounded unconvinced.

"Or Althea?" Tracy mused.

"No. That makes no sense. Why would she go to so much trouble to get you involved in this in the first place if all she wanted was to kill you? Besides, the witnesses described a man."

"It was dark. A tall woman with her hair up could easily look like a man."

Cameron shook his head. "I think it was the British, Tracy. Either Dorrien or Stevens. They're on the same team now, after all. And it's not our team. All this talk of 'cooperation,' it's total bullshit."

That much Tracy agreed with. "I know."

She squeezed Cameron's hand.

"You can't trust Jeff Stevens, Tracy."

"I know that too. I was planning on working with him, not trusting him."

Cameron looked confused.

"Jeff would never hurt me," Tracy explained. "But

if he sees finding Hunter and Althea as a competition between us—and I think he does—then he'll stop at nothing to win."

"So why work with him?"

Tracy smiled weakly. "Because I'll stop at nothing to win, either. And I usually do. In the end."

They talked for a few more minutes. Then Tracy started to feel tired. Kissing her tenderly on the top of her head, above the bandages, Cameron left, double-checking on his way out that no one was to be allowed past security.

Heading back to his hotel, Cameron couldn't help smiling to himself, thinking about the first time Tracy had woken up.

"The way you smiled at me," he told her today. "The look in your eyes when you said 'it's you.' I can't tell you what that meant to me."

Tracy had been affected by it too. "I don't remember," she told him. But her blushes told a different story.

She loves me, Cameron thought. *She's too scared to admit it yet. But she does.*

After Cameron left, Tracy stared at the ceiling above her bed for a long time.

Stop feeling guilty, she told herself sternly. *It's ridiculous to feel guilty.*

You can't control your dreams, Tracy.

No one can.

She did remember smiling. She remembered looking into those loving, familiar eyes and saying "it's you!" and feeling profoundly happy.

But the eyes weren't Cameron's.

They were Jeff's.

And yet Jeff hadn't visited her in the hospital. Cameron had.

Jeff hadn't checked up on her and flown thousands of miles to keep a constant vigil by her bedside.

Cameron had.

What Cameron offered her was something real. Something she could touch and hold on to and rely on. Something she could trust.

Jeff, on the other hand . . .

Jeff was just a beautiful dream.

Jeff landed at Charles de Gaulle red-eyed and exhausted. He'd had to change planes in New York, but he barely remembered being at JFK. Everything that had happened since Frank Dorrien called him was a blur.

Getting to Tracy. That was all that mattered now.

The rest of the world had faded to gray.

"Jeff."

Frank Dorrien was waiting as soon as Jeff stepped into the arrivals hall. Clean-shaven, apparently well rested, and sporting his usual civilian uniform of dark blue corduroy trousers, a perfectly pressed cotton shirt, tweed sports jacket and brogues, the General was like a creature from another planet.

"How is she?" Jeff blurted, pushing past him. "I have to get to the hospital."

Frank Dorrien grabbed his arm. "She's not there." Seeing Jeff's eyes widen in horror, he quickly explained, "She's not dead. Don't worry. About an hour after I spoke to you, she woke up."

Jeff felt his knees begin to buckle beneath him. The relief was so overpowering, he thought he might be sick.

"I have to see her."

Frank said stiffly, "I'm afraid that's not possible."

Jeff turned on him. "What are you talking about?" Shrugging off the general's hand he began walking towards the taxi rank. The general followed.

"This isn't my doing," he told Jeff. "If you want to blame someone, blame Cameron Crewe."

The mention of Crewe's name stopped Jeff in his tracks.

Frank explained that Cameron had flown in to

see Tracy and promptly banned everyone from her bedside. That Tracy had been voluntarily released into his charge and was now recuperating at one of Cameron's countless luxury properties, about an hour south of Paris.

"When you have as much money as Cameron Crewe, you can buy doctors, politicians, whomever you want," Frank observed bitterly. "Normal rules don't apply."

"I still need to see Tracy."

Jeff told Frank what he'd learned in Colorado. The general's eyes widened.

"Good God. Are you sure?"

"Quite sure."

"You still have the footage?"

"Oh yeah. I have it. I have copies of it too. All in very safe places."

The two men stood in silence for a while. Rushing travelers surged and jostled around them, like water in a stream gushing past two large rocks. At last Frank spoke.

"Don't tell her yet."

Jeff looked shocked. "What do you mean? I have to tell her. She has a right to know."

"And she will know. Just not right now."

Jeff opened his mouth to protest but Frank cut him off.

"Think about it. You don't know how news like that might affect her. She's only just emerged from a coma, Jeff."

Jeff hesitated. He hadn't thought about it that way.

"She's safe right now. Crewe's taking care of her."

That's what I'm afraid of.

"Let her rest. And while she's out of action . . ." Reaching into his jacket pocket he pulled out a brown manila envelope, smiling broadly, and handed it to Jeff. "*You* can go to Belgium and bring back Hunter Drexel."

Frank was clearly delighted that Tracy had been sidelined. The Americans were out of the running.

Jeff stared at the envelope. "What's this?"

"Your ticket to Bruges. Drexel's expected at a poker game there this Saturday. Playing under the name Harry Graham."

Harry Graham . . . why does that ring a bell?

"It's a stunning city," said Frank.

"I know."

Jeff and Tracy had pulled off a wonderful job in Bruges once, conning a vile wife beater out of one of the finest collections of Dutch miniatures in Northern Europe.

"Your train leaves in an hour," Frank said brusquely. "I'll ride to Gare du Nord with you and brief you on the way."

Chapter 24

Luc Charles's Saturday night poker games were legendary among the Bruges fine art community. At Charles's idyllic fifteenth-century converted monastery overlooking the Spinolerai Canal, the game was always seven card stud. Despite the fact Charles himself invariably came out on top—the self-made collector and owner of the most valuable collection of Dutch impressionists still in private hands was not a man who liked to lose—invitations to Luc Charles's poker night were much prized. To be offered a seat at Luc Charles's infamous baize-topped card table, rumored to have once belonged to Queen Marie Antoinette of France, and to sit beneath the Vermeers and the Rembrandts and the Hedas was to have reached the very pinnacle of Belgian society. Charles's money might be new—Luc's father was a baker from a Brussels suburb—but his home and art collection were old and grand enough to make even the snobbiest aristocrat's eyes water with envy, and their pupils dilate with longing. Fortunes were made and lost at Luc Charles's poker table, and the host was always happy to accept a painting in lieu of cash. At his own valuation, of course.

Tonight's players were a mixture of regulars and newcomers. Pierre Gassin, senior partner at Gassin Courreges, the most prestigious law firm in Brussels, was a familiar face, as was Dominique Crecy, the great modernist collector. Johnny Cray, an American trust fund baby on a tour of a place he pronounced "Yurrup," was a newbie. So was his friend, Harry Graham.

Graham was older, very thin, with badly dyed hair and a withdrawn, slightly moody manner.

"He looks ill," Luc Charles told Johnny Cray, pulling the young man aside. "His skin's positively yellow. Does he have blood poisoning?"

"No idea," said Johnny. "I only met him a week ago, at a small game in the country. He begged me to bring him tonight. I hope that's OK?"

Luc Charles grinned wolfishly. "It is if he loses."

"Oh, he will." Johnny's smile grew so wide it looked as if it were going to eat the rest of his face. "I've never seen a more reckless player."

"Reckless?"

"Like he's possessed. It's bizarre. With an average hand, he plays brilliant, thoughtful poker. But as soon as he thinks he's holding a winner? Boom!" Johnny made an explosion gesture with his fingers. "He loses it. I took fifteen thousand euros off him last week and that was at a tiny game. I heard he lost big at Deauville."

"How big?" Luc Charles's mouth started to water.

"Seven figures."

"In one night?"

"Fuck one night. On one *hand*," said Johnny.

Luc Charles walked back to where Harry Graham was admiring one of his portraits.

"Are you an art lover, Mr. Graham?"

The American shrugged. "I know what I like."

"A wonderful starting point," Luc smiled. Looking more closely at Harry, he asked, "We haven't met before, have we? I feel as if I know you from somewhere."

Unfortunately for Luc Charles, he'd been meeting a lot of Americans lately. Group 99, the tiresomely publicity-hungry rich-haters-cum-terrorists had been making a concerted effort to target the fine-art world, introducing a number of extremely high-quality fakes to the market in recent months. Even the top auction houses had been duped, including the mighty Christie's, who had sold what they believed to be an Isaac Israels painting for $7.2 million only to have Group 99 release a YouTube video revealing its true provenance. Heads had rolled, but the net result was that market confidence had been hit hard and insurers were particularly jumpy. Luc's insurers were owned by the American giant UIG (United Insurance Group). In the last month alone, Luc had received three "courtesy" visits from UIG execs. It wouldn't surprise him to have another show up at one of his poker games, hoping for some sort of inside track. And Harry Graham *did* look familiar.

"I don't think so." Graham turned away, glancing at his watch impatiently. "Shall we get started?"

"Certainly."

Luc Charles led the way to the card table. He was probably imagining things. The good news was that Johnny Cray's "reckless" friend was getting jumpy already.

That boded well for the night ahead.

From his hotel bedroom directly across the canal, Jeff Stevens had an almost perfect view through the sash windows of Luc Charles's drawing room.

With the aid of his trusty Meade ACF LX90 telescope, Jeff could see not only the players at Charles's table, but the hands of the ones with their backs to him. Poor old Dom Crecy was unlikely to leave the Charles residence tonight richer than he arrived, clinging on to his pair of kings like a drowning man clutching a branch in a tsunami. Jeff couldn't see Hunter Drexel's cards, but he had an excellent view of his face. Harry Graham, rather to Jeff's surprise, had chosen a seat directly opposite the window, which had been opened to let in the night air. It was the first time Jeff had seen Hunter's features in person, in the flesh as it were, and he found himself fascinated, trying to glean any information from his expressions, the look in his eyes.

Who are you? he found himself asking.

What are you thinking, right at this moment?

What do you want?

But like all good poker players, Hunter's face gave away nothing. Was he a terrorist or a victim? A good guy or a traitor? Was he really just playing cards to live, so he had enough cash to eat and hide and finish his story on fracking—or whatever it really was? Jeff had his doubts. If Hunter's plan was survival, he wouldn't be chasing down big stakes games like Luc Charles's seven card stud, or Pascal Cauchin's legendary Montmartre poker evenings.

No. There's some other reason he's doing this. Playing with billionaires. Risking exposure. No one needs to win millions of dollars just to survive.

Whatever Hunter's plan, he looked as if he were struggling tonight. And not just at cards. His face was almost unrecognizable from the pictures Jeff had seen from before his Group 99 abduction. Hunter looked thin and ill and exhausted and old.

Jeff kept watching.

Back at the modest bungalow they had rented on the outskirts of the city, Sally Faiers glanced anxiously at the clock.

She wanted Hunter home.

She had a bad feeling about tonight.

It didn't help that, even after everything she'd done for him, all the risks she'd taken, Hunter told her nothing. Like who Hélène was and why she'd left in such a hurry. Or why he had to go to this poker game tonight. Or what he planned to do with the money, assuming he won.

"I will win," he told her, through chattering teeth. It was a flash of the old Hunter, the cocky charmer she remembered. But a rare one. And he didn't look like a winner anymore. He looked like a desperate man, in need of a real doctor.

After two weeks together, Sally still didn't even know what Hunter's mysterious article was about, or where and when he was going to publish it.

"Soon," was all he'd tell her. "The less you know, the safer you are, Sal."

But Sally didn't feel safe. As she dressed Hunter's

wounds, tended his fevers and pumped him up with the illegal antibiotics she'd bought online, she felt further and further removed from reality. From the normal world she'd left behind in London. Her flat. Her job.

Ex-job.

All she had left was her own article, her own secrets. She tried to focus on writing, while Hunter was running around the city doing God knows what, but it was hard. Right now Sally couldn't imagine how today would end, never mind make any sort of plan for the future. Somehow her exposé of corruption in the fracking business no longer seemed as important and earth shattering as it had when it started. She felt isolated and riddled with doubt.

Even Tracy Whitney had stopped calling. It was as if Sally and Hunter were on a boat with no power, drifting deeper and deeper out to sea. Hunter claimed to know where they were going. But all Sally could do was sit and wait for them to sink, or starve, or go insane out here all alone.

A knock on the door made her leap out of her skin. Darting into the bedroom, Sally reached under the bed with shaking hands and grabbed Hunter's gun. Images of Bob Daley's head being blown apart rushed, unbidden, into her mind.

Flattening her back to the wall, she edged back

into the living room, towards the door. Adrenaline coursed through her body. She was ready to shoot when she suddenly caught a glimpse of who it was on the doorstep:

Monsieur Hanneau, their sweet, bookish next-door neighbor.

For God's sake. Feeling foolish and ridiculous, Sally slipped the gun under a cushion and opened the door. He probably wanted to borrow a cup of sugar or something. This was Belgium, not bloody Beirut.

"Hello, Monsieur Hanneau. I was just . . ."

The bullet was silent, but it blew a hole in Sally's chest the size of a grapefruit.

She was dead before she hit the floor.

Harry Graham lost the first two games. He won modestly in the third and grotesquely overplayed his hand on the fourth, ending up down several hundred thousand euros.

Luc Charles thought, *Reckless doesn't begin to cover it.* This fellow Graham clearly had money to burn.

At nine o'clock they broke for a meal—fat, juicy mussels in white wine and garlic, washed down with a local Belgian beer. Harry Graham barely touched his food. Understandable, given how much money he'd just lost, although Luc Charles got the unsettling impression that losing didn't seem to mean that much to Mr. Graham.

It's not the winning, Luc decided. *It's the playing. The high stakes. The risk. As long as his adrenaline's up, that's all that matters.*

"One more hand, Mr. Graham?" Charles asked, as a butler cleared away the plates.

It was a rhetorical question, but the American answered anyway, nodding brusquely.

"Of course. Always."

Forty minutes later, a murderous Luc Charles watched from the window as his guests took their leave. Pierre Gassin and Dom Crecy both left by car, their chauffeur driven Bentleys arriving discreetly at the side entrance to the monastery. Johnny Cray drove off in his own, matte-black limited-edition Lamborghini.

Cray's friend Harry Graham, the night's big winner, hopped into a water taxi. Luc watched his skinny, blond head get smaller and smaller before fading to black completely as the boat drifted down the canal, swallowed by the night.

In Harry Graham's pocket was a check made out to cash.

It was for 850,000 euros.

He played me, Luc Charles thought darkly. *The bastard played me.*

Luc never made bets above his personal limit of a hundred thousand per hand. Never. Yet somehow this silent stranger had lured him into it.

Johnny Cray had described Harry Graham as reckless. But the truth was, Harry had made Luc Charles reckless.

He made me a damn fool.

Luc Charles didn't know much about Harry Graham. But he intended to find out more.

A lot more.

As soon as Graham's boat was out of sight, Luc Charles picked up the phone.

Jeff Stevens's boat drifted quietly a few yards behind Hunter's.

Jeff's hotel kept two old-fashioned, gondola-style canal boats with long punts that were available to guests day or night. They employed three old men whose sole job it was to slide the wooden poles into the water and gently propel these vessels along Bruges's famous waterways.

It was quiet tonight. Jeff was the boatman's only customer, and even he didn't go far, asking to be let out after only a few bridges had passed. Hunter had stepped out at one of the many mooring spots along the Spinolerai into a barely lit cobbled street. Just managing to catch him before he disappeared from view, Jeff followed him towards Steenstraat. Drexel glanced around him briefly, but didn't seem to notice anything untoward. He turned right into the pretty cobbled square of Simon Stevinplein, then left into Oude Burg, where small crowds of tourists were still milling around, even at this late hour. Bruges's famous Belfry was lit from below, giving it a quasimagical glow that made the surrounding gabled houses even more fairy-tale-like than they were by day.

It's like Disneyland, Jeff thought, taking care not to lose Hunter as he weaved through the crowds on Breidelstraat, past the lace and biscuit shops, before coming to a stop outside a bar in Burg Square. Wedged next to the magnificent Gothic Basilica of the Holy Blood, Gerta's was the kind of hole-in-the-wall sliver of a place you could find in any European city, a haven for thirsty tourists. After one last glance around, Hunter slipped inside.

The bar backed directly on to the Basilica wall. That meant there was no way out, other than the way in.

I could take him right now, Jeff thought. *End this thing.*

But both Frank Dorrien and Jamie MacIntosh had been clear about his brief:

Follow. Gather intel. Do not confront.

The problem was that its frontage was so small, it was impossible for Jeff to see anything without either standing right by the window or actually going inside. Pulling his baseball cap lower over his face, he decided on the latter. As far as he knew Hunter didn't know who he was, still less what he looked like.

Jeff made straight for the bar and ordered a whisky. Only once the drink was in his hand did he look up.

Drexel was sitting at a table in the corner. He was with a woman. From the corner of his eye, Jeff could see that she was a brunette, somewhere in her thirties. She was attractive and well dressed, expensively dressed, in cream wide-leg pants and a gossamer-thin cashmere sweater. She wore a classic gold chain at her neck, and diamonds on her fingers, which she was jabbing accusingly at Hunter.

"Take it," he was saying, pushing something in the woman's direction. Without turning around and looking directly it was hard for Jeff to make out what it was, but eventually he realized it was a check. *Harry Graham's winnings.*

"I don't want it. I don't need it!" She was angry. Upset. "Do you think I came here for money?"

"I didn't say that." Hunter's tone was conciliatory.

"This was never about the money. Never!"

To Jeff's dismay, someone behind the bar turned up the music. He could no longer hear what the two of them were saying. Even worse, right at that crucial moment his phone rang, so loudly that both Drexel and the woman turned and stared at him.

Turning his face away, Jeff left a note for the barman and hurried back out into the street. To take the call. Only two people had this number. One was Tracy.

But it wasn't her.

"What the hell?" Jeff barked at Frank Dorrien. "I had Drexel sitting five feet away from me! Why are you calling?"

"Where are you?"

"In a bar. He's meeting a woman."

"A girlfriend?"

"I don't know. Could be. They seem close. He tried to give her money but she wouldn't take it. It could be Althea, Frank. I need to get back in there. They were talking . . ."

"Did he go to the bar straight from the game?"

Frank's tone sounded urgent.

"Yeah. Why?"

"And you had eyes on him the whole time?"

"Since he got to the Charles house, yes. What is it, Frank?"

"Sally Faiers is dead. Someone blew a hole in her torso the size of a rugby ball. About two hours ago."

Jeff exhaled slowly. Tracy had liked Sally.

"Jesus."

"I doubt he had much to do with it. Our guys are over there now, cleaning up. We can't have the Belgian police getting mixed up in this."

"Hold on," said Jeff. "How did you know? Was someone watching the bungalow? I thought you said I was alone here."

"Never mind that," Frank said dismissively. "Are they still in the bar?"

"Yes. I . . . shit. They're coming out."

Wordlessly, Jeff slipped the phone into his pocket without hanging up and stepped back into the shadow of the Basilica.

"Stay away from me!" The woman was crying. "You're a liar!"

"No, I'm not. I know what happened to Daniel. I *know*, Kate."

"I mean it. Stay away!"

With a sob, she physically pushed Hunter backwards, so hard that he slammed against the wall just feet from where Jeff was standing, frozen like a statue. Then she took off into the night like a gazelle, her long hair flying behind her

"Kate!" Hunter yelled after her, giving chase. "Come back! Kate!"

Jeff pulled out his phone the instant Hunter took off.

"Did you hear that?" he asked Frank Dorrien.

"Every word."

"What should I do?"

Frank hesitated for a second. Then he said "Forget Drexel. Follow the girl."

Chapter 25

"Are you sure you won't ride with me to the airport?"

Cameron was standing by his chauffeur-driven Mercedes in the driveway of his French château. Tracy had come outside to see him off.

"Or better yet, come to New York?"

"Soon, I promise." She kissed him. "I have a few loose ends to tie up here first."

After five days spent recuperating in Cameron's mansion outside Paris, sleeping, reading and generally being waited on hand and foot, Tracy felt better. Better, and bored, and itching to get back to the job of finding Althea and Hunter before Jeff stole too much of a march on her.

Greg Walton had visited her in person yesterday. Cameron had been persuaded, reluctantly, to let him in. What he had to say was disturbing, to say the least.

"We now know for a fact that Hunter Drexel visited Camp Paris on no less than four occasions in the days leading up to the shooting. Multiple witnesses place him there. He was posing as a theater producer by the name of Lex Brightman, and had offered jobs to some of the students. Including Jack Charlston."

"Richard Charlston's son."

"Exactly. Heir to Brecon Natural Resources and the first victim to be shot, after the poor teacher in the parking lot. There's no good reason for Drexel to be there, Tracy," Greg said grimly. "None that I can think of anyway."

"No," Tracy murmured. "Me neither."

"Tell me about Montmartre," said Greg. It was such a non sequitur, it caught Tracy completely by surprise. Which presumably had been his intention. "You were there, weren't you? When the shots went off."

"I'm guessing you know I was," said Tracy.

"Did Hunter show up at the poker game?"

"No. But he was expected. And he was still using the Lex Brightman persona. Obviously I wasn't the only person who knew that. Whoever was on that motorbike was there for him."

"Who told you that?" the CIA chief asked archly. "Jeff Stevens?"

Tracy sighed. There didn't seem much point in denying it now.

"How about we're honest with each other, Tracy. I know I can't trust the British. But I need to trust you."

"Fine," Tracy replied. "As long as it works both ways."

Greg grinned, and Tracy remembered what it was she'd liked about him in the first place. "I'll show you mine if you show me yours."

So Tracy filled Greg in on her conversation with Jeff, minus his unfounded suspicions about Cameron, and their private words about their son.

"MI6 have pictures of Hunter with a young French student. He may have been shot in the leg and this girl was helping him. They think he was heading for Belgium. That was the last I heard before . . ." She touched her head where her hair covered the stitches.

"Well, let me update you," Greg said. He wasn't grinning any-more. "The girl, Hélène Faubourg, is dead."

Tracy looked aghast. "How?"

"Poisoned, apparently. Her sister found the body, still slumped over a bowl of ramen noodles. She'd ingested enough polonium to kill an ox."

"Do we know who . . . ?"

"We never know who," Walton said darkly. "All we know is, you meet Hunter Drexel, you die. He did go to Belgium, by the way. Sally Faiers met him there. Drove him to Bruges."

"How is Sally?" Tracy brightened. "Is she talking to you directly now?"

"No. She's dead too."

Tracy listened horrified as Greg gave her the details.

"Someone went in before the police could get there. Cleaned the place up so there were no prints, no nothing. Except Faiers's corpse."

"Don't." Tracy winced. Somehow Sally's death made this whole nightmare much more personal. "What about Hunter?"

"Evaporated," Greg said. "We had a team on him. But the guy's slipperier than an eel in a vat of oil. We think he's left Belgium. At any rate he never went back to the bungalow again, where he and Faiers were staying."

Tracy processed all this in silence.

"Why was Agent Buck so anxious to keep me out of the hunt for Drexel?" she asked Greg Walton directly. "Every time I asked him anything, he shut me down."

"Because it was dangerous," Greg said simply. "When I brought you into this the idea was for you to track Althea via her computer trail. I wanted you safe on the other side of a screen. Not out in the field in harm's way."

"You sent me to Geneva, Greg," Tracy reminded him.

"I know. And maybe I shouldn't have. But this is different. Hunter Drexel is a dangerous man, Tracy," Walton said. "He's not who he seems to be. We think he's been part of Group 99 from the beginning."

"It's possible," Tracy admitted.

"More than possible. We believe he faked his own kidnapping to get Group 99 national attention. In our view he was complicit in Bob Daley's death—maybe he and Althea planned it together? We can't tie him to the Geneva bombing yet, but we will. We know he was at Neuilly. In all probability one of his 99 buddies killed Hélène Faubourg, a totally innocent student whose only crime was to try to help him. We think another executed Sally Faiers."

"Why?"

"My guess is that both those women knew too much. Saw through him, maybe, in the end."

Tracy rubbed her temples. She felt terribly tired all of a sudden.

"What do you need from me?"

"Number one, honesty. Whatever you learn from Stevens about Drexel, or anyone else, you share that intel with me or Agent Buck."

"Jeff hasn't contacted me since that night," Tracy said, unable to keep a note of disappointment out of her voice. Jeff must have known she'd been attacked. The British would have told him. Yet he'd made no attempt to visit her at the hospital, or afterwards. That hurt.

"He will," Greg said. "In the meantime, go back to Neuilly and any other contacts you have here in Paris who might be able to help us. Once the hysteria about the shootings dies down and the media moves on to the next story, my guess is Drexel will be back. I don't think he's done here."

It was a sobering thought.

Now that Cameron was leaving, Tracy could devote herself full-time to the hunt for Hunter Drexel. It wasn't only about Nick anymore, and what Hunter might be able to tell her about Althea. It was about Sally Faiers too. And Hélène Faubourg, and all the other people who'd lost their lives because they'd somehow gotten in Hunter Drexel's way.

Poor Sally. She loved Hunter the same way I loved Jeff.

The difference was, she trusted him.

Tracy wasn't about to make the same mistake.

"Promise me you'll get some rest. You won't push yourself too hard," Cameron said, closing the door of the car and leaning out of the window to say his goodbyes.

"I promise," said Tracy.

Uncrossing her fingers, she walked back into the house and began making calls.

Who do I know in Paris who might have seen Lex Brightman?

Where would a rich, gay, poker-playing New York theater producer hang out?

A few hours later, Tracy stopped by an old friend's jewelry boutique on the Left Bank.

Not that she thought Hunter would have been one of Guy de Lafayette's customers. But because Guy was *the* epicenter of Paris theater—land gossip, and the comings and goings of the left bank's rich and famous residents.

Tracy described Hunter to Guy.

"He may be going by the name Lex Brightman. Or Harry Graham, or any number of other pseudonyms. It's vital that I find him."

Guy said, "That's funny."

"What's funny?"

"Jeff said exactly the same thing to me a few days ago."

"Jeff?"

"Yes. He told me the pair of you are working together again. Something 'top secret.'" The old man gave a conspiratorial wink.

"Did he now?" said Tracy. *The sneaky little so-and-so. Back in Paris already and not so much as a call.*

"Oh, Tracy, darling, *do* tell me the two of you are back together again," Guy gushed. "I could die happy if that were the case, I really could."

Clasping his hands together, the diminutive jeweler hopped up and down like a small child in need of the bathroom and looked pleadingly at Tracy with his twinkling, impish eyes.

Tracy did not share his enthusiasm. "When was Jeff here?"

"He came to see me a few days ago, bless him. And my goodness he did look handsome! The man is ageless. You both are."

Tracy looked murderous.

Let's work together. It'll be just like the old days. So much for that baloney! Jeff was doing this on his own. Or worse, he was still acting as Frank Dorrien's lapdog. Well, two could play at that game.

Tracy felt a rush of righteous anger, conveniently forgetting that she, too, had sought out Guy on her own and had just agreed to report everything she learned back to the CIA.

The problem with using her old contacts to help Greg Walton was that they were Jeff's contacts too.

"So Jeff asked you for leads on the same man?"

"He did."

"And what did you tell him?"

"I sent him to Madame Dubonnet, of course." Guy smiled. "I understand your quarry is a gambler?"

"Among other things," Tracy said.

"Any serious poker players in Paris end up at Dubonnet's. Didn't Jeff mention it?"

Tracy said through gritted teeth, "It must have slipped his mind."

Madame Dubonnet was a toothless old hag who wore too much rouge, smelled of eau de violettes and Gitanes, and wore her blouse unbuttoned low enough to reveal a large expanse of crêpey cleavage. She had a deep, gravelly voice and a raucous laugh, and her gnarled, veiny hands were encrusted with diamonds as big as barnacles.

Despite her advanced years, however, she clearly considered herself to be sexually alluring. Tracy could instantly picture her being charmed by Jeff. And, no doubt, by the handsome Hunter Drexel, if Guy was right and he really had shown up here.

"Your friend told me you'd be coming." Madame Dubonnet talked down her long nose at Tracy. She was clearly not fond of the company of younger, more attractive women.

"My friend? You mean Guy?"

"Guy? Who is Guy? No! The American. Monsieur Bowers."

Mr. Bowers. Tracy smiled to herself. Jeff hadn't used that one in a long time.

"Lovely man." Madame Dubonnet's eyes positively glowed.

"When did Mr. Bowers stop by here, out of interest?" Tracy asked.

"None of your business," the old woman said tersely. "The point is that he warned me. 'She will come here asking questions about her lover,' he told me. And now you 'ave."

Tracy frowned. "My lover?"

"Bah, *oui!* Of course, your lover! Monsieur Graham. Not that you are 'is only girlfriend, of course. Any man rich enough to play at Albert Dumas's table keeps women like a beekeeper keeps bees. *Buzz buzz buzz.*"

Madame Dubonnet's wrinkled mouth puckered up grotesquely as she made the buzzing bee sound.

"Naturally I make no judgment," she added, looking at Tracy as a chef might look at a rat that had wandered into his kitchen. "But there are conventions here in Paris, even for the mistresses."

Tracy pieced things together. Jeff had guessed Tracy would go to Guy, and that eventually she would follow him here. So he'd pumped Madame Dubonnet for information on Hunter, then convinced the old hag that Tracy was some sort of bunny-boiling bit on the side, here to cause Harry Graham trouble.

"Madame," Tracy said firmly. "My friend Monsieur Bowers is mistaken. I am not Monsieur Graham's mistress. Or anyone else's mistress for that matter."

Ignoring Tracy's protests, Madame Dubonnet wagged an arthritic finger in her face, almost blinding Tracy with a five-carat sparkler.

"You know, Cherie, it is not a nice thing to try to *entrapper* a gentleman by threatening to go to his wife." Madame Dubonnet made a clucking sound with her tongue and shook her head from side to side, before pronouncing, "This, I do not approve of."

Tracy's eyes widened. *Boy, Jeff must have laid it on thick.*

"Madame. I assure you, you are mistaken. For one thing Monsieur Graham, as he calls himself, is no gentleman. For another, he has no wife. Although you may be right about the bee thing," she conceded, thinking back to what Sally Faiers had told her about Hunter's endless string of lovers. "In any case I am *not* his lover, as my 'friend' Mr. Bowers knows all too well. The truth is"—Tracy lowered her voice—"I'm working for American intelligence."

Madame Dubonnet smiled patronizingly. *"Vra-iment? Le CIA?"*

"That's right," said Tracy, relieved to have cleared up the misunderstanding. "I work for the CIA."

"And I am working for NASA, mademoiselle." The old lady cackled at her own joke. Then the lips pursed again for the last time. "As I said before, I do not discuss the private lives of my patrons. Marianne will see you out."

Jeff called Tracy just as she stepped out of Madame Dubonnet's apartment building onto the street.

"Darling! How's your head?"

Tracy exploded. "Don't 'darling' me. You told that old witch I was sleeping with Hunter Drexel!"

Jeff chuckled. "Ah, dear Madame Dubonnet. You've been to see her then?"

"Of course I have. You knew I would."

"Now don't be mad, angel. I didn't say you were sleeping with him. Not exactly."

"Well, whatever you said 'exactly' it was enough to get me kicked out of there. So what 'exactly' did she tell *you*? That you were so eager to hide from me?"

"Nothing!"

"Pull the other one, Jeff. I'm serious. She obviously

knew Hunter. She'd met him. What do you know? When was he last there?"

"I have no idea."

"You're lying."

"Tracy darling, what is the point of this conversation? If you refuse to believe a word I say?"

"Good point," Tracy said furiously, and hung up.

Jeff rang back immediately.

"I see you're fully recovered then?"

Tracy bit her lip. The urge to hang up on him again was almost overpowering, but she wanted to know what he knew.

"Yes, thanks. Nice of you to come visit me," she added caustically.

"I wanted to." Jeff sounded genuinely hurt.

"So why didn't you?"

"Something came up."

"Something always does," said Tracy bitterly.

"Hey, hold on," Jeff protested. "It doesn't help when your boyfriend guards the hospital like a Rottweiler and then spirits you off to his tower in the woods like bloody Rapunzel!"

Tracy took a deep breath and counted to three. "Where are you?"

Jeff told her.

"Meet me at l'Église Saint-Louis-des-Invalides in twenty minutes."

"l'Église les what now?" said Jeff.

"Just be there."

Little known to tourists, the church of Saint Louis nestled deep within the complex of Les Invalides, beneath its magnificent golden dome. Designed by architect Jules Hardouin-Mansart, the chapel was commissioned in the seventeenth century by Louis XIV as a sanctuary specifically for soldiers. Every stone, from its banner-hung walls to its crypt filled with the tombs of French generals, was steeped in military history. But this afternoon, like most afternoons, the church was almost deserted, with only a few quiet worshippers kneeling discretely in its pews or lighting candles of remembrance.

Jeff saw Tracy as soon as he arrived, kneeling alone in a side chapel. Making a sign of the cross he knelt down beside her and whispered in her ear.

"What are you praying for?"

"Strength," Tracy whispered back. "I tend to need it whenever you're around."

"How are you?" Jeff asked, ignoring the jibe.

"Fine."

"They told me you'd been in a coma."

Tracy thought, *And still you didn't come.* Out loud she said, "I'm fine, Jeff. We aren't here to talk about me. Where have you been?"

"Bruges."

Jeff had agreed to follow Frank Dorrien's advice and not tell Tracy about his trip to Steamboat. There would be time enough for that later.

"You saw Drexel?"

"Yes."

"And you know about Sally Faiers?"

Jeff shook his head grimly. "Yes."

A verger, busy polishing the tabernacle and the altar candle sticks, shot Jeff and Tracy a reproachful look. Jeff lowered his voice.

"Awful business."

"Any ideas who did it?"

"Well, it wasn't Hunter," Jeff whispered. "I was watching him when it happened. He won big at a poker game in the Old Town, then met up with a woman. Tracy, I'm pretty sure it was Althea."

Tracy's eyes widened. "Are you serious?"

Jeff described the woman Hunter had met and their interaction in as much detail as he could. "Your friend General Dorrien called to tell me about Sally's murder before I could hear any more. But I heard him call her 'Kate.' Twice."

Kate. A name. An actual name. It was the first time Althea had been anything more than a shadow. Not a lot to go on, perhaps. But it was something.

"They were fighting. If I didn't know better I'd have said it was a lovers' tiff. He was trying to give her money but she wouldn't accept it. She was upset when she left."

"You said you followed her?"

"Yes. Dorrien asked me to. But I lost her in one of the squares. The city's tiny but it's like a maze, especially at night."

"I remember," Tracy said. For a moment there was a flicker of warmth between them, a spark of shared nostalgia for another life. But it was soon gone.

"Your turn."

"I've got nothing to tell," Tracy said. "I've been recovering from a major head injury, remember? I've been off the case."

Jeff gave her a loving look. "You'll have to try that line with someone who doesn't know you, darling. You wouldn't have been to see Guy or Madame Dubonnet if you weren't working. And you wouldn't know about Sally Faiers either. So what's been going on?"

Tracy told him the CIA's latest theories. That Hunter Drexel was definitely involved in the Neuilly shootings. And that he probably had a hand in Sally's death as well. And Hélène's.

"I didn't know about the student. That's sad. . . ." Jeff frowned. But he seemed to hesitate.

"I'm sensing there's a but?"

"I don't know." He looked at Tracy intently. "Hunter's obviously involved with Group 99 somehow. He's not who he says he is."

"I agree."

"The Americans and the Brits both have him in the frame now. And they're probably right. But something doesn't add up."

"Right," Tracy whispered. "Like the fact that he didn't shoot Sally Faiers."

"Exactly."

"But Frank Dorrien knew she'd been killed within minutes."

Jeff nodded. "I thought about that. He could have been watching the house."

"In which case he'd have seen who did it. Yet no one was arrested."

"I thought about that too."

"But you still trust him?" Tracy looked deep into Jeff's eyes. Looking back at her, Jeff longed to tell her everything. It took every ounce of his willpower not to.

"You know me," he quipped. "I don't trust anyone. How about you?"

"I think Greg Walton's a good guy," said Tracy. She wasn't about to bring up Cameron's name again with Jeff. She'd learned her lesson last time. "I told him I'd pass on any intelligence you gave me, by the way. As we're being so 'open' with each other."

"Don't." Jeff said, more forcefully than he'd intended. "Whatever gets to Walton gets to Milton Buck," he explained, spitting out the FBI agent's name as if it were poison. "Never forget that, Tracy. Never."

Tracy was surprised. Jeff had as much reason to dislike Agent Buck as she did. After all, if Buck had had his way, Jeff would have been left to die at the hands of Daniel Cooper, nailed to a cross in a remote Bulgarian barn. Yet in the past it had always been Tracy who'd felt afraid of Milton Buck. Jeff had treated him almost as a joke.

Had something changed?

"I assume the British know about 'Kate'?" she asked, changing tack.

"Yes. I told Frank Dorrien everything I just told you. MI6 have been digging for a week, looking for any 'Kates' in Hunter's past."

"Have they found any?"

"A whole bunch. I'm telling you, Drexel makes Magic Johnson look like a Buddhist monk. But no one significant. Yet."

"All right," Tracy said, making another sign of the cross and standing up to leave. "I'll get on it."

Jeff put a hand on her arm. "Don't disappear on me, Tracy. I think Hunter came back to Paris because he's planning another attack of some kind. This 'story' nonsense is just a cover."

Tracy nodded. Hunter Drexel as the innocent, intrepid journalist was simply not believable anymore. Too many people had died.

"He's trying to get Kate, whoever she is, to help him. You mustn't get too close to this woman. If you raise her suspicions, you could be in very real danger."

"You think I don't know that? This time last week I was in a coma," Tracy reminded him. "I'm doing this for Nick, Jeff. That's the only reason."

Jeff watched as Tracy left the church, her head bowed, like any other anonymous war widow.

That's what she is, in a way, Jeff thought sadly. *Her life has been one long war. And she's lost so many people she loved.*

In that moment he felt utterly overpowered with love for her.

Even for Jeff Stevens, there were times when lies didn't come easily.

"Hi, you've reached Jeff. Leave a message."

Frank Dorrien was irritated. That was the third time today he'd failed to reach Stevens.

Frank was confident after Bruges that Stevens was back on board. That his tiresome maverick streak was under control. But that was before Jeff had met up with Tracy Whitney again.

Tracy had certainly been useful to Frank Dorrien, albeit unwittingly. Her connection to Stevens had provided MI6 with a huge advantage. But the intelligence she provided came at a price. When Tracy and Jeff got together, nothing was predictable. And the stakes couldn't be higher.

Frank Dorrien felt the first stirrings of real fear in the pit of his stomach, like sun-dazed butterflies slowly coming to life.

Glancing at his watch, Frank set off at a run towards Jeff's hotel.

"When did you last hear from Tracy?"

Milton Buck's entire upper body tensed with irritation and resentment. Who the hell did Cameron

Crewe think he was, interrupting him in the middle of an important meeting with French intelligence?

"I told you before. I can't talk now."

"I don't give a fuck what you told me, Agent Buck. I can't reach her and I want answers. Now!"

Arrogant asshole. I'm not one of your minion employees.

"I'll call you when I'm out of my meeting," Milton replied, through gritted teeth.

"Don't bother," Cameron snapped. "I'll take it up the food chain. God knows why I'm talking to the monkey anyway. We both know Walton's the organ grinder."

To Milton Buck's fury, he hung up.

Greg Walton was reassuring.

"I saw her two days ago. Everything's fine. I'm not expecting her to check in with us daily."

"Well, I am," Cameron Crewe said bluntly. The strain in his voice quivered down the phone line. "She always calls me back, usually within an hour. It's been a day and a night."

"She's working, Cameron. She's probably reestablishing ties with Jeff Stevens. That's what we asked her to do."

"That's what I'm worried about. Did you know she checked out of the Georges V?"

There was a long pause. "Are you sure about that?"

Cameron exploded. "My God, Greg. You're the CIA! You're supposed to be watching her."

"We'll find her," Greg Walton said. But all the confidence was gone now, like air from a pricked balloon. "I'll get my best team on it. Agent Buck . . ."

"Agent Buck is a goddamned moron," Cameron said furiously. "Forget it, Greg. You had your chance. I'll find her myself."

President Jim Havers spoke unnaturally slowly. As if by lingering over each word of the question, he could somehow postpone the answer.

"So you're telling me they're both gone?"

Prime Minister Julia Cabot replied tersely, "That's what my intelligence team is telling me."

"Whitney *and* Stevens."

"Yes."

"Together?"

"Apparently so."

"Shit."

A heavy silence descended between the two leaders. Julia Cabot broke it first.

"I don't suppose you feel like telling me what's going on, Jim?"

The president sounded angry. "What do you mean?"

"I mean who *is* Hunter Drexel?" The British Prime Minister spelled it out. "Who is he really?"

Jim Havers sighed heavily. "It's complicated, Julia."

"Uncomplicate it."

Another sigh.

"I can't."

"Well, that's a shame. Because I'd be prepared to wager good money that that's *exactly* what Whitney and Stevens are out there doing right now. And if they succeed, we'll *both* be hung out to dry."

Five minutes later, Greg Walton of the CIA and James MacIntosh of MI6 both received phone calls from their respective political masters.

The language each used was different.

But the message was the same.

Find them. Find them now. Or being fired will be the least of your worries.

Chapter 26

We will soon begin our descent into Geneva. Please fasten your seat belts and ensure any bags are stowed . . ."

Tracy zoned out as the chief flight attendant ran through the usual spiel. Sitting beside her in business class, Jeff was fast asleep. And by fast Tracy really meant fast—head thrown back, mouth open, snoring loudly as his chest rose and fell in the same steady rhythm it had been in since takeoff.

Tracy had taken countless flights with Jeff. Some were luxurious, sprawled out in sumptuous private jets. Others were markedly less so. But on every flight, without exception, Jeff had managed to fall asleep.

One memorable journey involved Tracy and Jeff having their limbs folded painfully into pallets of diamonds, like two double-jointed dolls. The pallets were then sealed with a small gap for air and wedged into a freezing cargo hold. For the next eight hours, neither of them could move a muscle. Simply breathing was difficult. And yet even on this flight from hell Jeff had somehow fallen asleep. His ability to switch himself off at will, like an electric toy, and slip into unconsciousness, was as impressive as it was infuriating.

Watching him now took Tracy straight back to the old days. Before all this madness. Before Nicholas. Before everything. With an effort she forced the memories out of her mind. She must stay in the present if she was to survive.

Today's flight was a point of no return. Tracy and Jeff were officially on their own now. They had boarded the Air France jet as Mr. and Mrs. Brian Crick, en route to their vacation in the pretty ski town of Megève. Annie Crick was a keen skier. Brian liked the mountains too. But he was there for the poker.

It was Jeff who came up with the theory. But with every day, Tracy liked it more.

Bursting into her hotel room in Paris, less than a day after their meeting at Les Invalides, he suddenly blurted out, "What if it isn't about the money?"

Tracy looked up wearily from her computer. For the last six hours she'd been painstakingly cross-referencing every Kate, Catherine or Kathleen who'd ever worked or slept with Hunter Drexel against databases from the CIA, MI6 and Interpol. Her eyes were crossing.

"What if what isn't about the money?"

"Poker. What if it's a cover for something else? What if the poker games are where he's meeting his conspirators? Where he's planning the next attacks?"

It was such an obvious question, Tracy couldn't quite believe she hadn't thought of it herself. That none of them had.

"All this time we've been assuming he's playing to win. So he could live off the cash, stay under the radar. But what if money has nothing to do with it?"

Tracy agreed to take a break from her fruitless hunt for Kate/Althea and to look into the other known players at Hunter Drexel's various games, in Romania, Latvia, France and Belgium.

There were some common threads. Most of the games were arranged by super-rich hosts like Pascal Cauchin or Luc Charles. Men who were absolutely on Group 99s target list. The energy sector, and in particular fracking, was well represented. So was fine art. Antoine de la Court, the dealer, had introduced

Hunter to Cauchin as Lex Brightman. Luc Charles was a legend in the fine-art world.

"Drexel could be using paintings to channel funds to or from Group 99," Jeff suggested. "We both know half the top dealers in Europe act as fences or money launderers."

"Look at this!" Tracy said excitedly.

A quick delve into Johnny Cray's background, the young American trustafarian who'd brought Hunter into the Bruges game, revealed a lengthy flirtation with radical leftwing causes. "Arrested at two antiglobalization rallies in the States. *Charged* over an alleged attempted bombing at Davos last year, at the economic forum!"

"What happened?" Jeff asked.

Tracy tapped away. "His parents got him off of that one. They donated like, thirty million dollars to some Swiss International Development slush fund."

She showed Jeff the numbers. Minimal further searching linked Johnny Cray's name to a slew of known Group 99 members and/or donors.

When Jeff learned a few days later that Cray was currently in Megève; and that he would be attending a high stakes poker game there at the chalet of Gustav Arendt, a local multimillionaire who'd made his fortune investing in African fracking ventures, he and Tracy booked their tickets.

"Wake up." Tracy tapped Jeff on the shoulder. "We're landing."

Jeff sat bolt upright, rubbed his eyes and smiled broadly.

"You look as lovely as ever, Mrs. Crick. Ready to hit the slopes?"

Tracy rolled her eyes. Jeff could make a game out of anything. But this was serious. The CIA or MI6 might catch up with them at any time. They'd risked everything on a hunch that Hunter Drexel would be at tomorrow night's game in Megève; *and* that somehow, between them, they could extract him from Arendt's chalet without bloodshed; *and* that when they did, Hunter would tell them the truth.

That was three very big ifs.

And it wasn't only Tracy's relationship with her CIA handlers that was on the line. She'd run out on Cameron Crewe too, checking out of the Georges V without leaving any message for him and destroying her old phone before she left Paris. She couldn't explain why, even to herself. Cameron had tried hard to take care of her. He'd even convinced her to take off with him to Hawaii, which was hugely out of character for Tracy. She'd wanted that at the time. Needed it, even. The idea of leaning on somebody else had been intoxicating. But that time had passed. Tracy was stronger now, and in any case she couldn't talk to Cameron while she was with Jeff. She just couldn't. Perhaps, once this was all over, there might be a way? A future for the two of them? But until then . . .

The plane's wheels hit the tarmac with a gentle bump.

"Welcome to Geneva."

With Jeff's insanely fast driving, it took them less than an hour on the Albertville-Chamonix motorway to cross the border back into France and arrive at Megève, an idyllic town in the French Alps, in the shadow of Mont Blanc.

Megève really comes to life in winter, when reliable snowfalls and a smattering of über luxurious boutique hotels make it the ski resort du choix for Parisians in the know. But it's breathtakingly beautiful in the spring too. Thanks to the glacier, late skiing is possible right into May.

Tracy was instantly charmed.

"Look at this place," she said to Jeff. "It's like a fairy tale."

Adorable, rustic wooden chalets and old stone buildings clustered around cobbled squares, their window boxes bursting with flowers. Surrounding the town, the green slopes of the Alps basked beneath blue skies, their tips still white and sparkling with a permanent cap of snow. Cafés spilled out onto pavements where diners—almost all of them French—ate warm, freshly baked bread and langoustines and sipped ice-cold Chablis in the sunshine.

The Cricks—Brian and Annie—were staying at Les Fermes de Mairie, a gorgeous, log-built mountain paradise and easily the smartest hotel in town.

"Look honey. They have an awesome spa. You want me to book us in for some treatments?"

Jeff was enjoying himself immensely as Brian Crick, the sort of loud, brash, vulgar American that set every French person's teeth on edge.

"That's OK." Tracy's Annie Crick was considerably more low-key. Her job was to be forgettable, a pale shadow of her larger-than-life, flamboyant husband. "I'm here to ski."

"Sure you are, sweetheart. Sure you are. And I'm here to make money! Ha ha ha!" Brian Crick laughed loudly enough for the entire lobby to hear him. "I'm in town to play poker up at Gustav Arendt's place," he told the receptionist. "I'll bet you know Gustav. Must be the richest guy in town, right?"

While the mortified receptionist checked them in, Tracy took a seat at the lobby bar. It was an old-fashioned affair, all brass and polished wood, behind which a vast picture window offered patrons a breathtaking view of the Alpine scenery. The mountains made Tracy think of Colorado, and of Nick, and Blake Carter. She realized with a pang of guilt that she almost never thought about Blake. Nick's death had used up every ounce of sorrow she had in her. But Blake had been a dear friend. Family really. Very few people had filled that role in Tracy's life.

Gunther Hartog.

Ernestine Littlechap, back at the penitentiary.

"You're friends of Monsieur Arendt?"

An Englishman had sat down beside Tracy and started talking. It took her a moment to remember where—and who—she was: *Annie Crick, loyally devoted wife of Brian Crick. A rich housewife from Ohio.*

"Not friends exactly. My husband knows him," she answered shyly. "He's come for the cards."

"Well, he's come to the wrong place if he wants to make money," the Englishman said, eyeing Tracy's enviable figure appreciatively. Even dressed down as Annie in a pair of wide-leg trousers and a taupe, high-necked blouse, she was easily the most attractive woman in the room. "Gustav Arendt's the richest man in Megève for a reason. He never loses."

Annie Crick laughed. "Everyone loses sometimes, Mr. . . . ?"

"Davies. Peter Davies."

They shook hands.

"Arendt doesn't. If your husband's smart he'll stay well away from that chalet tomorrow night."

The next day dawned bright and clear. Tracy spent the morning hiring skis and poles and organizing her lift pass. Jeff flitted around town as Brian Crick, buying watches and overpriced jewelry, flashing his money around, and generally having as many loud and obnoxious conversations as he could about poker, Gustav Arendt and his plans for the evening.

He met Tracy for lunch at a fondue restaurant up the mountain. It was deserted enough for Jeff to lower his voice and slip out of character for a moment.

"I'm exhausted," he grumbled.

"Shopped till you dropped, eh?" Tracy teased.

"I'm serious. Making yourself a target for Group 99's not as much fun as it sounds. I've spent half the morning shouting and the other half spending a fortune on crap I don't want."

"My heart bleeds."

"Plus I slept badly," Jeff added pointedly. Annie Crick had spent a very comfortable night in the couple's king-size bed. Brian had fared less well on the sofa. Not that it wasn't comfortable—Jeff had slept soundly on far worse—but lying so close to Tracy, unable to touch her or put his arms around her, was pure torture. He'd barely closed his eyes all night.

"Did you find out anything more?" Tracy asked.

Jeff nodded, taking a long sip of the cold beer he'd ordered.

"Firstly, your friend Peter was right. Gustav Arendt wins big, and often. So much so he rarely gets the same players up at the chalet twice. It's a case of once bitten twice shy. Rumor has it he has cameras hidden up there someplace, to spy on his opponents' hands."

"He cheats?"

Jeff shrugged. "Who knows? That's what they say. Secondly, I'm not sure if Drexel's gonna show tonight."

Tracy's face fell. "Why not?"

"I didn't say he isn't. I said I'm not sure. From what I hear, none of tonight's victims sound like our man. The players are supposed to be me; another rich energy guy, from Rome; our friend Johnny; and three others."

"Go on."

Jeff took another sip of beer. "One's a fine-art dealer from Geneva. Lars Berensen. Do you know him?"

Tracy shook her head. But it was interesting. Another art dealer couldn't be coincidence. Unless . . .

"Couldn't that be Drexel?"

"I don't think so," Jeff said. "Berensen's in his sixties, apparently. That's a stretch."

Tracy agreed. "What about the other two players?"

"A businessman named Ali Lassferly's expected. He's a possible—he doesn't exist on Google—although the guy I spoke to said he was French-Arabic."

"Drexel could pull that off," said Tracy.

"Maybe," Jeff conceded. "We'll know tonight I guess. I'm more interested in the last player."

"Who's he?"

"She. It's a woman. Apparently she's a widow living in St. Tropez. But she's American. And rich. You want to guess her name?"

The hairs on Tracy's arms stood on end. "Kate?"

Jeff leaned forward. "Close enough. Mrs. Catherine Clarke."

"Do you really think it could be her?"

"I don't know. But something's going down tonight. I'm sure of it."

"I should come with you," Tracy blurted.

"Absolutely not."

"It could be dangerous, Jeff."

"Exactly."

Tracy opened her mouth to protest but Jeff cut her off. "We have a plan. A good one. There's no reason to change it." Reaching into his jacket pocket he handed Tracy a new disposable phone. Just to be safe they were both changing handsets every few days.

"Keep it on. I'll call if I need you."

Gustav Arendt was in a foul mood. For three very good reasons.

Women.

Money.

And hemorrhoids.

Gustav's wife, Alisse, had found out last night about his mistress, Camille. Alisse was being tiresomely bourgeois about it, ranting and yelling, making unseemly comments about Camille's fake breasts and threatening divorce. Gustav couldn't understand it.

What do women expect when they marry a wealthy man? Monogamy?

Alisse's meltdown could not have come at a worse time. Gustav had already had a bad week, losing millions on a failed investment in the Ukraine. Land that he'd believed to be bursting at the seams with shale gas had actually produced pathetically meager returns. Gustav had fired his chief engineer, but that did little to stem his foul temper.

The hemorrhoids spoke for themselves.

The one bright spot in Gustav Arendt's otherwise black sky was the prospect of fleecing his guests at the poker game tonight. Looking out of the window at Chalet Mirabelle, he watched as the first of the players drove up.

There was Luca Androni, his fat, spaghetti-filled belly emerging first from his chauffeur-driven Range Rover.

Pig. Gustav Arendt disliked all his competitors in business, but he reserved a special loathing for Androni. It didn't help that, despite his obvious stupidity, the Italian had made out like a bandit in Ukraine. Luca Androni's shale gas fields directly abutted Gustav's, yet Androni had managed to extract millions of dollars from his land while Arendt's frenzied fracking had produced nothing more than a weak fart.

Gustav was going to enjoy relieving Luca of some of those millions tonight. Unlike Europe's increasingly indolent, lazy and grasping poor, he didn't need Group 99 to do his dirty work for him. Although, come to think of it, it surprised Gustav Arendt that a man like Luca Androni had *not* yet been targeted by Group 99. On paper, at least, he seemed like a perfect candidate for their loathsome brand of self-righteous communism. That was the problem with violent extremists. They were never there when you needed them.

The next player to arrive was Lars Berensen, swiftly followed by the ridiculous American fool Brian Crick. With his stooped shoulders, shuffling gait and bald crown, Berensen looked like an escapee from the local nursing home. But the art dealer was a lot sharper than his little-old-man shtick suggested. He had a painting under his arm tonight, to present to his client, Mrs. Clarke. No doubt the bitch had paid well over the odds for it. But that was Berensen's business. Gustav was not averse to his guests doing a little business up at Chalet Mirabelle, especially if they brought other rich stooges along to his poker table. Lars Berensen was responsible for inviting both the rich Widow Clarke and the Arab. Tonight, Lassferly. He'd earned his keep.

Brian Crick strode up to the chalet, talking loudly and clapping a hand across Luca Androni's meaty shoulders on the doorstep in a faux display of bonhomie.

"Good to meet you." Gustav could hear the American's booming voice from the window. "I heard a lot about you. Name's Brian. Brian Crick."

Gustav smiled. Mr. Crick would be a good deal quieter by the time he left tonight. And a good deal poorer.

Tapping the implant in his ear twice, Gustav waited for the familiar voice. Two floors above them, a technician sat in the eaves of the house, watching six separate camera feeds on a state-of-the-art screen.

"Testing."

Arendt nodded imperceptibly towards camera four.

Clear as a bell.

Tracy took a seat at the bar. The barman was arranging crystal glasses on a shelf.

She looked around for Peter Davies, but the Englishman wasn't here tonight. In fact the entire hotel was eerily quiet.

The barman turned around.

"What can I get you, Mrs. Crick?"

"I'll have a gin and tonic please. Gordon's if you have it, ice but no lemon."

"Coming right up."

Tracy glanced anxiously at her phone, then at the clock on the wall. It was still only seven o'clock. She thought about Jeff arriving at the game, waiting for Hunter Drexel, or Althea, to show up. She knew exactly how he'd be feeling right now, adrenaline pumping, nerves taut as a wire. Just like the old days.

For a moment she felt a flicker of guilt for what she was about to do.

But only for a moment.

This isn't a game, she reminded herself. *And these aren't the old days. However much Jeff wants them to be.*

I have a job to do.

Jeff sat at the card table twitching like a rabbit.

"I believe that's mine."

Gustav Arendt smiled smugly, spreading his second straight flush of the night across the soft green baize and reaching towards the pile of chips like a kid grabbing at candy. Jeff had seen some cheats in his time. But this guy was utterly shameless.

Not that Jeff cared about the cards.

Something had gone wrong. Very wrong.

Neither Catherine Clarke nor Ali Lassferly had shown up to the game. Nor, for that matter, had Johnny Cray. One down might have been coincidence, but three? Something was up.

Jeff wasn't the only one disappointed by the players' absences. Gustav Arendt was clearly pissed not to have three more fat wallets to plunder. But Berensen, the art dealer, looked close to tears. He kept glancing at the door, as if hoping against hope they would walk in, then back to the painting he'd brought with him, a carefully wrapped rectangle propped forlornly against the chalet wall.

Someone tipped the others off. But nobody told Berensen.

The situation was bad for multiple reasons. The first was that tonight's plan would have to be scrapped. Once again, their quarry had slipped through the net.

The second reason was far worse.

Drexel and his Group 99 friends know we're here.

They know who we are.

Do they know where we're staying?

Jeff's thoughts flew to Tracy, back at Les Fermes de Mairie. Was she safe? He longed to call her, but he couldn't leave the game until Arendt called a break, not without rousing suspicions.

At last, after what felt like an eternity to all of them, Luca Androni tossed his cards on the table in disgust and announced he was leaving.

"Me too." Jeff yawned loudly, still playing the part of bumbling Brian. "There's only so much beating a man can take in one night. Thanks for the hospitality, Gustav."

Pulling out a checkbook, Jeff left Arendt with what he and Tracy used to call a "bouncing bomb"—a beautiful forgery—for half a million dollars and hurried out into the night.

He called Tracy from the car but got no answer.

Strange.

"Start packing," he texted. "Clarke and Lassferly both no-shows. Back in ten."

Leaving the car engine running, Jeff sprinted into the hotel.

Ignoring the girl at the front desk trying to get his attention, he stepped into a waiting elevator and went straight up to the room, only to find his key card didn't work.

"Annie? Honey?" He banged loudly on the door.

Goddamn it, Tracy!

He took out his frustration on the girl at the front desk. "I've been locked out of my room," he fumed. "And I can't find my wife."

"I was trying to tell you earlier, Mr. Crick, when you came in. Mrs. Crick checked out earlier this evening. She paid the bill in full. I'm afraid I assumed you were both leaving Megève, as Mrs. Crick took all the luggage with her."

"All of it?"

"Yes, Sir."

Jeff's mind raced.

My laptop.

My second phone.

"If you still need the room I'd be happy to reactivate your cards . . ."

But Jeff was already running.

Tracy sat in the back of the cab, downloading the last of Jeff's files to her USB chip as they approached Grenoble. At this time of night the roads were clear. She should make the train in good time.

Poor Jeff. I hope he'll forgive me when this is all over.

Jeff. Cameron. Greg Walton. There were a lot of people Tracy would have to explain herself to. But she didn't care. The only person who really mattered was Nick.

Closing her eyes, Tracy focused on his face.

I'm close, darling. Really close. I'll do this for you, I promise.

Bringing Jeff down to Megève, the whole poker setup, had been complicated but necessary.

She had all the information she needed now.

It's time to finish this thing.

Jeff had never driven faster in his life.

Part of him wanted to strangle Tracy with his bare hands. But another part wanted to kiss her passionately and never let her go.

She hadn't changed. Not really. Not deep down. Whatever she said.

Tonight proved it, even if it also proved she'd been lying to him all along. Tracy knew where Hunter Drexel was. She probably knew who Kate was too. And it had nothing to do with any stupid poker game.

She's figured it out, damn her. And she's cut me out. She still doesn't trust me.

The entire poker game had been a setup. All of it—except for the part about Gustav Arendt being a cheat. Johnny Cray was never going to be there. As for Catherine Clarke and Ali Lassferly, whoever they were . . .

A sudden thought stopped Jeff in his tracks. Pulling over, he reached into the glove compartment and pulled out a pen and paper.

He wrote out each letter carefully.

A-L-I-L-A-S-S –F-E. . . .

I don't believe it. Jeff started to laugh.

Ali Lassferly was an anagram.

Of Sally Faiers.

Tracy's idea of a tribute, perhaps?

Pulling back onto the AutoRoute, his foot firmly on the accelerator, Jeff felt a momentary rush of joy. Tracy was still the same wonderful, smart, conniving, deceitful, perfect woman she'd always been. And here he was chasing her. Again.

Jeff glanced at the red dot on the satellite tracker he had wired to his dashboard and smiled. Tracy was heading for Grenoble station.

Thank God he'd slipped the tracking device into Tracy's phone.

Right behind you, my darling.

Jeff Stevens hadn't changed either.

Grenoble station was busier than Jeff expected so late at night.

The huge timetable boards mounted above the concourse announced the arrival and departure of a large number of trains, many of them international.

With the satellite tracker now clenched tightly in his hand, Jeff weaved his way through gaggles of tired travelers, closing in on Tracy's red dot.

It drew him in a straight line towards platform 13, where a train was waiting to leave. The sign at the barrier informed Jeff of its destination—Rome—and departure time. He had two minutes.

"*Billet.*" The surly inspector at the gate scowled at Jeff as he tried to push his way onto the platform.

"I'm late. I'll pay on board!" Jeff tapped frantically at his watch.

"*Billet,*" the man repeated, impassively.

Jeff contemplated punching him in his ugly, jowly, miserable French face, but he couldn't afford to be arrested. Not before he got to see the look on Tracy's face as he took his seat opposite her. *Fancy seeing you here, darling.*

Forget Hunter Drexel. It would be worth it for that look alone.

Turning around, Jeff sprinted to the ticket office,

practically combusting with frustration as he waited for the family in front of him to finish arguing about the fare.

"Je vous en prie!" he begged, waving large euro notes at them and pointing desperately to the Rome train. "Please! I have to catch that train. It's urgent."

Sprinting back to platform 13, he arrived just as the barrier was closing. That was when he saw her, in the same cream polo neck and tailored gray pants she'd been wearing earlier, with her hair tied back. She was right at the far end of the platform, in the front carriage of the train. Leaning out of the doorway, Tracy looked back to the concourse as the guard blew his whistle. Apparently satisfied, she retreated back inside the train.

Jeff waved his ticket at the guard.

"Mon billet."

The squat little man shrugged. "Sorry," he said in French. "Too late. Barrier's closed."

The train began to move.

Jeff's face darkened for a moment. Then he gave the man a beaming smile.

"I'm so sorry," he said. "I think you misheard."

Jeff's fist connected with the man's cheekbone with a satisfying crack. With a howl of pain, he dropped to the floor. Jeff vaulted the balcony and ran towards the train. It was gaining speed.

"Monsieur!" A guard yelled after him. *"Arrête!"*

But Jeff kept running, arms outstretched. He just managed to wrench open a door and jump inside before the train's increasing speed would have made it impossible. Half panting, half laughing, he doubled over, resting his head on his knees while he got his breath back.

I'm too old for this lark. Especially at this time of night.

Once he'd recovered, he straightened his tie, smoothed back his hair and walked calmly down the train towards Tracy's carriage. He was safe, for now at least. This was a high-speed train, not expected to stop until after they'd crossed the border into Germany. After a short break in Munich it would carry on south through Italy during the night, arriving in Rome by lunchtime tomorrow.

Plenty of time for Jeff to savor his triumph over Tracy—she was smart, but Jeff was smarter—and for him to convince her that, as she would never succeed in shaking him off, she may as well tell him the truth and let him help her. Capture Drexel and Kate.

For real this time.

Despite being an overnight train there appeared to be only one carriage of sleeping berths. Most of the cars contained ordinary seats, many with little RESERVED papers sticking up above the headrests.

People sipped coffee, or slept, or read news on their iPads. What little conversation heard was muted, a low murmur of French and German and Italian all mingled into one.

Jeff felt his excitement build as he reached the front carriage. The little red dot on his tracker gave a single solid beep and stopped flashing.

She was still here.

He'd found her.

He would be gracious in victory. After all, he still needed to win Tracy over. It wouldn't do to gloat.

He saw her leaning forwards, reaching into her purse for something. A phone.

Sliding into the seat beside her, Jeff waited for her to look up, then froze in horror.

"Are you all right?" A woman he had never seen before looked at him quizzically. "You look as if you've seen a ghost."

Jeff stared first at her, then at the phone in her hand. It was Tracy's phone. The one he'd given her at the fondue restaurant less than twelve hours earlier.

"That phone. Where did you get it?" he asked numbly.

"I have no idea," the woman frowned. "It's not mine. I found it just now. Someone must have dropped it into my bag by mistake."

Jeff's heart began to pound. Just then his own phone buzzed with a text.

He wrenched it out of his pocket.

Only one person had this number.

Sorry darling, Tracy wrote. *Enjoy Rome. T. x*

Frantically, Jeff accosted a passing guard.

"I'm sorry," he said in broken French. "There's been a mistake. An emergency. I have to get off the train."

The guard smiled. "I am sorry, Monsieur. The train will not stop until the border."

"You don't understand."

"No, Monsieur. *You* do not understand. If you need to see a doctor, we have one on board."

Jeff slumped down in his seat.

He didn't need a doctor.

He stared at Tracy's text for a full minute before getting up stiffly and walking into the empty train corridor to make his next call.

Frank Dorrien was deep asleep when his phone rang.

"I lost her."

Jeff Stevens's voice woke Frank instantly, like a glass of ice water in the face.

The general sat up in bed. "Where the hell have you been?"

"Never mind that," Jeff said. "Tracy's in danger. Real danger. I need your help, Frank."

Cameron Crewe stood in front of his son's grave.

It was a sweltering New York day, dank and humid and without the faintest whisper of a breeze. Sweat poured down Cameron's back, but he barely noticed.

The cemetery of St. Luke's Church in Queens was an unassuming square plot of land, much of it overgrown and weed-ridden, a tangle of rusty crosses and faded headstones. Many belonged to children. Forgotten children, it seemed. And yet there was something peaceful about the place, something beautiful and secretive. Cameron came here often, tending to Marcus's stone, a clean but simple marble slab.

So did Charlotte, Marcus's mother, although she hadn't been recently. In fact, according to the police, Charlotte's mother, Cameron's ex-mother-in-law, had officially reported her daughter missing last week. Cameron had promised to let the detectives know if he heard anything from Charlotte.

He hadn't.

He hadn't heard from Tracy either, not in more than two weeks. Everyone seemed to be disappearing, drifting out of Cameron's life as suddenly as they had once drifted into it.

Everything passes.

Nothing is forever. Least of all love.

Cameron's phone rang. He scowled at the intrusion. He must have forgotten to turn it off.

"Yes?" he snapped.

"We have a lead."

It was a man's voice. A voice Cameron hadn't heard in a long time. Too long.

"Where?"

"Italy. The Lakes."

"How soon can you be there?"

"Tomorrow. I need funds."

Cameron gave a cynical snort. *Don't you always?*

"I'll wire you another hundred thousand."

He hung up, trying to recapture the peace he'd felt a few moments ago, trying to feel Marcus's presence. But it was gone.

Mopping the sweat from his brow, Cameron turned and walked wearily back to his car.

Tracy smiled as the Airbus 300 soared up into the blue.

Poor Jeff. Eight hours on a train with no hope of rescue!

By now he'd no doubt found the most attractive woman on board and started chatting her up relentlessly. Anything to distract himself from being outwitted.

But he *had* been outwitted. They all had.

Tracy sipped her champagne gleefully.

The day of reckoning had come.

Chapter 27

L ake Maggiore was like a dream, a postcard image come to life. Tracy was staying in a small pension just moments from the shore. Every morning, after a delicious breakfast of fresh berries, local yogurt and sweet bread rolls that were a specialty of the house, she wandered down to the lake and swam. More often than not she was the only bather. The clear blue water was all hers. She felt like a queen, oblivious in those glorious moments to reality.

Flipping on to her back, gazing up at the cloudless blue sky, the Monte Rosa looming over her like a benevolent giant, Tracy imagined that she were someone else entirely. A princess, floating in a fairy-tale kingdom. Or a restless soul, newly arrived in paradise.

Was Nicky somewhere like this? Tracy hoped so. She felt close to him here, peaceful and calm. Which was odd, given the reason she had come here.

An old friend had tipped her off about Hunter Drexel resurfacing in Northern Italy. Antonio Sperotto was a gentleman thief from Milan, specializing in stolen ecclesiastical masters. He was also an inveterate gambler.

"Your man turned up at a poker game at Rocca Borromeo," Antonio informed Tracy. "At least I assume it's your man. He's going by the name of Lester Trent, and nobody's ever heard of him."

"Were you at the game?" Tracy asked.

"Not personally, no. A friend was there. Evidently Mr. Trent relieved one of the Agnellis of more than two hundred thousand euros. Caused quite a stir, I can tell you."

"Did this friend of yours talk to him?" Tracy asked. "What else did he find out?"

Antonio Sperotto chuckled. "My dear, these things aren't like book clubs. This is serious poker. There's no chitchat. Although apparently one of the Borromeo daughters wandered in at one point, which distracted some of the men."

"But not your friend, I take it?" Tracy teased. Antonio was so gay he would have made Liberace look macho. Most of his friends fit the same mold.

"Giovanni can appreciate beauty, darling, in all its forms," Antonio pouted. "But no. I suspect he was more distracted by the frescos. Did you know the Borromeo frescos are the oldest examples of nonreligious, Lombard Gothic work still in existence? They were painted in 1342, but the colors gleam as if it were yesterday!"

Tracy didn't know. She was more interested in Lester Trent.

"Trent appreciated the young lady," Antonio told her. "Although rumor has it he generally prefers his playmates a little further down the social scale. He likes professionals."

"Hookers?"

"That's what I hear," Antonio said. "Apparently he's had a string of girls ferried over to the place where he's staying."

Tracy thought about Sally Faiers, her love for Hunter and her loyalty. Sally had gone to Belgium to try to help Drexel and had been shot to death for her troubles. And now here he was, with Sally barely cold, already screwing around. In between planning his next act of murder on behalf of Group 99, no doubt.

Bastard.

"Where's he staying?" she asked Antonio.

"In a stunning medieval villa, the Michele, on another of the private islands. It's owned by the Viscontis, a local aristocratic family. He must have rented it from them."

"Visconti," Tracy muttered. "I feel like I've heard of them."

Antonio shrugged. "They're rich. Not quite in the Borromeos' league, but not short of a bob or two either. She owns a fabulous collection of diamond jewelry, one of the largest in Italy."

"That must be it." Tracy grinned.

A look of worry crept over Antonio Sperotto's face. "You're not going to try anything foolish, are you, Tracy?"

"Me? Never."

"This Drexel chap sounds like very bad news."

"He is," Tracy said seriously. "But he knows things, Antonio. Things I need to know."

"For God's sake be careful."

"I will." Tracy hugged him. "I promise."

The next step was to figure out how to get access to the Villa Michele, without alerting Hunter, or anyone else, to her presence. So far Tracy had seen no sign of MI6, the CIA or Group 99, but she knew for a fact that all three were devoting considerable resources to finding out what she already knew. It was only a matter of time before they showed up at the Lakes. Tracy needed to finish this before that happened, and before Drexel took off again.

Unfortunately, accessing the Visconti's villa proved harder than Tracy had anticipated. Partly because the house itself was a fifteenth-century fortress, with four-foot-thick, unscalable walls designed to keep out centurys' worth of marauders. And partly because it was situated on a small island, really just a rocky outcrop, in the extreme southern end of the lake. This meant it was close enough to the shore that anyone approaching by boat would be clearly visible from both of the major five-star hotels in town, as well as a good smattering of private homes along the lakefront. Not to mention the fact that the local police station faced the property almost directly, as if it were daring somebody to try and break in.

Despite these obstacles, within twenty-four hours, Tracy had a plan.

But before she took the final step, there was something she had to do.

Back at the guesthouse, Tracy called Cameron's private number from her new Italian phone. She was diverted straight to voicemail.

That's odd. He must be traveling.

She hung up.

She had called him to say goodbye. And to apologize. And to tell him she loved him. But none of these were things one could say to a recorded message.

Perhaps it's for the best.

Just as she was turning off her phone, it rang.

"Tracy?" Cameron's voice was heavy with worry. "Is that you?"

Tracy hesitated. She was already regretting calling him but it was too late now.

"Yes. It's me."

"Thank God. I've been out of my mind. At least one of you is OK."

"One of us?"

"Charlotte's gone missing," Cameron blurted. "My ex-wife. I've had the police here and . . . anyway, none of that matters. Where are you?"

Tracy took a deep breath. "It doesn't matter where I am. I'm safe."

"You're not safe! And it does matter."

He sounded utterly desperate. Tracy felt terrible.

"I called to say goodbye," she blurted. "And thank you. And I wish you happiness."

"Stop." Cameron's voice became stern. "Tracy, listen to me. We can talk about 'us' later. But right now I believe you are in grave danger. You've found Drexel, haven't you?"

Tracy was silent.

"If you've found him, trust me, it's because he *wants to be found*. It's a trap, Tracy."

"I don't think so," she said quietly. "I have to go."

"For Christ's sake, Tracy, wake up!" Cameron said desperately. "It's a trap! Hunter *wanted* you to find him."

"And why would he want that?"

"Because he knows you'll try to confront him alone. And when you do, he'll kill you." Cameron's tone softened again. "Please, darling. Tell me where you are. Tell me where Drexel is. I won't tell Walton or Buck, I swear it. I'll help you myself. Just don't do this alone."

Tracy's eyes welled with tears. She looked at her watch. In six more seconds he'd be able to trace the call.

"Goodbye, Cameron. And good luck."

She rang off, ripped the battery out of her handset and hurled it into the fire.

"You're late."

Frank Dorrien scowled at Jeff Stevens. They'd agreed to meet at the Café Italia on Locarno's Piazza Grande at noon. It was now 12:03.

"Hardly." Jeff glanced at his Patek Philippe and sat down. In linen trousers and a loose, short-sleeved shirt, topped off with a panama hat, Jeff was perfectly dressed for the warm weather. Unlike the general, who'd turned up in a twill shirt, a heavy tweed jacket and brogues with socks.

Jeff thought, *If the man got any more English they'd put him in the British Museum.*

"What do you mean 'hardly'? Late is late," Frank snapped. "You do realize it's entirely your fault we're in this situation as it is? Time is running out, Jeff."

"I know. I'm sorry."

"Sorry won't save Tracy. Or any of the other people Drexel and his Group 99 cronies are right now planning to kill."

"Jesus, Frank, I get it, OK?" Jeff's voice was breaking. "I fucked up. I thought Tracy and I . . ."

He left the sentence hanging.

Frank Dorrien took a sip of his tea and grimaced. It was lukewarm and disgusting, like every cup he'd had since he got to Italy. Unconfirmed sightings by British agents of Alexis Argyros near the Italian Lakes had been enough for James MacIntosh to fly Frank out there.

If Apollo was in Northern Italy, chances were that Drexel was there too. Although the Greek Group 99 leader was a target in his own right.

Ironically it was Frank Dorrien who had insisted that Jeff Stevens be brought along too.

"Absolutely not." Jamie MacIntosh was still smarting over Jeff's ill-advised decision to disappear with Tracy. "Mr. Stevens has made it quite clear where his loyalties lie. And it's not with us."

"I don't care about his loyalties," Frank said bluntly. "He's still our best chance of finding Tracy Whitney. And *she's* still our best chance of finding Drexel."

In the end, reluctantly, MacIntosh had agreed. The Americans had lost control of Tracy Whitney completely. Having Jeff Stevens on their team, combined with this new intelligence on Argyros, put MI6 in the driving seat once again.

If only we knew where we were going, Frank Dorrien thought bitterly.

"Argyros has gone to ground, for the time being at least," he told Jeff. "Right now our priority has to be finding Tracy."

"Agreed," said Jeff. "Where do you suggest we start?"

There were times when Major General Frank Dorrien could cheerfully have strangled Jeff Stevens.

"Where do *I* suggest . . . ? You're the one who's supposed to be able to outthink her, remember? Although after her little stunt on the train I'd say that theory's seriously in doubt."

Jeff looked miserably at his shoes.

"Think, man. Drexel's here, somewhere. Tracy finds him. She thinks she's the only one who knows he's here, but she's wrong. Argyros is right behind her."

"Or ahead of her," said Jeff. "Maybe Argyros has already found Hunter."

"Maybe. And maybe he's killed him. Or maybe, he never had any intention of killing him. Maybe he's here to meet Hunter as a compatriot. A friend. A co-conspirator. Maybe they're planning their next Neuilly together."

Jeff shivered. "Let's hope not."

"But Tracy doesn't know this," Frank continued. "She thinks she's alone."

"Right."

"So what's her plan? What would her next move be?"

Jeff closed his eyes, praying for inspiration. To his astonishment as much as Frank Dorrien's, it came.

Sitting up suddenly, he said, "I have an idea."

Tracy shut off the speedboat's engine as she drew up to the Villa Michele's outer wall.

She was dressed in sky-high platform heels, fishnet stockings and a skintight black Lycra dress that left little to the imagination. Her breasts, not usually her best asset, looked enormous this evening and very much front-and-center thanks to her amply padded bra. As it was not the sort of outfit that allowed one to conceal a gun easily, Tracy carried a small quilted purse, a cheap Chanel knockoff made of shiny, wipe-down plastic.

She felt cold, uncomfortable, and ridiculous. But her getup had done its job. The old man at the dock who'd rented Tracy the boat hadn't given her a second glance, still less asked for any ID. All the girls who went to the villa as Mr. Trent's guests paid cash on return. Hookers were good customers, regular, reliable and they rarely needed the boat for more than a couple of hours.

Tracy fit right in.

When she reached the Viscontis' island, the old man had explained, Tracy was to moor the boat by tying a heavy rope onto a large iron ring, bolted to the private harbor wall. Arriving in pitch-darkness it took her a while to locate said ring. When she did, it looked like something out of a medieval dungeon, rusted and creaking and huge. By the time she'd secured the boat, her hands were freezing and rubbed raw, and there were dirt and rust stains on her palms.

A real whore would have wet wipes in her purse, Tracy thought. *All I have is a pistol, a new cellphone, a recording device and some wire.*

Jumping out of the boat onto the thin strip of grass at the base of the wall, she wiped her hands as best she could on the turf. To her right, a set of steep stairs led up to a wooden door, that in turn led into the formal gardens and then to the villa itself. A CCTV camera directly above her head looked blindly out over the lake into the darkness. Tracy slipped beneath it to the foot of the stairs and began to climb.

She'd come prepared to pick the lock, but she found the wooden door had been left open. Cameron Crewe's voice rang in her ears. *He wants to be found. It's a trap!*

Maybe it was true.

If so, Hunter Drexel should be careful what he wished for.

Tracy's heart hammered against her ribs as she crossed the manicured, Italianate garden. She waited for alarms to go off, for a spotlight to suddenly catch her or guards to come running, roused from their drunken slumbers. The crunch of her feet on the graveled path sounded deafeningly loud to her own ears as she weaved her way in and out of the shadows of the poplars. According to her research there were no dogs at the villa. But Tracy still half expected to hear the heavy, panting breaths of slavering Dobermans, intent on ripping her limb from limb. She'd spent half of her adult life breaking and entering expensive homes, but the adrenaline never left her.

The last time she'd broken in anywhere was at Frank Dorrien's house. Tracy remembered now how triumphant she'd felt that night, finding the hard drive from Prince Achileas's computer, and the first images of Althea—Kate. Those pictures had proved that the general had lied, about Captain Bob Daley and his relationship with the dead prince, and about other things too. They were also still the only known images of Kate. The woman who had killed Nick, and claimed to know Tracy, but who remained as much of a mystery now as she had done when this all started.

With luck, in a few short minutes, that mystery would be solved. Tracy would be talking to Hunter Drexel face-to-face, finally learning the truth. The whole truth.

At last she approached the house itself. Crouching low beneath the height of the ground-floor windows, she flattened herself against a wall, scratching her legs badly on the rose bushes that clung to the villa like thorny limpets. Lights were on inside. Tracy listened. She could hear classical music—a sonata of some sort, coming from deeper within the house—but no voices. The whole place, in fact, was eerily quiet. Peaceful, but not in a good way. There was a faint smell of cooking, garlic and anchovies and lemon coming from a few yards away. Tracy saw that the French doors to the drawing room had been flung wide open to the garden, presumably to allow in the cool evening air.

She approached them cautiously, gun drawn, stealing herself for battle. She didn't want to kill Hunter, but she must overpower him. Hopefully he would talk to her of his own accord. He was a journalist, after all, in another life. A story teller. Not to mention a vain egotist. Those sorts of people invariably liked to talk. But Tracy wasn't about to take any chances.

With one last, deep breath, Tracy burst into the room.

Chapter 28

The room was empty.

At one end, a fire crackled gently in a vast Baronial fireplace. In front of it lay what looked like a recently discarded newspaper—today's *La Repubblica*—and a half drunk glass of scotch.

The music was coming from farther inside. Tracy followed it, keeping her back to the wall and her weapon drawn, inching her way along a long, parquet-floored corridor. Grand double doors at the end opened onto what looked to be a dining room. Tracy could see a long, rustic refectory table with a centerpiece of brilliant blue hydrangea flowers. Then suddenly, she froze.

There he was.

After all the reported sightings and grainy photographs, all the "what ifs" and near misses, Tracy was finally looking at Hunter Drexel. The blond hair was gone. He had reverted to his usual dark curls. And he looked stockier and healthier than he had in the pictures from Montmartre. Casually dressed in a sweater and jeans, with his back to Tracy, he was carrying a large bowl of salad over to the table like a man without a care in the world. He bore only the faintest traces of a limp and though he appeared to be alone, he was setting places for two.

Just as Tracy wondered *Who's he expecting?* Hunter's voice rang out loudly, bouncing off the ancient walls.

"Is that you, Miss Whitney?" He didn't look up, but continued setting the table. "Please, don't skulk around in the corridor. Come in."

Tracy moved forward, cocking the safety catch on her pistol with an audible *click*.

"You won't need that," Hunter said blithely, turning around and looking at her for the first time. "I'm unarmed. As you can see."

He held both arms out wide and smiled guilelessly. Tracy could see at once what had drawn Sally Faiers to him. That fatal, boyish charm. *Poor Sally.*

"I've been expecting you. I trust you'll join me for dinner?" He gestured to the seat at the head of the table.

Tracy played along. Lowering her gun, she placed it carefully beside her plate and sat down.

"You've gone to a lot of trouble, Mr. Drexel."

He gave a little bow. "I try."

"Will Kate be joining us?"

Hunter's eyebrow shot up momentarily.

He's surprised I know her name.

"Not tonight."

"Is she here? In Italy?"

Tracy threw out the question as if it were a casual inquiry about the weather. The whole situation was so surreal, she figured she might as well.

Hunter opened a bottle of Château Mouton-Rothschild with a satisfying pop.

"I don't know. The truth is I don't know where she is."

"But if you did, you wouldn't tell me, right?"

He filled Tracy's glass with a sigh, then sat down beside her. "It's not Kate you want, Miss Whitney. She's not the enemy. I'd rather hoped you might have figured that out by now, especially considering how much the two of you have in common. And what a fan she is of yours."

Tracy waited silently for him to continue.

"Kate worked for the CIA for many years, as a computer expert back at Langley. She was part of the team that tried to track you and Jeff Stevens, back in your heyday. You didn't know?"

Tracy shook her head. She'd suspected that Althea might be an intelligence agency insider, but it hadn't occurred to her that that might explain the link between the two of them. *She felt like she knew me because she'd tracked me all those years. But I never knew her.* It seemed so obvious now.

"Did Sally Faiers figure it out?" Tracy asked. "Is that why she was killed?"

A dangerous glint flashed in Hunter's eyes.

"I feel terrible about Sally. I loved her."

But even as he said the words, Tracy clocked him looking at her hooker dress appraisingly. She couldn't figure the guy out.

Seeing her confusion, Hunter said, "There's a lot you don't know, Miss Whitney."

"But you're going to enlighten me. Right?"

The smile was back, like sun breaking from behind the clouds.

"Let's eat."

Chapter 29

The meal was delicious, some sort of chicken and onion stew with olives and anchovies. To her surprise, Tracy realized she was hungry. She waited for Hunter to eat first before tasting her own food—after all the death and destruction he'd caused, poisoning would not be beyond him—and did the same with her wine. But before long they were both eating and drinking, and despite the gun still resting beneath Tracy's fingers, the tension between them had eased.

"How did you know I would come here tonight?" Tracy asked eventually, being careful to drink water as well as her wine.

"Because I invited you. Well, as good as invited you. Once I was sure you'd shaken off the CIA and the British, I let you know where I'd be. Made sure I was seen by a few of the right people. I knew you wouldn't be able to resist."

Tracy thought, *So Cameron was right. He did want me to find him.*

Aloud she said, "I could have shot you."

Hunter looked perplexed. "Why would you want to do that?"

"Oh, I don't now. Because of Neuilly? All those dead teenagers?"

"I had nothing to do with Neuilly," Hunter protested.

"British intelligence placed you there. Ours too."

"Then British intelligence is wrong!" He sounded genuinely horrified. "They've been trying to throw you off the scent, Miss Whitney, and it looks like they've succeeded."

Tracy looked at him skeptically.

"You didn't come here to kill me," Hunter said. "You came because you want to know the truth. And I let you come because I want to tell it."

"A confession?"

He grinned. "You still have me down as the bad guy, don't you?"

Tracy looked away. The truth was, she didn't know what she had him down as.

"I'm a journalist," Hunter said. "Telling the truth is my job. My problem has been finding somebody I trust enough to tell it to."

"And you think you can trust me?"

"What I think"—Hunter sipped his wine—"is that you're incorruptible. That sets you apart from just about everybody else in this sorry mess."

Tracy knew she was being flattered, but she let it pass. "I'm honored."

"Oh, I doubt that," Hunter said. "You think I'm a terrorist so I'd be surprised if my good opinion means much to you. But I'm going to talk to you anyway. I assume you're already recording?" He nodded knowingly at Tracy's knockoff Chanel purse.

Tracy dutifully pulled out the powder compact containing her tiny digital recording device and placed it on the table, next to her gun.

"Always one step ahead, aren't you Mr. Drexel?"

"In my line of work, if you're not one step ahead, you're dead," Hunter drawled. "Let's get started, shall we?"

Tracy sat, frozen, while he spoke, inhaling every word.

"It all began with a story for the *New York Times*." His deep, gravelly, smoker's voice echoed off the villa's vaulted ceilings. "That is, it was *my* story. I was writing it freelance. But my plan was to sell it to *The Times*. I'd been seeing a girl there."

"Fiona Barron," said Tracy. Two could play the one-step-ahead game.

Hunter looked impressed. "That's right. Fi. Anyway, Fi and I had a falling-out. And the editor wasn't my biggest fan either. To be fair to him, I guess I had been a bit of an ass. "

Tracy didn't probe. She could imagine.

"I wanted to build bridges at the paper. And the only way I knew how to do that was by writing something off-the-hook amazing. This was going to be *the* story that got me back in everyone's good books."

"So what was the story?"

"Back then, the story was fracking," Hunter said. "Specifically, corruption in the fracking industry. But, appalling as it was, that soon turned out to be the tip of a giant iceberg of shit. A 'shitberg' as I liked to call it."

He smiled but Tracy wasn't laughing. "Go on."

"Corporate corruption was being carried out on a massive scale, right across the globe. But it was the government involvement that really stank. Cash for contracts. Diplomatic bribes. Blind eyes turned to human rights abuses. There were CIA agents, sanctioned by Washington, showing up in China with suitcases literally stuffed with cash. Havers's administration were in it up to their dirty, white-collared necks. The president's obsessed with breaking the Saudis stranglehold on our economy. Jim Havers wants to go down in history as the man who broke America's oil addiction and he'll stop at nothing to do it. And I mean, nothing."

"So you planned to expose Havers?" Tracy asked.

"Among other people."

"You knew enough to end his presidency?"

"For sure. I noticed unmarked cars parked outside my apartment. All of a sudden I couldn't take a shit without the CIA knowing about it. Nobody had read my piece. It was all in my head at that point. But the government knew what questions I'd been asking and to whom. They wanted me dead."

Tracy frowned. "That's a pretty wild accusation. This was the same government who tried to rescue you in Bratislava, let's not forget. If they wanted you dead so badly, why go to the trouble?"

"They wanted me dead," Hunter repeated. "But they wanted it to look like an accident. So there were no shootings, no abductions. Instead there was a gas leak in my building."

"Come on," Tracy said. "Gas leaks happen all the time."

"Exactly. Except this one happened only in my apartment—nowhere else in the building. Enough carbon monoxide to kill a man three times my body weight in under an hour. I know this because that's how much they found in my cat's bloodstream when he died that night instead of me. I stayed over at a girlfriend's place."

Clearly Hunter was the one with the nine lives.

"A week later, I almost drove my car off the Atlantic City Expressway."

"What happened?"

"My steering wheel jammed. Next thing I know I'm shooting up an exit ramp and into a tree. I was lucky. Broke my collarbone, got a few bangs on the head, that was it. But if I hadn't made that ramp I'd have been dead for sure. Probably taken out a bunch of others with me. Afterwards, the guy in the shop told me someone had messed with my steering column, and put a slow leak in my brake fluid. Deliberate sabotage."

A nerve began to twitch in Tracy's jaw.

Deliberate sabotage. To the steering column.

It was exactly what Greg Walton told her had happened to Blake Carter's truck, the night of the accident. The night Nicholas died.

"The Americans weren't the only Western government playing dirty in the Shale Gas Wars," Hunter went on. "Everyone was at it. The British, the French, the Germans, the Russians. Opponents were silenced, taxes waived, and all the while the rich at the top of the industry grew richer, like fat mosquitoes gorging on the blood of some hapless animal. It was the sheer scale of the corruption that really shocked me. That and the fact that *no one* was reporting on it."

"Why do you think that was?" asked Tracy.

"I have no idea." Hunter refilled his wineglass. "Maybe no one else was looking. Or maybe people were looking, but someone was shutting those people up."

"Killing them, you mean?"

"Sometimes," Hunter said. "I'm sure that's what happened to Sally, by the way. She'd worked out a lot of this on her own, while I was on the run. Somebody decided it was time to stop the questions. Somebody with less concern for appearances than your masters at the CIA. But sometimes people were paid off. Which leads me to the next chapter in all this: Group 99."

Tracy leaned forward. This was what she'd waited for. This was where it all came together, where the pieces of the puzzle began to fit.

"So I'm writing my piece, uncovering all this dirty money and dirty politics around fracking, trying not to get killed. And as I'm doing my research I run into a bunch of different anti-industry groups. Most of them are environmentalists—well meaning, badly organized—doing their best to be a thorn in the side of the shale gas giants and the governments helping them to line their pockets. But then all of a sudden this one group pops up, and they're different from all the others."

"Group 99," said Tracy.

Hunter nodded. "Group 99 got interested once shale gas fields were discovered in Greece. Rumors were flying around that some former Greek royals had signed a vast, private deal to sell swaths of land for fracking. The family stood to make a mint, as did one or two corrupt government officials, and the frackers themselves of course. But there was to be no public benefit from exploiting this natural resource. Things were pretty bad in Greece at that time. The poor were at breaking point. That's when I first started hearing about Apollo—Alexis Argyros—and Althea, a Western woman, supposedly an American, who was raising money for this group, and maybe even running the show.

"Group 99 were a game changer. They had a totally different agenda from all the other antifracking groups. They didn't care about the environment. They wanted wealth equality, and to punish the greedy at the top of the tree. They also had a totally different MO. Remember, they were nonviolent at that time. They were smart, super smart, and tech savvy. They were well funded. They were highly organized but non-hierarchical. And they had global reach. The way I saw it, that put them in a unique position to attack the fracking industry, maybe even to bring it down, but at a minimum to end corruption at least in Greece."

Hunter drew breath for the first time in minutes. Tracy noticed for the first time how tired he looked. He'd waited a long time to tell his story, but now that it was finally happening, the effort seemed to drain all the energy out of him.

"Tell me more about Althea," Tracy said. "About Kate. You knew her identity all along?"

Hunter rubbed his eyes. "No. Not at the beginning. I knew Althea had been to visit Prince Achileas at Sandhurst. The Prince knew about his family's deal with Cranston and it clearly pricked his conscience. Althea got him interested in Group 99. I think the idea was that he was going to help them expose or sabotage the arrangement in some way. But he got cold feet. Anyway, I went to England. To meet him."

"You met Prince Achileas?" It was the first time Tracy had openly expressed surprise.

Hunter nodded. "Sure. I interviewed him for my piece."

"Did you meet Bob Daley then too?"

"Nope. Just the prince."

"Well, what did he say?"

"Not much, as far as fracking was concerned. He was very depressed by then. He hated Sandhurst. The boy was obviously gay, and having a tough time with that. Plus he was estranged from his father. And his commanding officer hated his guts."

"Frank Dorrien . . ." Tracy murmured under her breath.

"I was sad when I heard Achileas had topped himself," Hunter said, staring down at the wine dregs in the bottom of his glass. "Sad but not surprised. Bob Daley said the same thing about him, when we met later in the camp in Bratislava. The kid was a tortured soul. They were friends, believe it or not."

"I know," said Tracy.

"Anyway, Achileas never did tell me much about that Greek fracking deal. But he did talk to me about Group 99. He was quite fascinating on that subject, as it happened. And he showed me a picture while I was there, of the handler whom he'd met with: Althea. Not the greatest picture as you know. Grainy and her face is half in profile. But it was enough to shock the hell out of me."

"Because?"

"Because I realized then that I knew her. And that my story was about to get bigger than I'd ever imagined."

Chapter 30

"Her real name is Katherine Evans." Hunter looked at Tracy, propping his elbows on the table. "Kate. As soon as I saw Achileas's picture of her I knew. We were at school together."

"At *school*?" Tracy frowned. "But I thought you said she was CIA?"

"She was. But I knew her before that, at Columbia," Hunter explained. "We were in the same graduating class."

"So you were friends?"

Hunter took on a nostalgic expression. "More than friends. Kate was probably my first really big love."

Tracy was fascinated. "What was her background? Was she a radical in college?"

Hunter laughed. "Radical? Hell, no. If you could have picked one girl out of the yearbook least likely to get involved with an organization like Group 99, it would have been her. Kate's family were from Ohio. Good people, Christian, Republican. And rich. Her dad owned a local newspaper, but he'd made most of his money on Wall Street. Needless to say, he didn't approve of me one bit."

Tracy asked the obvious question. "So how does a nice, rich, Midwestern girl end up on the CIA's Most Wanted list?"

Hunter's face suddenly darkened. "She loses everything," he said bitterly. "That's how. The CIA destroyed Kate's life, so she figured she'd return the favor."

Tracy waited for him to explain.

"After Kate and I broke up she started dating a guy called Daniel Herschowitz. About a year later, she married him. I didn't know the guy well, but everybody said Dan was a great person. Solid, reliable. Everything I wasn't, basically." He smiled briefly. "He was also crazy smart, just like Kate. She was brilliant with computers—that's why they brought her in to track you—and Dan was some kind of math prodigy. They both got recruited into Langley before they even finished grad school."

The way he told it, it sounded like such a happy story. Gilded, gifted American couple fall in love and dedicate their lives to their country. Yet somehow, somewhere along the road between then and now, it had ended in tragedy. In terror and murder and misery.

Fighting to control her emotions, Tracy asked Hunter, "What happened? What went wrong?"

"I don't know all the details. But the summary is Dan was in Iraq, embedded on some deep cover mission for the agency. Something went wrong back home—some kind of security leak—and his identity was compromised. He managed to make contact with his handler and arranged to meet at a safe house in Basra. He got there expecting to be smuggled out of the country. Instead he was met by three Al Qaeda operatives, horribly tortured, and eventually beaten to death."

Tracy put a hand over her mouth. "Oh my God. But how did Al Qaeda know about the safe house?"

Hunter shrugged. "That's an open question. Kate's always been convinced it was an inside job. That the CIA sold Daniel out. She was still working at Langley at the time. She claims she hacked into files, right up to the director's office, that prove her husband was betrayed and murdered. But it was all covered up. The doctors said she was deranged with grief and she spent the next year in a secure mental facility in upstate Virginia."

"Jesus Christ."

"Yeah. It was bad. She was tortured by grief, destroyed by it. And everybody she trusted had betrayed her. That's what she believed anyway. What she still believes."

Tracy wasn't sure why, but she believed what Hunter was telling her. From the little she already knew about the CIA and the FBI and the way the intelligence community closed ranks when they felt under threat, Kate Evans's story sounded horribly plausible.

"When she finally got out of the hospital she was on a mission. The only thing she cared about was destroying the CIA. Getting payback on everyone who had conspired in Daniel's murder and what followed. That's what led her to Group 99 and everything that happened next. Kate never bought into their whole communist, punish the wealthy ideology. She's always been rich. She liked them because they were running rings around the CIA and costing the U.S. government millions of dollars. Plus she was a gifted hacker, with invaluable inside information on how the agency worked. Kate was the one who transformed Group 99 into a global force. She took a ramshackle bunch of angry kids from the slums of Athens and Paris and Caracas and got them organized, funded and ruthlessly focused."

Tracy sat back in her chair. For the first time, doubts began to creep in.

"You sound as if you admire her."

"I do."

"But what about the violence? The murders of all those innocent people?" With a supreme effort, Tracy forced Nick's face out of her mind. "What about Neuilly?"

"That wasn't her," said Hunter. "Kate expressly forbade the attack on the school. But by then she'd lost control to Apollo—Argyros—and his cronies."

"Henry Cranston, then."

"Cranston deserved to die," Hunter said flatly. "But Kate didn't plant that bomb either."

"She was there!" Tracy protested.

Hunter shook his head "She was set up. I'm telling you, it wasn't her."

"All right then," Tracy said. "Bob Daley. Kate personally authorized his murder. I heard the recording myself. She told Argyros to shoot him. That is a fact."

Hunter sighed heavily. "I know it is."

"So then how can you defend her? I thought Bob Daley was your friend."

"He was. I admit, Kate was wrong about Bob."

Wrong? The understatement was so shocking, Tracy wasn't sure how to react. *Wrong? They blew his brains out. The guy's skull exploded!*

Hunter stood up suddenly.

"Let's go outside. I could use some air."

They walked back along the corridor to the draw-ing room, the way Tracy had come in earlier, and out into the garden through the French doors. In the last hour the breeze had gone from cool to distinctly chilly. Tracy shivered in her skimpy dress. Darting back inside, Hunter grabbed a cashmere throw off one of the armchairs and draped it around Tracy's shoulders, making no reference to the fact that she'd brought her pistol with her and held it tightly in her right hand. She was beginning to trust Hunter more, but there were limits.

"Thank you," said Tracy.

Hunter reminded her in so many ways of Jeff. Both men were immensely charming, but both used their charm to manipulate others. *In this case, me.* It was a bizarre feeling, knowing you were being lulled into a false sense of security, but letting it happen anyway.

It struck Tracy that Hunter had been talking solidly for almost an hour, yet she still didn't know why Group 99 had kidnapped him or what his relationship to the group really was. As for Kate Evans, and her connection to Tracy and to Nick's death, she was still foundering in the darkness.

Below them, the still waters of Lake Maggiore shimmered silvery black. Above, poplar trees loomed and swayed like dark giants, their feathered fingers rustling ominously in the wind. On the other side of the lake the lights from the town twinkled prettily, cozy houses, bustling restaurants and hotels, an enchanting world of safety and normality and peace.

It's just a couple of miles across the water, thought Tracy, *but it might as well be outer space.*

She lived in a different world now. A world of torture and betrayal. Of lies and secrets.

A world of death.

Hunter walked beside Tracy along the graveled path. "I think you still have the wrong impression of me, Miss Whitney," he said. "Your friends at Langley have convinced you that I sympathize with Group 99. That I support their aims and objectives and approve of their methods."

Lifting up his shirt, he displayed a painful crisscross of scars, welts, knife wounds and burns cutting a swath across his chest, ribs and back.

"I experienced Group 99's methods firsthand. Believe me when I tell you, nobody hates them more than I do. These people kidnapped me. They beat me. They robbed me of a year of my life. Alexis Argyros, undoubtedly the most sadistic, straightforwardly evil human being I have ever met, is somewhere out there *right now*, tracking me down, still trying to kill me. And you honestly think I'm on his *side*?"

"I think you're on Kate's side," Tracy said quietly.

"That's different." Hunter's voice grew more urgent. For the first time this evening, Tracy heard anger there. "Kate is ill. The CIA made her ill."

"That's no excuse . . ."

"I think it is. The CIA broke her mentally. If they hadn't, Argyros would never have been able to manipulate her the way he did."

Tracy stopped walking. "What do you mean?"

"Argyros convinced Kate that Bob Daley was working for the CIA. That he was part of a joint British American task force in Iraq who deceived Daniel and left him there to die. Kate did order Bob's execution. But only because she believed he'd murdered her husband.

"The way I see it, the CIA and Argyros and his bully boys both have Daley's blood on their hands. Argyros is the one who turned Group 99 into violent terrorists, not Kate. He led his little group of angry boys exactly where they always wanted to go."

Angry little boys . . . who else had said that?

Tracy's mind rushed back to Geneva, to her first dinner with Cameron Crewe. She heard his voice now as if he were standing next to her: *Group 99 are just a bunch of angry young men . . . They aren't fighting for a cause. Fighting is their cause. They turn to violence because it makes them feel good. Simple as that. I call them the Lost Boys.*

They walked back inside. Hunter closed the French doors behind them and drew the drapes. Then he went over to the bar and returned with two cut glass tumblers of whisky.

"Here."

He handed one to Tracy. She looked at it for a moment but the time for caution seemed to have passed. She downed it in two swift gulps then asked him the question that had been forming in her mind all the time they were outside.

"Why were you kidnapped? You're working on your fracking story. The industry don't like it. The U.S. government don't like it. But Group 99 are kind of on your side, presumably? Anti-corruption, anti-wealth. Why did they abduct *you*?"

Hunter looked at her with renewed respect.

"Now *that*, Miss Whitney, is a good question. That is *the* question, don't you agree? Why *did* Group 99 abduct me?"

"And the answer is . . . ?"

"Simple. Although I'd really like you to get there yourself. I was kidnapped because somebody commanded it. Somebody very rich and very powerful. Somebody who knew I was on to them and had a lot to lose."

"Not President Havers?"

"No, no. Kidnap's far too messy. He'd have had me killed."

"Kate?"

Hunter shook his head.

Tracy frowned. "Then who?"

"Me."

Tracy and Hunter both spun around.

Cameron Crewe lounged in the doorway, smiling broadly. He had a drink in one hand and a Colt Python Elite in the other.

It was pointed directly at Tracy's head.

Chapter 31

"Gun please, darling."

Cameron was still smiling at Tracy. It was the same easy, warm smile she remembered, from Geneva, and New York, and Hawaii and Paris. The smile that had made her feel safe. That had brought her back to life after Nick's death.

It was true Tracy had never felt the same deep passion for Cameron that she had with Jeff. But Cameron had given her something else in their short time together.

Contentment.

Kindness.

Hope.

Now Tracy felt all three slipping through her fingers like so many grains of sand.

"Your gun, Tracy. Put it on the table, please. Slowly."

Cameron's tone was calm, gentle even. But his pistol was still pointed firmly between Tracy's eyes.

"Do as he asks," Hunter said softly.

Cameron watched like a hawk as Tracy stood up and carefully placed her gun on the walnut coffee table next to the fireplace. With each step she struggled to adjust to the new reality.

Cameron Crewe wasn't her protector.

He wasn't her friend.

He hadn't come here to "save" her from Hunter Drexel or anything else.

He was the one Tracy needed saving from.

"Thank you," Cameron said. "Now sit. You too."

He jerked his gun casually towards Hunter, who sat down next to Tracy on the couch. If Hunter was afraid he didn't show it, crossing his legs and making himself comfortable, as if the three of them were old friends settling in for a fireside chat.

Cameron turned to Tracy. "I'm sorry it has come to this, darling. I really am. I'd hoped for a different ending. But when you ran out on me after Paris . . . when you insisted on going after Drexel alone . . . you really left me no choice."

Tracy fought back an unhelpful urge to laugh. The entire situation suddenly seemed so ridiculous. The three of them here in this magnificent room, like characters in a play, acting out a scene. Except they'd all been given the wrong lines. Now Cameron was playing the evil terrorist, and Hunter the misunderstood hero.

And what does that make me? Tracy wondered. *The damsel in distress?*

I don't think so.

When she looked up at Cameron, there was no fear in Tracy's eyes. Only curiosity. Now, at long last, she was to learn the whole truth.

"So it was you?" she asked him. "You had Hunter kidnapped?"

"I did. A mistake in retrospect. I should have had him killed. But you live and learn."

Tracy had never heard him speak like this before, so callously. It was as if a completely different person had somehow invaded Cameron's body.

Was this the person Charlotte Crewe knew? The man that she tried to warn me about?

Was this why Charlotte had gone "missing"?

"So you were bankrolling Group 99? They worked for you?"

"Pond scum like Alexis Argyros will work for whoever writes them the biggest check. These people's life blood is greed. Greed and envy, prettily packaged as social justice. Isn't that right, Mr. Drexel?"

"It is. That's what I found out, after I spoke to Prince Achileas at Sandhurst," Hunter explained to Tracy. "Group 99 were taking bribes too. Even the so-called good guys were corrupt. Crewe Oil totally owned them, and Apollo and his cronies were making out like bandits from day one. They carefully targeted all Crewe's competitors but left him untouched. They took out Henry Cranston specifically so that Crewe would wind up with the Greek shale gas, and at a bargain price too."

"*You* murdered Henry Cranston?" Tracy could no longer hide her shock. "Is that why you were in Geneva?"

Cameron shrugged. "I'm a businessman. I protected my business interests."

"By bombing your competitors?"

"If necessary. I wouldn't waste your tears on Henry though, darling. Believe me, he wasn't worth it."

Tracy stared at him. She didn't say a word but her face spoke plainly: *Who* are *you?*

How was it possible that she'd read a person so wrong, so terribly, fatally, completely wrong?

Jeff had tried to warn her, but she'd assumed he was simply jealous.

She owed Jeff an apology.

She wondered if she would live to give it to him.

"Let me get this straight," Tracy said. "Hunter knew that you controlled Group 99?"

"Yes."

"And that you were using them to launch attacks on your competitors?"

"And on governments where he wanted to exert leverage," Hunter interrupted, "including the U.S. and Britain. It was Cameron who recruited Kate into Group 99. He got close to Greg Walton, wormed his way in as a CIA asset, and then helped orchestrate the devastating cyberattack on the Langley systems, as well as a whole slew of embarrassing government leaks."

"But . . . you were a donor to Jim Havers's election campaign," Tracy said. "You supported him."

"Openly, yes. And he supported me. But there's no such thing as trust in politics. Or in life for that matter. One must keep one's friends close but one's enemies closer."

Hunter said, "The day I was kidnapped, I was on my way to Crewe's offices. I wanted to confront him with the evidence, to hear his side of the story. By then I already knew that Group 99 were receiving major cash injections from a U.S.-based source. Althea— Kate, as I later learned—was being set up to look like that person. But she was obviously a cover. I quickly realized there had to be someone else behind her, someone far wealthier, and with far more to gain. Crewe made sense. His fracking interests had miraculously never been hit by Group 99, yet his competitors had all suffered heavy losses. Cameron had both the means and the motive to buy control of Group 99 and that's exactly what he did. Within two years, Crewe Oil became the most profitable fracking company on earth."

Cameron nodded appreciatively at Hunter's description of his boardroom prowess.

"He was smart about it too," Hunter went on. "He made sure he developed excellent connections on both sides of the fence. Back in the U.S. he had the CIA eating out of his hands. They already considered him an asset, so it never occurred to them to dig in that particular backyard. As for the Havers administration, Crewe Industries had made a vast contribution to the president's campaign. Plus everyone in the fracking industry saw him as one of the good guys. He had all these charities, all these NGOs . . ."

"That's right," said Tracy, turning to Cameron. She was still clutching at straws, trying to piece something back together of the Cameron Crewe she first met, the man she'd liked from the first moment she saw him. "You gave back. You did. You cared about the local communities where you operated."

He looked back at her pityingly.

"It's a charming idea, Tracy. But no."

"Most of them weren't charities," Hunter explained. "They were fronts. Money laundering operations designed to help fund a variety of terrorist or extremist groups, often with conflicting aims. Crewe's policy was a simple one: he gave cash to everyone. So there was Group 99, who specifically opposed the wealthiest one percent; but he also supported extreme rightwing, anti-immigration groups. He gave money to political separatists, pro-Islamic groups, anti-Islamic groups, republicans, nationalists. The idea was to do everything possible to destabilize the regions he'd targeted—and that could be anywhere that was rich in shale gas. Poland, Greece, China, the U.S.—and then exploit that political uncertainty to push out his competitors. In my piece I called it 'chaos economics.' "

"Chaos economics!" Cameron grinned. "That's very good. I like that."

"It was brilliant," Hunter said, turning to Tracy. "It worked. Of course it was also utterly morally repugnant. Cameron here is an object lesson in shameless greed. Human misery, the innocent suffering of others, means nothing to him. Frankly I wouldn't wipe the guy off my shoe."

The smug smile disappeared from Cameron's face.

"Spare me the high-handed lectures," he snarled at Hunter. "The simple fact is that most countries have no idea how to capitalize on their own natural resources. Either they don't have the infrastructure to do it, or they don't have the political will. Fracking is a vote loser. But someone was going to make a fortune out of all that shale gas. That much was certain. All I did was do my best to make sure it was me."

"By funding murder and terrorism?" Tracy shot back at him. "By helping sadists and killers take over a peaceful organization like Group 99?"

Cameron rolled his eyes. "Oh, please. Don't be so naïve, darling. Group 99 were itching to blow somebody's head off long before I came along. They were always going to turn to violence in the end, with or without my help. Argyros and his cronies are base, bloodthirsty animals. Just look at what they did at Neuilly. They would have started killing people sooner or later."

"And all you did was make sure it was sooner," Tracy observed caustically. Although inside she felt desolate and ashamed.

I trusted you! I fell in love with you. At least, I thought I did.

How can this be happening?

Hunter looked at Cameron quizzically. After his exchange with Tracy, his smug smile was back.

"You do realize you're mentally ill?" Hunter said.

Cameron turned slightly and leveled his gun squarely at Hunter. "Be quiet," he snapped. "No one's interested in your opinion. You can see why I had to have him kidnapped," he said to Tracy. "Here was this self-important nobody, this womanizing gambling addict, planning to destroy not only me but my company, everything I'd worked for."

Hunter laughed. His lack of fear seemed designed to antagonize Crewe. It was working. "You're a psychopath."

"I SAID BE QUIET!" The gun shook in Cameron's hands. "I'm talking to Tracy, not you."

"I'm not a psychopath," he told Tracy, looking suddenly vulnerable. "At least, no more than you are. No more than anybody who goes through what we've been through and realizes they have nothing left to lose. After Marcus died, everything changed."

For a split second Tracy's heart went out to him and she felt at one with him again. The old connection between them, the spark that had been lit so unexpectedly in Geneva, came back. Cameron had lost Marcus, and Tracy had lost Nicholas, and that had been enough to bring them together, to fuse them emotionally for a time. Because for a time, losing Nicholas had been the only thing in Tracy's life. The only event, the only emotion, the only thought, the only point to her existence. Cameron had found her in that moment—or had she found him?—and they'd fit together like two pieces of a puzzle.

But no more.

It wasn't only that Cameron had clearly never been the man Tracy thought he was. That he was deranged and dangerous, a killer. Tracy was different too.

The pain of Nick's death would never leave her. But it wasn't the only thing anymore. There was a whole world out there, a world full of other people, other lives, other hopes and dreams. Tracy might not know those people. But they mattered. Humanity mattered. Truth mattered. At least to her.

Cameron kept talking.

"Before Marcus's death, I had a life outside the business. But afterwards, Crewe Oil was all I had left. People talk about morality, about justice, about right and wrong, about *God*." He snorted derisively. "It's all nonsense. Life and death are arbitrary. When Marcus died, I knew there was no God. No justice. No right or wrong. No mercy. Continuing to act as if there were would just have been . . . irrational."

He looked at Tracy pleadingly, as if willing her to understand.

"Tell me about Althea," Tracy asked him, playing for time. "About Kate Evans. You recruited her?"

"Yes. We met at a conference in New York. Looking into her eyes was like looking into a mirror." Cameron sighed nostalgically. "Not like you and me. There was no physical attraction. But I recognized Kate's despair from the outset. Her need to lash out against a world that had robbed her of the only thing she cared about. This woman didn't care if she got shot. She didn't care what happened to her. My purpose was Crewe Oil. Kate's was destroying the CIA. But we understood each other, Kate and I. She was prepared to follow my directions, at least at first."

"Did you tell her to kill my son?" Tracy glared at Cameron, forcing herself to keep her voice steady.

"No!" He sounded genuinely horrified. "Absolutely not. I had nothing to do with Nick's accident, Tracy. You must believe that."

Tracy studied his face, looking for any sort of clues. Did she believe it? She didn't know. She didn't know anything anymore.

"Think about it," said Cameron. "Why would I lie?"

"Because it's what you do?" Hunter interjected.

Cameron swung around furiously. For one awful moment Tracy thought he was going to shoot Hunter then and there. But he held back. For the moment at least he was more interested in Tracy.

"After Bob Daley's execution, I lost contact with Kate completely," he went on. "Group 99 had already served their purpose for me. I have no idea why Kate decided to involve you, and I sincerely wish she hadn't. What we had was real, Tracy. That night in Geneva. Hawaii . . . I developed feelings for you. Real feelings. Feelings I thought I would never have again."

Tracy held up a hand. "Please, don't."

"It's the truth. I tried to keep you close. To control the situation. I still hoped, somehow, to spare you. But when the Brits brought in Jeff Stevens, and the two of you began closing in on Drexel together, I knew there was no hope. Once you found Hunter, he would tell you the truth about me. Between you, you would make sure his story got published. I couldn't let that happen. But I did love you, Tracy. I did want . . ."

Before he could finish, Hunter exploded off the couch like a missile. With an earsplitting noise that was half scream, half roar, he launched himself at Cameron. Tracy watched as if in slow motion as Hunter flew through the air, head down, arms outstretched, reaching for Cameron's gun like a rugby player diving for the ball.

It was so unexpected, it took Cameron a fraction of a second longer to react than it should have.

But not long enough.

Tracy saw Cameron's expression change from surprise, to anger, to determination. Then a shot rang out like a single clap of thunder.

The bullet hit Hunter at such close range, he seemed to stop in midair, as if someone had pressed freeze frame on a movie, or an unseen hand had reached down and grabbed him from above. Then, like a sack of rocks, he dropped to the ground.

Tracy stared down in horror.

Lying on his back, his arms spread wide, Hunter's lifeless eyes gazed emptily upwards, at nothing.

Chapter 32

There was no time for tears. No time for shock. No time for anything.

Hunter Drexel was dead, and in a few seconds Tracy would be too.

Tracy's gun was still on the coffee table, about twenty feet away. More in desperation than in hope, she made a run for it.

"Oh no you don't."

Cameron lunged after her, grabbing hold of the back of her leg. Tracy felt herself falling forwards, with the same slow-motion sensation she'd had for the last, agonizing minute, as if she were watching this happen to someone else, yet somehow remained utterly powerless to stop it. Her head smashed painfully into the table. Blood gushed down her forehead into her eyes, partially blinding her. Cameron tightened his grip on her legs as Tracy's fingers scrambled desperately for the gun. By some miracle she grasped it, gripping the cold black metal for dear life. But there was no chance to shoot. Cameron was on top of her now, his full body weight pressing Tracy down against the hard wood of the table, crushing her, squeezing the breath from her body like air from an old set of bellows. Blood, warm and thick, oozed from the gash on her forehead.

"Don't fight me, Tracy. Don't make this harder."

Tracy could feel Cameron's breath in her ear and his heartbeat hammering against her back.

She managed to twist her body slightly to one side, just enough to bring a knee up into Cameron's groin. It was a move she'd learned years ago from a friend of Gunther's, Tai Li, a martial arts expert whom Gunther had said she and Jeff ought to meet.

"Self-defense can be important in your line of work, my dears," Gunther had told them. "Spend a few hours with Tai. You won't regret it."

That was a long time ago. Tracy still remembered how she and Jeff had dissolved into giggles during Sensei Li's classes. Tai Li was old and wizened, with a face like a pickled walnut—although, as Jeff used to say, a walnut would have had more of a sense of humor.

The old man took Jujitsu *very* seriously, barking instructions at Tracy and Jeff like a drill sergeant. Tracy remembered almost none of what he'd taught her. But this particular move had stuck with her, and it had come in handy more than once.

Cameron yelped in pain and rolled off her. His gun had dropped to the floor in the melee. Tracy kicked it aside, sending it skidding across the parquet floor like a puck on an ice rink.

"Bitch!" he hissed. The pain had made him angry.

It was now or never. Aiming her gun towards Cameron's leg, Tracy fired. But this time he was too quick for her, knocking her arm upwards, so the gun flew out of her hand and the bullet lodged uselessly in the ceiling. Shards of plaster rained down like snow. The next thing Tracy knew Cameron had grabbed her by the shoulders. He was forcing her down on to the table but this time on her back, so that she was looking up at him. Sweat poured from his forehead and dripped onto Tracy's skin. His face, the same face she had loved and that had made love to her just weeks earlier, was unrecognizable now, contorted in an ugly combination of anger and pain. His blond hair stuck to his scalp like the wet pelt of a dog.

He is a dog, Tracy told herself. *An animal, wild and deadly and without compassion.*

His hands began to close around Tracy's neck, the fingers coiling around her windpipe like a boa constrictor. "I'm sorry, Tracy," he told her, wheezing with the effort of holding her down. "I never wanted this."

To her own surprise, Tracy felt panic start to sweep over her like an icy wave.

She'd told herself countless times since Nick's death that she no longer feared her own. But now, as Cameron's grip tightened and she fought and gasped for breath, her body's survival instinct took over. She felt frightened, and angry.

Who was this man to rob her of life?

Who was he, Cameron Crewe, to decide who lived and who died? Whose lives mattered and whose did not? What truths got to be told and what hidden?

No. Tracy wouldn't allow it!

But there was nothing she could do.

Her legs flailed wildly, uselessly. Her arms, pinned down by Cameron's knees, twitched and jerked pathetically of their own accord in a grotesque dance of death. Froth was forming at her mouth as she strived vainly to free herself from his choking grip, her energy failing with each oxygen-starved moment. Tracy could feel her eyes bulging, the blood racing around her skull as if her head were about to explode. In the movies strangulation was quick, a few seconds of struggle and then peace. But this wasn't like that at all. She hadn't blacked out. Instead she could do nothing but look up and watch as a man she had once thought she loved murdered her, slowly and painfully, the effort of snuffing out her life visible in his flared nostrils and ugly, popping veins.

Frustrated himself by how long it was taking, Cameron began to shake her violently like a terrier with a rat between its jaws. *He's trying to break my neck,* thought Tracy. She visualized her brain bouncing off the walls of her skull, like a soft pupa inside its cocoon. The pain was excruciating. She no longer thought of survival. Only of the agony being over.

And then, just like that, it was.

There was no bang. At least none that Tracy heard. Instead the bullet sounded like nothing more than moving air, a gentle *whoosh*, as if somebody—God?— were blowing her a last merciful kiss.

Cameron Crewe opened both his eyes wide in surprise. Then he fell on top of Tracy, his arms sliding off her neck and hanging, doll-like, by his side.

The last thing Tracy remembered was the agonizing sensation of air flooding back into her starved lungs, like swallowing a fistful of razor blades.

Then she passed out.

Chapter 33

LONDON, THREE MONTHS LATER . . .

Tracy strolled through Kensington Gardens, enjoying the autumnal beauty of the park and the surprisingly warm September sun on her back. She was wearing striped pants tucked into riding boots, a navy-blue sweater with a matching blue scarf, printed with an anchor motif, and an open trench coat. Her dark hair was shoulder length now, the longest it had been since before Nick died, and her cheeks shone pink with health as she walked. She was still slim—too slim, according to her doctors—but her figure was starting to soften at the edges. She was no longer the skeletal creature she'd been in June, during the height of her pursuit of Althea and Hunter Drexel.

It was late morning on a weekday. London children

were back at school and their parents back at work after the long summer. But the park was still busy. Locals walked their dogs, trainers warmed up with their clients beneath the beech trees, retired couples wandered hand in hand or read their newspapers on slatted wooden benches. And of course the ubiquitous tourists swarmed in chattering huddles around the palace, hoping for a glimpse of Will and Kate, or at least the chance to take a selfie outside what had once been Princess Diana's London home.

Tracy felt at home here too. In this park. In this city.

She had always loved London. Nicholas was conceived here, and although she had fled the city soon afterwards, haunted by her broken marriage to Jeff, she knew now she had left a part of her heart behind. Colorado had been a new start, a new life for her and Nick. Thanks to Blake Carter, that too had been a joyous time in Tracy's life. But with Nick gone and her work with the CIA now at an end, it was time for a new chapter to begin.

Tracy had flirted with the idea of returning to New Orleans, where she grew up. Or Philadelphia, where she'd been happy for a short time as a young woman. Before her mother's suicide. Before prison, and Jeff and Nicholas. Before her real life began. But it was London that spoke to her most strongly, London that seemed to be calling her home.

Climbing up the hill from Kensington High Street, Tracy skirted the palace, making a left along the path that led towards the Princess Diana Memorial playground and Notting Hill beyond. A man in an old-fashioned tweed coat stood up from one of the benches and waved as she approached. Tracy waved back, quickening her pace towards him.

"It's sweet of you to do this." She greeted him warmly with a smile and a hug. "I'm sure you've got many more important things to be doing today than having lunch with me."

"More important than lunch with Tracy Whitney?" Major General Frank Dorrien raised a bushy eyebrow. "I don't think so. At any rate, I can't think of anything more fun. Shall we?"

He crooked his elbow, offering Tracy his arm. It was an old-fashioned gesture, chivalrous, and, Tracy now knew, typical of Frank. She was embarrassed to think how completely wrong she'd been about him.

He'd had nothing to do with Prince Achileas's death, although he admitted to disliking the boy.

"It had nothing to do with his being gay. I couldn't give two hoots about that. It was his support for Group 99 I couldn't forgive, especially coming from his background. Even before they turned violent I despised what 99 stood for. Envy and bitterness, dressed up as social justice. But it was after they kidnapped Bob Daley that the gloves really came off, at least as far as I was concerned. Bob was a wonderful man and he'd been a friend to Achileas. How he could continue to flirt with them after that . . ." Frank shook his head angrily.

It was Frank who'd saved Tracy's life at Villa Michele. Frank who'd shot Cameron Crewe and put an end to his reign of terror. Later, he explained to Tracy how he and his bosses at MI6, right up to the prime minister, had come to suspect both the U.S. government and Cameron Crewe of playing a double game when it came to Group 99. He also filled in some of the blanks left by Hunter Drexel, about Kate Evans's motivations for involving Tracy in the first place.

"As you know, Kate was part of the American team charged with tracking you down, back when you and Jeff were still top on everybody's wanted list. She'd always admired your ingenuity, your ability to stay one step ahead of the agency. I think she came to see you as emblematic. Someone who had played the CIA at their own game and won. A sort of antihero, if you like. She admired you."

"She had a funny way of showing it," Tracy said.

Frank Dorrien shrugged. "She wasn't mentally well. You mustn't forget that."

In one way, all this had been good to know. It finally closed a circle. But in another way it left Tracy bereft. Now she might never know who was responsible for

Nick's death. Frank Dorrien was quite certain that Kate had done nothing to hurt him.

"There's not a shred of evidence linking her to that accident," Frank told Tracy. "Indeed we're as sure as we can be that she was in Europe at the time. Greg Walton fabricated all of that nonsense to give you a motive to help him."

"So if not Kate, then who?" Tracy asked.

Frank took her hands kindly. "Maybe nobody. Maybe it truly was an accident, Tracy."

That was the hardest part for Tracy now. Living with the maybes.

Today though, life felt bright and the future possible. Tracy and Frank walked on through the park together, slowly. Tracy was officially fully recovered from her ordeal on Lake Maggiore. But her doctors had warned her to take it easy, and for once she was heeding their advice. The strain of the last six months had taken a toll that Tracy hadn't been aware of until it was over.

Now, reluctantly, she'd been forced to admit that she wasn't twenty-three anymore. Stress and exhaustion no longer bounced off her like stones skipped across a river. They hit. And they hurt.

"You look lovely," Frank said. "Very French."

Tracy smiled. "It's the scarf."

"It suits you."

For a few minutes they walked on in companionable

silence, Tracy leaning into Frank like a sapling bending in the wind. Then Tracy said, "You know, I don't think I've ever properly thanked you."

"For what?"

Tracy laughed. "For saving my life that day. If you hadn't showed up . . . if you hadn't shot Cameron . . ."

"Yes, well," Frank Dorrien said gruffly. "I should never have allowed things to get that far in the first place. We should never have lost track of you."

"Jeff should never have lost track of me, you mean," Tracy said archly.

"No, no," said Frank. "I can't have that. I was team leader. The buck stopped with me."

Tracy thought, *He's so British. So clipped and reserved. Heaven forbid he show any emotion, or take any credit for his own heroism.*

They'd reached the top of the hill now. Frank led them to an empty bench so that Tracy could get her breath back.

"I take it you've seen this?"

He handed her a copy of today's *Times*.

"No!" Tracy took it delightedly. "I mean I've read the piece online, obviously. But I haven't seen a hard copy. All the newsagents I passed on the way here had sold out."

No one had been more astonished than Tracy to

learn that Hunter Drexel was still alive—that he'd survived Cameron's point-blank bullet that night at the villa. After all, she had watched Hunter go down with her own eyes, seen his empty gaze. Had anybody asked her, Tracy would have sworn on oath that Hunter was dead. But apparently he'd been wearing body armor underneath his clothes during dinner. Ironically to protect himself from *her*, not Cameron Crewe. But it had saved his life just the same.

Tracy was relieved to learn Drexel was alive. But she still had mixed feelings about him, and about where his loyalties really lay. He'd refused to tell MI6 anything about Kate Evans location, and seemed determined that she should evade justice for the murder of Bob Daley—supposedly his friend—as well as for the other Group 99 cyberattacks she organized. And though he hadn't been involved in Sally Faiers's death, or Hélène Faubourg's, to Tracy's mind he'd bounced back from both these tragic events in a manner that did not endear him, nor engender trust.

On the other hand, he'd been through hell and risked a lot to bring Crewe Oil to justice and to expose the truth about both the global fracking industry and Group 99.

Unfortunately, it wasn't the whole truth.

Tracy opened the paper eagerly and scanned the

first four pages, all of which were devoted to Hunter's article. It contained a great many bombshells, but the most shocking part for Tracy was what it omitted.

No mention was made of President Havers's involvement in corrupt practices, still less was there any allusion to the botched Bratislavan rescue attempt. Instead a false story had been concocted about Hunter escaping while in transit from one Group 99 camp to another. Even worse, he claimed to have been working *alongside* the CIA while on the run from Group 99, helping to lure the group's leader, Alexis Argyros, aka Apollo, into a trap that resulted in his ultimate death via drone strike. Names and locations had all been withheld as "classified," making the story conveniently impossible to verify. And meanwhile Greg Walton and his team came out of the whole thing smelling of roses while Hunter was hailed as a hero.

Tracy shook her head. "I still can't believe he sold out."

"Oh, I wouldn't say that exactly," said Frank. "The Havers administration was never as bad as Drexel painted them. At the end of the day, all they did was arrange a few off book, handshake deals to promote U.S. interests. We were just as bad."

"I'm sure you were," said Tracy. "But someone ought to be saying so!"

"Sally Faiers tried," Frank reminded her. "Look what happened to her."

Tracy handed him back the paper. They walked on.

"Do you think the Americans killed Sally?" Tracy asked.

Frank shook his head. "No. We're pretty sure Crewe ordered the hit in Bruges. And on Hélène. Hunter had confided in both of them, you see."

"Kate wasn't mentioned in the article," said Tracy. "After everything we went through! They don't even talk about Althea."

"Drexel insisted on keeping her out of it." For the first time, Dorrien sounded as outraged as Tracy was. "That was his quid pro quo, for keeping his mouth shut about Bratislava and the president. We know he gave her well over a million dollars in poker winnings, presumably to start a new life somewhere. And at the end of the day it was in everyone's interests to let her drop, to focus on Argyros. The drone strike on Apollo was a success. Letting Althea slip through the net was a failure. With Crewe and Argyros both dead, Group 99 have been cut off at the knees. Hunter Drexel's a hero, and so's the President. Everyone's a winner."

"Tell that to Bob Daley's widow," Tracy said bitterly. "Or the parents of those poor kids at Camp France."

"I agree, my dear," said Frank. "It's not fair. But then life so rarely is, wouldn't you agree? Ah, here we are. *Chez Patrick.* I hope you're hungry."

They'd turned a corner into a charming cobbled mews. A few yards in front of them stood an extremely pretty French restaurant, with blue and white canvas awnings hanging over outdoor tables, simple wicker bistro chairs and window boxes overflowing with Sweet William perched above the open door. A glorious smell of garlic and white wine wafted down the mews towards them, making Tracy's mouth water.

Inside, Chez Patrick was bustling. An elderly Frenchman took Tracy's coat and scarf. He was reaching for Frank's heavy tweed coat when Frank's phone rang.

"Sorry," he mouthed to Tracy, darting back into the mews. "You go in. I won't be long."

Leaving him to his phone call, Tracy followed the maître d' through the restaurant. Weaving her way through gingham-clothed tables and past chattering diners, she arrived at a table tucked away round a corner, in a little alcove all its own.

Jeff Stevens looked up and smiled.

"Hello, Tracy."

Chapter 34

Tracy turned and bolted out of the restaurant.

She looked up and down the mews in search of Frank Dorrien. But Frank had gone.

He set me up. The bastard set me up.

By the time she turned around, Jeff was standing outside. In a dark suit that off set his gray eyes perfectly, with his curly dark hair ruffled by the wind, he looked as handsome as he had the day Tracy first saw him, in a train compartment en route to St. Louis. Tracy remembered that first meeting as if it were yesterday. She had just pulled off her first ever job, stealing Lois Bellamy's jewels for a crooked New York jeweler named Conrad Morgan. Jeff, posing as FBI Agent Thomas Bowers, had scammed her into handing them over; and Tracy had scammed him right back.

But of course, it wasn't yesterday. Decades had passed since that train journey. Decades of adventure and excitement, of love and loss, of exquisite joy and unbearable pain. Nicholas's life, and death, lay between then and now, an unbridgeable Grand Canyon of grief that Tracy could never cross, no matter how much she might want to.

"Please," Jeff said reproachfully. "Don't run away. Have lunch with me."

"I can't believe Frank did this," Tracy muttered furiously.

"You mustn't blame Frank," Jeff said. "I begged him. I told him I needed to see you."

"And I told him, very plainly, that I didn't want to see you," Tracy said.

Jeff's wounded expression was like a punch in the stomach.

Softening her tone, Tracy said, "It's a bad idea. You know it is."

"It's only lunch."

Tracy gave Jeff a knowing look. When it came to the two of them, there was no such thing as "only lunch" and they both knew it.

"We do need to talk," Jeff pressed her.

Tracy hesitated, just for a second, and Jeff smiled. He knew he had her.

The food was delicious. Nothing too rich and creamy, the way French food sometimes could be. Tracy had a langoustine salad that positively exploded with flavor, and Jeff had a fortifying steak frites, washed down with a good Burgundy for courage.

He knew he was going to need it.

For the first half an hour they talked about the case. About Hunter and Kate and the drone strike that had killed Alexis Argyros. About the fracking industry and corruption and the duplicitous nature of politicians.

"If only more people were as honest as us, eh, darling?" Jeff quipped.

Tracy loved his sense of humor and she envied it. She wished she could still laugh at the world the way Jeff could. She used to laugh a lot.

"I love you, Tracy."

Tracy's head whipped back as if she'd been stung. This was so out of left field, so unexpected. She looked at Jeff almost angrily.

"Stop."

Jeff's eyes were locked on Tracy's. "Why?"

"You know why. It would never work."

"Why wouldn't it work?"

"Because we're completely incompatible!"

"That's horseshit. We're totally compatible."

"We drive each other crazy," said Tracy.

"I know." Jeff grinned. "Isn't it wonderful?"

Tracy couldn't help but smile at that. But the light mood didn't last long. Reaching across the table, Jeff took both Tracy's hands in his.

"Tell me about Nicholas."

Tracy frowned. "What do you mean? Tell you what?"

"Everything. What he looked like when he was born. What his favorite breakfast cereal was. What position he slept in."

"STOP!" Tracy shook her head violently. She tried to snatch her hands away but Jeff tightened his grip. Other diners turned to look at them. It was painful to watch Tracy, twisting and writhing to get away from him, like an insect with its wings on fire.

"I can't talk about him," she pleaded. "Not with you. Not like that."

"Like what?"

Tracy swallowed hard. "As if he were still alive."

She gazed down at the tablecloth, avoiding Jeff's eyes. He gave her a few minutes, then reached for her hand again.

"You can talk about him, Tracy. You have to talk about him," Jeff said gently. "If you don't let the grief out, it will kill you in the end. It will poison you from the inside out like battery acid. Just like it did to Cameron Crewe."

Tracy looked up sharply. "Maybe that's what I want. Maybe I want it to kill me."

Jeff said, "I don't believe that. You know that's not what Nick would have wanted."

Angrily, Tracy brushed away tears. "You don't understand, Jeff. If I let the grief out, if I let it go, I'm scared I'll be letting *him* go."

"You'll never let him go," Jeff said. "Neither of us will."

"Yes, but . . ."

"This isn't just about you, Tracy!" Jeff cut her off, not angry exactly, but exasperated. Desperate. "*I* need to talk about him. To learn about him, about his life. I missed it. I missed all of it, and I can never get those years back. If you don't talk to me about him, what am *I* left with? How can I grieve?"

Tracy felt terrible. The pain etched on Jeff's face was every bit as real as her own. How had she not noticed it before? In Paris, or Megève, when they'd spent time together? It must have been there. Was it because Jeff's face had reminded her so much of Nicholas, she'd stopped seeing him as a person in his own right?

Yes. That was it.

But she saw him now. Jeff, her Jeff. Reaching up, she stroked his cheek.

"I'm sorry. I'm so sorry."

Jeff kissed her hand. "Don't be sorry. Just talk to me. Please. Talk to me about our son."

And so, falteringly at first, Tracy talked. She talked until they'd finished their meal. She talked when Jeff paid the bill. She talked as their coffees turned cold, and the restaurant emptied, and at last the manager came over and politely informed them that they were closing now, to prepare for the evening's dinner service.

Outside, the sun glowed low and red over the mews. Crisp, golden leaves swirled around Tracy and Jeff's legs and crunched beneath their feet as they walked hand in hand back up towards Notting Hill Gate.

"Will you stay in London for a while?" Jeff asked.

She nodded. "For a while, yes. Maybe for good. I'm still thinking. How about you?"

"I'm still thinking too."

The love hung in the air between them like a living thing, a ghost.

Tracy looked up into Jeff's eyes and said what they were both thinking.

"I don't know if we can go back. I love you, but . . ."

He stopped her with a kiss.

"We can't go back. We can only go forward. But we don't have to do it alone."

For a moment, Tracy let herself hope that he might be right. "I should go."

Jeff stuck out his hand for a cab and helped Tracy inside.

"Don't disappear on me now."

"I won't." Tracy smiled. "I promise."

"Tomorrow's the great adventure, Tracy," Jeff said, tapping the door as the driver pulled away. "And it's coming whether we want it or not."

He watched as Tracy's taxi eased into the London traffic and drove out of sight.

Epilogue

J eff waited in the darkness.

It was very late, almost two A.M., and the parking structure was deserted.

He started to panic that he wasn't coming. That this would be the one Saturday night when the bastard didn't come here, to this rundown out of town mall, to meet his informant. But just as Jeff was giving up hope, he appeared, perfectly dressed as always in an expensive suit and tie. He waited until his "source" crawled in, ragged and dirty and desperate for the drug money he was about to earn for betraying some underworld figure or other. Then he glanced around briefly and made his approach.

The two men spoke for five minutes. Then the suit handed over a crisp white envelope, just as he always did, and the addict scuttled away.

He was almost at his car when he felt the cold metal of Jeff's gun pressed against the back of his ear.

"Who are you?"

He was trying to sound calm, but Jeff could hear the fear in his voice and smell it on his skin.

"What do you want?"

"The truth," Jeff said. Reaching into the man's pocket, he extracted his gun. "Turn around."

Milton Buck did as he was asked.

"Back up against the wall."

Buck took two steps back, glaring at Jeff defiantly. The FBI agent had always loathed Jeff Stevens. The man clearly viewed himself as some sort of a Robin Hood, when in fact he was nothing more than a common thief. "What's this about Stevens?"

"I saw you. On the hospital CCTV feed. You were there the night Nicholas died."

Milton Buck shrugged. "So?"

"So it was you. I went to Steamboat Springs. I did my research. You were the one who sabotaged that truck. You expected Nick to die, but when he didn't, you went to the hospital and tampered with his anesthetic. You killed a decent man and an innocent child. You murdered my son."

Milton Buck hesitated for a moment. He contemplated denying it, but there was clearly no point.

"Does Tracy know?"

"No. She thinks it was an accident. The truth would kill her."

Milton Buck glared at Jeff defiantly. "What do you want? An apology? Well you won't get one. Not from me. My job is to defend America, Stevens. To protect our national interests. My mission was to neutralize the threat of Group 99, at the time a *global* treat to economic stability. We believed Tracy was a direct link to Althea. We needed her to do her duty. But she refused. Repeatedly. So I did *my* duty. Sometimes that means making tough decisions. And yes, sometimes it means people have to die."

Jeff paused for a long time. Then he nodded, lowering his gun. "You're right."

Milton Buck frowned. This was not at all what he'd expected. "What?"

"I said you're right." Jeff smiled. "Sometimes people do have to die."

Raising his arm, Jeff fired two bullets between Milton Buck's eyes.

Then he turned and walked away.

Acknowledgments

My sincere thanks go to all the Sheldon family for putting their trust in me once again, and especially to Mary—thank you for your support and kindness over these last few years—and Alexandra, whose input to *Reckless* in particular has been invaluable. Thanks also to Luke Janklow, who puts the "gent" in agent, Mort Janklow, and everyone at Janklow and Nesbit, especially Hellie Ogden in London and the lovely and astute Claire Dippel in New York. Huge thanks to all at HarperCollins, especially my editors, May Chen in New York and Kim Young in London for all your insights, hard work and oh, the *time* you all spent helping me to get this book right. It is the literal truth to say that I could not have finished *Reckless* without you. I am truly grateful. Finally, thanks to my family, for their endless love, especially my husband, Robin. I adore you.

This book is dedicated to Belen Hormaeche, one of my oldest and dearest friends. Bels, you are like a sister to me. Thank you for always being there. T xx